SCANDINAVIAN FOLK BELIEF AND LEGEND

THE NORDIC SERIES Volume 15

1   *British Diplomacy and Swedish Politics, 1758–1773*
by Michael Roberts

2   Henrik Ibsen, *Peer Gynt*, translated by Rolf Fjelde.
A thoroughly revised version of Fjelde's translation, with new
appendixes

3   *The Finnish Revolution, 1917–1918*
by Anthony F. Upton

4   *To the Third Empire: Ibsen's Early Drama*
by Brian Johnston

5   *A History of Scandinavian Literature*
by Sven H. Rossel

6   *Viking Art*
by David M. Wilson and Ole Klindt-Jensen

7   *Finland and Europe:*
The Period of Autonomy and the International Crises, 1808–1914
by Juhani Paasivirta

8   *Socialism and Abundance:*
Radical Socialism in the Danish Welfare State
by John Logue

9   *Scandinavia during the Second World War*
edited by Henrik S. Nissen

10   *Scandinavian Language Structures:*
A Comparative Historical Survey
by Einar Haugen

11   *The Welfare State and Beyond: Success and Problems in Scandinavia*
by Gunnar Heckscher

12   *Scandinavia in the Revolutionary Era, 1760–1815*
by H. Arnold Barton

13   *Between East and West: Finland in International Politics, 1944–1947*
by Tuomo Polvinen

14   *Mannerheim: Marshall of Finland*
by Stig Jägerskiöld

SCANDINAVIAN FOLK BELIEF AND LEGEND

Reimund Kvideland
Henning K. Sehmsdorf
editors

UNIVERSITY OF MINNESOTA PRESS
MINNEAPOLIS / LONDON

Published by the University of Minnesota Press
111 Third Avenue South, Suite 290, Minneapolis, MN 55401-2520
http://www.upress.umn.edu
Printed in the United States of America on acid-free paper
Designed by Gwen M. Willems
Ninth printing 2018

Library of Congress Cataloging-in-Publication Data

Scandinavian folk belief and legend.

(The Nordic series ; v. 15)
Bibliography: p.
Includes index.
1. Folklore — Scandinavia.   2. Legends — Scandinavia.
I. Kvideland, Reimund, 1935– .   II. Sehmsdorf,
Henning K.   III. Series.
GR205.S23   1987   398.2′0948   86-25039
ISBN 978-0-8166-1503-2 – ISBN 978-0-8166-1967-2 (pbk.)

Illustrations for parts II-IX are from Olaus Magnus's
Historia de Gentibus Septentrionalibus (History of the
Northern People, 1555) as follows: part II—bk. 2, chap. 3;
part III—bk. 3, chap. 16; part IV—bk. 3, chap. 15;
part V—bk. 3, chap 10; part VI—bk. 3, chap. 21;
part VII—bk. 2, chap. 15; part VIII—bk. 5, chap. 22;
and part IX—bk. 7, chap. 20.

To
Kristian, Katrin, Elin, Käthe,
and Johann

Contents

Preface   xxi

Introduction   3

PART I   The Human Soul

1   The Power of Thought   43
1.1 When Your Nose Itches   43
1.2 When Your Toe Throbs   43
1.3 When Your Ears Ring   44
1.4 My, What an Appetite She Has!   44
1.5 When Your Right Eye Itches   44
1.6 The Riding *Hug*   44
1.7 The Woman Who Nearly Killed the Horse   45
1.8 The Girl Who Thought of Her Sweetheart   45

2   Changing Someone's Mind   46
2.1 To Make a Girl Love You   46
2.2 Love Magic   46
2.3 The Love Potion   46
2.4 Three Drops of Blood   47
2.5 Eileiv the Fortune-Teller   47
2.6 Uglehe'en   48
2.7 He Wanted the Farmer to Follow Him   48

3   The Evil Eye   49
3.1 The Bewitched Child   49
3.2 English Disease   50
3.3 Anders Provst   50
3.4 The Farmer in Krakerås   51
3.5 Setting Up a Loom   51
3.6 The Woman Who Had an Evil Foot   52

4   Envy   52
    4.1 Envy Kills   52
    4.2 A Prayer against Envy   52
    4.3 Knock on Wood   53
    4.4 Envy Corrodes a Stone   53

5   The Nightmare   54
    5.1 The Woman Who Thought the Nightmare Was Her Husband   55
    5.2 The *Mare* in the Shape of a Cat   55
    5.3 The *Mare*   56
    5.4 He Spoke Too Early   57
    5.5 Married to the *Mare*   57

6   Longing   58
    6.1 Snowshoe-Pernille   58
    6.2 The Dead Husband Longs for His Namesake   59
    6.3 The Dead Child Complains   59

7   *Hug*-message   60
    7.1 The Day My Mother Died   60
    7.2 The Shipwrecked Fisherman   60
    7.3 Her Father Came to Her   61
    7.4 The Shipwreck of the *Olivia*   61
    7.5 My Son, Get Up and Come with Me   62
    7.6 An Omen of Death   63
    7.7 He Escaped the Fire   63

8   The *Vardøger*   64
    8.1 She Heard Her Husband   64
    8.2 He Saw His Mother   65
    8.3 A Father's Visit to His Daughter   65

9   The *Fylgje*   66
    9.1 How to Reveal Your Character   66
    9.2 Grandmother's *Vardøger* Scared the Cows   67
    9.3 The Evil *Fylgje*   67
    9.4 Seeing the *Vardøger* to the Door   68
    9.5 Meeting One's *Fylgje*   68
    9.6 The Old Man Met Himself   69
    9.7 The Dead Man Wanted His Leg   69
    9.8 The Cap of Victory   69
    9.9 The Shirt of Victory   70
    9.10 He Stopped the Fire with a Caul   70

10   The Finn Messenger   71
    10.1 The Skipper and the Finn   71
    10.2 They Touched His Jacket   71
    10.3 The Finn Brought the Silver Spoon   72

11   The Dream Soul   73
     11.1 The Barrel in the Mound   73

12   Werewolves and Man-Bears   74
     12.1 Their Firstborn Would Have Been Werewolves   75
     12.2 The Child Drove Away the Werewolf   75
     12.3 Now I am Free   76
     12.4 The Tailor Understood the Howling of the Wolves   76
     12.5 The Werewolf Attacked His Wife   77
     12.6 The Finn and His Wolfskin   78
     12.7 The Lapp Carried a Belt under His Skin   78
     12.8 The Man-Bear Raised the Child   79
     12.9 They Shot His Grandfather   79
     12.10 Scolding the Bear   80

13   Death   80
     13.1 Opening a Door to Let the Soul Out   80
     13.2 They Saw Her Soul   80
     13.3 The *Fylgje* of the Dead   81

PART II   The Dead and the Living

14   Heaven or Hell?   87
     14.1 Easy to Pull   87
     14.2 The White and the Black Bird   87
     14.3 One Black and One Brown Horse   88
     14.4 The Heavy Coffin   89

15   The Living in the Land of the Dead   89
     15.1 Two Friends   90

16   Return of the Dead Lover   91
     16.1 The Bride Who Came Back   91
     16.2 "Gárún, Gárún, Gray I Am Growing 'round My Pate"   92

17   The Midnight Mass of the Dead   93
     17.1 The Christmas Mass of the Dead   94
     17.2 The Dead Grabbed Her Coat   94

18   The Revenging Dead   95
     18.1 The Woman at Haugen   95
     18.2 The Milkmaid's Verse or the Draug's Verse   96
     18.3 John from Skorravik   96
     18.4 He Had to Marry the Dead   97
     18.5 He Wanted the Child Named after Himself   98
     18.6 The Girl Who Stole the Thighbone   99
     18.7 The Funeral Singer   99
     18.8 A Murderer Brought to Justice   100
     18.9 He Swept with Seven Brooms   100

19   Binding the Dead   101
     19.1 They Rammed a Pole through Her Chest   101
     19.2 Throwing Soil on the Coffin   102
     19.3 He Shot the Dead in the Head   102
     19.4 You Have Not Bitten the Thread from the Needle Yet   103

20   The Friendly Revenant   104
     20.1 She Had Food and Drink Ready for Him   104
     20.2 "Your Name Is Written in the Book of Life"   104
     20.3 The Dead Gave Advice   105
     20.4 Cold Death Is Dreary   106
     20.5 The Dead Mother Nursed Her Child   106

21   The Dead Not Properly Cared For   107
     21.1 The Skull   107
     21.2 They Forgot the Shroud for the Child   108
     21.3 He Needed a Shave   108

22   The Dead Needs Reconciliation   109
     22.1 "I Was Enemies with My Neighbor"   109
     22.2 He Had Accused Her Falsely   110

23   Greed   111
     23.1 She Walked Again in the Storehouse   111
     23.2 Counting His Money   111

24   Suicide   112
     24.1 He Took His Own Life   112
     24.2 I Am Neither in Heaven Nor on Earth   113

25   Murdered Children   113
     25.1 Baptizing Murdered Children   114
     25.2 "The Bucket Is Tight!"   115
     25.3 Dancing the Calves to Death   115
     25.4 "Shut Up, Big Mouth!"   116
     25.5 "My Mother Wears Gold"   117
     25.6 I Was Meant for Marrying   118

26   The Boundary Ghost   118
     26.1 The Servant Girl Helps the Boundary Ghost   118
     26.2 The Pedlar Returned the Boundary Stone   119
     26.3 Giving False Witness   120
     26.4 The Boundary Ghost Screams   120
     26.5 Returning Stolen Land   120
     26.6 "Where Should I Put It?"   121
     26.7 The Minister's Dog   121

27   Ghosts   122
     27.1 Fooling Around   122

27.2 The Ghost without a Head   122
27.3 "Is My Eye Red?"   122
27.4 The Spook in the Grain House   123
27.5 Keeping Company with a Ghost   124
27.6 Ghosts Dancing   124
27.7 The Farmhand Who Danced with the Ghost at Kittebuske   125

PART III   Healers and Wise Folk

28   Healing Humans   131
    28.1 Kari Vrisdaughter   131
    28.2 Jens Kusk   132
    28.3 The Child Who Would Not Utter a Sound   133
    28.4 Olav Huse   134
    28.5 To Stop Bleeding   135
    28.6 May Bleeding Be Stanched   135
    28.7 Against Fever   136
    28.8 Against Snakebite   136
    28.9 Against Rickets   137
    28.10 Healing a Sprain   138
    28.11 Against Frostbite   138
    28.12 Against Inflammation   139

29   Healing Animals   140
    29.1 Against Loss of Spirit in Animals   140
    29.2 Healing a Dried Up Cow   141
    29.3 To Heal a Bone Fracture   141
    29.4 Against Finn Shot   142
    29.5 Turid Klomset   142
    29.6 The Quack   143
    29.7 Against Homesickness in Animals   144

30   Protecting House and Home   144
    30.1 Locking Doors   144
    30.2 Opening Locks   145
    30.3 Quenching Fire   145
    30.4 Wasp Spell   146
    30.5 The Finn Who Exorcised the Rats   146
    30.6 To Keep the Fire Burning   147
    30.7 To Aid in Childbirth   147

31   Binding the Thief   148
    31.1 To Strike Out a Thief's Eye   148
    31.2 The Cat Did it!   149
    31.3 Caught in the Act   149

32 Wind and Weather   150
    32.1 Three Knots in a Handkerchief   150
    32.2 If You Rule Today, I Rule Tomorrow   151
    32.3 The Finn Boy   151
    32.4 To Make the Rain Stop   152
    32.5 Rain from a Clear Sky   152

33 The Trickster   153
    33.1 Maliser-Knut   153
    33.2 The Smith Who Hypnotized People   154

PART IV   Witchcraft

34 Revenge and Envy   161
    34.1 Sticking Pins into a Girl   161
    34.2 Øli Skogen   162
    34.3 Inger Petterst   163
    34.4 The Lapp Woman   163

35 Magic Shot   164
    35.1 Shooting the Trollman   164
    35.2 The Wizards of the Westman Islands   165

36 The Whirlwind   168
    36.1 The Witch in the Whirlwind   168
    36.2 Haying with a Whirlwind   169

37 Food Magic   170
    37.1 Ragnhild Blikka   170
    37.2 Lisbet Nypan   171

38 Stealing Milk   171
    38.1 Milking with a Knife   171
    38.2 Brandy from a Knife Handle   172
    38.3 Witch Butter   173
    38.4 Churning   173
    38.5 Hallvor Drengmann's Son   174
    38.6 The Neighbor Who Stole the Milk   175

39 Troll Cat   175
    39.1 The Troll Cat   176
    39.2 To Bring a Troll Cat to Life   176
    39.3 Marte Holon   177
    39.4 Shot with Silver Button   178
    39.5 The Carrier   179

40 The Witches' Sabbath   180
    40.1 Steinar Aase   180
    40.2 The Burning Mill   181

41   Magic Flight   183
  41.1 The Serving Boy   183
  41.2 Seeing Witches Fly   184
  41.3 Riding the Minister's Wife   185
  41.4 Fastri Hopen   187

42   The Witch's Daughter   187
  42.1 The Little Girl Who Was a Witch   188
  42.2 The White Snake   189

43   Social Sanction and Persecution   190
  43.1 The Trial of Quive Baardsen   191
  43.2 Ingerid Eirik's Daughter Kaaljørju   193
  43.3 Hilde Oluf's Daughter Blindheim   195
  43.4 Two Witches   196
  43.5 The Witch Who Wanted to Take Holy Communion   198
  43.6 Mette Bundet   199

PART V   The Invisible Folk

44   Origin and Hope for Salvation   205
  44.1 The Origin of the *Hulder* Folk   205
  44.2 The Origin of the Invisible Folk   206
  44.3 The Mound Folk Hope for Salvation   206

45   The Dangerous Encounter   207
  45.1 The Changeling   208
  45.2 The Unbaptized Child   208
  45.3 Burning the Changeling   209
  45.4 The Old Changeling   209
  45.5 Where Are You Going, Killkrack?   211
  45.6 Taken into the Mountain   212
  45.7 Dancing with the Elves   212
  45.8 The Boy Who Was Lured by the Elves   213

46   The Fairy Lover   214
  46.1 The Hill Man   214
  46.2 Courted by a *Hulder*   215
  46.3 He Had to Go with the Forest Sprite   215
  46.4 The Girl and the Elf King   216
  46.5 Sleeping with a Forest Sprite   217
  46.6 The Interrupted Wedding with a Hill Man   217
  46.7 Taken into the Hill   218
  46.8 Married to a *Hulder*   219
  46.9 The Abducted Bride   220
  46.10 The Boy Who Had a Child with a *Tusse*   220
  46.11 Married to a Wood Sprite   221

47   Good Neighbors and Friends   222
   47.1 The *Tusse* Folk Help with the Harvest   223
   47.2 The Mound Folk Give Advice in Sewing   224
   47.3 The *Huldre* Folk Tell the Date   224
   47.4 The Wood Sprite Woke Him Up in Time   225
   47.5 Calling the Dairymaid   226
   47.6 Midwife to the Mound Folk   227
   47.7 She Threw Away the Shavings   228
   47.8 The Grateful *Huldre* Mother   228
   47.9 Rynjus Is Dead   229
   47.10 The Mound Folk Gave The Cake   230
   47.11 Trading Fire and Tobacco with the Mound Folk   230
   47.12 Moving the Stable   231
   47.13 Binding the Cattle of the Mound Folk   232
   47.14 Playing with the Children of the Mound Folk   233
   47.15 The Boy Who Teased the Man in the Hill   234
   47.16 The Cross Prevented Theft by the Mound Folk   234
   47.17 The Hill Folk Borrowed Scissors and Knives   235
   47.18 The Troll Hat   235
   47.19 The Drinking Horn   236
   47.20 Hey, Look at the Pussycat!   237

48   The Spirit of the Farm   238
   48.1 The *Tusse* at Vreim   239
   48.2 The *Nisse* Who Stole Fodder   239
   48.3 The Heavy Burden   240
   48.4 When the *Nisse* Got No Butter on His Christmas Porridge   241
   48.5 Now Håkan Is Hot!   242
   48.6 The Farmhand Who Stole the *Tomte's* Porridge   242
   48.7 The *Tomte* Who Baked Bread   243
   48.8 The *Tomte* Took Care of the Horse   244
   48.9 How the *Nisse* Learned to Take a Rest   244
   48.10 The *Nisse's* New Clothes   245
   48.11 The Troublesome *Haugbo*   246
   48.12 The *Tunkall* at Tengesdal   246
   48.13 The *Nisse* in the Church Tower   247
   48.14 The *Nisse* Woke Up the Ship's Mate   248

49   The Spirit of the Mill   248
   49.1 The Mill Troll   248
   49.2 A Little Man Held the Mill Wheel   249

50   The Spirit of the Mine   249
   50.1 The Silver Mother at Nasa   250
   50.2 Klett Mountain   250
   50.3 He Lost His Eyesight   251

50.4 They Got Help Finding the Ore   251
50.5 The Lady of the Mine Warned Them   252

51   The Water Sprite   252
51.1 Learning to Play the Fiddle   253
51.2 She Whistled the Tune   254
51.3 He Gave a Gnawed Off Bone to the Water Sprite   254
51.4 They Had to Keep Dancing   254
51.5 The *Näck* Longed for Salvation   255
51.6 The Hour Has Come, but Not the Man!   256
51.7 The *Nøkk* in Horse Shape   257
51.8 Riding the *Nøkk*   257
51.9 Seven Women on a Horse   258
51.10 The *Näck* as a Working Horse   258
51.11 Binding the *Näck*   259

52   The Spirits of the Sea   259
52.1 The Cattle of the Mermaid   260
52.2 He Gave a New Mitten to the Merman   260
52.3 A Duel of Wits   261
52.4 The Mermaid and the Fisherman   261
52.5 The Mermaid at Stad   262
52.6 The Wind Knots   262
52.7 The Revenge of the Mermaid   263
52.8 The Seal Woman   264
52.9 This One Suits Me, Said the *Draug*   266
52.10 The Kitchen Boy Beat His Mitten on the *Draug*   267
52.11 The *Draug* Shunned the Excrement   268
52.12 The Dead Fight the *Draug*   268
52.13 The Sea Serpent   269
52.14 He Met the Sea Monster   269
52.15 The Harbor on *Utrøst*   270
52.16 Swine Island   271

53   The Wild Hunt   272
53.1 He Rode with the *Oskorei*   272
53.2 The *Oskorei* Fetched the Dead Man   273
53.3 Joen's Hunt   273
53.4 Horn's Hunter   274
53.5 The Chase of the Hind   274

PART VI   The Devil

54.1 To Exorcise the Devil   281
54.2 Corporal Geremiæson's Contract with the Devil   282
54.3 Christen Pedersen's Contract with Satan   282
54.4 You Can Take a Joke, Can't You?   283

54.5 Making the Devil Carry Water in a Basket   284
54.6 Ignorant Use of the Black Book   285
54.7 Burning the Black Book   286
54.8 Last Man Out   286
54.9 The Devil Took the Shape of a Fly   288
54.10 Petter Dass Traveled with Satan   288
54.11 Traveling with the Evil One   290
54.12 Driving on Three Wheels   292
54.13 The Devil as a Dance Partner   293
54.14 They Danced to Their Death   294
54.15 The Devil as a Card Player   294
54.16 The Devil Took the Bride   295
54.17 The Devil Flayed the Dead   295

PART VII   Trolls and Giants

55.1 The Giant's Toy   301
55.2 The Visit to the Old Troll   302
55.3 THe Ogress's Hole on Sand Island   302
55.4 Trolls Shouting   303
55.5 Håstein Reef   303
55.6 The Trolls Scared a Fisherman   304
55.7 How to Scare Off a Poacher   304
55.8 Married to a *Jätte*   305
55.9 The Mowing Competition with a *Jutul*   306
55.10 The *Jätte's* Wife Borrowed the Butter Churn   306
55.11 The Master Builder   307
55.12 Gydja and the Trolls   308
55.13 The Troll and the Church at Skrea   310
55.14 The *Jätte* Who Moved to Norway   310
55.15 The Church at Ketilsfield   311
55.16 The Cleft in Horje Mountain   311
55.17 The Troll Who Was Turned to Stone   312
55.18 The Trolls Could Not Move the Faeroe Islands   312
55.19 The Ogress Drowned in the Ocean   313

PART VIII   Buried Treasure

56.1 A Spell for Binding Treasure   319
56.2 To Find Buried Treasure   319
56.3 The Fortress at Sømnes   320
56.4 I Will Catch Up With Him   321
56.5 Seven Headless Roosters   321
56.6 The Treasure at Fagrikoll   322
56.7 The Boy Who Raised the Treasure   322

56.8 The Black Hen   323
56.9 The Blood of Seven Brothers   324
56.10 Plowing with a Hen and Harrowing with a Cat   324
56.11 Buried Money   325

PART IX   History as Seen from the Village

57   Kings, Settlements, and Boundaries   331
57.1 Holger the Dane   331
57.2 King Hjørd on Jørstad   332
57.3 The King and the Crofter's Daughter   332
57.4 The Boundary Dispute   333
57.5 The Boundaries of Klagstorp and Tåstorp   334
57.6 The Borders of Sigdal, Krødsherad, and Snarum   334
57.7 The Boundaries of the Icelandic Bishoprics   335

58   Churches   335
58.1 Finding a Building Site for the New Church   336
58.2 Indulgences for Work on the Church   337
58.3 The Holy Image at Røldal Church   337
58.4 They Could Not Move the Church Bells   338
58.5 The Church Bell at Bergume   338
58.6 The Journeyman Who Cast the Bell   339

59   Saint Olav   339
59.1 Saint Olav's Spring at Torvastad   340
59.2 Saint Olav in Suldal   340
59.3 The Troll Hag Spinning on Her Wheel   341
59.4 Saint Olav at Reinsfell   342
59.5 Saint Olav and the Master Builder   342

60   The Black Death   344
60.1 The Pest Aboard a Ship   344
60.2 The Pest and the Ferryman   345
60.3 The King's Messenger Spread Cholera   345
60.4 Binding the Great Death   346
60.5 Here You Shall Stand!   346
60.6 Sacrifice to Stop the Black Death   347
60.7 They Burned the Pest   348
60.8 God Bless You!   348
60.9 Førnes Brown   349
60.10 Now It Will Be Fun to Live   349
60.11 The Black Death on Kirjala   350
60.12 Hukebu Haukeli   350
60.13 The Survivors   351
60.14 She Rang the Church Bell   351
60.15 The Deserted Church in Landet   351

61   War Times   352
   61.1 The Comet   352
   61.2 The Sound of Drums   353
   61.3 The Swedes in Mannfjord   353
   61.4 The Guide Who Led the Enemy into Death   354
   61.5 The Forest Moves   355
   61.6 The Witch Who Blunted the Swedish Guns   355
   61.7 Feathers Turned into an Army   355
   61.8 Children Dressed Up as Sheep   356
   61.9 Charles XII, King of the Swedes   356
   61.10 A Louse on a King   357
   61.11 Charles XII and the Finnish Soldiers   357
   61.12 Tordenskjold   358
   61.13 The Women Who Carried Their Husbands out of Captivity   359
   61.14 They Killed the Child in the Cradle   359
   61.15 The Kalmycks   360
   61.16 Fooling the Enemy   360
   61.17 The Minister at Finnby Church   361
   61.18 The Man Who Killed the Corporal   361
   61.19 They Took His Silverware   362
   61.20 The Swedes in Ure   362
   61.21 He Did Not Stay the Night   363
   61.22 Home from the War   363
   61.23 The Boy from Luoma   364
   61.24 The Soldier and the *Jusska*   364
   61.25 Darnel Soup   365
   61.26 The Hungry Soldiers   366
   61.27 The Norwegian and the Swede   366

62   Squires and Landowners   367
   62.1 The Rich Lady on Torget   367
   62.2 Lady Anna of Pintorp   368
   62.3 The Sunken Manor   369
   62.4 Sir Fleming on Svidja   369
   62.5 Sir Fleming's Death   370

63   Thieves and Outlaws   370
   63.1 Til, Til, Tove   370
   63.2 The Outlaws Who Kidnapped the Girl   372
   63.3 The Master Thief Who Did Both Good and Evil   372
   63.4 The Outlaw on Grasøya   373
   63.5 How to Catch a Thief   373
   63.6 Shoemaker Point   374

PART X   Urban Folklore Today

64   Outsiders and Strangers   379
   64.1 Potatoes in the Living Room   379
   64.2 Rat Meat at the Restaurant   380
   64.3 Spider   380
   64.4 The Snake in the Banana   381
   64.5 A Torn Off Finger   381

65   The Supernatural   382
   65.1 The Dead Woman   382
   65.2 An Omen of Death   383
   65.3 I Saw Jesus in Vadstena   383
   65.4 Jesus' Second Coming   384
   65.5 Jesus as Hitchhiker   385

66   Horror Tales and Antitales   386
   66.1 The Murdered Boyfriend   386
   66.2 The Trip to Mallorca   387
   66.3 A Knife in the Heart   387
   66.4 There Was Blood on the Stairs   388
   66.5 Blenda Washes Whiter   388
   66.6 It Was a Dark, Dark Night   389

67   Adulterers and Thieves   389
   67.1 A Terrible Revenge   389
   67.2 Grandmother Was Stolen   390
   67.3 A Turkey under Her Hat   391
   67.4 Free Tickets   391

Bibliography   395

Index   419

Preface

Today folklore and folklore studies enjoy wide interest both on college campuses and among general readers. A knowledge of our own ethnic background as well as of other traditions broadens our horizons and helps us understand ourselves and the world we live in. This book surveys the folk belief of Scandinavia as manifested in legends, memorates, dites, magic formulas, rite descriptions, and other documents. It demonstrates the remarkable uniformity of folk belief in preindustrial Scandinavia and also notes regional differences. It presents central aspects of the traditional worldview rather than the prose narrative tradition recognized as literature. Consequently folktales that represent a concept of supranormal experience different from that of legends and related texts have not been included here. We are currently working on a collection of Scandinavian folktales.

To date there exists no collection of legends and other texts covering the folk belief of Scandinavia as a whole. Reidar Th. Christiansen's *Folktales of Norway* (1964), Jacqueline Simpson's *Icelandic Folktales and Legends* (1972), John Lindow's *Swedish Legends and Folktales* (1978), and John F. West's *Faroese Folk-Tales and Legends* (1980) limit themselves to the folktale and legend tradition of the respective countries, and there are no English-language editions of Danish or Swedish-Finnish traditions.

In selecting our texts, we have emphasized faithfulness to belief tradition rather than to literary quality. Some of the better-known texts, for example, those published by Peter Chr. Asbjørnsen during the nineteenth century, have not been included here because they were edited to conform to the literary standards of the time. The majority of texts in this book were gleaned from standard printed sources and some are from folklore archives.

Henning K. Sehmsdorf translated the Danish, Norwegian, and Swedish texts, and Patricia Conroy, the Icelandic and Faeroese texts. We have attempted to reproduce this material in simple and straightforward English. It must be kept in mind, however, that oral and written texts constitute two quite different media. Collectors and editors necessarily influenced the final printed texts.

The book results from a collaboration that spanned two continents, and we would like to acknowledge those who helped us. First, we want to express gratitude to our colleagues in the Department of Folkloristics and Ethnology at the University of Bergen and the Department of Scandinavian Languages and Literature at the University of Washington in Seattle. In particular, our thanks to Bente G. Alver (Bergen), who has read through much of the material, and to Bengt af Klintberg (Stockholm), who has given us valuable advice and whose editions of legends and magic formulas in Sweden have been of immeasurable help. We also wish to thank Ebbe Schön (Stockholm), Ann-Helene Skjelbred (Oslo), Gustav Henningsen, Bengt Holbek, Carsten Bregenhøj (Copenhagen), and Hallfreður Örn Eiriksson (Reykjavik) for many good suggestions.

Finally, our thanks to the Norwegian Information Service in New York, The American-Norwegian Marshall Fund, the Norwegian Ministry of Foreign Affairs, the Norwegian Research Council, and the Universities of Bergen and Washington for the invaluable financial support and leave time which made this book possible.

SCANDINAVIAN FOLK BELIEF AND LEGEND

Introduction

Tradition in Rural Society

The bulk of the legends and other texts in this book represent rural oral traditions and folk beliefs of preindustrial Scandinavia. Most were collected from oral sources between the mid-nineteenth and early twentieth centuries. The final chapter, however, contains samples of narratives that are told in Scandinavia today, demonstrating the continuity of tradition as well as the changes wrought by the industrialization and urbanization of Scandinavian society.

When we speak of Scandinavia, we mean Denmark, the Faeroe Islands (some 220 miles north of Scotland), Iceland, Norway, Sweden, and Finland. The Finns differ from the rest of the Scandinavians in ethnic background and language, but Finland was ruled by Sweden until 1809, and social and cultural ties between the Finns and their neighbors to the west have remained strong. During the Middle Ages, large portions of the southwestern coastal district of Finland were colonized by Swedish farmers. Today their numbers are dwindling rapidly, but large pockets of Swedish speakers remain along the coast. Even now Swedish continues to share with Finnish the status of an official language. The texts from Finland included in this volume were all recorded in Swedish and represent the tradition of the Swedish-speaking community.

By the mid-nineteenth century, the population of Scandinavia numbered roughly seven and a half million, of which three and a half million fell to Sweden, one and a half each to Denmark and Norway, and one million to the Swedish province in Finland. In addition there were some sixty thousand people in Iceland and perhaps twenty thousand on the Faeroe Islands. Whereas in Britain and on the Continent the Industrial Revolution had caused a large part of the population to converge in mushrooming towns and cities, in Scandinavia the majority as yet subsisted on what they could produce by farming, lumbering, and, in the coastal areas, fishing. There were few cities of any considerable size. In 1800 Copenhagen had one hundred thousand inhabitants, Stockholm seventy-five thousand, and Norway boasted of only one significant trade center—Bergen, which had a population of fifteen thousand. No more than one-tenth of the Scandinavian population lived and worked in urban areas. Commerce played a relatively small part in the national economies. The only exports were grain from Denmark, bar iron from Sweden, tar from Swedish Finland, and fish and timber from Norway. Until the 1850s there were no major commercial banks in the North.

During the second half of the nineteenth century, commerce and industry developed more rapidly and communications improved. In Norway and Sweden, roads were built to open up the valleys and make traffic across the mountain passes possible. A system of packet boats along the Scandinavian coasts and short railroad lines in the southern parts of Sweden and Norway provided the first public means of transportation. In Sweden steam-powered saw mills allowed the export of timber to grow and eventually eclipse that of iron, and the repeal of the British Naval Acts in 1849 led to a rapid development of a merchant fleet in Norway. Bit by bit textile factories appeared throughout Scandinavia. By 1872 cheap grain from Russia and the U.S. began flooding Scandinavian markets, causing prices to drop by half. But within a decade, the Danes learned to process their grain into beer, which they exported successfully. They also switched to animal production, developed beet sugar on a large scale, and pioneered in shipbuilding and engineering. Norway responded to the drop in grain prices by increasing their milk production and further expanding shipping, eventually deploying one of the world's larger merchant fleets. Sweden began producing high-quality but inexpensive steel, and by the beginning of the twentieth century, the highly industrialized Sweden of today had emerged. The agricultural population fell rapidly until, by 1910, less than half of the labor force was so employed. In the rest of Scandinavia, industrialization occurred more gradually but just as surely and with it came the social and cultural changes that dismantled traditional society.

Throughout preindustrial Scandinavia, a similar socioeconomic stratification can be observed. Both Sweden and Denmark were parliamentary monarchies. Until the early nineteenth century, Norway was governed as a province of Denmark, and Finland, as a province of Sweden. In the spring of 1814, when Denmark was forced to cede Norway to Sweden as a result of the Napoleonic Wars, an assembly of civil servants, farmers, town representatives, and military officers hastily met at Eidsvoll. They fashioned a constitution in a few short weeks and, on May 17, declared Norway a "free, independent, and indivisible realm," to be governed by a limited form of monarchy. The Danish regent, Christian Frederik, was elected king, but by August he was forced to abdicate in favor of the Swedish crown prince Carl Johan (formerly the French marshal Bernadotte), who threatened to take by force what had been pledged to Sweden by treaty. Carl Johan agreed to accept the Norwegian constitution, however, and the two countries were joined in a dynastic union that lasted until 1905, when Sweden finally gave way to the Norwegian independence movement, which had been growing steadily throughout the century. Iceland, although granted home rule in 1904, remained Danish until World War II, when, in 1944, it declared itself a republic. At the same time, the Faeroe Islands achieved autonomy except in foreign relations, which to this day remain in the hands of the Danish government. In 1808–9 Finland was wrested from Swedish control by Russia, which was seeking to strengthen its borders in the Northwest. Even the most patriotic Finns accepted submission to the growing power of the czarist empire as inevitable, and it was not until the general disruption of the status quo during World War I, and specifically in the Russian Revolution of 1917, that Finland was able to declare itself independent. The nationalist movement in Finland involved the struggle not only for political freedom but also for an indigenous Finnish culture that could hold its own against Russification and Swedish cultural hegemony. The rise of Finnish as a national language played an important role in this process.

Social organization in Scandinavia, below the national government level, was by counties, districts, and parishes, to which the individual farmsteads belonged. In Denmark and Norway, most of the large estates were owned by nobles and wealthy bourgeoisie, but, by the mid-nineteenth century, half of the land had passed into the hands of independent farmers (*bonde*) and other middle-class owners. This transformation was largely due to the so-called Laws of Enclosure passed successively between the 1750s and 1820s (in Sweden) to replace the patchwork of widely dispersed fields with a more unified system of middle-sized farms. The new owners acquired their holdings by exchange or by lease and outright purchase. In Norway, where less than four percent of the land is arable anyway, there were never many large estates and consequently no rural aristocracy to speak of. The same is true of Iceland and the Faeroe Islands.

Besides the landowning farmers, the largest part of the rural population consisted of cotters (Danish/Norwegian, *husmenn,* Swedish, *torpare*), as well as laborers and servants. Cotters were tenants of small holdings, which they received in exchange for their labor. The required services left them little time or energy to devote to their own fields. Nevertheless, they were better off than the laborers who worked for room and board and perhaps for a few pieces of clothing and some seed to plant around the shack supplied by the *bonde.* The tenancy system was enforced by various ordinances. Measures passed in Denmark between 1733 and 1764 made acceptance of tenancy compulsory (*adscriptio glebae*), and a decree passed in Norway provided that the children of cotters, except for the eldest boy and girl, had to serve in their home parish at fixed low wages. In Sweden similar laws gave extensive legal and disciplinary rights to the landowners. Still, this nearly proletarian population continued to grow rapidly. By the beginning of the nineteenth century, cotters outnumbered freeholders in Denmark, and in Sweden they composed forty percent of the entire population by 1850.

Although the household, made up of the farmer and his family, including cotters, laborers, and servants, constituted the basic social unit in the rural areas, there were other important elements in the hierarchy of rural society. At the top of the scale we find, besides the wealthy landowners, the bailiff. He was usually a man of means and served as the representative of the county government, wielding virtually absolute power in his district. It is not surprising that in legendary tradition the bailiff often appears as a cruel and unjust man, a reputation he shares with the owners of the large estates. The rural folk had little contact with the central government above the level of the bailiff.

Another figure of considerable authority among the rural folk was the minister. In Catholic times the clergy contributed significantly to the development of oral traditions and belief. Saints' legends and exempla, used by priests to illustrate their sermons, lived on as popular narratives. Monks and nuns, who usually received little more than rudimentary theological training, acted as healers and combined invocation of divine help with magic in their medical practice. And belief in the satanic powers of witches had been official church dogma since before the fifteenth century. With the Reformation, established by royal edict in most of Scandinavia during the 1530s (1541 in Iceland), the clergy was stripped of its economic prerogatives. Monasteries were dissolved and most of the church lands and properties sold. The minister became financially dependent upon tithes and voluntary contributions, and often he must have been rather poor. But socially the clergy continued to enjoy a strong position, teaching the people from the pulpit and maintaining control over schools and even over the universities. It is worth noting that the early poets of Scandinavia were frequently clergymen, and they were also the first to pay attention to the oral traditions of the folk and to publish them.

But in spite of his authority, the minister, too, is treated as an ambiguous figure in legend and folktale. He was rarely born in the parish in which he served and remained an outsider by virtue of his social background and education. After the Reformation, the minister's university education was frequently rendered as proof that he had been trained at the Black School at Wittenberg (the town of Martin Luther) and possessed the Black Book which gave him magical power. It was believed that he could not only exorcise the devil but employ the devil's services for his own purposes — such as, travel through the air. Thus the minister at times appears as the defender of the folk who dupes and defeats Satan, but often he is treated as a buffoon or as one wielding equivocal powers.

Well below the landowners, bailiffs, ministers, and farmers, we find another important social group consisting of itinerant laborers and craftsmen. During the haymaking and harvesting, a farmer would often hire additional help. The seasonal laborers would sleep in outhouses and barns, and were fed at the farmer's table. Usually they received no actual wages, and at the end of the season they had to move on, often surviving by begging. Craftsmen, such as shoemakers and tailors, were better off. The farmstead was largely self-sufficient, and the spinning, weaving, and sewing were tasks of the farmer's wife and women servants. Nevertheless, specialists in making clothes and shoes would move from farm to farm and there ply their craft, for a few weeks at a time, in return for room, board, and wages.

Temporary laborers and itinerant craftsmen were often good storytellers and did much to transmit traditions from one place to another. A similar role was played by the soldiers returning from service in the town garrisons or from abroad. The soldiers were usually the sons of cotters and laborers. Normally each landlord was required to provide one soldier for each one hundred acres he owned, and naturally he would dispatch one of his workers rather than his own son.

Upon returning, the soldier would receive a small house to live in, and often he would function as an elementary teacher. Universal elementary education was introduced in Denmark in 1814, in Sweden in 1844, in Norway in 1860, and in Finland, although less comprehensively, in 1865. But for a long time, rural children received only rudimentary instruction; teachers visited farms on a rotating basis for a few weeks at a time, and even the teachers knew little beyond the basics in reading and writing. Secondary education, let alone university study, was available only in the larger towns or cities and was usually reserved for the children of the well-to-do. It was a major advance when N. F. S. Grundtvig, a Danish minister and later bishop, founded the first folk high school in 1844. Geared specifically to the needs of the rural population, the folk high school was in session during the winter months, when the young were not needed as much on the farm. The folk high schools were introduced in Norway in 1865 and in Sweden three years later. They continue as an important element in the Scandinavian educational system today.

A final group to be mentioned here were pedlars, who hawked their wares at farms and at marketplaces in town, and beggars, usually old and jobless, sick or insane. Some of the beggars came from the local community and they were generally well treated; others wandered from village to village and farm to farm. These strangers were usually feared. Often they were accused of thievery, or worse, suspected of using witchcraft to harm crops, livestock, and even the farmer and his family, if they had not been generous enough in doling out food, clothing, or shelter for a night or two. Among the itinerant beggars were individuals who either could not or would not work, gypsies, Finns, and Lapps—all strangers in the eyes of the established community and therefore suspect.

Daily life on the farmstead was stable and often isolated. Nevertheless, regular contacts with the outside world were provided by traders, craftsmen, soldiers, beggars, and occasional visitors, bringing new impulses capable of transforming tradition. Ownership of the land passed from father to son and typically remained in the same family for many generations. The work rhythms were dictated by the exigencies of the soil and the shifting seasons. The folk lived close to nature and believed they were a part of it. In the worldview of the rural population, beliefs taught by the church merged with those native to Scandinavia and surviving in folk tradition. Christianity was late in coming to Scandinavia, making few inroads before 1000 A.D. The Norse religion (like that of the Finns and Lapps) was this-world oriented, and both the old sky gods and the earth bound elves (*alfir* and *disir*) were seen not as transcendent but as being in and of nature. The ancient god Odin, for example, was adept at manipulating the forces of nature through magic. His powers were not supernatural like those of the Christian God, but preternatural. In recent Scandinavian folk traditions, both orientations, one vertical, involving the transcendent deity, the other horizontal, relating humans to the "powers" of nature, exist side by side. We can see this duality in the practices of reputed witches and wise folk and in the underlying, multifarious concepts of the human mind and soul (*hug*), as well as in many church-sponsored rituals surrounding central events in the seasonal and life cycles of the individual, within the context of rural life.

From the perspective of the church, the spirits of the farm, forest, field, river, lake, sea, and air were typically seen as evil, and blessings, exorcisms, amulets, and other sacred devices were used to protect the human community. Today it is easy to dismiss the people's belief in these spirits, along with the church's response to them, as mere superstitions, but that is quite beside the point. Perceiving their daily environment in prescientific but eminently practical terms, the people responded to nature in the way they experienced it, namely as animate and possessed of will and thus capable of aiding humans but also of doing them harm. The farm spirit (Danish/Norwegian, *nisse*, Swedish, *tomte*), for example, ensured the prosperity of house and farm, but if crossed he would steal the farmer's hay, grain, or cattle, depriving him of his wealth and delivering it to a more fortunate neighbor.

The relation between the human community and the spirits of nature thus depended upon mutuality and respect. If asked to move his cow shed because the animal droppings bothered the *haugbo* ("mound-dweller") living underneath the shed, the farmer would usually comply. If his wife was asked to act as midwife to one of the "invisible," she would go. But there were also traditional devices to keep the "invisible" at bay if they became too intrusive. Anything made of steel was considered to have protective properties, as were fire and light and certain seeds and herbs. A mother might place a pair of scissors in the cradle to keep her child from being "changed" or the young girl tending cattle at a remote mountain farm might tie herbs in her hair to keep from being pestered by a would-be fairy lover. Also, newborn children were in danger of being carried off by the "invisible," who would exchange them for their own offspring. This tradition served to explain the dangers surrounding childbirth and common infant diseases, such as mongolism, atrepsy, or rickets, which we now attribute to poor nutrition and other causes. One practical consequence of this belief was that special care was taken to keep the newborn child under constant supervision. Even adolescents and adults could be carried off and "taken into the mountain." Mental depression and other psychological disorders were explained in this way. Or the watersprite (Danish/Norwegian, *nøkk*, Swedish, *näck*) might cause the careless bather to drown in a river or lake, or the spirit of the seas (*draug*) might cause the fisherman to go down with his boat. Although dangerous, the "powers" of nature were also considered to be good neighbors and friends, capable of giving advice and practical aid. In oral tradition we find numerous stories about the "invisible folk" helping their human neighbors, such as the *hulder* alerting the dairymaid to a fire or to a loose cow; we hear about elves teaching a girl to sew or helping a young man repair a tool and about the *nøkk* teaching the aspiring fiddler to play his instrument. We hear of the "subterranean" folk who come to the aid of soldiers during a war. We even hear of successful marriages between the "invisible" and human folk, as well as of brief erotic encounters between them.

In general, sickness was considered to have supranormal origin— that is, to be caused by the "invisible" or by human beings seeking revenge for some real or imagined wrong. In this folk tradition, we find elaborate rituals and spells fusing divine power with magic to drive out hostile influences from the afflicted person or animal. The folk concept of the mind or soul (Danish, *hu*, Norwegian, *hug*, Swedish, *håg*) is fundamental to this context. Unlike the Christian notion of the soul as a spiritual element that separates from the body at the moment of death, the *hug* is continuous with the physical self, representing a person's thought, will, desire, and feeling. The many projections of the *hug* include traditional notions regarding dream experience, including the nightmare, as well as belief in an invisible presence accompanying and preceding the person (Danish/Norwegian, *vord*, Swedish, *vård*). The *hug* could "wander" about without the individual being aware of it, often with dire consequences, but it could also be sent deliberately, for example, in the case of magic flight or other uses of magic. Specialists in the controlled use of the *hug* were called wise folk or witches, depending on whether their skills were considered useful or threatening to the community.

The "unseen" world also included the dead, who continued to "live" in the grave until they finally faded from memory. Oral tradition suggests that the dead were often feared, but relations with them could be friendly. A dead mother's longing for her child might inflict sickness upon the infant (*elsk*); a drowned sailor might haunt the villagers, demanding that a newborn boy be named after him so that he could live on in him; a child born out of wedlock and killed would often torment the mother; and the dead who had not been prepared properly for burial would come back to demand their due. Inversely, thieves or murderers had to "walk again" until they had expiated their crime. But the dead could also give advice, help settle a dispute, or assure a family of their spiritual welfare. Occasionally we hear of a dead spouse returning at night to share in the comforts of his or her accustomed bed and board.

In dealing with the dead, as with the "invisible" folk, respect and caution were called for, and analogous devices and rituals were applied to "lay" the dead and protect the living against unwanted intrusions. In medieval literature we find the revenant (*draug*) being bound to the grave by having a pole rammed through his or her chest, decapitated, or removed from the house through a specially cut hole, which is then walled up again so that he or she cannot get back in. In later folk tradition, it is more typical to keep the dead away by seeding flax around the house, placing a hot griddle on the threshold, or, more constructively, bringing something to the grave that symbolically satisfies the needs of the restless dead.

In the course of an individual's lifetime, there were ritualized events of special significance. Before baptism the infant was considered heathen, and not until its forehead had been sprinkled with holy water was it safe from being "changed" by the "invisible" folk. By the same token, the mother was heathen by virtue of having conceived the child and had to be "churched" in a special purificatory rite (Danish/Norwegian, *kirketagning*, Swedish, *kyrkotagning*). Similarly, confirmation at age fourteen acknowledged the adolescent's progression into adulthood and self-responsibility as a Christian, to be followed in due time by the ceremonies of marriage and, finally, by the sacrament of the funeral. All these church-sponsored rituals instilled in the individual the knowledge that the various stages of the passage through life had not only personal and socioeconomic importance but also sacred significance. Each event marked a transition in the person's life, a period in which special dangers were posed both by the devil and, from the Christian perspective, by the "invisible."

Folk and religious tradition also met in the annual calendar of the liturgical year and popular feast days. Before the time of Christianization, the agricultural year had been divided into two seasons, summer and winter. Each season was then divided by its festival, midsummer and midwinter (*Jul*). After the introduction of Christianity, the church, instead of banishing the folk festivals, paired them with holy days. Thus *Jul* became Christmas, and the midsummer feast became associated with Saint John (the Baptist). The calendar was also filled with numerous saints' days, most of which were lost again after the Reformation. Besides its liturgical significance, the church calendar had its practical use in helping the farmer remember to plant crops, harvest, slaughter, brew, et cetera. In Denmark and southern Sweden, the coming of spring was acknowledged with festive processions "bringing in summer" and by dancing around the maypole decorated with the first green foliage of the year. In Sweden the evening before St. Valborg's Day (May 1) was celebrated with the lighting of bonfires. In this instance, as in the case of Christmas and Saint John's Day, it is the evening before the holy day that has become most important in folk tradition. Christmas Eve is celebrated with eating and drinking and the giving of gifts; Christmas morning the Christian folk go to church. Midsummer Night (June 23) is still the most popular festival throughout Scandinavia. Easter was a purely church-related holiday, but it too was surrounded with traditions about the "other world." The night before Easter, as on Midsummer Night, witches met with Satan on the Blue Mountain (Danish, *Bloksberg*, Norwegian, *Blåkollen*, Swedish, *Blåkulla*) to celebrate the Black Sabbath. Another important folk feast to remember here is Saint Olav's Day (*Olsok*, July 29), supposedly the day the missionary king Olaf Haraldsson died on the battlefield at Stiklestad in Norway. On the Faeroe Islands, *Olsok* continues to be celebrated by communal dancing and the singing of the medieval ballads that tell about the life of the king.

The Storyteller and Oral Tradition

Today the bulk of legends that have been published take the form of complete narratives or stories. However, recent fieldwork suggests that legends are more typically presented in a kind of dialogue or informal conversation. Unfortunately, there is no empirical evidence to prove that this also applies to the way stories were told in the past. But it is noteworthy that we have much more information about storytellers specializing in folktales than in legends. The two forms of storytelling are by no means the same; the legend has always been less dependent upon the specialist for its transmission.

No doubt there were situations in which a legend was recited in its complete form, for example, when a child or an outsider was told it for the first time. This would occur when it was deemed important to impart knowledge of given norms or rules or to tell the history of the family and clan. Detailed descriptions of how legends were traditionally told are rare. Ivar Klokker from Hardanger (Norway), for example, is quoted by Pastor Hertzberg during the nineteenth century: "When the old folk in Hardanger got together at festive occasions, their talk almost always turned to enumerating their ancestors and family, and telling stories about them."

From the end of the nineteenth century we know about several tellers of legends, but, again, we lack precise information about how they told them. Johannes Skar writes about Hallvor Aakre from Setesdal (Norway): "He could sit all week and tell stories, evening after evening. He knew about all the farms and the families living there. . . . He told about strong men and their deeds, about the invisible folk and beliefs and witchcraft." He had learned from his grandfather how to tell stories, but Snorre Sturluson's medieval sagas of the Norse kings influenced his style.

Rikard Berge took down the entire history of the Villands-Clan in Hallingdal (Norway) from Nils Lyingsslåtten (born in 1827), "from Blank-Ola on down through the years, told with such vividness and skill that I have never heard the Norwegian language used better." Berge writes that Nils presented his stories with a freshness and color that made the audience listen not only with their ears but also with their eyes. About another storyteller from the 1890s, Sveinung Sørensen, Rikard Berge states that "he raised the simplest legend up to an elevated epic style. . . . His style possessed vigor, an economical and chiseled form. . . . He dramatized the legends, especially stories about strong men; he changed his voice for each character. . . . He savored the story . . . spinning out an epic thread and holding on to it firmly."

In the classic Norwegian legend collections of P. Chr. Asbjørnsen, we find detailed descriptions of the storyteller, but we know from Asbjørnsen's diaries and notebooks that these descriptions are entirely fictional and thus represent a literary genre.

In the important study of tradition bearers on Gotland (Sweden) during the mid-nineteenth century, Ragnar Bjersby emphasizes that on the whole there is little empirical evidence upon which to base the study of legend performance in the past, but he does provide us with some interesting details about the storytelling situation. For example, he quotes a description from a funeral: "When the festive dinner had ended . . . I happened to be looking into the small bedroom, and there I found entertainment. The sexton was sitting in the middle of the floor, yes. Snoblom on a bed by the door, and there was a whole bunch of older women, and they were telling ghost stories by the dozen. . . . Everybody had one story or another to offer, but best was the old, whitehaired sexton" (Bjersby, 1964, p. 128). The telling of legends during wakes and funerals has been well documented (Inger Christiansen, 1968). It was typically part of all festive get-togethers, such as weddings, Christmas parties, and work feasts. Nevertheless, one must take care not to exaggerate the importance of festive occasions for transmitting legends and folk belief. In the evening, when the folk gathered in the kitchen, all types of traditions were exchanged. Most of the daily work was carried out in unison, which gave many opportunities to talk about traditional knowledge. Legends and folk beliefs were shared by everyone and were told and talked about under many different circumstances as an integral part of everyday life. This meant that stories were usually referred to or told only in an abbreviated form—everybody knew what they were all about. As Norwegian folklorist B. Hertzberg Johnsen was able to document in recent fieldwork studies of a specific local legend, informants had heard the story in its complete form only once (Johnsen, 1980, p. 189). This tendency toward abbreviation of the narrative in the typical performance situation may help to explain the fragmentary nature of many legend texts found in the archives.

If we have but little conclusive data about the storyteller, we have even fewer genuine descriptions of legend performances as an interaction between storyteller and audience. But some of the texts do indicate that collectors had witnessed this type of interaction. In *Historiegubbar på Dal* (Storytellers in Dal, 1866), the Swedish author August Bondeson gives a fictionalized description of storytellers. In his depiction of Anders Backman (born in 1826), he suggests that the audience participated in the performance through commentaries:

Once, when Anders had finished a story about a giant, Mother Stina had something to say:

"What's become of the giants now?"

"Hm, there've never been any giants," said the miller, a young fellow who didn't believe in this sort of thing.

"Yes, but the giant on Bare Mountain, he existed. I've been there and seen the passages in the stone and his cave there," said Mother Stine.

At this point Bondeson broke off the discussion, afraid that the doubter was going to disrupt the mood. Even though this description is fictional, it probably reflects an actual storytelling situation. Rikard Berge has given us an animated depiction of his informant Nils Lyingsslåtten. In the dialogue between Berge and Nils we have perhaps a fairly realistic picture of a traditional legend performance:

When he had asked [Berge] about the harvest and cows in Telemark, Nils suddenly turned to the folk there and asked whether they could get on with the cattle deal they had been negotiating. Møkjal and Nils were neighbors, and now Møkjal was taking the cattle to the mountain pasture and he wanted to have "Kveikreid" along.

But then the tall man straightened up. They did not want to let that cow go; one animal by that name had to remain on the farm.

"It's strange," said Nils, sort of dreaming to himself, "my father also wanted to have that 'Kveikreid' name among his cows. Yes, indeed, he did."

"That's some old nonsense," said Møkjal, turning to the wife and daughter to negotiate further. I stuck with Nils and soon found out what the name "Kveikreid" was all about.

On Rygg they were good friends with the mound folk, he said, so they got a cow from them on loan. Her name was "Kveikreid" and she milked the bucket full every time. Then the mound woman said to the women on Rygg:

"But if someone dies in our family, then we'll have to have the cow back; until then you can have her," she said. And they owned her for many years; but one morning she just disappeared; her stall was empty and since then nobody has seen "Kveikreid." Only the name hung on at the farm, and the cow by that name has always brought prosperity to the cow shed.

"But you've never come across the mound folk?" I asked.

"Oh, sure, of course. The mound folk are just like other people." Once he was out herding cattle, when he saw a mound boy and his mother.

"They were dressed just like the folks here. I thought it was my own mother, I did," said Nils, and so he asked her when he came home:

"What were you and Ola doing on the northern field?"

"We've haven't been there at all," she said. Then he knew for sure that he had seen the mound folk. Møkjal got more and more talkative, the women all the more eager to sell and old Nils got more irritated all the time.

In a recent folkloristic study from Sweden, we have a similar description of the proletarian writer Jan Fridegård who was the son of a cotter and grew up on a large manor. Ebbe Schön writes that Fridegård based much of his writing on firsthand observations of the storyteller and his milieu. Fridegård evoked "not only the particular style and technique of the storyteller but also the reactions of the audience: appreciative comments, expressions of doubt or dislike, the storyteller's counter response, or the response of someone else picking up the thread to tell another story" (E. Schön, 1978, p. 116). What follows is a memorat retold by Fridegård in *Lyktgubbarna* (The Will-o'-the-wisp, 1955, p. 8–9, quoted by Schön, p. 160–161):

It was dangerous on the hill, so it was not a good idea to go up there alone. You could run afoul of an elf or a wood sprite before you knew it. That would be the end of you.

My father told a story about a boy who sat drinking coffee by the edge of the meadow that you can see on the other side of the field. Suddenly he saw the elves dancing, a ring of tiny elves. Stupid and brutal as he was, he jumped up and hit them with his whip. They disappeared but the boy got sick and could not walk home on his own. The horses got home by themselves, but the boy was lying in the field, swollen and in pain.

"Did he get well?" one of my brothers asked.

"Like hell he did! They sent for Madame Tapper, as she was called. She was to melt lead over him, but the lead flew into the walls and ceiling.

"I can't help you," Madame Tapper said angrily, "you must really have upset them. They won't accept the sacrifice."

And he died the next day.

"Now what is one to think about something like that?" my mother asked then.

"Believe anything you want, but it's the truth. Go and ask Madam Tapper, she's still alive, as you know."

"Oh, I know that there's much that's hidden. I don't have to ask her."

It has been argued that the best among folk singers, storytellers, and fiddlers came from the lowest strata in society, most of them cotters, day laborers, fishermen and servants (Bø et al., 1981, p. 17–18). This was the view held by Danish folklorist Evald Tang Kristensen who said, for example, that "folk traditions are mostly preserved by poor folk, and it seems that increased material comforts in life are causing this spiritual inheritance to be lost." In *Gamle kildevæld* (Old Wellsprings, 1927), Kristensen described the milieu in the home of Ane Jensdatter (1830–97), who lived in Lund Moor in the parish of Gjellerup and was one of his more important informants:

> It was a place that lay far from the beaten path, not many strangers ever came there. They lived in great poverty. The mother sang to the children when it got dark in the evening, while the knitting needles moved rapidly, because they had to save light, and the lamp was lit only when it became absolutely necessary. They worked all day, and if everything went as it should, the work lasted until the children became sleepy. Then the mother began with her songs and stories, and sang and sang and sang, until the little ones knew it all by heart, just as if it had been put into print. (p. 34)

Clearly it was Kristensen's goal to document that the poorer folk also possessed their own culture. Nevertheless, one should take this view of the tradition bearer with a grain of salt. Perhaps the role of the poor in this regard has been exaggerated and reflects instead the sociopolitical views of the collector and scholar. However important the role played by the landless and poor was in transmitting folk belief, stories, and songs, it must be remembered that these collective traditions belonged to all the folk, including the landed farmers, and that it shaped their daily existence as much as that of the poor.

Genre Analysis and Function

It is imperative to differentiate between the various genres of folk tradition in terms of content, form, function, distribution, and degree of interaction. A jocular verse does not have the same function as a magic formula. A migratory legend may be based on folk belief from another time or place and is not necessarily representative of folk belief in the area in which it was collected. For the folklorist genre analysis is first of all a critical tool. For the people who live in the tradition, the different genres are time-tested forms of communication. By utilizing generally accepted genres, even socially problematical messages can be expressed in an indirect but unambiguous manner.

One of the most important genres is the legend, which is also one of the most difficult to define. Since the Brothers Grimm, it has been customary to contrast the legend with the folktale. In the introduction to *Deutsche Sagen* (German Legends, 1816), they write: "The folktale is more poetic, the legend is more historical"; and in the second edition of *Deutsche Mythologie* (German Mythology, 1844), Jakob Grimm puts it this way: "Looser, less fettered than the legend, the folktale lacks that local habitation which hampers the legend, but makes it more homelike. The folktale flies, the legend walks, knocks at your door; the one can draw freely out of the fullness of poetry, the other has almost the authority of history."

It is often said that the legend has a firm, stereotyped form, but in fact the complete form is transmitted only in certain situations, for example, when the legend is told to someone who is not familiar with it, as mentioned earlier. More often the legend is referred to only summarily. According to Linda Dégh, the recital of the legend usually takes the form of a conversation. Similarly, Leopold Schmidt maintains that only the content of the legend is fixed and that its form depends on the circumstances in which it is communicated (Schmidt, 1963, p. 108).

The criterion of belief has been employed to characterize the legend. But this may be of little use because belief sometimes changes, when social conditions and the level of scientific knowledge change, and varies from person to person. A legend does not become a folktale just because people cease believing in it, as Max Lüthi writes (Lüthi, 1961, p. 24). Empirical investigations have demonstrated that the attitudes among participants in a legend performance can vary from belief to disbelief and from a positive response to aggressive rejection. Linda Dégh and Andrew Vázsonyi summarize the problem as follows: "Every legend states something. . . . This is distinctive in comparison with tale categories. . . . As much as it seems proven that the personal belief of the participants in the legend process is irrelevant, it also seems to be a rule that general reference to belief is an inherent and the most outstanding feature of the folk legend" (Dégh 1976, p. 119).

We are left, then, with a relatively vague description of the legend as a story about events, including historical events, placed in a supranormal context. Most often the legend is told with the tacit assumption that it is a true story, that it is in agreement with accepted belief and localized in known surroundings and ascribed to trustworthy persons. But the form of the legend found in books — this edition included — is a function of the process of collecting and editing rather than representative of how the legends were told in their natural context.

Traditionally legends have been divided into three main groups: mythical, historical, and etiological. The concept "mythical" is less than satisfactory, however, because it harks back to an outdated idea that the legends are the remains of an older mythology. Furthermore, supranormal elements are no less basic to the etiological legends and to most of the historical legends.

In contrast to local legends, migratory legends are spread over a relatively large area but are always tied to specific localities and persons. The storyteller typically insists that the legend did not come from the outside but rather that it originated right in his own milieu and spread from there.

Legends are often characterized as a form of literature. This view derives partly from collectors and editors giving preference to texts of high literary quality. Another factor may be that in the process of recording, the informant is obliged to produce a complete text for the benefit of an outsider — the collector. But in actual performance it is the personal style of the storyteller that lends aesthetic quality to the legend. The legend does not boast of introductory or concluding formulas, as in the folktale, nor does it always have a developed plot.

C. W. von Sydow distinguished between legends and the so-called memorat. Today the memorat is defined as a personal story about a supranormal experience told by either the individual or a third person quoting him or her. The supranormal experience reported in a memorat often occurs in darkness and usually under conditions of fatigue, stress, or a state between sleeping and waking. Psychologists suggest that in supranormal experiences, visual, tactile, and auditory perceptions and other personal factors combine with the traditional framework of beliefs as well as with social norms of behavior. For example, some men have been drinking and playing poker until late at night. One of the players drops a card on the floor. When he bends down to pick it up, he sees a black dog with glowing eyes and jaws crouching under the table. The men understand that this is the devil, and the drinking and card playing stops immediately. The traditional belief that card playing and drinking are identified with the devil is suddenly actualized. The game breaks off and the balance of social norms is restored.

Most often a supranormal experience is spontaneously interpreted in terms of collective belief. But it also happens that the individual is not sure what the supranormal experience means. The experience remains on the level of the *numen*, and when he or she tells about it to others the result is thus a *numen*-memorat. The experience may then be interpreted by third persons and assimilated into accepted belief. Legends containing similar motifs often influence the retelling of what has happened.

Nevertheless, it sometimes occurs that an individual insists upon an interpretation that differs from the collective tradition, in which case we get what may be called a personal memorat. Personal memorats are easy to identify; they have no parallels or variants in the collective tradition.

Memorats are our most important source for the study of folk belief. They tell about socially accepted supranormal experiences. Wherever we find memorats, we can assume that legends describing the same experience represent actual folk belief in that geographical area.

It has often been suggested that memorats are eventually stylized to the degree that they become legends. But the fact that they contain legend motifs is not sufficient proof. Memorats and legends express two different attitudes toward supranormal experience, and there is no empirical evidence documenting the evolution from one genre to another.

A story about a personal experience or memory that is not supranormal in character is called a chronicat. It has the same relation to historical legends that the memorat has to legends about the supranormal. During the past few years, the chronicat has been expanded to include ethnohistorical materials and has thus become an important source for the expanding field of oral and ethnic history.

The fiction is another major category of prose narrative. They tell about beings not believed in by adults who try to get children to believe in them for pedagogical reasons. For example, parents try to scare children away from playing near a well by telling them that the well sprite will take them. Children occasionally experience the well sprite and tell memorats about it. What is a fiction for one group becomes a belief for another.

Descriptions of various ritualized actions are also an important source for the study of folk belief. These ritual descriptions do not have a firm structure; they constitute a verbalization of an action rather than a narrative genre.

Often we encounter tradition in the form of general statements about supranormal and other circumstances and events. This is not an ethnic genre but, rather, a "collector's genre," which gives a brief and summary description of a larger context. These statements have been termed dites. Dites about folk belief have to be scrutinized carefully by comparing them with memorats and ritual descriptions before they can be accepted as valid documentation.

The magic formula is the last genre that we will consider. It can be described briefly as verbal sequences designed to achieve specific goals through the power of the word. Magic formulas vary from epic narratives to unintelligible combinations of words, letters, and signs. They can be subdivided into four categories, namely, conjurations, which address a direct command to a harmful power; ritual formulas, which describe a given purpose to be achieved through ritual action; epic formulas, which consist of narratives involving magical beings and sympathetic magic; and secret formulas, which combine incomprehensible words, series of letters, and signs and are usually applied through the act of writing.

A good number of magic formulas, usually the less complicated variety, were commonly used by people who applied them to everyday needs, such as, healing minor ailments and protecting the family, livestock, and house against evils of various kinds. The majority of magic formulas, however, were in the hands of specialists who were called upon in more serious cases. Magical formulas were, of course, also used to do harm and therefore were both respected and feared. The source of magic formulas was partly oral tradition and partly printed or handwritten compilations called Black Books.

Magic formulas can also be found in legends. For example, see the stories of witches giving life to troll cats (nos. 39.1–39.2) flying to the Black Mass (no. 41.1, and the legends about healers plying their craft (no. 28.1) or about the baptism of the revenant child (no. 25.1).

Entertainment is an important dimension in all the genres we have discussed, but it is rarely, if ever, primary. William Bascom's classic distinction between the four functions of folklore is still relevant here and can be applied to the various genres. In reciting and talking about legends and supranormal experiences, the folk transmit and reaffirm collective belief. As stated previously, memorats in particular support belief in supranormal beings and their relations to the human world.

Legends also confirm the existing social structure and underlying norms. For example, until recently the work rhythm was normally dictated by the rising and setting of the sun, and consequently people went to bed relatively early. In folk tradition this is expressed by the belief that the "invisible" folk demanded that their human neighbors keep quiet after a certain hour; they would punish them if they were disturbed. At times this belief was used by servants or laborers against employers who insisted that they work beyond a reasonable hour. The example implies a form of social criticism frequently found in folk tradition. The criticism is normally directed against employers, landowners, and other people in power, such as the tax collector, sheriff, or minister. Legends provide a compensatory escape from social hardships and injustice, without necessarily propounding social change. In general, folk tradition is conservative rather than reformist, but there are exceptions to the rule. For example, sometime during the seventeenth century, the migratory legend "The Army of the Huns" was used to raise a revolt against the authorities in both Norway and Sweden.

Another major function of legend tradition is to create a sense of identity and enculturation. Rarely, as in the case of stories about "Holger the Dane" or about the Swedish king Charles XII, does legend tradition take on national significance. Typically legends relate the individual to the familiar local milieu, the village or farm. Generally speaking, legend tradition instills in people a larger worldview and sense of territoriality, that is, a feeling for the geographic and cultural space in which they live.

Finally, legends have an etiological function. They explain natural phenomena, such as rock formations, holy springs, and lakes; they reveal the meaning of place-names and the origin of buildings, in particular, churches; and they illuminate special family traits and traditions. For example, a well-known legend about the Black Death accounts for the allegedly large-pored skin of a family in western Norway by relating it to the experience of a little girl who survived the plague by hiding in a bed filled with bird down (ML 7090, Christiansen, 1958, 10–11). Typically a legend has several functions. For example, the traditions about the "invisible" folk enforcing a reasonable bedtime involves elements of collective belief, the sanctioning of social norms, and an explanation of nocturnal disturbances.

Collections and Editions of Folk Legends and Belief

The oldest extant evidence for legend motifs and folk beliefs in
Scandinavia can be found in the poems of the Elder Edda, which were
compiled in written form in about 1270 A.D. but composed variously
between 700 and 1100 A.D. In them reference is made to troll
women, dwarfs, elves, the walking dead, guardian spirits, shapeshifting, magic flight, and the *hug*. Stories about supranormal beings
abound in the Icelandic sagas and *Landnámabok* (The Book of Settlement) from the twelfth century. In the thirteenth-century *Heimskringla*
(History of the Norse Kings) by Snorre Sturluson, many legends are
woven into the narrative by the author. Some twenty-five years before Snorre, Saxo Grammaticus used both Danish and foreign legend
material to document the history of his people.

An interesting pictorial documentation of legend tradition can be
found on frescoes decorating ceilings and walls in medieval churches.
Popular motifs include the devil in many forms, witches stealing milk
and churning butter by magic, sea maidens, and Saint Olav fighting
the trolls.

The first sustained folk life descriptions appear in histories written
during the sixteenth and seventeenth centuries, of which Olaus Magnus's *Historia de gentibus septentrionalibus* (The History of the Northern
People, 1555) is probably the most noteworthy. Between the end of
the sixteenth and the beginning of the nineteenth centuries, clergymen
and other government officials compiled visitation books and
topographical descriptions containing a wealth of information about
the folk, their customs and beliefs, and a certain number of legends.
In the 1590s, for example, Bishop Jens Nilsson from Oslo recorded
the well-known story about the man who invited himself to share a
drink with the "invisible" folk (no. 47.19). In Denmark the physician
Ole Worm initiated the collecting of popular traditions with the help
of the clergy. Stimulated by Worm's example, Johannes Bureus,
Gustav II Adolph's teacher, began similar efforts in Sweden.

Two other interesting works from the period are Jakob Birkerod's
Folketro og Folkeskikk, særlig fra Fyn (Folk Belief and Customs, especially from Fyn, 1734, published by I. M. Boberg in 1936), and Erik
Pontoppidan's *Everriculum fermenti veteris* (Sweeping Out the Old
Sourdough, 1736, translated from Latin and published by Jørgen Olrik in 1923). Whereas Birkerod allows folk traditions to speak for
themselves, Bishop Pontoppidan identifies folk belief with supersti-

tion analogous to paganism and papism, all of which he wished to "sweep" from the minds of his countryfolk.

It is not until the nineteenth century that the first self-contained editions of folk legends appear. The great example here is the work of the Grimm Brothers in Germany whose *Deutsche Sagen* (German Legends) were published in 1816–18. The Grimms combined literary and oral sources in their editions. In principle they were committed to publishing the legends in their oral-tradition form, but in fact they retold many of them in their own style. Following the model of the Grimm Brothers, the Danish librarian J. M. Thiele excerpted legend material from a great variety of literary sources, and he collected oral traditions; like the Grimm Brothers, he edited his material. The four volumes of *Danske folkesagn* (Danish Folk Legends) were published between 1818–23. The Grimm Brothers and Thiele in turn inspired the Norwegian clergyman Andreas Faye to publish *Norske sagn* (Norwegian Legends) in 1833. Faye reproduced unchanged the legends he culled from literary sources, but he reformulated the texts he collected from oral sources to correspond to the literary style. Faye's primary motivation was to provide appropriate subject matter for the writers and poets of Norway. J. S. Welhaven, for example, based a number of his most successful romances on Faye.

The Norwegians Peter Christen Asbjørnsen and Jørgen Moe emulated the editorial principles developed by the Grimm Brothers. They took a middle position between scholar and traditional storyteller, wishing to preserve intact the texts they collected from their informants but, at the same time, wanting to retell them in a form that was acceptable to the educated reader. Thus, while translating the folktale texts from dialect to the written Dano-Norwegian, they incorporated not only a great number of proverbs and dialect words current in folk speech but also reshaped the overall sentence structure to approximate rural Norwegian. Their *Norske Folke-Eventyr* (Norwegian Folktales, 1841–42 and 1852) became the classic collection of Norwegian folktales. Asbjørnsen continued the work on his own with subsequent editions of Norwegian legends, beginning with *Norske huldreeventyr og folkesagn* (Norwegian Fairytales [memorats] and Folk Legends, 1845–48, new edition 1859). Asbjørnsen placed the legends in the context of fictional frame stories describing Norwegian nature, folk life, and storytelling events. The frame stories were based on observations made by Asbjørnsen while collecting oral traditions, but he felt free to recombine his data as he saw fit. Asbjørnsen's model for the placement of the legends within a fictional context was

Thomas Crofton Crooker's *Fairy Legends and Traditions of Ireland* (1825), which he encountered in Wilhelm Grimm's German translation of the same year (*Irische Elfenmärchen*).

In Iceland, Jón Árnason and Magnús Grímsson published the first, small edition of *Íslenzk æfintýri* (Icelandic Folktales [and legends]) in 1852. Six years later the German legal historian Konrad Maurer contacted Árnason and Grímsson and encouraged them to continue their work, which eventually resulted in the publication of Árnason's *Íslenzkar þjóðsögur og æfintýri* (Icelandic Folk Legends and Tales) in 1862–64. Konrad Maurer published his own collection of Icelandic Legends in *Isländische Volkssagen der Gegenwart* (Icelandic Folk Legends of the Present, Leipzig, 1860). Árnason collected some texts directly from oral tradition, but most of them were contributed by collaborators throughout Iceland, many of whom were his former students at the Latin School in Reykjavik. Árnason published the texts in the form he received them, but wherever he thought the collectors deviated too far from folk speech, he revised the texts accordingly.

In the meantime V. U. Hammershaimb had already published the folk legends of the Faeroe Islands in *Færoiske Sagn* (Faeroese Legends, 1846), which appeared in the learned Danish journal *Annaler for Nordisk Oldkyndighed og Historie* (Annals for Nordic Archeology and History). It was followed by a general collection of Faeroese folk traditions, including a section on folk legends, published in *Antiquarisk Tidsskrift* 1849–51 (Antiquarian Journal, 1852), and another major work, *Færøsk Anthologi* (Faeroese Anthology, 1891). For Hammershaimb collecting folk traditions was closely tied to the effort of formulating a written Faeroese language; his collections in fact constitute the first literary writings in Faeroese. His example was followed by Jakob Jakobsen who published *Faerøske Folkesagn og Æventyr* (Faeroese Folk Legends and Tales) in 1889–1901. In a similar fashion, Ivar Aasen published collections of Norwegian folk traditions in *Prøver af Landsmaalet i Norge* (Samples of Dialects in Norway, 1852) to demonstrate the viability of dialect-based Norwegian as a written language. Parallel efforts were made in Sweden and Swedish Finland, where legends were published in dialect form, as, for example, in the journal *Svenska landsmål och svenskt folkliv* (Swedish Dialects and Folklife, first published in 1878), as well as in volume 6 of the Swedish-Finnish collection entitled *Nyland* 1896).

G. O. Hyltén-Cavallius is the first Scandinavian scholar to give a detailed ethnological description of a province. In *Wärend och Wirdarne* (Warend and Its People, 1864–68), Hyltén-Cavallius not only presents a wealth of folk traditions, including legends, but also analyzes his material on the basis of the romantic premises that had been dominant in folklore studies since the brothers Grimm.

It might be useful to enumerate the most important collections of traditions and legends to appear in the various Scandinavian countries from the 1870s to the present. Svend Grundtvig, best known for his editions of folk ballads, also collected other materials, which were published in *Gamle Danske Minder i Folkemunde* (Old Danish Traditions, 1854–61). Grundtvig's large, unpublished collections of legends, which he accumulated between 1839 and 1883, were eventually published by H. Ellekilde in 1944. The teacher Jens Kamp, stimulated by the interest he encountered in folk high school circles, published *Danske Folkeminder* (Danish Folk Traditions, 1877). A substantial manuscript about folk belief in Denmark was printed posthumously in 1943, under the title *Dansk Folketro* (Danish Folk Belief).

No doubt the most prolific collector of folk traditions in Denmark has been Evald Tang Kristensen. For more than fifty years, he journeyed on foot through most of his home province (Jylland) and faithfully recorded legends, folk beliefs, tales, songs, and every other imaginable aspect of the folk culture. During his lifetime he published seventy-nine books, in most instances acting as his own publisher. His main collection of Danish legends, *Danske sagn* (first series, 1892–1901, second series, 1928–39), included more than 22,000 texts. Four volumes of the monumental *Jyske Folkeminder* (Folk Traditions from Jylland, 1871–97), as well as *Danske skæmte-sagn* (Danish Jocular Legends) and *Gamle Folks Fortællinger om det Jyske Almueliv* (Old Folks' Stories about Life in Jylland, 1891–1902), also contain numerous legend texts. In recording the texts from his informants, Kristensen approximated the written norm of Danish, although he colored it with the folk speech of Jylland. In the beginning, Kristensen did not pay much attention to the individual storyteller because it was his view that the texts represented a collective tradition. But eventually he changed his mind and began to document the traditions as part of the everyday life and milieu in which he found them. In *Gamle Kildevæld* (Old Well-Springs, 1927), he provided a valuable photographic record of some of his most important informants. In a new edition of this work (1981), the photographic images have been supplemented with Kristensen's own detailed biographic notes gleaned from his diaries and other sources.

Other legend collections worth mentioning include *Udvalgte sønderjydske Folkesagn* (Selected Folk Legends from South Jylland, 1919) by

F. Ohrt, and two legend collections by Anders Uhrskov, *Folkesagn* (Folk Legends, 1922) and *Sjællandske sagn* (Legends from Sjælland, 1932). In addition, numerous volumes describing folk life in specific localities throughout Denmark have appeared in the series *Danmarks Folkeminder* (Danish Folk Traditions, 1908).

In Norway Andris Eivindson Vang, a schoolmaster in Valdres and a personal acquaintance of Asbjørnsen, followed the latter's example in publishing *Gamle Reglo aa Rispo ifraa Valdres* (Old Folktales and Legends from Valdres, 1850), followed by *Gamla Segner fraa Valdres* (Old Legends from Valdres, 1870). Vang's collections were the first in Scandinavia to be published in dialect. Johan E. Nilsen, on the other hand, followed the model of Ivar Aasen in publishing *Søgnir fraa Hallingdal* (Legends from Hallingdal, 1868) in *nynorsk* (New Norwegian) rather than in dialect.

One of the more important collectors of folk belief in Norway was Joh. Th. Storaker. His earlier materials were published in the journal *Folkevennen* (The Friend of the People), edited by the sociologist Eilert Sundt. After Storaker's untimely death at age thirty-five, the remainder of his collections was published in the 1920s by Nils Lid.

Another important collection is the eight-volume *Gamalt or Sætesdal* (Old Traditions from Setesdal, 1903–16) by Johannes Skar, which surveys the whole gamut of folk traditions in an area that preserved them intact until quite recently. Setesdal, next to Telemark, has been considered the richest source for the study of folklore in Norway. Skar writes in the dialect of the region he describes.

The Norwegian folklorist who can be compared to Evald T. Kristensen in terms of both the quantity of material collected and the approach is Rikard Berge. Berge also occupies an important place in the history of Norwegian folklore research. Among his legend editions, we should name *Norske eventyr og sagn* (Norwegian Folktales and Legends, collected in collaboration with Sophus Bugge, 1909–13) and *Norsk sogukunst* (The Art of Norwegian Folk Narrative, 1924). In the latter he combines legend texts with broad descriptions of the storytellers and their milieu.

Other important regional collections, some of them up to ten volumes long, include Tov Flatin's from Numedal, Torkell Mauland's from Rogaland, Andreas Mørch's from Sigdal and Eggedal, Sigurd Nergaard's from Østerdalen, Knut Strompdal's from Helgeland, Knut Hermundstad's from Valdres, and Halldor Opedal's from Hardanger. Most recently Olav Bø, Ronald Grambo, and Bjarne and Ørnulf

Hodne published a new edition of Norwegian legends, *Norske segner* (1981).

Many of the above works were published in the series *Norsk folkeminnelags skrifter* (Publications of the Norwegian Folklore Society), which, since its inception in 1921, has produced one hundred twenty volumes. Most of the volumes printed in this series contain legends.

Herman Hofberg published the first collection pretending to represent the legend tradition of Sweden. In *Svenska folksägner* (Swedish Folk Legends, 1882) he aspires to a style that would appeal to a broad, middle-class readership. His language, which is heavily influenced by the romantic literary style of the period, is far removed from the idiom of the rural folk. Eva Wigström's *Folktro och sägner från skilda landskap* (Folk Belief and Legends from Various Provinces, 1898–1914) and J. A. Lundell et al.'s *Sagor, sägner, legender, äventyr och skildringar av folkets levnadssätt på landsmål* (Folktales, Legends, Saints' Legends, and Folk Life Descriptions in Dialect, 1881–1946) also include traditions from different geographical areas of Sweden, but unlike Hofberg, these collectors reproduce their texts in dialect. Waldemar Liungman draws upon his own collections, archives, and printed sources to compile the massive *Sveriges sägner i ord och bild* (Swedish Legends in Word and Image, 1957–69). Liungman's unfinished work is a bold attempt to systematize the entire Swedish legend tradition.

An important scholarly series of folktale and legend editions was published by Gustav Adolfs Akademien under the title *Svenska sagor och sägner* (Swedish Folktales and Legends). Twelve volumes have appeared so far.

Folklorists in Sweden have been as active as those in Norway, compiling regional collections of folk legends as well as other forms of tradition. The most productive folklorist has been Carl-Martin Bergstrand, who has published twenty volumes from southwestern Sweden. Eva Wigström's collection from Skåne, Sven Rothman's from Östergötland, Elias Åström's from the same region, Elin Storckenfeldt's from Västergötland, K. E. Forsslund's from Dalarna, Edvard Olson's from Värmland, and Olof P. Pettersson's from Lappland are some examples. An important, recent all-Swedish edition of legends, with up-to-date introductions and commentaries, is Bengt af Klintberg's *Svenska folksägner* (Swedish Legends, 1972).

The folk traditions of Swedish Finland have been published in virtually complete form in *Finlands svenska folkdiktning* (Finland's Swedish Folk Literature). V. E. V. Wessman has published three volumes of texts in this work, namely *Historiska sägner* (Historical Legends, 1924),

Kulturhistoriska sägner (Cultural-Historical Legends, 1928), and *Mytiska sägner* (Mythical Legends, 1931).

In Iceland a number of collections have appeared since the publication of Árnason's. The most comprehensive is Sigfús Sigfússon's *Íslenzkar þjóðsögur og -sagnir* (Icelandic Folktales and Legends, 16 volumes, 1922–58). A new, scholarly edition of Árnason's classic work by Árni Bøðvarsson and Bjarni Vilhjálmsson, in six volumes, was published in 1954–61.

Excellent, scholarly editions of magic formulas are available in the various Scandinavian countries. In Denmark the representative work is Ferdinand Ohrt's *Danmarks Trylleformler* (Danish Magic Formulas, 1917–21); in Norway A. Chr. Bang's *Norske Hexeformularer og magiske Opskrifter* (Norwegian Magic Formulas and Recipes, 1901–2; in Sweden Em. Linderholm's *Signelser och besvärjelser från medeltid och nytid* (Blessings and Conjurations from the Middle Ages and Modern Times, 1917–40); Swedish–Finnish material is included in V. W. Forsblom's *Magisk folkmedicin* (Magic Folk Medicine, 1927); and Icelandic material can be found in Nat. Lindqvist's *En islandsk svartkonstbok från 1500-talet* (An Icelandic Black Book from the 16th century, 1921).

Among recent English-language editions of Scandinavian legend collections, we should note Reidar Th. Christiansen's *Folktales of Norway* (1964), John Lindow's *Swedish Legends and Folktales* (1978), and Jacqueline Simpson's *Icelandic Folktales and Legends* (1972) and *Legends of Icelandic Magicians* (1975), as well as John F. West's *Faroese Folktales and Legends* (1980).

Legend and Folk Belief Research

The most comprehensive survey of the history of Scandinavian folklore research is Inger M. Boberg's *Folkemindeforskningens historie* (The History of Folklore Research, 1953). Recent overviews include *Leading Folklorists of the North* (edited by Dag Strömbäck et al., 1971); the papers given at the seminar "Folklore och nationsbyggande i Norden" (Folklore and the Concept of the Nation in Scandinavia) held by the Nordic Institute of Folklore in 1979 and published in *Tradisjon* (1980); Magne Velure's "Hovuddrag i nordisk folketruforskning, 1850–1975" (Main Trends in Nordic Folk Belief Research, 1850–1975), published in *Fataburen* (1976); the papers given at the congress "Nordic Tradition Research—Schools and Lines of

Thought," printed in *Studia Fennica* (1983), which includes an updated version of Velure's survey and a survey of prose narrative research by Bengt Holbek; and Elsebeth Vinten's *Islandske folkesagn og eventyr. Indsamling, tradition og traditionsmiljø* (Icelandic Folk Legends and Tales. Collecting, Tradition and Milieu, 1980).

Early Scandinavian research concerning the legend and folk belief reflected the view developed by the Grimm Brothers that contemporary tradition constituted the survival of pre-Christian myths. This view implied that tradition was progressively disintegrating and becoming more and more fragmentary. As a consequence researchers were more interested in reconstructing the beliefs of the past than in studying tradition as an element in contemporary culture. Asbjørnsen's article on the "Wild Hunt" (1852) was probably the earliest example of this tendency. He speculated that the nocturnal riders are the remnants of the pagan gods; but he also suggested that they might be the dead—a view that was echoed in the folk belief of his time. The achievement of Hyltén-Cavallius, whom we previously mentioned, was that he was the first Scandinavian scholar to place the study of folk traditions in their ethnological context.

The next important phase in the development of research is identified, on the one hand, with the British anthropological school—in particular, Edvard Tylor—and, on the other, with the so-called mythological school identified with Wilhelm Mannhardt and his students. Tylor applied Darwin's concept of evolution to the phenomenon of religion, tracing its development from animism to monotheism, and introduced the term survivals in his influential *Primitive Culture*, which appeared in 1871. Mannhardt argued in *Wald- und Feldkulte* (Cults of Forest and Field, 1875–77) that nature spirits were vegetation deities appeased by popular rites and that contemporary customs were in fact degenerated fertility rituals of the past. Mannhardt was the first to use questionnaires as part of a systematic effort to collect folk traditions; he asked Sophus Bugge and Asbjørnsen to do the same on his behalf in Norway.

Tylor, Mannhardt, Andrew Lang, and James Frazer, in whose *The Golden Bough* (1890) the concept of fertility rites was applied universally, shaped Scandinavian scholarship for the next two generations. N. E. Hammarstedt investigated various customs from healing methods to bread-baking and Christmas and wedding festivities, applying the comparative method of Frazer and especially of Mannhardt. Henning F. Feilberg was mainly influenced by H. Spencer's manistic teaching that the worship of dead ancestors lies behind all religion.

Feilberg is best known for his theory that the origin of *jul* and the belief in the "invisible" folk is in the worship of the souls of the dead. His most important works include *Jul* (1904), *Bjærgtagen* (Taken into the Mountain, 1910), *Sjæletro* (The Soul, 1914, and *Nissens Historie* (The History of the House Spirit, 1913). On the whole, however, Spencer's influence was greater in Finland (e.g., with Kaarle Krohn and some of his pupils) than in the rest of Scandinavia. In Swedish-Finnish folklore research, the ideas of the sociologist Edvard Westermarck were of some importance — for instance they influenced Gunnar Landtman's work "Hustomtens förvantskap och härstamning" (The Relations and Origin of the Housespirit, 1922), Gabriel Nikander's "Fruktbarhetsriter under årshögtiderna hos svenskarna i Finland" (Fertility Rites in the Seasonal Festivals of the Swedes in Finland, 1916), and K. Rob. V. Wikman's numerous studies on folk belief. All three scholars were critical of the notion of the "invisible" deriving from a cult of the dead and of the exaggerated emphasis on fertility cults.

In Sweden the ideas of Mannhardt and Frazer were continued by Hilding Celander, who, in his *Nordisk jul* 1 (1928) and other works describes the origin of Christmas as a threshing feast. Also, M. P. Nilsson interpreted the mid-winter celebration as a fertility feast, quoting Snorre's *Sagas of the Norse Kings* as evidence, but he modified Celander's analysis to include the fertility of animals.

Another Swede, Åke Campbell, criticized the theory of survivals, however, asking whether all forms of tradition should be interpreted as evidence of an older system of folk belief. Taking the example of play and jokes in contemporary tradition, he questioned the hypothesis that they represent degenerate forms of originally serious rites. Could not jocular elements be an integral part of tradition at all times? (Campbell, 1925, p. 42). These are the beginnings of the kind of source criticism that became central to folklore studies in the twentieth century.

The most prominent Mannhardtian in Norway was Nils Lid. His *Joleband og vegetasjonsguddom* (Christmas Sheaf and Vegetation Deity, 1928) and similar works are detailed studies of agricultural customs and beliefs based on the German folklorists' theories. Lid came to the conclusion that the tradition of customs was constant and primary, whereas the underlying beliefs changed with time. Methodologically speaking, Nils Lid combined the approach of ethnology with an emphasis on etymological studies.

An entirely different emphasis is found in the Dane Axel Olrik's studies of the form of prose narratives. In *Nogle Grundsætninger for Sagnforskning* (Some Principles Concerning Legend Research, 1921), he does not focus on the legend alone, to be sure, because genre analysis had not yet progressed far enough to make precise distinctions possible. Olrik's primary goal was to establish a morphology of popular prose narrative as a whole, including the legend. In *Nordens Gudeverden* (The World of the Nordic Gods, 1926–51), Olrik, like the survivalists, treated the legend mostly from a perspective of reconstructing a past tradition, in this case, that of myth and heroic legend.

Serious criticism of the evolutionist theory of survivals began with the Swedish scholar Carl Wilhelm von Sydow, who demonstrated that tradition comprises different genres that are of varying value for the study of folk belief and must be distinguished accordingly. As previously mentioned, von Sydow introduced the terms memorat and fict, both of which have proved to be highly fruitful in folklore research. Von Sydow's distinction of genres was patterned on the morphology of species in botany, implying an inner developmental mechanism — an idea that has since been relinquished. The current view is that genres are ideal types abstracted from the various forms actually found in tradition. Von Sydow fought the important theoretical battles, and his students, notably Gunnar Granberg and Albert Eskeröd, applied his theories to detailed analyses of legend and folk belief.

In Granberg's *Skogsrået i yngre nordisk folktradition* (The Wood Sprite in Recent Nordic Folk Tradition, 1935) the emphasis is not on the question of tradition's origin but rather on its relation to the natural environment and its occupational context. Granberg was the first to use statistical analyses to separate collective tradition from personal experience narratives, as well as from migratory motifs. Granberg modified von Sydow's concept of the memorat to mean only those personal narratives that describe supranormal experience.

Albert Eskeröd argues in *Årets äring* (The Annual Harvest, 1947) that tradition reflects the dominant interests of various economic, age, and social groups. He emphasizes the importance of dividing the source material into categories of varying usefulness and reliability, distinguishing not only belief, custom, and the various forms of folk literature but also "the traditional empirical knowledge supported by actual experiences of nature and the particular character of tools and implements" (1947, p. 355). Eskeröd defines folk belief ahistorically as "belief in supernatural, supranormal beings, forces and contexts" (1947, p. 44). He refutes the theories of Mannhardt and his followers concerning vegetation divinities and cults. Eskeröd was accused by C. M. Edsman of lacking historical perspective (1949, p. 21–44), but Eskeröd maintains that contemporary belief and custom provide their own adequate historical explanation. He argues that unless contradicted by specific evidence in the older material, we can assume the continuity of tradition (1947, p. 31). Eskeröd supplants the theory of survivals with a theory of universal origins based on psychological factors actualized in situations of critical importance within the context of everyday working life. Eskeröd was thus the first to apply the theories of Malinowski and Radcliffe-Brown to the analysis of Scandinavian traditions.

In 1952 Eskeröd's contemporary, the Norwegian Svale Solheim, published *Norsk sætertradisjon* (Traditions of Norwegian Mountain Farming), a work in which he too places legends and folk belief in the context of the work experience, but, unlike Eskeröd, Solheim pays scant attention to theoretical considerations. He interprets folk belief as the mirror of social and work conditions. The folk's battle with a harsh natural environment and social injustices provide the basis for Solheim's analysis.

In the study of folk beliefs surrounding healing through magic, three works ought to be mentioned. I. Reichborn-Kjennerud's five-volume *Vår gamle trolldomsmedisin* (Our Ancient Magical Medicine, 1928–47) surveys all aspects of magic healing in Norway, in both a historical and a systematic perspective. In this instance, however, the tradition is not placed in its social context. The Swede Carl-Herman Tillhagen, by contrast, describes the practice of the healer in his social milieu in *Folklig läkekonst* (The Art of Folk Healing, 1958). Lauri Honko's *Krankheitsprojektile* (Illness Projectiles, 1959) focuses on "magic shot" as the cause of illness. Honko treats predominantly the Finnish tradition, but he includes European and non-European materials for the purpose of comparison. Honko approaches his study from a historical and psychological perspective.

Another work by Lauri Honko, *Geisterglaube in Ingermanland* (Spirit Belief in Ingria, 1962), continues Eskeröd's functional analysis of preternatural traditions in the context of everyday life but is also influenced by Finnish research as exemplified by Martti Haavio. Honko has been strongly influenced by cultural anthropology, social psychology, and sociology. He studies the actualization of belief and ritual in the social context and the consequences this has for the individual. The problem of genre analysis as developed by von Sydow, Granberg, and Eskeröd is taken up by Honko in the article "Genre Analysis in Folkloristics and Comparative Religion" (1968), in which he develops the generally accepted view of genres not as fixed phenomena but as abstractions, as "ideal types." This view is reflected prominently in the work of Brynjulf Alver (1967), Åke Hultkrantz (1968), Bengt af Klintberg (1968), Juha Pentikäinen (1968), and Magne Velure (1972).

Since the 1920s, Norwegian scholars have been particularly active in discussing the historical legend. In *Norske ættesogor* (Norwegian Family Sagas, 1922), Knut Liestøl studies the legend cycle about the Skraddar family from Åseral (Vest-Agder), Liestøl's own home village. After a careful examination of the underlying tradition in form and subject matter, Liestøl concludes that the main events as described in the legend cycle are in accord with documented history but that the reading of these events by the tradition bearers is often nonhistorical. These studies were preparatory for a subsequent work, *Upphavet til den islandske ættesaga* (1929; translated into English as The Origin of the Icelandic Family Saga, 1930), in which Liestøl applies the same approach in documenting the historical base of the Icelandic saga and the role of legend tradition as a background to saga literature. Rikard Berge, in an article entitled "Folkesegni og den historiske kritiken" (The Folk Legend and Historical Criticism, 1922), arrived independently of Liestøl at the same conclusions regarding the historicity of legend tradition.

Liestøl's method was historical rather than folkloristic. Two Norwegian historians who were inspired by him, Halvor Nordbø and Lars Reinton, investigated two other cycles of family legends and came to opposite conclusions. Nordbø wrote a doctoral dissertation investigating family legends in Telemark, *Ættesogor frå Telemark* (1928), and found them unreliable as historical documents, both in detail and in the overall outline of events. Lars Reinton, on the other hand, traces the legend cycle about a specific family in Hallingdal dating back uninterruptedly to the 1600s. In *Villandane. Ein etterrøknad i norsk ættesoge* (The Villand Family. A Study of Norwegian Family Legends, 1939), Reinton compares legends that were collected between 1860 and 1930 with historical records and finds them remarkably consistent. Brynjulf Alver has suggested that the reason for the noteworthy agreement between the stories about the Villand Family and historical documentation may be that they had not yet entered collective tradition. This is consistent with Alver's view propounded in his article "Historiske segner og historisk sanning" (Historical Legends and Historical Truth, 1962) that the historicity of the legends does not rest with the external facts but rather with the interpretation of the events as perceived by the folk. In other words, contrary to the students of the historical legend before him, Alver's approach is folkloristic rather than historical.

Alver's methodological perspective is continued by Bjarne Hodne in his doctoral dissertation, *Personalhistoriske sagn* (Personal-Historical Legends, 1973), in which he analyzes legends about known criminals collected from all parts of Norway, dating from 1672 to 1850.

Two other studies to be mentioned here are Kjell Bondevik's *Studier i norsk segnhistorie* (Studies in Norwegian Legend Tradition, 1948), which investigates among other things the Battle of Kringen in 1612 between Norwegians and Scotsmen, focusing on traditional motifs such as the device of rolling logs on the enemy, and Olav Bø's *Heilag Olav i norsk folketradition* (Saint Olav in Norwegian Folk Tradition, 1955), which studies the far-flung traditions about the Norwegian national saint.

The growing interest in legend study during the 1950s led to an international discussion about the need to develop national as well as international legend indexes. In Scandinavia two important indexes have been developed, one by the Norwegian Reidar Th. Christiansen, which covers the more common Norwegian legends of the migratory type (The Migratory Legends, 1958), and the other by Lauri Simonsuuri, which focuses on Finnish legends but also includes German and Scandinavian material (*Typen- und Motifverzeichnis der finnischen mythischen Sagen* [Catalog of Types and Motifs of Finnish Mythical Legends, 1961]). Carl-Herman Tillhagen played a major role in the international work with legend typologies (1963, 1964), and he took the initiative for a comprehensive Swedish legend index, which is now being compiled by Bengt af Klintberg. The Danish folklorist Vibeke Dahll has prepared a useful overview of the status of Scandinavian legend indices and typology in *Nordiske sagnregistre og sagnsystematik* (Nordic Legend Catalogs and Legend Systemization, 2d edition, 1973).

Recently folk belief and legend research has tended toward the analysis of sociocultural patterns exemplified through detailed analyses of specific complexes. The English school of anthropology identified with Mary Douglas and others has been a major influence here. Examples of Scandinavian research along similar lines include Ann-Helene Skjelbred's *Uren og hedning. Barselkvinnen i norsk tradition* (Unclean and Pagan. The New Mother in Norwegian Tradition, 1972), in which she discusses the traditionally ambivalent attitudes toward conception and childbirth; Jonas Frykman's *Horan i bondesamhället* (The Whore in Rural Society, 1977), a historical study of the position of the unwed mother; and Orvar Löfgren's "Fetströmming och lusmörtar" (Folk Beliefs and Cognitive Systems among Swedish Peasant Fishermen, 1975), as well as his dissertation, *Fångstmän i industrisamhället* (Fishermen in Industrial Society, 1977), in which he analyzes folk belief and worldview in a small fishing community in southern Sweden. Both Frykman and Löfgren are less interested in folk belief itself than in how tradition reflects social realities.

Another dimension of this perspective concerns the role of folk or alternative medicine in contemporary society. Folk medicine was previously studied as a historical phenomenon; now the emphasis has shifted to the question of why large segments of the population today continue to avail themselves of alternative medical practices even though a well-developed official health system is available to them. The researchers in the forefront of this line of inquiry have been Bente Alver, Birgitte Rørbye, and Lauri Honko. Recent articles by these scholars were published in *Tradisjon* (no. 8, 1978). Further discussions can be found in the book-length study *Botare* (Healers, 1980) by Alver, Rørbye, af Klintberg, and Anna-Leena Siikala.

The continuation of legend tradition in an urban, post industrial setting has received some scholarly attention in the past few years, mostly in the form of articles by Bengt af Klintberg (1973, 1976), Magne Velure (1979), Carsten Bregenhøj (1969, 1978), Reimund Kvideland (1973, 1980), and Hans Ohlsson (1976).

Many of the contemporary legends (or urban legends, as they are usually called) are American in origin, but due to modern communications and travel they have become as international as the older migratory legends. Modern legends often express a sense of insecurity and frustration with contemporary life, ranging from trivial concerns to more basic social problems. Thus there are legends about the difficulties people have in dealing with the many new and often exotic foodstuffs appearing on the grocery shelves, or about the conflicts arising when members of other races enter a racially homogeneous and exclusive social milieu, or about the culture shock resulting from the increased mobility of modern life, or about the widespread fear of seemingly uncontrollable and dangerous groups such as terrorists, motorcycle gangs, and punks. Many legends express anxiety over modern technology, the rapid pace of social change, and the general feeling that people are losing control over their own lives. In much of contemporary narrative tradition we see a conflict between the progressive internationalization of modern life and the need for local identity and territoriality. On the whole the culture mirrored in contemporary legends differs radically from the stable rural world depicted in the older legend tradition.

Much of the work done by Scandinavian folklorists during the last decade or so has been based on intensive fieldwork. Collecting and systematizing oral traditions in archives has been central in Scandinavian folkloristics from the beginning. The historical-geographical method developed by Finnish scholars, for example, required the accumulation of a large body of variants. With the advent of functional analysis and social psychology, however, scholars found it necessary to go beyond the archives into the field and there find the context in which tradition functions. One of the problems raised by the increased attention to the social role of folklore is that the researcher's own preconceived notions may be challenged. Thus the shifting focus from the literary and structural analysis of texts to the analysis of sociocultural values and attitudes expressed in texts may lead to the conclusion that the researcher's theoretical assumptions are too narrow. In ethnomedical research, for instance, the concept of illness as a malfunctioning—in which the body is analogous to a machine—is pitifully inadequate. This line of research leads to larger existential questions, such as, which social factors determine whether we consider ourselves healthy, who defines the role of the patient, and how we should view the interaction between patient and healer. Regarded in this way, folklore studies could lead to a revision of the medical practices authorized by the official health care system, a process that is now beginning in the Scandinavian countries.

Whereas earlier research thus focused on diachronic viewpoints, modern folklore studies have turned to synchronic perspectives with fruitful results. It is too early to determine to what degree these perspectives can be applied to the study of the older legend tradition and folk belief. However, this much is clear: the concept of tradition itself has been significantly expanded to include all aspects of collective culture. Tradition is no longer regarded as an identifiable, separate product but as a dynamic, continuous process involving everyone. This applies as much to contemporary urban society as it does to the preindustrial rural past.

PART I
The Human Soul

Part I illustration: The devil carrying off
the soul of a dying man. Mural
painting, ca. 1520, from a church in
Sæby, Vendsyssel (Denmark).

I n Scandinavian folk tradition the human soul is usually referred to as *hug* (Danish *hu*, Swedish *håg*). Occasionally we come across the cognate of the English term (Danish *sjæl*, Norwegian *sjel*, Swedish *själ*). By the time the latter was introduced to Scandinavia by missionaries from England and Germany, almost a thousand years ago, it had acquired overriding Christian meanings. According to Saint Paul, the soul is primarily a spiritual element identified with the godhead and therefore dichotomous to the physical self. The term *hug*, by contrast, does not imply any such meanings. Rather, it refers to the mental life of the individual — to personality, thoughts, feelings, and desires.

There are various and complex conceptions of the *hug* imbuing the greater part of Scandinavian tradition, from the medieval literature of Iceland to more recent folk belief and legend. It was believed that the *hug* could affect both animate and inanimate objects — including other people — either consciously or unconsciously. The deliberate manipulation of the *hug* is the basis of all magic. The *hug* can manifest itself invisibly or it can take on a shape (*ham*). In some instances, the shape assumed by the *hug* has developed into an independent supranormal being, as exemplified by the many traditions about the nightmare (*mare*).

Other important projections of the *hug* include the *vord* (Swedish *vård*), which is a kind of presence accompanying the individual; the dream-soul, which leaves the body during sleep; the *vardöger* or *fyreferd* (Swedish *förfäl*), a visual or auditory experience presaging a person's approach; and the free-soul, which is the soul sent from the body in magic flight.

See Else Mundal, *Fylgjemotiva i norrøn litteratur* (1974); Dag Strömbäck, *Sejd* (1935), and "The Concept of the Soul in Nordic Tradition," *Arv* 31 (1975), 5–22; Bente G. Alver, "Conceptions of the Living Human Soul in the Norwegian Tradition," *Temenos* 7 (1971), 7–33; Nils Lid, "Magiske fyrestillingar og bruk," *Nordisk kultur* 19 (1936), 3–76; H. F. Feilberg, "Sjæletro," *Danmarks folkeminder* 10 (1914); Åke Campbell, "Det onda ögat och besläktade föreställningar i svensk folktradition," *FmFt* 20 (1933), 121–46.

1. The Power of Thought

If a person sneezed, yawned, hiccuped, or felt a tickling sensation, someone was thinking about him or her. Another person's *hug* had entered his or her body. It was considered irresponsible to let one's mind wander because it could bring harm to someone else. Sickness was often explained as resulting from a *hug* which had entered the body of the sick person or animal.

1.1 *When Your Nose Itches*

When your nose itches, someone is thinking of you.

> Collected by Edvard Grimstad in Gudbrandsdal, Oppland (Norway). Printed in Grimstad, *Etter gamalt. Folkeminne frå Gudbrandsdalen* 3 (1953), 13.

1.2 *When Your Toe Throbs*

A throbbing sensation in your big toe means that someone is thinking about you. If it is the big toe of your right foot, it is a man; if it is the big toe of your left foot, it is a woman.

> Collected by Peter Lunde in Eikjen, Vest-Agder (Norway). Printed in Lunde, *Kynnehuset. Vestegdske folkeminne* (1924), 197.

1.3 When Your Ears Ring

When your ears ring, someone is talking about you. If the right ear rings, they are saying something nice. If the left ear rings, they are saying something nasty.

> Printed in Just M. Thiele, *Danske folkesagn* 3 (1860), 141.

1.4 My, What an Appetite She Has!

Grandmother sat looking at the old woman and thought to herself: "My, what an appetite she has!"
At once the woman got nauseated and started throwing up. She was sick for several hours, until grandmother recalled what she had been thinking. Then the woman got better.

> To avoid the effects of envy, as exemplified in this memorat, people would customarily offer food to anyone who observed them eating.
> Ms. in ULMA 8:0 saml. Printed in Åke Campbell, "Det onda ögat, *FmFt* 20 (1933), 142.

1.5 When Your Right Eye Itches

When your right eye itches, something bad is going to happen to you.

> Collected by V. U. Hammershaimb on the Faeroe Islands. Printed in Hammershaimb, "Nogle færøiske talemåder," *Antiquarisk Tidsskrift 1849–51* (1852), 305. Reprinted in Hammershaimb, *Savn* (1969), 187.

1.6 The Riding Hug

Some people have a stronger *hug* than others. The strongest *hug* is called a "riding *hug*." It can be so powerful that if you are visiting a farm, the farmer's cattle might get sick. To make them well again, you must go to the barn and lift the animals up or put your arms around them and pet them. Then they will be healed at once.

> This *dite* was collected in Konsmo, Vest-Agder (Norway). Printed in Joh. Th. Storaker, *Mennesket og arbeidet i den norske folketro* (1938), 74.

1.7 The Woman Who Nearly Killed the Horse

So, you do not believe that thoughts can be dangerous? A woman nearly killed my father's horse. She did not mean to, but she had powerful thoughts. She lived someplace along the road to Särna. My father often traveled from Särna down to Falun, and her house was right by the road. She was a witch. When she saw the horse, she thought to herself what a big animal it was. At that moment the horse collapsed and was ready to die. But the woman came running.

"I didn't mean to do it, I didn't!" she cried.

And she breathed on the horse here and there until the animal got up and was as good as new. It was a big, reddish brown horse. So, you see, thoughts really can be dangerous.

> The human breath was thought to possess healing power. (Cf. no. 28.8)
>
> See Herman Geijer, "En gosses märkvärdiga upplevelser," *Svenska landsmål* (1913), 99–142.
>
> This memorat was collected by Herman Geijer from a shoe-maker in Gärdebyen, Rättvik, Dalarna (Sweden). Printed in Karl-Erik Forsslund, *Med Dalälven från källorna till havet. I. Österdalälven. 8. Rättvik* (1922), 125. Reprinted in Dag Strömbäck, *Folklore och filologi* (1970), 272.

1.8 The Girl Who Thought of Her Sweetheart

One evening a young girl decided to go dancing. She hurried on her way. When she got close to where the dance was being held, she came to a creek. While the girl stared down into the water, a man rose to the surface and handed her a big knife. She took the knife and the man vanished. She knew him at once; it was a man who was away at sea at the time.

A few years later, the man returned and married the girl. One day he saw the knife, recognized it, and asked his wife whether she had tormented him that night long ago. When she admitted how she had gotten the knife that evening, he stabbed her to death.

> The man's response shows that it was the strength of the girl's longing that forced his *hug* to appear on the surface of the water. According to tradition, conjuring the *hug* in this manner caused great emotional strain on the person called and could be quite dangerous for him or her.
>
> Collected in 1922 at Närpes folk high school, Österbotten (Finland). Printed in V. E. V. Wessman, *Sägner* 3.2 (1931), 562.

2. Changing Someone's Mind

It was possible to affect someone's thoughts and feelings with the help of magic. *Hug*-turning, as it was called in folk tradition, mostly concerned the act of making someone love you or of ridding yourself of an unwelcome passion. But experts in magic also resorted to *hug*-turning when practicing revenge.

2.1 To Make a Girl Love You

To turn a girl's *hug*, kill a starling, take its heart, and sew it into a little piece of cloth. Then put it between the big toe and the second toe of your right foot and, thus, step on the foot of the girl you love—she will be yours.

> This is a description of a ritual involving sympathetic magic. (cf. no. 34.1.) The heart has traditionally been looked upon as the seat of life and of the passions.
>
> Collected by Lars M. Fjellstad in Elverum, Hedmark (Norway). Printed in Fjellstad, *Gammalt frå Elvrom* (1945), 73.

2.2 Love Magic

If a guy can catch a live swallow, cut out its tongue, and, with the tongue in his mouth, kiss a girl, she will be consumed by such desire that she will not give him peace until they are married.

> The heart and tongue of the swallow are common ingredients in magic rituals.
>
> Collected by Jeppe Aakjær in Jylland (Denmark). Printed in Aakjær, *Jyske folkeminder* (1966), 94.

2.3 The Love Potion

A boy from Heiæ in Fjotland mixed something into a drink—I think it was urine—and gave it to a girl. He wanted her very much but was not sure whether she was willing. They got married.

> This ritual is based on the idea that even bodily secretions—urine, sweat, blood, and saliva—contain the *hug* (pars-pro-toto).
>
> Collected by Peter Lunde in Fjotland, Vest-Agder (Norway). Printed in Lunde, *Kynnehuset. Vestegdske folkeminne* (1924), 3.

2.4 *Three Drops of Blood*

The great-grandfather of the man who told this story supposedly hailed from a town called Halden. He was a spry and good-looking fellow. Once, he got a big apple from a girl. When he cut it open, he found three drops of blood inside. He quickly threw the apple away, because he understood right away that the girl wanted to turn his *hug* to her.

> Collected by Peter Lunde in Bjelland, Vest-Agder (Norway).
> Printed in Lunde, *Kynnehuset. Vestegdske folkeminne* (1924), 3.

2.5 *Eileiv the Fortune-Teller*

Eileiv the fortune-teller lived in the mid-nineteenth century, in the township of Sau. He was a wise man, had second sight, and could do amazing things.

Once, Eileiv visited a farm in Bø. He had a falling-out with a servant girl, and, by the time he left, he was steaming mad. The girl's wooden shoes stood right by the door and Eileiv spat into them. When the folks on the farm discovered Eileiv's spittle, they gave it to the pig running around in the yard—just for a joke. But as soon as the pig had lapped up the spittle, it became wild and drunk. It took off after Eileiv and finally caught up with him. Eileiv turned around, gave the pig a box on the ear, and said:

"Get yourself home, you aren't the one supposed to come."

Another time Eileiv was at a dance in Nes. He asked a girl to dance with him. She was not too keen on the idea and refused. Then Eileiv threw himself down on a bed, and, before anyone knew what was happening, the girl followed him to the bed, took off all her clothes, and lay down beside him. Everyone at the dance was watching. It took quite a while before the girl recovered consciousness. By that time, she was really cross. All the people laughed at her and were greatly entertained.

> Eileiv the fortune-teller was well known in Telemark, not only for his power of magic but also for his wit. Many legends are told about him.
> See Ørnulf Hodne, "Trolldomssaken mot Spå-Eilev, "*Norveg* 24 (1981), 7–40.
> Collected by Kjetil A. Flatin in Seljord, Telemark (Norway).
> Printed in Flatin, *Tussar og trolldom* (1930), 96–97.

2.6 Uglehe'en

There was a man from the Finn Woods called Uglehe'en. He knew a lot of magic.

One night he arrived at a farm. Tired and exhausted, he sat down on the edge of the fireplace. A girl named Marit was cooking porridge.

"Get out of here, you ugly bum," she said, "you're in the way." She probably did not mean anything by it, but he took it amiss.

"Sure, I'm ugly all right. But no matter how ugly I am, you're going to be so crazy about me that you will follow me anywhere."

Well, the girl just laughed. She did not think she would be running after him very soon. He slept there that night, and the next morning he got up early and left. He did not stop until late in the day when he came to another farm. There he stopped to rest. A little later the same day, the girl began to feel so queer. She could not help herself: she had to go after him. She knew this was ridiculous and resisted as hard as she could, but go she must. It was late at night when she got to the farm where Uglehe'en was staying. Everybody had gone to bed by the time she knocked on the door.

"Well, I'll let you go this time," he said, "but I imagine you won't be making fun of old folks again."

> Uglehe'en, a transient wise man, is remembered in a number of legends. (Cf. nos. 34.1–34.4.)
> Collected by Sigurd Nergaard in Elverum, Hedmark (Norway). Printed in Nergaard, *Hulder og trollskap. Folkeminne fraa Østerdalen* 4 (1925), 61–63.

2.7 He Wanted the Farmer to Follow Him

One summer day during haying season, a farmer was in his barn unloading hay. A beggar came in and asked for a little something. The farmer answered that he did not have time just then. Time was short and the weather good, he said. The poor man kept on begging and would not give in. Then the farmer got mad and said that he had better get out of there, and quickly too; he did not have time to listen to his whimpering and whining in the middle of the haying season. But now the beggar got angry and spiteful.

"You're going to be sorry," he said. And he left.

The farmer had taken off his shoes and put them aside on the threshing floor. But when the beggar left, the farmer saw him spit in one of the shoes.

"I better watch out for him," the farmer thought, and when he was done with the load, he put the foot of the horse into the shoe the beggar had spit on. Believe me, that horse went crazy! It took off after the beggar like a shot, almost as if to run him down. You see, the beggar knew how to cast spells. He had wanted the farmer to follow him, but he got the horse instead.

I do not know how things turned out in the end. If the beggar was not able to undo the spell, the nag probably trampled him into the dirt. Or maybe he is still walking around with that crazy horse trailing behind.

Collected by Torkell Mauland in Jæren, Rogaland (Norway). Printed in Mauland, *Folkeminne fraa Rogaland* 2 (1931), 34.

3. The Evil Eye

It was generally believed that the power of the *hug* could be transferred to another being or object through sight, touch, or the spoken word, often with the intent to do harm. Hence, the expressions evil eye, evil hand, evil foot, and evil tongue.

3.1 The Bewitched Child

There was a mother who had a one-year old child. The child was quite sick, and some knowledgeable folk said it was the English disease. They told her to see a physician or take certain medicines that had cured other children. But one day a beggar woman came to the house, a gypsy of the kind we do not see around much anymore. She knew right away what was wrong with the child. Other people were behind it; the child had been bewitched by the evil eye. The mother believed her, because the child had been ill for more than six months. But the beggar knew a cure.

She told them to dig a grave on the south side of the cemetery and place the child in it, naked and on its back, turning it to the east and then to the west, at high noon. Then they were to fill in the grave and replace the sod exactly the way it had been before. The next day at noon, the mother carried a shovel and the grandmother carried the child, and they went to the cemetery, where they did what the gypsy had told them to do. The mother undressed the child and the grand-mother dug the grave. Later, she closed it up again.

The man who told this story watched them dress the child and fill in the grave, but he did not see the actual ceremony.

> The child is healed through a ritual involving symbolic death. (Cf. no. 28.3.)
>
> This memorat from Himmerland, Jylland (Denmark) was pub-lished by *Daglige Nyheder* on June 2, 1880, on the basis of a report first printed in *Nordjyllands folkeblad*. Reprinted in Jens Kamp, *Dansk folketro* (1943), 211–12.

3.2 English Disease

A mother must be careful lest a woman of loose morals cast an eye on her child when it is undressed. If this were to happen, the child could get the English disease or some other sickness, which only a wise woman can cure. Even the father of the child, if he were to have an affair with such a woman, could make the child sick just by look-ing at it.

> In this *dite* the harmful power of the evil eye is related to an in-fraction against social and moral norms. In general sickness was explained as resulting from either demonic or moral causes. (Cf. no. 28.9.)
>
> See Jonas Frykman, *Horan i bondesamhället* (1977), 25–54.
>
> Collected on Falster (Denmark). Printed in Jens Kamp, *Danske folkeminder* (1877), 364.

3.3 Anders Provst

There was an old man named Anders Provst. He was said to have the evil eye. If he bid on an animal but did not get it, things never went well for the owner afterward.

Be that as it may, one summer Anders Provst came over to my place. It was the year I was doing some building. He wanted me to sell him a certain cow. It was a really good milking cow. Well, I said no; it was quite out of the question. We were expecting a lot of guests, and we had only four cows all told. He insisted that he want-ed to buy that cow, but I wasn't going to have anything to do with it.

Well, the cow had a calf in good time, but then, afterward, it choked on the first bite of fodder it took. Things went from bad to worse. The cow got constipated and there was nothing we could do. We even tried passing a live frog through her. It seemed that the frog scraped her out a bit, but, enough of that, the cow died on me. When we cut her open to take a look, we found that first bite of fodder in the stomach, which we call the King's Hat. It was lodged on one side and was all rotten.

Whether Anders Provst was to blame for all this, I will leave unsaid.

> The unsuccessful healing ritual described in this memorat is a form of sympathetic magic.
>
> Collected by E. T. Kristensen in Jylland (Denmark). Printed in Kristensen, *Jyske folkeminder* 8 (1886), 292–93.

3.4 The Farmer in Krakerås

Many years ago there was a farmer here in Krakerås. There was something odd about him; he could do things.

He was in the cow shed one day and petted one of the animals.

"What a nice cow," he said.

After that the cow would not give any milk for a long time.

They had a foal and once he took it by the neck.

"What's the matter with you?" he asked.

The foal remained lying there and never got up again.

> The text exemplifies both the evil hand and the evil tongue.
>
> Ms. in ULMA 5033. Printed in Åke Campbell, "Det onda ögat," *FmFt* 20 (1933), 137.

3.5 Setting Up a Loom

When setting up a loom, be sure to lock the door. Otherwise someone might bring an evil foot to the weaving.

> Collected by Eva Wigström from a woman in Skanörs Ljung, Skåne (Sweden). Printed in Wigström, *Folktro och sägner* (1898–1914), 443. Reprinted in Wigström, *Folktro och sägner*, edited by Aina Stenklo (1952), 32.

3.6 *The Woman Who Had an Evil Foot*

As I mentioned a little while ago, some people have an evil foot. If you meet one of them on your way to work, you can be sure that something will go awry.

A few weeks back, the man in charge of the blasting in the stone pit here met such a woman. Do you think that he could get any of his explosives to detonate? No way! But the next day everything worked like greased lightning.

> Collected by Eva Wigström from a woman in Skanörs Ljung, Skåne (Sweden). Printed in Wigström, *Folktro och sägner*, (1898–1914), 7. Reprinted in Wigström, *Folktro och sägner*, edited by Aina Stenklo (1952), 36.

4. Envy

A particularly powerful manifestation of the *hug* is referred to in folk tradition as "envy" (Danish *avind*, Norwegian *ovund*, Swedish *avund*). People feared envy. It was believed that this emotion had a strong, adverse effect on human beings and animals, as well as on inanimate objects.

4.1 *Envy Kills*

Old Stina was a dangerous woman. She came to my grandmother's cow barn once to help her with one of the cows that was having a calf. Stina wanted that calf, but she did not get it. A few weeks later the calf died, and the cow died soon after. My grandmother was sure that Stina had killed them both with her envy.

> According to folk tradition, the things most often subject to envy are cattle and the various products of the farm.
> This memorat was collected in Wilhelmina parish, Lappland (Sweden). Ms. in ULMA 8:0 saml. Printed in Åke Campbell, "Det onda ögat," *FmFt* 20 (1933), 140.

4.2 *A Prayer against Envy*

I swear by my faith that the Virgin Mary herself milked cows. She heeds the dairymaid and chases away all evil from my animal. I make the sign of the cross on your back, and no envious woman will have power over you. I pour the last drop of milk through the collar that ties you. May witchcraft and demons and envy come to naught!

> This magic formula combines conjuration and ritual to protect the animals against various hostile influences, including envy. The Virgin Mary is invoked as the patron of cattle as well as of the dairymaid. Milking through the collar of the cow was a general protection against the demonic. The last drops of the milk were thought to contain the "good fortune," that is, both the quality and the quantity, of the milk. A few drops were always left in the bucket to ensure a continued supply.
>
> See Svale Solheim, *Norsk sætertradisjon* (1952), 129–39, 288–319.
>
> Collected by V. U. Hammershaimb on the Færoe Islands. Printed in Hammershaimb, "Barneviser og ramser," *Antiquarisk Tidsskrift 1849–51* (1852), 315. Reprinted in Hammershaimb, *Savn* (1969), 197.

4.3 Knock on Wood

When sitting at a table and talking about something you or someone near and dear owns, you had better knock softly on the underside of the table and wish that it will be yours to keep for a long time. Otherwise, "something" will be envious and try to take it away from you.

> Here envy is not identified with a person but with an unspecified "power."
>
> See Iørn Piø, *Bank under bordet* (1963), 13–31.
>
> Collected in East Jylland (Denmark). Printed in Jens Kamp, *Danske folkeminder* (1877), 401.

4.4 Envy Corrodes a Stone

Envy is powerful. Someone once asked a witch whether she believed that there was magic.

"No, I don't believe so," she said, "but envy, envy! Envy will corrode even a stone."

And that must be true.

Once there were two men out walking. They were neighbors, and their names were Olav and Uv. Uv was prosperous, but Olav was poor. Olav became so envious of Uv that he nearly wasted away.

So they walked on. Uv understood only too well what Olav was thinking. Uv wanted to test Olav. He picked up a stone and hid it. Olav thought Uv must have found something special and asked:

"What did you find this time?"

"Oh," said Uv, "I'm not telling a soul. What I found can't be bought for money."

Olav almost burned up with envy. Then they came to a shack. Uv did not want to drag the stone along anymore so he stuffed it under a log when Olav was not looking. Olav went about, year in and year out, they say, sick with envy of what Uv had found. Uv knew this and when he happened to pass by the shack again, he remembered to look for the stone. But all that was left was a bit of dust.

So you see, envy will corrode even a stone.

> This rare legend dramatically demonstrates that envy can affect even inanimate objects.
>
> Collected by John and Hallvor Lie from their grandmother in Veum, Telemark (Norway). Printed in J. and H. Lie, *Gaamaalt etti bestemor*, edited by Rikard Berge (1925), 33.

5. The Nightmare

The dream experience commonly referred to as a nightmare was interpreted as the visitation of someone's *hug*. Sexual dreams play a large part in this context. The *mare* is usually described as a weight on the sleeper's chest. Both human beings and animals could be "ridden" by the *mare*.

In time the *mare* developed into a separate supranormal being. It was believed that a woman could ease birth pains by crawling through the fetal membrane of a foal. But her offspring would become a *mare*, if female, a werewolf, if male. (Cf. no. 12.1.)

> See Carl-Herman Tillhagen, "The Conception of the Nightmare in Sweden," *Humaniora: Essays honoring Archer Taylor*, edited by W. D. Hand and G. Holt (1968), 317–29; David Hufford, "A New Approach to the Old Hag: The Nightmare Tradition Reexamined," *American Folk Medicine*, edited by W. D. Hand (1976), 73–85; D. Ward, "The Little Man Who Wasn't There: On Encounters with the Supranormal," *Fabula* 18 (1977), 212–25; Bengt Holbek and Iørn Piø, *Fabeldyr og sagnfolk* (1967), 186–99; K. Visted and H. Stigum, *Vår gamle bondekultur* 2 (1971), 366–68; I. Reichborn-Kjennerud, *Vår gamle trolldomsmedisin* 2 (1933), 17; 4

(1944), 143–52; Dag Strömbäck, "Ein Beitrag zu den älteren Vorstellungen von der *mara*," *Arv* 32–33 (1976–77), 282–86.

5.1 The Woman Who Thought the Nightmare Was Her Husband

In the old days, people were bothered by the *mare* more often than they are today. But I was really plagued by her one night in Veadal.

I had locked the door and been in bed for some time. Then she came. She held me down so that I could not move, not even my hand or a single finger, nor could I talk or scream. I thought it was my husband, I seemed to feel his beard and chin. When I finally got my speech back, I said:

"How can you be heartless enough to come in here and lie on top of me, scaring me out of my wits, and not even talk to me?!"

But there was no answer and soon I realized that I was all alone in my bed. I folded my hands and said the Lord's prayer. Then I put on my underclothes, got a light, and searched in every corner and under the bed. But there was no one in the room.

> In this memorat a woman apparently dreams of her husband but subsequently interprets the experience as a visit by the *mare*.
> Collected by Halldor O. Opedal in Eidfjord, Hardanger, Hordaland (Norway). Printed in Opedal, *Makter og menneske*. *Folkeminne ifrå Hardanger* 1 (1930), 99.

5.2 The Mare in the Shape of a Cat

Once the *mare* came to me as a cat. It was at night. I had just gone to bed. I had not been asleep yet and lay wide awake. Then I suddenly heard something padding across the floor. I thought it was the cat; it pads like that. It came closer to the bed, and suddenly it came up to me. It came from the foot of the bed and lay on top of me, pinning me down. I could not move a finger. I did not know what to do except to pray. Then it disappeared.

The *mare* comes to you when you sleep. She lies on top of you so that you can not breathe. You feel like you are going to choke.

> It is not unusual that the *mare* takes on the appearance of a cat or some other animal.

Collected by Andreas Mørch in Sigdal-Eggedal, Buskerud (Norway). Printed in Mørch, *Frå gamle dagar. Folkeminne frå Sigdal og Eggedal* (1932), 44–45.

5.3 The **Mare**

The *mare* is a troll that looks like a beautiful woman. At night, when everyone is asleep, she comes in and lies down on top of you and presses down so hard on your chest that you can not breathe or move your arms and legs. She sticks her fingers into your mouth to count your teeth, but by the time she gets them all counted, you can not breathe and you die. You must try to get her off, and if you manage to shout "Jesus," she has to flee. People think they are lying in bed wide awake and see a *mare* coming to their bed and lying down on top of the covers, but still they can not do anything to defend themselves. At night she might even be in the room unseen. To find out, take a knife, wrap it in a handkerchief or garter and pass it from hand to hand around yourself three times, reciting:

Mare, mare mine, hear!
Are you now inside here,
Do you forget that whack-ho
That Sigurd Sigmundarson gave you
on your snout, my dear?
Mare, mare mine, hear!
Are you now inside here,
out you must go,
bearing rocks and stones,
and everything within here!

If the knife lies uncovered after the third turn, the *mare* is not inside the house. But if the knife is covered, she is inside, and you must wrap the handkerchief or garter around the knife two more times and do the same as before, if you want to get the *mare* out. To prevent her from getting into the bed, it is a good idea to turn your shoes so that the heels are pointing toward the bed and the toes away—then she will not have an easy time trying to climb in!

> In this description the *mare* manifests itself as a demonic being that is capable of killing. Steel and particularly sharp knives were normally used as protection against evil. Here the knife is used to discover and drive out the invisible *mare*. Sometimes a knife would be suspended over the bed to keep the *mare* away.

Collected by V. U. Hammershaimb on the Faeroe Islands. Printed in Hammershaimb, "Færöiske folkesagn," *Antiquarisk Tidsskrift 1849–51* (1852), 203–4. Reprinted in Hammershaimb, *Savn* (1969), 147–48.

5.4 He Spoke Too Early

A couple of tailors were visiting a farm. One evening they were working in the common room. The servant girl was spinning. After they had been sewing for a while, the spinning wheel gradually slowed down and the girl seemed to dissolve into a haze. Finally, only her clothes were left.

The tailors knew right away that the girl was a *mare*. They decided to wait there until she came back. Around half past nine, the spinning wheel began turning once more and bit by bit the girl regained her human form while slipping back into her clothes. Then one of the tailors said:

"I believe you are a *mare!*"

"Oh, thank you for saying that! Now I am free! But if you had waited just a little longer, I would have gotten my little finger back. Now I'm going to lose it."

He had spoken to her too soon; her little finger had not yet materialized.

People believed that a nightmare was freed from the spell when someone spoke to her or revealed that she was a *mare*.

> This legend has been recorded only in Skåne, Sweden, but the underlying belief that one could free a person from being a *mare* by speaking to her is widespread in Scandinavia.
>   Collected in 1933 by Valter Åberg from Bengta Kristiansson in Vanstad parish, Skåne (Sweden). MS. in LUF (3761), 1–2. Printed in Bengt af Klintberg, *Svenska folksägner* (1972), 242–43.

5.5 Married to the Mare

A farmer's son was being tormented by the *mare*. One evening he asked the farmhand for help. Together they plugged up every hole in his bedroom except one through which the *mare* could slip in. As soon as the farmhand noticed something out of the ordinary, he was to get up and plug up that hole, too. And that is what he did.

The next morning they found a girl in the bed. Nobody recognized her. Nor did she herself know where she had come from. The farmer's son married the girl, took over the farm, and had many children with her. But one day he showed her the hole through which she had come in, and she slipped out again and was seen no more.

> This legend combines the motif of the swan maiden with that of the *mare*. It is known in most of Scandinavia.
>
> See Helge Holmström, "Sägnerna om äktenskap med maran," *FmFt* 5 (1918), 135–45.
>
> Legend type: ML 4010.
>
> Collected by E. T. Kristensen in Lille-Tåning, Jylland (Denmark). Printed in Kristensen, *Danske sagn* 2 (1893), 245.

6. Longing

According to widespread belief, a person could get ill in body and mind from being longed for by someone else. Usually the longing, traditionally called *elsk* (love), was of an erotic nature. The lover might be a human or a supranormal being. But even the dead were known to impose an *elsk* on a surviving relative and thereby make him or her sick, or a living person could long for the dead and keep the loved one from finding peace in the grave.

> See I. Reichborn-Kjennerud, *Vår gamle trolldomsmedisin* 2 (1933), 9–10, 16–17, 108; 4 (1944), 142–43; Nils Lid, "Magiske fyrestillingar og bruk," *Nordisk kultur 19. Folketru* (1935), 15–16; Svale Solheim, *Norsk sætertradisjon* (1952), 485–86.

6.1 Snowshoe-Pernille

In Sandalsnesa there was a girl whom people called Snowshoe-Pernille. About a generation back, a "hill man" put an *elsk* on her. So she got a soldier to sleep with her. Then she threaded a rope through a hole in the wall and tied a pair of snowshoes to the other end. Whenever she pulled the rope, the snowshoes could be heard scraping against the outside wall. She would pull the rope, without the soldier noticing it, so he would think that one of the hill folk was after her.

You see, when a girl who had the *elsk* did not give in to a "hill man," she lost her mind—unless she was rescued by a soldier.

> The "hill man" was a supranormal being. One traditional remedy against an *elsk* inflicted by such a lover was to sleep with a fully armed soldier for three nights. The remedy was to be magical,

ritually extending the protective power of the soldier's arms to the girl.

See Svale Solheim, *Norsk sætertradisjon* (1952), 485–86; I. Reichborn-Kjennerud, (1944), 142–43.

Collected by Ola Sandnes in Indre Sunnfjord, Sogn and Fjordane (Norway). Printed in Solheim, *Norsk sætertradisjon*, 486.

6.2 *The Dead Husband Longs for His Namesake*

The woman who told this story was employed at Gare in Spangereid. It was around 1863. She was in the service of a woman who had been a widow but was remarried. This woman gave birth to a son while she was there, and they named the child after the first husband.

The baby cried a lot. They thought it was because the dead man drew him, so they took the child and carried it to the church in the middle of the night. They thought the child would quiet down once it had been taken there.

> In this memorat, the dead person drawing the child is not its father. But by naming the child after the first husband, a relationship was established between them. The dead man longs for his namesake.
>
> Collected by Peter Lunde in Vest-Agder (Norway). Printed in Lunde, *Kynnehuset. Vestegdske folkeminne* (1924), 88.

6.3 *The Dead Child Complains*

There was a woman who had a little child, but it died. She grieved for the child early and late, crying herself to sleep every night. Once she dreamed that many little children walked past her, each carrying a green branch in its hand. She wanted to see her own child and waited for it to come, but it did not appear. After a long time, when all the other children had gone by, it finally came.

"Why didn't you come before this?" she asked.

"It's your own fault, Mother," answered the child, "because all the tears you cry for me fall on my body until I am so wet and heavy that I can hardly move."

Then the mother woke up, and she understood that her dream had been a sign to her not to cry anymore.

> This legend expresses society's sanction against excessive grief for

the dead. The motif of the dead complaining of the *elsk* can be found in Eddic poetry and in folk ballads.

Collected from Johanne Marie Kristensdatter in Søheden, Jylland (Denmark), Printed in E. T. Kristensen, *Danske sagn* 2 (1893), 312.

7. *Hug*-message

Throughout Scandinavia there are folk traditions about the *hug* of a person appearing to his or her family or friends with a message of death or of some mortal danger. The *hug* could manifest itself in the person's own shape, by sound, as a premonition, or in a dream.

See Eyðun Andreassen, "Varsel om ulukker på sjøen på Færøyane," *Tradisjon* 7 (1977), 75–89.

7.1 *The Day My Mother Died*

One night a few years back, I woke up with the feeling that something was standing near my bed and wanted to talk to me. I could both see it and not see it. It appeared to be wrapped in a brown garment, the same color as soil. Suddenly I knew that it must be my mother. Just then I saw a blinding white light over by the wall. I have never seen anything like it. At that very moment, my mother died in Hårup, and an hour later I was informed that she was dead — I had visited her that same evening and had just fallen asleep when I was suddenly awakened by that feeling.

In this memorat the message of the mother's death is accompanied by the anticipation of her burial, as well as by the promise of a blessed afterlife in the Christian sense, which is symbolized by the white light.

Collected by E. T. Kristensen from Søren Hansen, Hårup, Jylland (Denmark). Printed in Kristensen, *Danske sagn* 2 (1893), 414.

7.2 *The Shipwrecked Fisherman*

One evening a fisherman was sailing home from the city. A storm broke, and his boat went down during the night. The same night the storm threw all its might against the double doors of the entrance to the drowned man's home. The latch was worn and perhaps not fully engaged. It sprang open. The storm raged into the entrance, whipped along the four walls, and then suddenly withdrew. The suction pulled open the door to the inner room. The fisherman's wife woke up, believing that her husband had come home. A cold puff of air hit her in the face. She thought that it came from his cold clothes. She called out his name, but because no one answered, she took a light, threw on some clothes, and went down to the shore. The feeling that her husband had come home would not leave her. She had felt the cold air from his clothes as he walked past. Yes, she even believed that she had seen him. When people came the next day to bring the news of his death, she said that he had already been there during the night to bid her farewell.

Collected in Nyland (Finland). Printed in A. Allardt, *Nyländska folkseder och bruk* (1889), 113. Reprinted in V. E. V. Wessman, *Sägner* 3.2 (1931), 1.

7.3 Her Father Came to Her

One night a long time ago, a woman in the fishing village of Vik saw her father, whom she knew was at sea at the time, standing by her bed. He was dripping wet. She thought that she perhaps had been dreaming. But the next morning, she found wet tracks on the floor, and she clearly saw a mark where he had turned on his heels when he walked away.

The very same night her father drowned at sea.

Collected by Eva Wigström from a woman called "Hönsgumman" in Skåne (Sweden). Printed in Wigström, *Folktro och sägner* (1898–1914), 193–94. Reprinted in Wigström, *Folktro och sägner*, edited by Aina Stenklo (1952), 64.

7.4 The Shipwreck of the Olivia

My uncle—he was worse than my brother. He saw this when Napoleon went down with his ship *Olivia* in 1912:

He had been out getting peat, he said. When he got down to the beach at the inner end of the fjord, my uncle saw Napoleon—he was the skipper—and twelve men behind him. He knew Napoleon well and some of the men, too—two of them who died were from our village. Water was pouring off them—they were dressed in sou'westers and oilskins—they walked right through the tide.

My uncle put down his willow basket. He knew that if he turned away, it would disappear and he would not see any more. It was an awful sight. The sea was pouring from their oilskins.

The *Olivia* had gone down, but nobody knew about it. She sank by Sørisland. Nobody knows what happened. But my uncle said that when he got home, Mother said to him, "Something has happened to you—you have *seen!*"

"Give me some water!"

"You shall have it. Tomorrow you can tell us what you saw!"

"The *Olivia* is gone—shipwrecked!"

Nobody knew anything about it. He said that the *Olivia* had gone down, man and mouse.

"How do you know that?" my brother asked him.

He answered, "Because I saw them!"

And that is how it was. The *Olivia* never returned. He saw her. Yes, strangely enough.

> Collected by Eyðun Andreassen, sometime between 1965 and 1974, on the Færoe Islands. Printed in Andreassen, *Tradisjon* 7 (1977), 77.

7.5 My Son, Get Up and Come with Me

Gunleik Heggtveit (born in 1725) from Brunkeberg was a very prosperous man and he had many children. One of his sons was named Sveinung. Sveinung was staying at Hestskodike the last summer his father was living.

One night toward the end of that summer, Sveinung was sleeping alone in the barn at Hestskodike. Around midnight he woke up. He saw his father standing on the loft, leaning over the railing and looking down at him. His father said:

"Sveinung, Sveinung, my son, get up and come with me."

Sveinung thought it was strange for his father to be there at night, but he got dressed and followed him outside. Gunleik slowly headed west toward Brunkeberg Church and Sveinung followed him. He talked to Sveinung about this and that and gave him advice on how he should manage his life. There was this girl, Aaste by name. Sveinung had proposed to her. He must not marry her, his father said, because she would cause him nothing but trouble. And he told him about another girl he should marry instead.

They walked and talked for quite a while, but when they came to Sothaug, Gunleik suddenly vanished, and Sveinung stood there by himself on the road. Only then did it occur to him that there might be something wrong. He went straight to Heggtveit to find out what was going on. He found out that his father had died about three hours before, at the same time when he had appeared to him in the barn at Hestskodike.

> In this legend the message of death is combined with advice to the surviving son.
> Collected by Kjetil A. Flatin in Seljord, Telemark (Norway). Printed in Flatin, *Tussar og trolldom* (1930), 144.

7.6 An Omen of Death

If a person appears where he or she really is not, that person will soon die.

A few days before Grandmother died, my mother came to me and said that Grandmother was going to die soon.

"I was in the storehouse and looked out through the window," she said, "and I clearly saw your grandmother walk along the path to the field. This seemed a little strange to me, because I didn't think that she was well enough to walk that far, nor did I know of any errand she could have there. But when I came back to the entryway, there stood your grandmother washing some cups."

That same evening Grandmother took to bed, and two days later she was dead.

> In this memorat the manifestation of the *hug* functions as an omen rather than as a message.
> Collected by Edvard Grimstad in Skjåk, Oppland (Norway). Printed in Grimstad, *Etter gamalt. Folkeminne frå Gudbrandsdalen* 3 (1953), 33.

7.7 He Escaped the Fire

My father had journeyed to the great market in Själevad, as was his habit every year. We did not expect him home for several days. But late one evening when our faithful old servant was making his nightly rounds, he met the master standing in the middle of the farmyard. And right afterward he saw a bird in one of the outbuildings. When he tried to catch it, fire sprang from it. The servant knew that a bird like that was an omen of fire, and he kept watch all night. The next morning he told my mother about his visions during the night. He was worried about having seen the master. But my mother comforted him and told him that she, too, had had a vision. My father had appeared to her and told her that he had been saved from mortal danger.

Later we found out that there had been a great fire at the market. At the same time my father had been seen at home, he was pulled from the window of the house where he was staying. The house was all ablaze.

Collected by Eva Wigström from a woman in Norrland (Sweden). Printed in Wigström, *Folktro och sägner* (1898–1914), 18–19. Reprinted in Wigström, *Folktro och sägner*, edited by Aina Stenklo (1952), 208–9.

8. The *Vardoger*

Another form of *hug*-message is the *vardøger* (Swedish *vård*), which announces that a person is about to come. The *vardøger*, too, manifests itself in the person's own shape or by sounds usually associated with that person's arrival.

See Lily Weiser-Aall, "En studie om vardøger," *Norveg* 12 (1965), 73–112.

8.1 She Heard Her Husband

The *vardøger* is a strange thing. Many folks have one.

Gudbrand Molandssveen—the man who made the clearing for the railroad station—often traveled to Gjøvik to buy merchandise for his store. Now Gudbrand was someone who had a *vardøger*. His wife often heard him coming back at night, even though he was not yet there. She was so used to this that whenever she heard his *vardøger*, she would get up and fix some food for him. At the time, Gudbrand would be somewhere near Lunne, about fifteen minutes away.

This is a migratory legend associated with historical people in various locations.

Collected by Knut Hermundstad from Simen Lofthus in Etnedal, Oppland (Norway). Printed in Hermundstad, *Gamletidi talar. Gamal Valdreskultur* 1 (1936), 117.

8.2 *He Saw His Mother*

Embret Mo once told how he saw his mother's *vardøger* when he was a boy.

At the time, they were living on a cotter's farm in the township of Herad. A little way up on the hillside lay a sawmill. His father was the foreman there. It was not very far to walk and his mother would usually go up there during the day with his father's food.

One day when she had gone to the mill, Embret stood by the window waiting for her. Suddenly he saw her walking down the hillside. He thought that she was coming back a bit early; he had not expected her quite yet. But he stood there and watched her getting closer. She had a wooden container in one hand. Walking along the path to the house, she passed right by the window where he was standing and turned into the entryway. He heard her enter and take hold of the door handle. Then it became quiet. He waited for a while, but she did not come. He went out to look for her but she was not there. He thought it was strange that he could not find her. She could not just have vanished into thin air. He searched and called for her but to no avail. So he went inside again and stood by the window. Then he saw her up on the hillside, as she had been the first time. She was walking down with a wooden container in her hand. Now he really got confused. How she could just be coming back now was more than he could understand. He stood there and stared at her as she came down the hill again, walked past the window, and turned into the entryway. But this time she came inside.

"What happened to you a little while ago, Mother?" he said.

"A little while ago?"

"Yes, you came into the entryway, and then you just disappeared!"

"I haven't been in the entryway until now. I just came down from the saw mill, you know."

So he told her the whole thing.

"Oh, you have seen my *vardøger*," she said.

> This memorat was collected by Sigurd Nergaard in Elverum, Hedmark (Norway). Printed in Nergaard, *Hulder og trollskap. Folkeminne fraa Østerdalen* 4 (1925), 108–9.

8.3 *A Father's Visit to His Daughter*

When we lived in Høve, my father was supposed to come for a visit. He longed to see us because he had not been to our house since we moved there.

When I came into the dining room, I saw him standing in the door to the hall entrance. He was wearing his knit scarf and his traveling clothes. "You are already here!" I exclaimed.

But at that very moment he disappeared. Right after that a young girl came in, and I asked her whether the coach had arrived because I had not heard anything. No, no one had arrived, she answered. Half an hour later, they came, and my father stood in the door in the same position, wearing the same clothes I had seen him in earlier. Even the colors were the same.

Strangely enough, when I saw him the first time, I had the feeling that I was seeing something out of the ordinary, but I was not frightened.

> Collected by E. T. Kristensen from Mrs. Rønne, Stevns folk high school, Sjælland (Denmark). Printed in Kristensen, *Danske sagn*, N.R. 2 (1928), 491–92.

9. The *Fylgje*

The *fylgje* (cf. the verb *fylgja*, "to follow") is a projection of the *hug* that accompanies the person. It takes either human shape or that of an animal. Normally, only animals or people with second sight can see the *fylgje*. In medieval literature, notably the Icelandic sagas, the *fylgje* also had a protective function, which was later assumed by the Christian angel. In recent tradition, belief in the *fylgje* spills over into that of the *vardøger* (Swedish, *vård*), and is often called by that name.

> See Else Mundal, *Fylgjemotiva i norrøn litteratur* (1974).

9.1 How to Reveal Your Character

The *vardøger* is an animal that accompanies or precedes you. If you want to know what kind of *vardøger* you have, there is a way to find out. You take your sheath knife, roll it up in a kerchief, and wrap it tightly. Then you pass this bundle from hand to hand, first in front of you, then behind you, three times. While moving the bundle, you say:

"A horse as *vardøger!*"

If your *vardøger* is a horse, the knife will lie outside the kerchief by the time you have passed it the third time. If it is not a horse, the knife will still be wrapped in the kerchief. You proceed this way until you discover your *vardøger*, naming animal after animal until you find the right one.

> The animal shape of the *fylgje* (or *vardøger*) revealed a person's character. A coward's *fylgje* would appear as a rabbit, a sly person's as a fox, et cetera.
>
> Collected by Andreas Mørch in Sigdal-Eggedal, Buskerud (Norway). Printed in Mørch, *Frå gamle dagar. Folkeminne frå Sigdal og Eggedal* (1932), 43.

9.2 Grandmother's Vardøger Scared the Cows

Grandmother thought that her *vardøger* was a wolf or a dog. The cattle acted very strangely whenever she came into the cow shed. As soon as she approached the barn at feeding time, the cows would stand between the cribs, stare toward the aisle, and bellow. But when she came inside, they fell silent. They were seeing her *vardøger*.

> Collected by Andreas Mørch in Sigdal-Eggedal, Buskerud (Norway). Printed in Mørch, *Frå gamle dagar. Folkeminne frå Sigdal og Eggedal* (1932), 43.

9.3 The Evil Fylgje

An old woman from Mark parish here in Leksvik said that as a child she heard the following story from an old woman.

In her youth this woman was invited to a dance. It was toward the end of the summer. She did not really feel like going, she said, but she went anyway, after finishing her evening chores. When she was near the house, she decided to take a pee before going in. She crouched behind a big tree right by the house. It was late in the evening. She sat there wondering whether she should go back because deep down inside she really did not want to go to the dance. But, it is funny, when you have been invited to a party by people you want to please, you feel obligated to go. Then she got the idea to peep in through the window. The dancing had already begun, but there were not many couples on the floor, maybe five or six.

Just inside the window, a tall wretch was swinging his partner. She knew him quite well. He was the scoundrel who starved his horses during the winter. She caught a glimpse of something following behind him in the dimly lit room. It was a horse that was nothing but skin and bones, swaying from side to side, so emaciated that it could barely stand. Next there came another couple, and the man leading his partner was a fat glutton from a big farm further down in the parish. His *fylgje* was a fat pig plodding along on all fours. The man in the third couple was nicknamed "Roswold the fox" because he tried hoodwinking everyone he talked to. A fox was slinking along behind him. Next came a fellow with a lively girl in his arms. He was called "lady killer" because he ran after all the girls in the parish. He was followed by a cock.

The girl almost fainted on the spot when she saw nothing but evil *fylgje* in animal shapes mingling with the dancers. So she returned home and never went dancing again.

> In this legend the people at the dance are characterized in negative terms. The story may possibly have the didactic function of warning against frivolous activities like dancing.
>
> Collected by Edvard Kruken in Leksvik, Nord-Trøndelag (Norway). Ms. in NFS Kruken 8, 46–48.

9.4 Seeing the **Vardøger** *to the Door*

When someone leaves the house, you had better make sure that his or her vardøger gets out, too.

When I was a boy, my aunt in Enderud always saw me to the door. She followed me outside whenever I left for school. She wanted to make sure that my *vardøger* did not stay behind.

People still use this saying when seeing someone to the door: "I've got to let out your *vardøger*."

> According to folk belief, if the *fylgje* (or *vardøger*) was separated from the person, the result would be sickness, even insanity.
>
> See Lily Weiser-Aall, "En studie om vardøger," *Norveg* 12 (1965), 83–89.
>
> Collected by Sigurd Nergaard in Åmot, Hedmark (Norway). Printed in Nergaard, *Hulder og trollskap. Folkeminne fraa Østerdalen* 4 (1925), 158.

9.5 Meeting One's **Fylgje**

If a person meets his or her own *fylgje*, it is a sure sign that he or she will die soon.

The motif of a person meeting his or her own *fylgje* (or *vardøger*), an omen of imminent death, is known both from medieval literature and from recent tradition.

See Else Mundal, *Fylgjemotiva i norrøn litteratur* (1974), 131.

This *dite* was collected by Jens Kamp in Copenhagen (Denmark). Printed in Kamp, *Danske folkeminder* (1877), 383.

9.6 The Old Man Met Himself

One evening an old man from Vårdö came home from work and met himself. A week and a half later, he was dead.

Collected in Vårdö, Åland (Finland). Printed in L. T. Renvall, *Åländsk folktro, skrock och trolldom* (1890), 23. Reprinted in V. E. V. Wessman, *Sägner* 3.2 (1931), 563.

9.7 The Dead Man Wanted His Leg

There is another story from the same district about a man named Magnús. He had a severe case of leprosy and was bad-tempered to boot. People were transporting him to the doctor one time. They got as far as the farm called Borg in the Mýrar district, where they were allowed to spend the night. From there they took him to the Ánabrekka, where one of his legs fell off, and he died shortly afterward. The archdeacon's wife, who told this story, lived at Borg. She had an eerie feeling. That night she dreamed that he would return there unless his leg was brought to the cemetery the next day.

It was said that Magnus's *fylgje* had appeared in her dream.

The *fylgje* of the dead man appearing in this legend is to be distinguished from the revenant returning from the grave. (Cf. nos. 21.1–21.2.

Collected by Konrad Maurer in Iceland. Printed in Maurer, *Isländische Volkssagen der Gegenwart* (1860), 83–84. Icelandic version printed in Jón Árnason, *Íslenzkar þjóðsögur og æfintýri* 1 (1862), 359. Reprinted in new edition 1 (1954), 344–45.

9.8 The Cap of Victory

The cap of victory was an omen of good luck for the child born with it. It was a sign that the child would become something useful.

The fetal membrane, which sometimes covers the head of the child at birth, was considered a bringer of good luck. Someone born with a caul was able to quench fire, could not be injured by magic or weapons, and generally would be successful in life. In tradition, beliefs surrounding the caul have blended with those concerning the *fylgje*. Some scholars have argued that the term *fylgje* is derived from *fulga* (English caul).

See Jan deVries, *Altgermanische Religionsgeschichte* 1 (1970), 222–24; Lily Weiser-Aall, "Die Glückshaube in der norwegischen Überlieferung," *Saga och sed* (1960), 29–36.

This *dite* was collected by Peter Lunde in Fjotland and Eikjen, Vest-Agder (Norway). Printed in Lunde, *Kynnehuset. Vestegdske folkeminne* (1924), 30.

9.9 The Shirt of Victory

In Væver, Musse, there lived a man named Ole Hansen. His oldest son was born with a shirt of victory.

If he walked three times around a burning house, the fire would not spread to another building. Nor could anyone shoot him, as long as he carried his shirt of victory in his pocket.

Collected by E. T. Kristensen from Jørgen Mortensen in Musse parish, Lolland (Denmark). Printed in Kristensen, *Danske sagn*, N.R. 6 (1936), 315.

9.10 He Stopped the Fire with a Caul

When I was a boy, people used to clear forests by burning them. The last time I took part in a slash burning, I was fifteen. It was my last year at home.

My father had just started the fire, and the flames were shooting up.

"Wait a minute, Frimann," shouted an old man, "I'll run around the clearing so that the fire won't get out of hand."

"You fool, you think that'll work?"

But the old fellow ran once around the burning and, can you imagine, the fire stopped at the line where he had run. It did not get any farther. Explain that, if you can. I remember it as if it happened yesterday. The man had a caul in his pocket. A child of his had been born with a caul and the old folks blindly believed that it could stop fire. He had stuffed the caul with some cotton so that it looked like a cap.

In this memorat, the caul itself is used as a magic device. (Cf. no. 30. 3).
Collected by Elis Åström in 1951 from Ida Oliv, Västra Ny, Östergötland (Sweden). Printed in Åström, *Folktro och folkliv i Östergötland* (1962), 20.

10. The Finn Messenger

The folk tradition about the Finn who sends his *hug* on a journey while his body lies in a trance has its origin in Lappish shamanism. Although recorded mostly in Lappland in northern Norway and Sweden, variants have been reported as far south as Denmark.

See Ernst Arbman, "Shamanen, extatisk andebesvärjare och visionär," *Primitiv religion och magi*, edited by Å. Hultkrantz (1955), 52–55.

10.1 The Skipper and the Finn

Once there was a skipper from Vestervig who sailed to Norway. Winter came and forced him to stay in Norway for some time. He put up in the house of some people in Finnmark. When Christmas came, his landlord asked him whether he would like to know what they were having for dinner on Christmas Eve in Vestervig. Indeed, he would really like that, he said. He would even give him a pint of brandy for his trouble. They came to terms, and the Finn drank half the pint and talked for a while. Then he drank the other half and lay down on the floor. His wife took a quilt and covered him. There he lay, trembling, for about half an hour, and then he woke up. He told him what they were eating for supper, and to prove that he had been there, he produced a knife and fork, which the skipper recognized as the very same he used at home in Vestervig.

Legend type: ML 3080.
Collected by E. T. Kristensen from the teacher P. Christiansen, Kvols, Jylland (Denmark). Printed in Kristensen, *Danske sagn* 2 (1893), 274.

10.2 They Touched His Jacket

There was a Finn who worked as a hired hand in Lofoten. One day he sat talking with some workers, and he said that if he wanted to, he could easily take a quick trip home. They could not believe it. Well, he said that he would prove it to them. He crawled under the floor in the room and told them that under no circumstances were they to touch his jacket. There was no sign of life from the Finn for a long time, so one of the men touched his jacket. It felt empty.

A while later the Finn appeared once more, and he had a silver spoon in his hand as proof that he had really been home. But, he told them that he had been in a terrible storm in Vestfjord and had just barely survived. That was when the man had touched his jacket.

> Legend type: ML 3080.
>
> Collected by Knut Strompdal in Vefsn and Sømma, Nordland (Norway). Printed in Strompdal, *Gamalt frå Helgeland* 3 (1939), 66.

10.3 The Finn Brought the Silver Spoon

Johan Benedikson once had a hired hand in Lofoten who was a Finn. When Johan left home that year, his wife, Gurina, was with child. Johan was a little concerned about leaving, but since it was a matter of earning their livelihood, he had no choice.

One morning when they were sitting in their shack at the fishing grounds in Lofoten, Johan said how nice it would be to know how things stood at home. They had heard so much about Finns being versed in witchcraft, and one of the men asked the Finn whether he could find out. Sure, he said, he could manage that. Then he lay down on the floor, and they heard only that he mumbled to himself while he seemed to crawl into his jacket. It took a while before the Finn stirred again. His jacket was lying there, but it looked somehow shrunken. Then all at once the jacket began to move, and the Finn was there again. Yes, everything was alright at home. Gurina had given birth, and she was sitting and feeding the child. To prove that he had been there, he had brought back a silver spoon.

Johan was amazed because he recognized the spoon. When he came home the next spring, his wife told him how the spoon had disappeared during the winter. A little girl had been holding the spoon when a black cat came in through the door, took the spoon, and scampered off before they could do anything about it.

> Legend type: ML 3080.
>
> Collected by Knut Strompdal in Vefsn and Sømma, Nordland (Norway). Printed in Strompdal, *Gamalt frå Helgeland* 3 (1939), 66–67.

11. The Dream Soul

In folk traditions about longing, the nightmare, the *fylgje*, and other manifestations of the *hug*, dreams are presented as passive experiences of the sleeper. In the so-called Guntram legend, by contrast, the soul of the dreaming person is active. It leaves the body, usually takes the shape of a small animal, and explores the world. Its experiences are then remembered by the sleeper as a dream. In most variants the dream soul finds a treasure, a motif which has been lost in Norwegian tradition, however.

This migratory legend was first recorded by Paulus Diaconus (died 797) about Guntram, king of the Burgundians (561–92). The motif of the dream soul in animal shapes does not occur in the memorat tradition of Scandinavia.

> See Hannjost Lixfeld, "Die Guntramsage (AT 1645 A)," *Fabula* 13 (1972), 60–107.

11.1 The Barrel in the Mound

Once, some men were traveling together. One Sunday morning they set up their tent in a beautiful green field. The weather was bright and sunny. They settled down to sleep, in a row, inside the tent. The one who was lying closest to the entrance could not fall asleep, and he looked around. He saw a bluish haze over those furthest inside the tent. The haze passed through the tent and went outside. The man was curious, so he followed it. It passed slowly over the field and finally came to an old, bleached skull of a horse. There were a lot of flies around it, filling the air with the buzzing of their wings. Now the vapor floated into the skull. After a long time it came out again. Then it drifted farther across the field, until it came to a small creek. It seemed to want to cross over. The man placed his riding crop over the creek, which was so narrow that the shaft could reach from one bank to the other. The vapor crossed over the water on the crop. It continued on for a while, until it came to a mound in the field. It disappeared down inside the mound. The man stood close by and waited for the vapor to come out again. It was not long before it did. Then it traveled back the same way it had come. The man put his crop across the creek and the vapor passed over it just as it did before. It did not stop until it reached the innermost man in the tent. It disappeared there. Then the man lay down and fell asleep.

At the end of the day, the travelers got up and gathered their horses. They chatted while they were saddling up. The man who had been lying furthest inside the tent said:

"I wish I had what I dreamed about today."

"What's that? What did you dream about?" asked the one who had seen the vapor.

"I dreamed I was walking across a field, and I came to a big beautiful house. A lot of people were gathered there and they were singing and having a grand time. I spent quite a while in this house and then I continued on across the fine, even field. I came to a big river. I tried for a long time to get across but I couldn't. Then I saw a terribly big giant coming. He had a huge club in his hand, and he placed it over the river. I crossed the river on the club and continued on for a long while. Finally I came to a large burial mound. The mound was open and I went in. Inside I found a large barrel full of coins. I stayed there for a long time examining the coins — never before had I seen such a pile. After that I left and went back the same way I had come. I came to the river, and the giant put his club over the river again. I crossed on the club and headed home for the tent."

The man who had followed the vapor began chuckling to himself and said:

"Come on, pal, let's have a quick look for the money." The other man laughed and thought he was crazy, but he went with him anyway. They walked along the same way the vapor had gone. They came to the mound and dug it up. Inside they found a jar full of coins. Then they went back to the tent and told their companions the whole story about the dream and the vapor.

Collected by Magnús Grímsson, minister at Mosfell, from "an old woman in Borgarfjörður" (Iceland). Printed in Jón Árnason, *Íslenzkar þjóðsögur og æfintýri* 1 (1862), 356–57. Reprinted in new edition 1 (1954), 342–43.

12. Werewolves and Man-Bears

Throughout most of the world there are traditions about human beings changing into wolves or bears. In this instance it is not a matter of the *hug* separating from the body and taking on another shape; rather, the whole person is transformed, body and soul, into an animal being. The transformation may be self-induced or may be due to hostile magic. In medical context the phenomenon has been characterized as a form of insanity (lycanthropy). Both werewolves and man-bears are well known from medieval literature. The so-called berserks often formed the bodyguard of early Scandinavian kings and chieftains.

> See Ella Odstedt, *Varulven i svensk folktradition* (1943); Bengt Holbek and Iørn Piø, *Fabeldyr og sagnfolk* (1967), 165–75; Nils Lid, "Til varulvens historia," *Saga och sed* (1937), 3–25; reprinted in Lid, *Trolldom* (1950), 82–108; Dag Strömbäck, "Om varulven," *Svenska landsmål* (1943–44), 301–8; reprinted in Strömbäck, *Folklore och filologi* (1970), 255–63; Odd Nordland, "Mannbjørn," *By og bygd* 11 (1957), 133–56; Montague Summers, *The Werewolf*, 2d edition (1966); M. Kriss, *Werewolves, Shapeshifters, and Skinwalkers* (1972); *Atlas över svensk folkkultur II. Sägen, tro och högtidssed 2*, edited by Åke Campbell and Åsa Nyman (1976), 74–79.

12.1 Their Firstborn Would Have Been Werewolves

If a woman crawls naked through the caul of a foal, she will give birth without any pain, but her firstborn will become a *mare* or a werewolf.

Four women from Greve wanted to make use of this remedy, so they took a caul and went to a beach. But when they had undressed, some men from the town came by, and they chased the women back to town, naked.

> The reaction of the men in this legend is not a prank but a countermeasure to a magic ritual that would have serious consequences for the women's offspring.
> See Ella Odstedt, *Varulven i svensk folktradition* (1943), 115–66.
> Collected by E. T. Kristensen from Kristoffer Jensen, Ramsömagle, Sjælland (Denmark). Printed in Kristensen, *Danske sagn 2* (1893), 231.

12.2 The Child Drove Away the Werewolf

Werewolves were known to attack pregnant women.

A werewolf came to a woman's house once, but fortunately she had her little boy at home. Since a male child can easily overcome a werewolf, she asked the child to take a wooden ladle and drive the unwelcome guest out the door.

> Persons who had become werewolves because their mothers had eased their labor pains with the foal's caul were known to attack

pregnant women. If a werewolf could tear the fetus from the womb and eat the child's heart, it would be released from the spell.

Collected by E. T. Kristensen from K. Ericksen, Copenhagen. Printed in Kristensen, *Danske sagn* 2 (1893), 230.

12.3 Now I Am Free

There was a man in Foss who turned into a werewolf and killed sheep and cattle. But one fine day he recovered and got married. One morning his wife asked what he wanted for breakfast.

"You don't have to worry about me," he said, "I'll have breakfast in the woods."

Toward evening he came home looking ragged and tired. She thought that he had been drinking.

The next day they went out to work in the fields. At noon the man went to the woods. But before he left, he said:

"If a wolf comes and attacks you, just call my name."

A while after he left, there came a huge and dangerous-looking wolf. He attacked the woman, but she called her husband's name. The wolf changed right before her eyes — and there stood her husband with a piece of her dress in his mouth.

"You've done well," he said, "now I am free."

> In some instances, a person became a werewolf only periodically, in others, the transformation was permanent. Freeing the werewolf by calling the man's name is in keeping with pars-pro-toto magic. The name is magically identified with a person or thing. (Cf. nos. 41.4, 55.11, 59.5.)
> See Ella Odstedt, *Varulven i svensk folktradition* (1943), 141–45. Legend type: ML 4005.
> Collected by Ragnar Nilsson in Foss, Bohuslän (Sweden). Printed in Carl-Martin Bergstrand, *Bohuslänska sägner* (1947), 119.

12.4 The Tailor Understood the Howling of the Wolves

It was possible to force someone to take the shape of an animal. It was done by magic.

There is a story about a tailor who had been changed into a wolf, but when the spell was broken, he became a man again. Since then he understood the howling of the wolves. One evening he and the farmer he was working for stood on the steps to the house. They were talking.

"How the wolves are howling! I wonder what they are saying?" said the farmer.

"Well, they're saying that they're going to kill your mare tonight, so you'd better take her inside."

But the farmer didn't listen to him and left the mare in the field during the night. By the next morning the wolves had come and killed her.

> See Ella Odstedt, *Varulven i svensk folktradition* (1943), 14, 93–95.
> Collected by Werner Karlsson in 1930 from Mathilda Gränz in Lenhovda parish, Småland (Sweden). The story is derived from a broadside printed in Lund in 1846.
> Ms. in ULMA (2817:1), 54. Printed in Odstedt, *Varulven i svensk folktradition*, 94. Reprinted in Bengt af Klintberg, *Svenska folksägner* (1972), 247.

12.5 The Werewolf Attacked His Wife

One summer a married couple from Vassland in Kvas were out in the hills haying. Later the same day, after they had piled a few loads around the haypole, they sat down to eat. But then they got into a fight.

After a while, the man got up to leave, but first he said to the woman:

"If something should come, just climb on the haystack, and take the rake with you."

She sat there for a moment, thinking that her husband had just gone off to relieve himself.

But then a wolf came after her with gaping jaws, and she jumped up on the haystack and defended herself with the rake. She screamed and hollered for her husband but to no avail. The wolf became angrier and angrier and leaped at her so fiercely that he reached the hem of her skirt and bit off a piece. Then he ran away.

Toward evening, the woman had to return home without her husband. A little ways from the house there was a pen. They were keeping a calf in there. When she walked by it, she saw that the calf was lying there dead and half eaten.

When she got in the house, she found her husband in bed, sick. So she had to go out again and tie up the cattle by herself, and it got late before she was done.

When she came back, her husband had gotten worse. She had to sleep next to the wall. During the night her husband threw up. The next morning when she got up, she saw the mess on the floor. There were calf hooves and hair — and the piece from her skirt. Then she understood what kind of a husband she had. He was a werewolf.

> Collected by Tore Bergstøl in the 1920s in Vest-Agder (Norway). Printed in Bergstøl, *Atterljom. Folkeminne frå smådalane kring Lindesnes* 3 (1959), 20–21.

12.6 The Finn and His Wolfskin

When a Finn wanted to become a werewolf, he took the afterbirth of a wolf and pulled it over his head.

Once there was a Finn who was such good friends with a farmer that he showed him his wolfskin. He even pulled on one of the sleeves to show him how it worked. The farmer wanted the Finn to pull the skin over his head, too, but the Finn didn't want to go that far.

"If I put the skin over my head, I become a wolf — not only skin deep but also in my *hug*," said the Finn.

He would not be able to control his actions then.

> Most of the legends describing people who voluntarily turn themselves into werewolves are about either Finns or Lapps. This text suggests two similar rituals whereby one becomes a werewolf; the first involves the afterbirth of a wolf, the second, a wolfskin. There are certain parallels between these rituals of self-transformation and shamanistic practices.
>
> See Ella Odstedt, *Varulven i svensk folktradition* (1943), 30–57; Nils Lid, "Til varulvens historia," *Saga och sed* (1937), 3–25.
>
> Collected by Knut Strompdal in Velfjord, Nordland (Norway). Printed in Strompdal *Gamalt frå Helgeland* 3 (1939), 63.

12.7 The Lapp Carried a Belt under His Skin

A man went hunting one autumn, after it had snowed. He came across a bear track leading straight to the door of a Lapp hut. When he peered into the hut, he saw an old Lapp sitting there, smoking his pipe. The hunter got scared and ran. But when he looked back, he saw a bear trotting after him. He knew right away that it was the old Lapp who had changed into a bear. He climbed up into a tree, and when the bear came after him, he fired. The bear said:

"Oh, drat!" and then he was silent. He was dead.

When the hunter flayed his prey, he found a tin belt and a pouch with a tinderbox under the bear's skin.

Olof Jakobson told me this story, and he said that the belt and pouch are stored in the cathedral in Uppsala.

> In European folk tradition, the belt is often described as the means by which a person changes himself into a wolf or bear, as well as the sign by which the shape-shifter is recognized as such.
>
> See Ella Odstedt, *Varulven i svensk folktradition* (1943), 30–57; Nils Lid, "Til varulvens historia," *Saga och sed* (1937), 6–8.
>
> Collected by Levi Johansson in 1930 from Hans Hansson in Frostviken, Jämtland (Sweden). Ms. in NM EU 17841, *Sägner och memorat* 6, 541. Printed in Bengt af Klintberg, *Svenska folksägner*, 249–50.

12.8 The Man-Bear Raised the Child

A pregnant woman met a bear in Kleppland Woods. The bear attacked and killed her, tore the child out of her body, and took it with him. The child followed the bear. A few years later, the bear was shot. The hunters caught the child and took it home, but it died soon afterward. It was hairy on one side like a bear, but on the other side, it was smooth-skinned, like a human being.

> There are widespread folk traditions about wild animals bringing up human children. In the folk ballad about Little Lavrans (ballad type: A 24) it is said that a man-bear is released by raising the child he has taken from the mother's womb. (Cf. no. 12.2.)
>
> Collected by Peter Lunde from Gunder O. Vestrus in Søgne, Vest-Agder (Norway). Printed in Lunde, *Folkeminne frå Søgne* (1969), 32.

12.9 They Shot His Grandfather

They once shot an unusually large bear up in Dreyja. While they were flaying the animal, a young Finn came by. He stopped and watched them for a while. Suddenly he burst into tears. They had killed his grandfather, he said.

> It is not clear whether the Finn recognizes his grandfather by the bearskin or by some other means.
>
> Collected by Knut Strompdal in Drevja, Nordland (Norway). Printed in Strompdal *Gamalt frå Helgeland* 3 (1939), 66.

12.10 Scolding the Bear

People thought that a Finn named Tomas, who came from Rammen, could change himself into a bear.

One day a bear got into the cattle at a farm where the Finn often hung around. The girl who was tending the cattle thought right away that it was Tomas who had taken a bear shape. She ran up to him and shouted:

"Shame on you, Tomas, you don't wash, you don't comb your hair, and you don't go to church, you God-denier and killer of poor folks' cows!"

The bear turned tail and ran back to the woods without taking any cattle that time. They were convinced that it was Tomas because the girl had recognized him and had scolded him so.

> Collected by Knut Strompdal in Vevelstad, Nordland (Norway). Printed in Strompdal, *Gamalt frå Helgeland* 3 (1939), 65–66.

13. Death

The Christian notion that the immortal soul separates from the body at the moment of death is also found in folk tradition. Characteristically, however, the soul is described in material form, as a puff of air or smoke, as a light, or as a white shape leaving the body. In Iceland, the departing soul is at times called the dead man's *fylgje*.

> See Else Mundal, *Fylgjemotiva i norrøn litteratur* (1974), 136.

13.1 Opening a Door to Let the Soul Out

When life had fled from the body of a dying person, one opened the door just a crack. That way the soul would be free to go.

> This *dite* was collected by Edvard Grimstad in Gudbrandsdalen, Oppland (Norway). Printed in Grimstad, *Etter gamalt. Folkeminne frå Gudbrandsdalen* 3 (1953), 34.

13.2 They Saw Her Soul

The soul of a dead person is sometimes visible the very moment it is separated from the body.

About fifty years ago, an old spinster died in Leiret. She had always been a good person, and she was content when she saw the end approaching. She was lying sick, during the summer, and the window stood open. The very moment she departed this life, people saw a white shape leaving the body and rushing out through the window. A handkerchief lying on the windowsill was swept along by the gust of air and fell to the ground in the garden.

The old folks said that it was her soul that had left her body.

> Collected by Sigurd Nergaard in Elverum, Hedmark (Norway). Printed in Nergaard, *Hulder og trollskap. Folkeminne fraa Østerdalen* 4 (1925), 98.

13.3 The Fylgje of the Dead

Sometimes when someone dies a kind of wraith or spirit is seen where he died or perhaps somewhere else. It is pale gray and usually looks like a puff of smoke. It cannot be seen except in the dark, and it goes wherever the air currents take it. It does no one any harm. This is the *fylgje* of the dead person.

> Collected by Magnús Grímsson, minister at Mosfell (Iceland). Printed in Jón Árnason, *Íslenzkar þjóðsögur og æfintýri* 3 (1958), 407.

PART II
The Dead and the Living

Part II illustration: "The shadows of
drowned men." Olaus Magnus, *Historia
de Gentibus Septentrionalibus* (History
of the Northern People, 1555),
book 2, chapter 3.

ccording to folk belief, the continuity of the *hug* and the body was also maintained in death. The "living dead" continued to exist in the grave and interaction with the living ranged from cautious neighborliness to outright hostility. By and large, however, fear of the dead dominates this tradition. Continued contact most often implied some unfinished business between the dead and the living, a debt not paid, a crime not atoned for, or perhaps a funeral rite that had not been properly observed. The legends about the dead reflect the typical mix of church-sponsored and other beliefs.

14. Heaven or Hell?

When someone died, people were concerned whether the dead person would find peace in the afterlife and, particularly, whether he or she would go to heaven or to hell. There were many omens and signs connected with the moment of death and with burial, but their interpretation varied from place to place and from time to time.

Some legends describe popular beliefs regarding the fate in store for people who have made a pact with the devil. Characteristically, many of the individuals claimed by the devil at the moment of death are wealthy. Those stories can be read as a form of social protest and sanction.

> See Louise Hagberg, *När döden gästar* (1937), 100–104.

14.1 Easy to Pull

When the horse pulled the dead easily, people would say:
"He was easy to pull. He must be happy."

> Collected by Peter Lunde in Eikjen parish, Vest-Agder (Norway). Printed in Lunde, *Kynnehuset. Vestegdske folkeminne* (1924), 42.

14.2 The White and the Black Bird

We are not alone. There is both a good and an evil power by our side. And when death approaches, good and evil omens appear just before we die. If one's life has been compassionate, the omen will be

good. But it will be evil if one's life has been ungodly. The good
omen will be a bright spirit; the evil omen will be dark.

Once there was a dean at the church in Brunskog. He predicted
that he would die in the church. Two birds would appear, one white,
the other black and they would fight each other. If the white bird
won, the congregation should celebrate the funeral feast. But if the
black bird won, they should not celebrate.

And it came to pass just as the dean had foreseen. He died in
church and two birds appeared who fought each other. But the white
bird won. And so they held the funeral feast.

> The legend reflects the pre-Christian belief in the *fylgje* (Cf. nos.
> 9.1–9.10.), which here has been assimilated to the Christian con-
> cept of a continuous battle between the powers of good and evil.
> See Louise Hagberg, *När döden gästar* (1937), 92–93, 108–11;
> Carl-Herman Tillhagen, *Fåglarna i folktron* (1978), 20–23.
> Collected in 1898 by Nils Keyland from Per Persson, Sand-
> sjöberg, Östmark parish (Sweden). Ms. in NM HA Sägner 3.
> Printed in Bengt af Klintberg, *Svenska folksägner* (1972), 169.

14.3 One Black and One Brown Horse

Sammel Håka's daughter was not much better than her father, although she married well. When they buried her, it was quite frightening. She had ordered that one black and one brown horse were to
pull the hearse. But, whatever the reason, two black horses were
hitched up instead.

If anyone thought the horses could pull the wagon, they were mis-
taken. The horses struggled until they were streaming with sweat,
but they could not budge the wagon. Finally they had to unhitch one
of the black horses and put a brown one in its place. And then it
worked.

On the way to church, a storm broke. It was terrible. It swept the
hats right off the funeral guests. And when the minister spoke over
the dead, the doors were torn open and a sudden wind blew out all
the candles so that it became pitch black in the church. You see, the
daughter had signed a contract with Perkel.

> According to af Klintberg, Sammel Håka (Samuel Haakonson)
> lived during the eighteenth century. Born of a poor family, he
> became one of the richer farmers in the area. Various legends
> about him explain that he must have had help from the devil. His
> daughter inherited Samuel's satanic reputation.

It was generally accepted that the last wish of the dead must under any circumstances be respected.

The weight of the coffin was interpreted in various ways. A heavier than normal coffin meant that the devil was sitting on it. An unusually light coffin indicated that the soul of the dead had left the body and was already in heaven or in hell.

It was considered dangerous to call the devil by his proper name. Therefore a noa-name (a substitute word replacing a taboo word), such as Perkel, was customarily used instead.

See Louise Hagberg, *När döden gästar* (1937), 377–79; Bengt af Klintberg, *Svenska folksägner* (1972), 320.

Collected in 1911 by Sven Rothman from Per Gustaf Johanson, Källhagen, Västra Hargs parish (Sweden). Printed in Rothman, *Östgötska folkminnen* (1941), 92.

14.4 The Heavy Coffin

There was a man in northern Sweden who owned a lot of land. He was a very ungodly man, and he treated his workers badly.

Once he went on a trip and fell ill while staying at an inn. And there he died a horrible death. When he gave up the ghost, there was such a stench in the room that neither the minister nor the servant could stand it. The room became so hot that the wallpaper was singed.

When they were going to bury him, they could not make the horses move; they would come to a halt every few steps. The minister walked in front and sang, but still they could not move the coffin. So they fetched half a company of soldiers in uniform. The soldiers marched ahead, and then the horses followed.

Collected in 1870 by J. E. Wefvar in Vårdö (Finland). Printed in V. E. V. Wessman, *Sägner* 3.2 (1931), 4.

15. The Living in the Land of the Dead

The motif of the journey to the other world exists in a large complex of folktales (AT 470) and legends. The latter can be divided into two major types; one emphasizing the message from the other world, the other the mutual promise of two friends to invite each other to their weddings.

See Leander Petzoldt, "AT 470: Friends in Life and Death. Zur Psychologie und Geschichte einer Wundererzählung," *Rheinisches Jahrbuch für Volkskunde* 19 (1969), 101–61.

15.1 Two Friends

Once there were two boys who were close friends. They made a pact to invite each other to their weddings. If one of them died before both had gotten married, the one who was still alive was to come to the other's grave at the time of his wedding and blow on a clay pipe. Then the dead would wake up and come to the wedding.

Some time later one of them died. When the other was about to get married, he went to the grave, as they had agreed, and blew on a clay pipe. The dead man arose and went along to the wedding. After sitting at the wedding reception for a little while, he asked the bridegroom to follow him to the grave. Well, the bridegroom went with the ghost—because it was, of course, just a ghost. After they had walked for some time, they somehow came to a meadow where a whole herd of cows was grazing. It seemed that all the grass on the meadow had been eaten down so that only black dirt was left, but still the cows were so fat that no one had ever seen fatter cows. So the bridegroom asked the dead man whether he knew why the cows were so fat when they had such poor pasture.

"Yes," said the other one, "these cows here belong to people who are satisfied with what they have even though they have but little."

After they had walked a bit further, they came to a meadow where the grass was so tall that it reached up to their knees, but still the cows seemed terribly skinny. Then the living man asked:

"Why are these cows so skinny even though they have such good pasture?"

"They belong to envious people," answered the dead man. "They always begrudge others what they have and are never satisfied with what they have themselves."

For some reason the bridegroom then fell asleep. When he woke up, he had been sleeping for seven hundred years. Everything had changed; it seemed to him that he had come to a different world. His money was not good anymore, and nothing was the same as it had been before.

> The wedding plays a relatively minor role in this story, which focuses on the visit to the land of the dead. The vision of the other

world has a moralizing tone. The motif of the fat and the skinny cows is reminiscent of the Pharaoh's dream in Genesis 41:15–22.

In the folktale a person's absence from the land of the dead has little or no effect on his or her future life. In the legend, by contrast, he or she usually falls to dust upon returning. In the present narrative, however, these patterns are combined. See also the American legend about Rip van Winkle.

Collected in 1894 by J. A. Björkström in Kullå, Borgå (Finland) for the Swedish Literary Society in Finland. Printed in A. Allardt and S. Perklén, *Nyländska folksagor och -sägner* (1896), 77. Reprinted in V. E. V. Wessman, *Sägner* 3.2 (1931), 61.

16. Return of the Dead Lover

The dead lover returns to bring a message, to take revenge, or to respond to the grief of his beloved. The most famous interpretation of this popular motif is found in G. A. Bürger's ballad "Lenore" (1774). (Cf. AT 365.)

See Will-Erich Peuckert, *Lenore* (1955).

16.1 The Bride Who Came Back

Once, a bride and a bridegroom were separated. She died, and he did not find out. Later that day he saw her; she came along, driving a horse and wagon, and asked him to go for a ride with her. He asked her why, but she did not answer and just started driving. They drove in silence for a long time, but when she finally took him back, she said:

"The moon is shining, the dead is driving, and yet my beloved does not understand."

At that moment she disappeared. Then he knew that she was dead and that he had seen her ghost. She had been dressed in everyday clothes, and that is why he did not understand.

Collected in 1915 by V. E. V. Wessman from Wilhelmina Wikström, Förby, Finnby (Finland). Printed in Wessman, *Sägner* 3.2 (1931), 25.

16.2 "*Gárún, Gárún, Gray I Am Growing 'round My Pate*"

Once there was a couple who lived on a farm, but no one knows what their names were or what the farm was called. They kept two servants, a man and a woman. His name was Sigurður and hers Guðrún. Sigurður was interested in Guðrún and proposed to her, but she would not have anything to do with him. One winter they went to church on Christmas Eve. They had only one horse, which their boss had lent them. Off and on they rode double, and while they were riding, Sigurður began a conversation with Guðrún: "I wonder whether we'll ride together like this another Christmas Eve?" She said no, that would not happen. They squabbled a bit about that, and then he said: "We'll ride together on Christmas Eve next year whether you want to or not!" After that they fell silent, and no one knows if anything else of interest happened during their trip.

Toward the end of that same winter, Sigurður took sick and died. He was transported to the church and buried. Time passed and it was Christmas again. On Christmas Eve the couple was getting ready for church and they asked Guðrún to join them, but she did not want to. She told them she would stay at home, and that is what she did. As soon as they had left, she cleaned the farmhouse and arranged everything the way she liked it. Next, she lit a candle and threw an overcoat over her shoulders. Having done that, she sat down and began to read a book. After she had read for a short while, she heard some knocking. She picked up the candle and went to the door. There she saw an apparition in the form of a man and a horse with gear, which she recognized as the minister's saddle horse. The newcomer addressed her and told her that she must go riding with him. She had a suspicion that this was Sigurður, her co-worker. She put down the candle and followed him. He asked whether she wanted a hand, but she told him that she did not need help from him and mounted the horse herself. Instantly he was in the saddle in front of her. They headed along the road to the church and neither one said a word to the other. But after they had ridden for a while, he began to speak: "Gárún, Gárún, gray I am growing 'round my pate." She answered: "Shut up, you fool, and keep going!" No one knows whether they said anything else to each other before they reached the churchyard. He stopped someplace by the wall and they both dismounted. Then he spoke:

"Bide a bit, bide a bit, Gárún, Gárún,
while I shift Old Nellie, Nellie,
eastward of the churchyard, churchyard.

Then he disappeared with the horse, and she flung herself over the
wall and ran up to the door of the church. Just as she was about to
enter, someone grabbed her from behind, but her overcoat was lying
unfastened over her shoulders, so whoever grabbed her got only the
coat, and Guðrún escaped into the church, where she at once fell onto
the floor and fainted. This all happened at the high point of the
celebration of the mass. People rushed over and tried to revive her.
She was carried into the farmhouse near the church and looked after.
She came to after a while and told all about what had led to her arrival. The people went to the stable to see about the minister's horse.
They found it there, dead, with every bone in its body broken and
the hide stripped from its back. Remnants of the overcoat were found
by the church door—it had been torn to shreds, and the shreds lay
strewn all about. After that Sigurður's grave was fixed so that he
would lie quietly.

> Collected by Páll Jónsson in 1861 from Guðrún Guðmundsdóttir
> on Hvammur Island. Printed in Jón Árnason, *Íslenzkar þjóðsögur og
> æfintýri* 3 (1958) 352–53, 642.

17. The Midnight Mass of the Dead

The stories about the midnight mass of the dead constitute a type
of migratory legend. As early as the fourth century A.D. in stories
about saints' lives, the midnight mass is celebrated by angels, the
blessed dead, and the saint. Another version, possibly based on popular tradition, is found in Gregory of Tours's *De gloria confessorum* (sixth
century), in which the midnight mass is attended by the dead and ordinary people rather than by angels and saints. In folk legends the
story is consistently focused on the fear of the dead and on the narrow escape of the unwitting observer.

> See Lutz Röhrich, *Sage* (1966), 36–38; Brynjulf Alver, "Dauings-
> gudstenesta," *Arv* 6 (1950), 145–65; Bernward Deneke, *Legende
> und Volkssage. Untersuchungen zur Erzählung vom Geistergottesdienst*
> (1958); Louise Hagberg, *När döden gästar* (1937), 653–61.
> Legend type: ML 4015.

17.1 The Christmas Mass of the Dead

Late one Christmas Eve in the end of the eighteenth century, a man from the Ingå Islands was on his way to the mainland with a load of fish. When he came to the church at Ingå, he saw lights in the windows and heard the sound of singing.

"That's strange," he thought, "the clocks on the islands must be slow. They're already celebrating the early Christmas service. I'm going to let my horse rest for a while and go into the church myself."

He tried, but the gate to the churchyard was locked. "Boys will be boys," the man thought and climbed over the wall.

Once inside the church, the man walked almost all the way up to the transept. There he sat down in a pew and took part in the singing. But when he looked around, he saw that everyone there, even the minister by the altar, was dead. When they sang the last verse, he thought it best to leave. Just as he walked through the gate, he heard a loud noise. Turning around, he saw the lights in the church go out and heard screams and a rushing in the air as if from many birds. When the man got home, he threw up blood and lay sick for seven weeks.

> Collected in 1902 by V. E. V. Wessman from Karl Bergström in Sibbå (Finland). Printed in Wessman, *Sägner* 3.2 (1931), 13.

17.2 The Dead Grabbed Her Coat

The dead would gather in church before the regular service began. In any case, this was their custom on Christmas morning.

In the old days when the church was still at Saltnes, it happened that a woman from Vik was on her way to church early one Christmas morning. When she passed by Halsmoen, she saw candlelight in the church. She thought she might be late, so she hurried. Well, she got to church, but as she walked down the aisle, she could see that all the pews were already filled with people. She made her way to the place reserved for the folk from Vik and sat down next to another woman.

Entering the pew, she looked around at the other people there. She knew some of them; others she did not. But everyone she recognized were people already dead. Then she turned toward the woman by her side. It was a neighbor who had died some time ago. Before the woman could collect her thoughts, the dead woman said:

"I tell you, you must hurry out of the church, or you will be in trouble."

The woman got out of the pew, but, at the same moment, the dead started slowly from the pews and followed her. And just when the woman got to the door, they grabbed ahold of her coat. It was a wrap without sleeves. The woman quickly undid the clasp holding the wrap together. And that is how she saved herself.

> Collected by Ragnald Mo in Saltdal, Nordland (Norway). Printed in Mo, *Eventyr og segner. Folkeminne frå Salten* 2 (1944), 96.

18. The Revenging Dead

Some of the walking dead are considered especially dangerous. If there is an unresolved conflict or crime, or if the grave is disturbed, the dead might seek revenge or demand restitution. If a couple refuses to name their new born child after a particular dead person, he or she might take revenge on the child itself. Even a chance meeting with a revenant could cause sickness or other harm, the underlying assumption being that the dead generally resent the living.

See Louise Hagberg, *När döden gästar* (1937), 545–84.

18.1 The Woman at Haugen

A man who was called Andres lived on Haugen in Nordbygdi in Seljord. He was married twice, but he did not get along with his first wife at all. They often quarreled and beat each other.

After she died, she walked again and made Andres's life miserable. Every night after he had gone to bed, he could see her through the window, walking down the barn bridge, just as she had done when she was alive. She came across the yard and through the door, no matter how well he locked and bolted it. She came right to his bed and squeezed in beside him.

So one evening Andres took a big logging ax into bed with him. When his dead wife came back, he raised himself up and struck the ax into the beam overhead. Then he told her to go to hell. She disappeared at once, and he never saw her again.

Andres was a giant of a man, wild as a Turk, and a beast.

One of the more common means of protecting oneself against the revenant was with a sharp-edged tool. Here the use of the ax is combined with a curse.

See Louise Hagberg, *När döden gästar* (1937), 622.

Collected by Kjetil A. Flatin in Seljord, Telemark (Norway). Printed in Flatin, *Tussar og trolldom* (1930), 142–43.

18.2 The Milkmaid's Verse or the Draug's Verse

I swear it's true and give my vow,
that the Virgin Mary milked a cow;
and she the prayers of a milkmaid heeds,
and every draug from Bessie beats.
The sign of the cross I'll put on your back,
preserving you from envious attack.
It caused the milk through the bucket to leak—
may shame on draug and spells and envy be wreaked.

It is unusual that the dead (draug) are held responsible for the loss of milk in a cow, as is the case here.

Collected by V. U. Hammershaimb on the Færoe Islands. Printed in "Barneviser og ramser," *Antiquarisk Tidsskrift, 1849–51* (1852), 315. Reprinted in Hammershaimb, *Savn* (1969), 197.

18.3 Jón from Skorravík

A man by the name of Jón, from Skorravík on Fellsströnd, had a child by his own daughter. He wanted a fellow named Guðmundur Teitsson to marry her, but Guðmundur was not eager to do so because of the incest. During the autumn, the three sailed out to Stykkishólmur. At dusk, when they were just beyond Hrapp's Island, such a fierce storm struck that the boat was overturned—but in reality it was Jón who caused it, for it was his idea to drown both his daughter and Guðmundur. His daughter did drown, but Guðmundur was able to get up on the keel of the boat and hang on. Jón knew how to swim and grabbed Guðmundur's foot, but it is impossible to say whether he meant to drag Guðmundur from the keel back into the water or whether he was desperately trying to save his own life. Since Guðmundur was a determined man and did not want to die, he kicked his foot out so hard that Jón went under. But when Guðmundur drifted ashore he saw Jón there, risen from the dead, and he was attacked by him. That same evening, Bogi Benediktsson, who was living on Hrapp's Island and owned property there, grew restless, and he could not figure out why. So he sent some of his men down to the beach to see what had been washed up on shore. There they found Guðmundur lying unconscious — his eyes were bloodshot and his body was bruised all over. A long time went by before he could stand to open his eyes in daylight, and he always shuddered to think of that horrible experience. This story is from a woman who has heard it more than once from Guðmundur himself.

Collected by Konrad Maurer in Iceland. Printed in Maurer, *Isländ-dische Volkssagen der Gegenwart* (1860), 66–67. Icelandic version in Jón Árnason, *Íslenzkar þjóðsögur og æfintýri* 1 (1862), 256. Reprinted in new edition 1 (1954), 247.

18.4 He Had to Marry the Dead

In the olden days, there were bone houses in the cemeteries. That is where they threw the bones they found when digging up old graves.

One day a hen disappeared at the minister's place and nobody could find it. Toward evening an old hand at the farm heard that the hen was missing. He said that he had seen it by the bone house that day, so he thought it must still be there. Now, nobody would dare go to the bone house that late in the evening. But the farmhand said he was not afraid. He would go and look for the hen.

It got dark. He groped around among the piles of bones as best as he could, looking for the hen. Suddenly he got ahold of a cold, hard hand. It grabbed him and held on. He pulled and struggled, but could not get free. Then he shouted for help.

They heard his screams at the farm, and they knew it was urgent, but no one dared go there. Finally the minister took a light and went himself. He found the old man beside himself with fright, barely able to tell him what had happened. The minister thought about it for a while. Then he got an inkling of what might be going on.

"Is there anyone you have wronged or betrayed in your life?" he asked.

"Oh, yes; I'm afraid there is," said the farmhand. "When I was young I had a sweetheart. I deceived her, and they say that she took her life because of it."

"Did you promise to marry her?"

"Yes, I suppose I did."

"Then there is only one thing to do. What you have promised, you must keep."

So the minister married them, the living and the dead. When that was done, the old man was released.

Collected by Sigurd Nergaard in Elverum, Hedmark (Norway). Printed in Nergaard, *Hulder og trollskap. Folkeminne fraa Østerdalen* 4 (1925), 95–96.

18.5 He Wanted the Child Named after Himself

Lars Osnes from Ulstein was married to Johanne Roppen. Johanne bore a son, and she wanted to name him Elling after her father. It was winter then, during cod season. One stormy day two boats from Ulstein with many fine men on board disappeared at sea. There was great sorrow in the village when it happened.

Johanne was not related to any of the men who were lost. Nonetheless, she was disturbed at night. She thought that she saw a man in an oilskin come into her house and walk over to the cradle where her little boy was lying. He was not baptized yet. This happened night after night.

Johanne went to the woman next door and asked her for help. Her name was Lisbet Osnes.

"Well, I suppose you know what he wants," said Lisbet.

Yes, Johanne did, to be sure. "He wants me to name the boy after him, but the child is to be christened Elling after my father," Johanne said.

"I'm going to give you some advice," said Lisbet. "Heat up a baking griddle until it is red-hot and put it by the threshold before you go to bed tonight."

Johanne did that. She had just fallen asleep, when she was suddenly awakened by a horrible scream coming from the doorway. The dead man had burned himself.

She neither heard nor saw him again. But the little boy became sickly. He would not thrive anymore. He remained a half-wit all his days, and they called him Crazy Elling.

This is supposed to have happened around 1850.

It was quite normal to name a child after a grandparent. In this narrative, the revenant's demand that the boy be named after him, even though he is not a relative, reflects his desire to live on in the child. There were a number of proven means by which to protect the unbaptized child against this or other demands of the dead, such as the use of a hot iron, spreading sulfur or gunpowder about the house, or sowing flax seed. If the child got sick or did not develop normally, it was assumed that the parents had not succeeded in protecting the child.

Collected in 1938 by Martin Bjørndal from Berte Hareid, Sunnmøre (Norway). Printed in Bjørndal, *Segn og tru. Folkeminne frå Møre* (1949), 92–93.

18.6 The Girl Who Stole the Thighbone

When they made brandy in the olden days, they put a human bone into the vat to improve the taste.

A girl went to the cemetery one Thursday evening to get a bone from a grave, although she was very afraid of the dark. She took a thighbone. But after that night, she never had any peace. The fellow whose bone she had taken walked again, screaming, in the night. He was big and tall. He had been a grenadier in his time. Wherever she went, he followed right behind her, screaming.

"Itt! Itt! Itt!" he screamed in a nasty voice. And the girl was beside herself with fear.

Her mother told me about it.

Collected in 1912 by Sven Rothman from Mother Andersson in Godegård, Östergötland (Sweden). Printed in Rothman, *Östgötska folkminnen* (1941), 9–10.

18.7 The Funeral Singer

It happened that people, before they died, hired someone to sing at their funeral.

There is a story about a man in Vefsn who was so much in demand as a funeral singer, that a woman hired him beforehand to sing at her funeral. The man had a high and clear voice. But when the day of the woman's funeral came, the man did not have time, and they had to get someone else.

That night when he had finished his work and was resting in bed, the dead woman came into his room. He clearly saw her come in and walk over to a loom and put down her mittens. And then she came and was going to strangle him. The man was big and strong, but he barely managed to shake off the dead woman. People thought that she was angry because the man did not sing at her funeral.

> It was customary to sing hymns before leaving the house with the coffin, as well as when the funeral procession passed by neighboring farms. This was considered a farewell by the dead represented by the funeral singer hired for that purpose.
>
> See Bjarne Hodne, *Å leve med døden* (1980), 83–84; Louise Hagberg, *Når döden gästar* (1937), 310–18.
>
> Collected by Knut Strompdal in Vefsn, Nordland (Norway). Printed in Strompdal, *Gamalt frå Helgeland* 2 (1938), 54–55.

18.8 A Murderer Brought to Justice

A farmer, Kavela Eirik, in Bjärnå had a serving girl. He slept with her, and she got pregnant. One day he asked her to put her head in his lap, he wanted to pick the lice out of her hair, he said. But then he stuck a knife into her neck and she died. After that he put her under a big pile of twigs on Kankomalmen. But she walked again and unhitched the horses. It got so bad that no one could pass by the farm, nor did anyone dare find out what was going on. Finally they asked a minister to come. He cut himself at the root of his thumb with his penknife. He said that he would write in blood whatever she told him, and then she would stop walking. This is what she answered:

"Kavela Eirik murdered me, and I want to be buried in sacred soil."

She told him that she was under the big pile of twigs. They dug her up and brought the bones to the cemetery. But the farmer was put in prison and punished. After that she stopped unhitching the horses.

> Collected by V. E. V. Wessman in 1915 in Finnby (Finland). Printed in Wessman, *Sägner* 3.2 (1931), 35–36.

18.9 He Swept with Seven Brooms

A long time ago, at a farm in Uthuslia, there was a dead woman who walked again. During her life her husband had treated her badly, and people said more than once that he would get his in return. And as soon as she was dead, he got it! Almost every night she came and leaned over his bed; and when he went outside, she followed him. She did not do or say anything; she just stared at him. However that may be, he almost went mad. He had never been afraid in his life. But now he hardly dared walk outside in broad daylight. Then someone told him that he should sweep with seven brooms and sow flax seed all the way from the door of the house down to the road. This he did, and ever since then, he has been left in peace.

> Sowing flax seed around the house, on the road, or by the grave was a common means of protection against revenants. Flax seed was also placed in the coffin itself. In popular explanations, the protective power of the flax stems from the belief that the Christ child was swaddled in a linen cloth made from flax. According to another explanation, the dead were required to count or pick up the seeds—a task they were incapable of mastering. The advice to sweep with seven brooms relates to the magic power of that number.
>
> See Louise Hagberg, *När döden gästar* (1937), 626–29; V. J. Brøndegaard, *Folk og flora* 2 (1979), 308–12.
>
> Collected by Sigurd Nergaard in Østerdalen (Norway). Printed in Nergaard, *Hulder og trollskap. Folkeminne fraa Østerdalen* 4 (1925), 92–93.

19. Binding the Dead

The relationship of the living to the dead was always ambivalent, ranging from concern to fear. In many situations fear was the dominant emotion, as witnessed by numerous stories about how to bind the dead to the grave by magic or by mechanical means.

> See Louise Hagberg, *När döden gästar* (1937), 622–35.

19.1 They Rammed a Pole through Her Chest

In Ris there was an evil woman by the name of Ma-Rams. She made a lot of trouble when she was alive and walked again after she died. Finally she was bound in her grave near Ovsted Church. That place is called Ma-Ram's Hole to this day. People remember a big wooden pole stuck in that hole. It had been rammed right through the body of Ma-Rams. If someone rocked the pole, she would say:

"Move it again and I'll beat you bloody until you're dead."

But if someone rocked it once more, she would pull him or her down the hole and wring his or her neck.

Something similar, by the way, happened at Østbirk where Slante-Lars, the minister there, bound someone in the grave.

> There are instances of corpses being bound in the grave with a stake rammed through them dating back to the *Saxo Grammaticus.* And there is evidence that the custom was practiced in Scandinavia during the Middle Ages. This is not to be confused with the tradition of placing a pole on the coffin if the minister could not be present at the burial; it would be removed later, when he performed the rite of throwing soil on the coffin.
>
> See *Saxonis Gesta Danorum* (1931–57), bk. 1, chap. 8.3, bk. 5, chap. 11.4; Gunnel Hedberg, "Straffredskap," KLNM 17 (1972), column 284; Louise Hagberg, *När döden gästar* (1937), 634–35; Bjarne Hodne, *Å leve med døden* (1980), 123–24.
>
> Collected by E. T. Kristensen from Rasmus P. Randlev in Tåning, Jylland (Denmark). Printed in Kristensen, *Danske sagn* 5 (1897), 298.

19.2 Throwing Soil on the Coffin

After the minister had thrown a handful of dirt on the coffin, someone in the family would do the same — but secretly so that the minister would not notice. Then the dead had to stay where he or she belonged.

> According to Christian belief, the soil thrown on the coffin symbolizes that the body is transitory. But the folk also interpreted the act as a magic ritual designed to bind the dead to the grave. The magic aspect was strengthened if a relative secretly threw some dirt on the coffin, too.
>
> See Louise Hagberg, *När döden gästar* (1937), 398–400.
>
> Collected by Johan Skrindsrud in Nord-Etnedal, Oppland (Norway). Printed in Skrindsrud, *På heimleg grunn. Folkeminne frå Etnedal* (1956), 65.

19.3 He Shot the Dead in the Head

In Kattbeck near Wichterpal lived on old tramp called Ado, who had the job of burning charcoal on the farm. Once, he got careless and let the coal burn to ashes. Afraid he would get a beating, he hanged himself. His shack was given to another tramp named Hans. But the dead man returned, holding the rope in his hand and making noises about the house. One evening when the moon was out, Hans

saw him standing by the door. He walked up to him, taking care not
to let the dead man's shadow fall on himself—if that happened, Hans
would be in his power. Then Hans cut a small silver coin into nine
pieces, and, with that, he shot the dead man through the head. He
disappeared with a great noise and never showed himself again.

> One method of ridding oneself of a revenant was to shoot him or
> her, preferably with silver. The coin is cut into nine pieces be-
> cause of the inherent magic power of that number.
>
> Collected in Wichterpal, Estland. Printed in C. Russworm,
> *Eibofolke oder die Schweden an den Küsten Ehstlands und auf Runö*
> (1855), 264–65. Reprinted in V. E. V. Wessman, *Sägner* 3.2
> (1931), 51.

19.4 You Have Not Bitten the Thread from the Needle Yet

There was a sorcerer whose name was Finnur. He was wicked and
malevolent, and everybody was afraid of him. When he died, no one,
neither man nor woman, wanted to ready the body and wrap it in a
shroud. Even so, there was one woman who said she would give it a
try. She was about half done when she went out of her mind. Then
another woman volunteered, but she did not pay any attention to
how the corpse carried on. When she was nearly finished, Finnur
said:
"You haven't bitten the thread from the needle yet."
She answered:
"I'll break it, not bite it, damn you," and snapping the thread from
the needle, she broke the needle into several pieces and stuck them
into the soles of the corpse's feet.
There is no mention that he ever did anyone else harm after that.

> According to Hagberg, in Sweden it was believed that one should
> never put the pins that hold the shroud together between one's
> teeth. Perhaps the dead sorcerer would have walked again or
> gained power over the woman, if she had done so. Plunging nee-
> dles into the dead person's soles is a well-known device to keep
> the dead from walking.
>
> See Louise Hagberg, *När döden gästar* (1937), 202–4. Collected
> by the minister Skúli Gíslason. Printed in Jón Árnason, *Íslenzkar
> þjóðsögur og æfintýri* 1 (1862), 226. Reprinted in new edition 1
> (1954), 219.

20. The Friendly Revenant

Under certain circumstances, contact with the dead could be constructive, even welcome. Lifelong emotional bonds between the dead and the living were not easily severed. Besides, at times the dead could give useful advice or convey messages.

20.1 She Had Food and Drink Ready for Him

Torolv Hillestad often went home at night. His wife was happy when he came. She had beer and food ready on the table every night so that she did not have to get up.

"Oh, are you here, my dear Torolv?" she said. "There is a bowl of beer and food for you on the table. How are you living? How are you getting along?" she asked.

"Tolerably well, so far," said Torolv, "but I'm afraid it's going to get worse later on."

Torolv had been a reckless man.

"If I weren't so good to the poor, there would be no mercy for me," he said.

They were mowing in the hills, the farmhand and he.

"You mustn't mow there," the farmhand said, it's not your hayfield."

"If you want to get rich, you can't be afraid for your soul," said Torolv.

"I always run into the devil here," he said one time when he was crossing Hillestad Creek. He dreaded crossing that creek.

> Torolv's concern about the future shows that he as yet exists in a liminal world between the living and the dead. The story reflects the ambiguity in judging a man who has been a thief but kind toward the poor.
>
> Collected by Johannes Skar in Årdal, Setesdal, Aust-Agder (Norway). Printed in Skar, *Gamalt or Sætesdal* 1 (1968), 488–89.

20.2 "Your Name is Written in the Book of Life"

My second wife came to me after she had died. During her lifetime, I had bought a Bible, and one day when we were reading in it, we came to the words: "Their names are written in the Book of Life." We prayed together that our names might be written in that Book.

Sometime later she died. But she came back one night and stood in the doorway and said:

"Per."

I did not answer.

"Your name is written in the Book of Life."

I raised myself up in bed.

"Tell Peder Jensen that his name is also written in the Book of Life."

With that she disappeared through the door. Later I delivered the message.

> The dead wife appearing to her husband in this legend must be considered a messenger from heaven rather than a revenant in the ordinary sense of the word.
>
> Collected by E. T. Kristensen from Niels Kristiansen, Vole, Jylland (Denmark). Printed in Kristensen, *Danske sagn* 5 (1897), 323–24.

20.3 The Dead Gave Advice

My mother told this story about her brother, Hans, who had wanted to sell a building lot. One evening Hans went fishing. My mother lay awake all night at home thinking about the deal. Sometime that night her deceased mother came in, walked over to the bed, and said:

"Tell Hans that he must not sell the lot; one of the children should inherit it."

I asked my mother whether she might not have been dreaming this. She answered:

"No, if it's the last thing I say, I was wide awake."

> The notion of the dead returning to give advice at a moment of crisis or decision, is well known in tradition. At times the living would even seek counsel with the dead, calling them up or talking to them at the grave.
>
> See Louise Hagberg, *När döden gästar* (1937), 540–44.
>
> Collected by Kristian Bugge in 1902 from Otto Ruberg in Brevik, Vestfold (Norway). Printed in Bugge, *Folkeminne-optegnelser* (1934), 68.

20.4 Cold Death Is Dreary

Two years ago some men drowned between the coast and Eyjar. All of them were either from Mýrdalur or from Eyjafjöll. They had been on their way to Eyja for the fishing season. Toward evening a sharp southeaster had sprung up. People think that is when they perished. That night a woman at Eyjafjöll dreamed that a man came to her and said:

Rough it was when night drew nigh.
Death, cold death is dreary.
There was I carried, where many tarried
on the sands of the land of the living.

> Here the dead man brings the message that he and the rest of the crew have drowned. Similar messages or omens are commonly reported even today.
>
> See Eyðun Andreassen, "Hamferð. Varsel om ulukker på sjøen på Færøyane," *Tradisjon* 7 (1977), 75–89.
>
> Collected by the minister Skúli Gíslason. Printed in Jón Árnason, *Íslenzkar þjóðsögur og ævintýri* 1 (1862), 231–2. Reprinted in new edition 1 (1954), 224.

20.5 The Dead Mother Nursed Her Child

If the mother of an infant dies, people keep watch during the first few nights after she has been buried. If the child cries, the mother cannot rest in her grave but hurries back to put it to her breast. But no good ever comes of that because the child gets sick or is crippled and becomes lame.

It happened in Vinuun, in the parish of Døstrup, that two girls who kept watch with a child went to the kitchen to get a bite to eat. When they came back, they saw something white lying over the cradle, and they could hear distinctly that the child was sucking and making a gurgling sound.

> The love of the mother transcended death but was not without danger to the child. An infant who had lost its mother was more likely to get sick or fail to develop normally. This was often explained as resulting from the dead mother nursing the child. Vice versa, the crying of the child kept the mother from finding peace in the grave. (Cf. nos. 6.2–6.3.)
>
> See Louise Hagberg, *När döden gästar* (1937), 146–50.

Collected by Pastor J. L. Knudsen, Røddinge, Sønderjylland (Denmark) from pupils at the folk high school. Printed in E. T. Kristensen, *Danske sagn* 5 (1897), 315.

21. The Dead Not Properly Cared For

The preparation of the dead person for burial was not primarily determined by aesthetic or hygienic criteria but rather by considerations for the well-being of the dead in the afterlife. Of special concern were the provisions for unborn children whose mothers died in childbirth. The stories function to enforce certain norms of proper treatment of the dead.

See Louise Hagberg, *När döden gästar* (1937), 127–33; Bjarne Hodne, *Å leve med døden* (1980), 57–62.

21.1 *The Skull*

Once when a grave was being dug in a cemetery, another burial place was uncovered. As was the custom, everything was buried again, along with the coffin. That night the wife of the farmer responsible for the cemetery dreamed that a woman came to her and recited:

I've wandered the churchyard until I'm weary,
within me joy grows dull.
Why, oh, why, my dearest deary,
can't I ever find my skull?

Later the farmer's wife had the area searched, and the skull was found outside the cemetery wall, where it had been left by some dogs that had gotten at the skeleton when no one was paying attention. She had the skull buried and then slept undisturbed.

Collected by the minister Skúli Gíslason. It is "a legend that is common in southern Iceland." Printed in Jón Árnason, *Íslenzkar þjóðsögur og æfintýri* 1 (1862), 238. Reprinted in new edition 1 (1954), 229–30.

21.2 They Forgot the Shroud for the Child

There was a woman in Tostrup who died in childbirth. She was buried, but they forgot to give her a shroud for her child. One evening when Jens Krog was walking by the cemetery, she climbed over the wall and said:

"Give me a shroud for my baby."

Jens did not get scared. He unbuttoned his trousers, took out his pocketknife, and cut a large piece from his shirt. He gave it to the woman, and she returned the same way she had come.

> Collected by E. T. Kristensen. Printed in Kristensen, *Jyske folkeminder* 8 (1886), 212.

21.3 He Needed a Shave

Somewhere there was a dead man who had been put into the coffin without first being shaved. So he came back and haunted that place for some fifteen years. No one knew what was amiss or why he did not stay in the grave. They had a room they used for guests, but nobody was able to sleep in it because the dead man walked there at night. Whenever someone was staying overnight, the ghost came and pulled the blanket off him.

Once, a workingman came and asked for quarters for the night.

"We would like to offer you lodging, but we don't have any room. It's been spooking up there for fifteen years. You wouldn't dare sleep there," they said.

But he said, "Sure, I'll sleep up there. I'm not afraid of any ghosts."

He went to bed, but at midnight the ghost came in through the door and put his shaving gear on the table. Then he went over to the workingman lying in the bed and pulled the blanket off him.

The workingman said to him, "What do you want?"

The ghost answered, "Well, I want you to shave me."

"Sure," said the man, "but where do you have your knife?"

The ghost took the knife from the table and gave it to the man to shave him. And he shaved him then. When he was finished the ghost asked:

"Shall I shave you too?"

But the man answered, "No, I just got a shave myself."

Then the ghost took his gear and disappeared. And he never came back again.

Collected by J. A. Björkström in 1894 in Nickby, Sibba in Nyland (Finland). Printed in A. Allardt and S. Perklén, *Nyländska folksagor och -sägner* (1896), 74–75. Reprinted in V. E. V. Wessman, *Sägner* 3.2 (1931), 20.

22. The Dead Needs Reconciliation

If a person died before atoning for a wrong he or she had committed, the person would not find peace until it was rectified. In this way society enforced sanctions against various injustices.

22.1 "I Was Enemies with My Neighbor"

Something was amiss at the church in Årdal. A skeleton would grab people by the shoulders and they could not get rid of it. Some people went mad, and no one dared walk past the church after nightfall.

"I suppose you're man enough to carry the skeleton," they would say if someone boasted and showed off—then he would shut up immediately.

There was a young man who was the quiet sort, but he never seemed afraid of anything. They asked him if he would dare take on the skeleton.

"Well, I've been thinking about it," said the boy.

So he went to the cemetery. The others stood outside the wall. It did not take long before the skeleton hung on his back and put its arms around his neck. He tried to shake it off, struggling and pulling, but the skeleton hung on.

"What is it you want?" asked the young man.

"I was enemies with my neighbor and didn't get to straighten it out. Would you carry me to his grave and ask him to forgive me?" he asked.

So the young man carried the skeleton to the dead neighbor's grave and asked.

"As truly as God forgives me, I will forgive you," said the dead neighbor. Then the skeleton fell from the boy's shoulders like dust. Hatred had held him together until then.

Legend type: ML 4020.
Collected by Johannes Skar in Setesdal, Aust-Agder (Norway). Printed in Skar, *Gamalt or Sætesdal* 1 (1961), 490.

22.2 He Had Accused Her Falsely

This is a story that Johanna, the wife of Kappars Jakob, told me. It is about how she twice saw her father-in-law after he had died.

You see, it was like this. Johanna had an illegitimate child before she married Jakob. People said that this boy of hers was treated badly at the farm of her in-laws. They did not want their son to get involved with Johanna and bring her to the farm because of the child. And they did not treat Johanna any better than they treated the boy.

Once, her father-in-law accused Johanna of stealing seven loaves of bread, and after that he accused her of many things. Johanna said again and again that she was as innocent as a newborn child. She would even swear a holy oath at the Lord's table when she went to confession. But her father-in-law did not believe a word of it and called her a thief and worse.

Well, her father-in-law died, and then things went better for Johanna because Jakob was a good man. One night they were lying in their bed, by the door, Johanna on the outside and Jakob next to the wall. She was wide awake, she saw a man come right up to the bed. He touched her with his hand.

"Lord," said Johanna, "I was so scared, I thought the blood would stop in my veins."

In the morning she told Jakob about it. But Jakob said the next time she saw the man, she should ask him who he was and what he wanted.

So the next time the man came and touched her in bed, she asked him:

"Who are you and what do you want from me?"

The ghost answered that he was her father-in-law and that he could not rest in his grave unless Johanna forgave him for having made false accusations against her when he was alive. Johanna said to him:

"I forgive you in Christ's name."

Then the ghost disappeared and Johanna never saw him again.

Collected in 1905 by H. R. A. Sjöberg in Replot (Finland). Printed in V. E. V. Wessman, *Sägner* 3.2 (1931), 17–18.

23. Greed

Greed was considered such a character flaw that the dead who were guilty of it were forced to walk again, consumed with their unwillingness to share their money or other possessions.

23.1 She Walked Again in the Storehouse

There was a woman in Eggedal. She was stingy toward the poor and did not give full measure to the tenants when she sold them food; it was her job to distribute sausage, other meat, and animal feed to the cotters in exchange for their work.

She walked again after she died. She would busy herself in the storehouse, weighing blood sausage with a rusty iron weight. There were many who saw her. She would walk in the fields with a rake. She could not find any peace in the grave, even though she had been dead many years.

> Collected by Andreas Mørch in Sigdal-Eggedal (Norway). Printed in Mørch, *Frå gamle dagar. Folkeminne frå Sigdal og Eggedal* (1932), 47.

23.2 Counting His Money

Once, the farmer of a prosperous farm died, and, around the same time, all his money and his finest possessions disappeared — silver tableware and many other precious things. And nobody could sleep in the farmer's bed; those who slept there after his death were always found dead the next morning.

One time, a man came and asked if he could stay there. The wife said she could not allow it and told him how things were with the bed and said she had nothing else that she could offer him to sleep in. The man said he was not afraid and asked if he might sleep in the bed — and in the end he got his way.

That evening the man went out into the cemetery, dug up some earth, and rolled around in it until he was all dirty. Next he went in and got into the bed. In the middle of the night, the door was opened and a head peered in; then a voice said, "Here it's nice and clean!" The man knew this was the farmer returned from the dead. The ghost entered the room, pulled two planks out of the floor, removed a great deal of money, and tossed it back over his shoulder. This went on most of the night. When the night was nearly over and day was about to break, the man jumped out of the bed and headed for the cemetery. There he saw an open grave and jumped into it. After a while the ghost came and asked the man to get out of the grave. But the man said he would not unless the ghost showed him where he was hiding the valuable things that had disappeared when he died. The ghost said he would not, but he let himself be talked into it, since there was no other way for him to get back into the grave. He took the man out along the wall of the cemetery and pulled up some turf. There, in front of them, appeared a trapdoor. He raised it, and they went down into the underground chamber. The ghost showed the man all the treasures there and then wanted to get back into his grave. But the man refused steadfastly to let him unless he promised never again to rise up from the grave. The ghost promised, and so the two of them went back to the grave. The ghost crawled in, and the man rearranged everything as well as he could. Then he went back to the house and got back into bed. In the morning everyone gathered around him, anxious to see if he was alive. Then he told them about the valuable things and how he found them. He was given half of everything.

> Collected west of Skarðströnd (Iceland). Printed in Jón Árnason, *Íslenzkar þjóðsögur og æfintýri* 1 (1862), 264–65. Reprinted in new edition 1 (1954), 255.

24. Suicide

In general suicide was considered "dishonest." The dead person was normally refused burial in sacred soil. It was believed that a person who had committed suicide was condemned to walk again for as long as he or she would otherwise have lived.

> See Peter Ludvigsen, "Selvmord—sagn og virkelighed," *Tradisjon* 7 (1977), 91–102.

24.1 He Took His Own Life

Some fifty years ago, around 1860, a farmer in Tenala lost some money. He accused a herding girl of having taken it. Then he killed her and hid her in the barn. When he got home and took off his boots, he found the money there. It had slipped through a hole in his trouser pockets.

Well, the farmer started brooding, and he had no peace night or day. At last he took his own life. After his death he often showed himself to other people. One time when I was in the woods looking for a cow, I saw an old man without a head. He ran after me and carried a sack on his back. Many others have seen him, too.

Collected in 1910 by V. E. V. Wessman in Pargas, Bromarv (Finland). Printed in Wessman, *Sägner* 3.2 (1931), 31.

24.2 I Am Neither in Heaven Nor on Earth

In a wood called Højes Ris in the parish of Lunde in Svendborg, there is a hill referred to as Jæbbe's Hill to this very day. The former owner of the hill was called Jeppe. But it was another Jeppe who hanged himself on a tree there on the hill. This Jeppe who had committed suicide could not find any peace in the grave. He walked every night. The old folks remember many people who had seen him, among them a plucky young fellow who saw Jeppe when he walked past the hill one night. He started talking to Jeppe and said: "Where are you these days?"

"Well, I am neither in heaven nor on earth, but somewhere in between," answered Jeppe.

Collected by E. T. Kristensen from H. Hansen in Ørridslev, Fyn (Denmark). Printed in Kristensen, *Danske sagn* 5 (1897), 78.

25. Murdered Children

A major group of "walking dead" tales relate to murdered children. The terms *utburd* (Norwegian) and *utböling* and *utkasting* (Swedish) have their background in the pre-Christian custom of exposing undesired, weak, or misshapen children so that they would die. Other names indicate the manner in which the dead manifests itself, for example, by shouting. In recent tradition we hear about children born out of wedlock, killed, and hidden in the house or somewhere outside. Swedish statistics from the seventeenth and eighteenth centuries show that murder of infants was the most common form of homicide. Legends often tell how the dead child is discovered and the mother brought to punishment, thus enforcing the sanction against extramarital pregnancy.

The legends reveal two strata of different ages. The older layer points to the concept of baptism as the decisive means of salvation. This is apparent in the legend type most frequently found in Norway and western Sweden in which the murdered child screams until someone baptizes it. Later it became more important that the dead be buried in sacred ground, and this is reflected in the child complaining until taken to the cemetery. Another means of ridding oneself of the *utburd*, one which did not concern itself with the spiritual welfare of the child, however, was simply to burn the remains of the murdered infant.

> See Louise Hagberg, *När döden gästar* (1937), 558–71; Juha Pentikäinen, *The Nordic Dead-Child Tradition* (1968), and "The Dead without Status," *Temenos* 4 (1969), 92–102; Jonas Frykman, *Horan i bondesamhället* (1977); Bo Almquist, "Norska utburdsägner i västerled," *Norveg* 21 (1978), 109–19; *Atlas över svensk folkkultur II. Sägen, tro och högtidssed 2*, edited by Åke Campbell and Åsa Nyman (1976), 94–101.

25.1 Baptizing Murdered Children

In Herøyvika by Korsnes there is a rather large pond they call the millpond. Once a mill stood there on the hill. The millpond was haunted in the old days. Folks saw little boys walking around the pond and people driving past heard children crying in the woods.

Late one evening a woman was walking from Tysnes to Korsnes. When she came to the millpond, she heard the same strange voices many others had heard before her. They whimpered and cried so painfully. She listened for a while, but then she understood what it was. She said loudly and distinctly so that it echoed in the forest:

"I baptize you Sigrid or Jon, in the name of God the Father, God the Son, and God the Holy Ghost."

As soon as she had said those words, it was silent, and since then nobody has noticed any ghosts at the millpond.

> Because it was impossible to know whether the *utburd* was a boy or a girl, it was important to include both a boy's and a girl's name in the baptismal formula. Most often they are Anna (Johanna) and Jon, which are the names given in the liturgical text of the Catholic baptismal formula.

See Juha Pentikäinen, *The Nordic Dead-Child Tradition* (1968), 217–21.
Legend type: ML 4025.
Collected by Johan Hveding in Tysfjord, Nordland (Norway).
Printed in Hveding, *Folketru og folkeliv på Hålogaland* (1935), 73.

25.2 "The Bucket Is Tight"

There was a girl who killed a child in secret and stuffed the body into a bucket. Eventually the girl got married. But during her wedding night, when the dance was well under way, they heard a child speaking from the cellar beneath the floor:

The bones are long
The bucket is tight.
Let me come up and dance with the bride!

When they looked they found the dead body of the child.

> This is the most common legend in Sweden about murdered infants.
> See Juha Pentikäinen, *The Nordic Dead-Child Tradition* (1968), 212–16.
> Collected in 1936 by Carl-Herman Tillhagen from Agda Westman (born 1895) in Ytterlänäs (Sweden). Ms. in NM EU 29685, Sägner och memorat 9, 755. Printed in Bengt af Klintberg, *Svenska folksägner* (1972), 188.

25.3 Dancing the Calves to Death

There was a farmer in Vissefjärda. I won't say where he lived, but he could never keep his newborn calves alive. The calf lived the first night, then death took it, and nobody knew how it happened. One time they had a calf and there was a shoemaker staying with them. They talked to the shoemaker about how it might be that they could never keep any of their calves.

"I'll take care of that," said the shoemaker.

When evening came, they carried the calf into the room where the shoemaker was sitting. By the way, it was customary in earlier days to take a newborn calf inside.

The shoemaker sat for a while, sewing. Just then a little one appeared. He was not much more than one foot in height, dressed in gray he was, and he took the calf and began dancing with it. The shoemaker could not believe his own eyes. After a while the little fellow came over to the shoemaker and said:

"Shoemaker, you sew — and I, I am dancing with the calf."

And then he went back and kept this up until he danced the life out of the calf. The shoemaker thought this was uncanny.

"What are you?" he said to the little fellow.

"I live in the bucket at the servant girl's feet," he said.

"Well, well," said the shoemaker, "is that so?"

And then the little fellow disappeared.

The next morning, when the farmer came in, the calf was of course lying there, dead.

"There you are," he said, "what good could you do?"

"Just wait," said the shoemaker.

He ordered them to make a big fire in the oven, and they did, and then the shoemaker went to the bed of the servant girl, tore open the foot end, got the bucket, put a pin in the lock, and threw the bucket into the fire. Then it began to wail in the bucket.

"Take out the pin, take out the pin," it screamed.

But they only stoked the fire until it was all burned up.

You see, it was like this: the farmer had gotten the servant girl pregnant and when the child came, they killed it and put it in the bucket and hid it at the foot end of the servant girl's bed so that it could not get out. Then the little one took its revenge by killing all their calves. But after that day all the calves were left in peace.

> Collected by E. Johansson and A. Holmström in 1933 from Johan Sjödin (born 1858) in Vissefjärda (Sweden). Ms. in LUF (4702), 16–18. Printed in Bengt af Klintberg, *Svenska folksägner* (1972), 189–90.

25.4 "Shut Up, Big Mouth!"

They say that there was a dead child in Dyreskardet, south of Halsarne. A girl bore a child, but did not want anyone to know about it, so she killed it and buried it among the rocks near the pass. Since then people heard strange cries there. Perhaps the dead little thing could not rest in peace because it had not been baptized. But there was no one who knew for sure, and people wondered whether it was a *hulder* calling.

One Sunday evening some girls went by the pass, and the mother of the child was among them. Then they heard a terrible scream, much louder than before. So the child's mother turned around and shouted:

"Shut up, you big mouth in the hills!"

But as soon as she had said that, they heard terrible laughter and then these words:

"My mother calls me 'big mouth in the hills'!"

All the girls heard it, and they became suspicious. Later the mother confessed everything.

> Collected by Torkell Mauland from K. J. Steinsnes in Rogaland (Norway). Printed in Mauland, *Folkeminne fraa Rogaland* 1 (1928), 155.

25.5 "My Mother Wears Gold"

At Onagerði, the parsonage in Viðareiði, a servant woman bore an illegitimate child and killed it in secret. There was a poor farmhand at the parsonage nicknamed Písli. She took a stocking leg from him, put the child into it, and then buried it. Some time later the same woman married, and they held a big wedding. While they were dancing the bridal dance, the dead child came rolling in in a stocking leg, jumped into the ring and sang:

My mother wears gold.
I am dancing in wool.
I am dancing in Písli's stocking leg.

Then he rolled in front of his mother's feet, but she fainted and was carried out, and there was a hasty end to the wedding.

> The dead child is referred to in Faeroese tradition as *ni agrisur*, which literally means "pig from below." The term is also used in reference to house spirits.
>
> A stocking leg is a special kind of footless stocking used on the Faeroe Islands.
>
> The fact that the verse sung by the dead child is in Danish rather than in Faeroese suggests that the legend originated in Denmark. This is quite remarkable because the dead child is unknown in later Danish tradition.
>
> See Bo Almqvist, "Niða(n)grisur. The Færoese Dead-Child Being," *Arv* 27 (1971), 97–120.
>
> Collected by Jakob Jakobsen, probably from Viðoy (Faeroe Islands). Printed in Jakobsen, *Færøske folkesagn og æventyr* (1898–1901), 225.

25.6 I Was Meant for Marrying

Once there was a woman who had a child, and she exposed it so
that it died. Later she had another child, and it was a little girl. This
one was not taken out to die, but grew and thrived until she was of
marriageable age. The time also came when a man turned up to ask
for her hand, and a little while later, he married her. There were a lot
of people at the wedding, and everyone was having a good time. After the wedding had been going on for a while, people could hear
sounds at the window and someone chanting:

I should have done the churning,
had a home brand new;
I was meant for marrying,
just like you.

People thought that this verse was sung to the bride. It must have
been the bride's sister, the one left to die, who sang.

> Collected by Jón Árnason from the painter Sigurður Guðmunðs-
> son, Reykjavik (Iceland). Printed in Árnason, *Íslenzkar þjóðsögur og
> ævintýri* 1 (1862), 225. Reprinted in new edition 1 (1954), 218.

26. The Boundary Ghost

Ownership of land was the very basis of rural life. Magic rituals
accompanied the placing of boundary stones, and stealing land by
moving such a stone was severely punished. According to medieval
Norwegian law, anyone stealing land was declared an outlaw. In recent tradition the thief is forced to walk again after death, struggling
in vain to return the boundary stone to its proper place.

> See Olav Bø, "Deildegasten," *Norveg* 5 (1955), 105–24; Louise
> Hagberg, *När döden gästar* (1937), 571–73.

26.1 The Servant Girl Helps the Boundary Ghost

The old man on the farm was lying dead on his bier. But a few
mornings later, people noticed that the socks on his feet were full of
mud and worn. They knew then that the farmer walked again at
night. The servant girl was not afraid, however, and she said that she
would go out at night and take a look.

There was bright moonlight and she saw him walking by the property line. The servant girl quickly walked up to him and said:
"I'm going to help you, grandfather."
"Yes," he said, "wherever I say 'illegal' you pull up the boundary marker, and wherever I say 'legal' you put it down."
They got done by morning, and then everything was the way it was supposed to be. Then the dead man said:
"Now I will show you a place where you will find a treasure. You're to have it for helping me."

Collected in 1932 by Erik Lehmann from Klara Andersson, Almvik, Halling (Sweden) (born 1865). Ms. in NM EU 5438. Printed in Bengt af Klintberg, *Svenska folksägner* (1972), 799.

26.2 The Pedlar Returned the Boundary Stone

If one walked straight up to a boundary ghost and placed the stone wherever he pointed, he would leave you in peace.
There was a farm where the boundary ghost was screaming all night. Then a pedlar came to the farm and wanted to stay there for the night. When it got to be evening, the ghost began to shout, and the folks on the farm poured out their trouble to the pedlar.
He thought that it was possible to get rid of the ghost. All they had to do was walk up to him and talk with him. But the farmer thought it was no use.
"Are you afraid of the ghost?" asked the pedlar. "There is nothing to be afraid of!"
"No one would dare talk with him," said the man.
"There's nothing to it. I will go to him," said the pedlar.
So he went out. The boundary ghost was shouting and screaming. The pedlar walked down to him, but the farmer stood in the yard and watched. He thought he was crazy. When the pedlar reached the ghost, he said:
"Now you must tell me where the stone was lying before, and I'll put it back in place. But you must promise never to come back again!"
Then the pedlar put the stone where the ghost pointed, and ever since then, they have been rid of him.

Collected by Peter Lunde in Bjelland, Vest-Agder (Norway). Printed in Lunde, *Kynnehuset. Vestegdske folkeminne* (1924), 120.

26.3 Giving False Witness

For a long time there were ghosts in Fårbæk in Haderup parish so that no one dared to use the road. Finally a minister in Ryde said he would bind them. He got the coachman at Rydhane to drive him to Fårbæk and he asked him to wait there until he came back. The minister went up a slope and down the other side. Then the coachman heard him asking:

"Where are you going?"

"I'm going to Fårbæk to give witness about a boundary line," was the answer.

"You should have given witness when you were still alive, then you would have had peace after death," said the minister.

From then on there were no more ghosts at that place.

> Anyone giving false witness in a boundary dispute was damned to "walk again." The same was true of surveyors and representatives of the law who took bribes. A frequent motif is that people put soil from their own fields into their shoes and then swore an oath that they were standing on their property.
>
> Collected by E. T. Kristensen and printed in Kristensen, *Jyske folkeminder* (1886), 202.

26.4 The Boundary Ghost Screams

There was a ghost along the boundary between Tronstad and Greipstad. People had seen him near Stare Pond several times. He was struggling with a stone. Sometimes he managed to lift it high up into the air, and then he would laugh. But the stone would always sink down again, and then the ghost would scream horribly.

> Collected by Peter Lunde in Vest-Agder (Norway). Printed in Lunde, *Kynnehuset. Vestegdske folkeminne* (1924), 119.

26.5 Returning Stolen Land

Once a shopkeeper had put up for the night on a farm in Sevel and had just gone to bed when he felt something tugging on the sheets. He thought that someone was trying to play a trick on him and reached down to catch the culprit but got hold of an ice-cold hand. He let go in a hurry, jumped out of bed, and ran into the main house, where he upbraided the people for putting him up in such a devil-ridden bed.

Sometime later it became clear what had been going on: one evening, when the farmhand went out to feed the horses, something in the shape of a man came up to him and asked that he do him a favor. He had once owned the farm and plowed too close to his neighbor, he said, but if the farmhand would now drive to the field and plow as many furrows in the snow as he had plowed in the soil, he would find peace. Later, when the snow was gone, they could plow the furrows and add them to the property of the man he had wronged. This was done and he never bothered them again.

> Collected by E. T. Kristensen and printed in Kristensen, *Jyske folkeminder* 8 (1886), 201–2.

26.6 "Where Should I Put It?"

There was a man who walked again on Bundegård's field in Krejbjærg because he had moved a boundary stone. People could hear him shout in the night:
"Where should I put it? Where should I put it?"
One evening there were some young people gathered outside of town and they heard him, too. One of them, a brash young man, shouted back:
"You devil! Put it where you found it!"
And after that, no one ever saw him again.

> Collected at Jebjærg folk high school in Jylland (Denmark). Printed in Kristensen, *Danske sagn* 5 (1897), 423.

26.7 The Minister's Dog

Once there was a surveyor at Torsbjærg, west of Vorde Church. He had put some boundary markers in the wrong place. Many people had heard him walking after his death—dragging his chain behind him every night.
One dark morning I had been out to move the horses and was on my way home when I heard a chain rattling terribly. I remembered all the old stories, and I was more scared than I had ever been before. But when I got closer, I discovered that it was the minister's dog.

> The story offers a good example of how tradition shapes perception.
> Collected by E. T. Kristensen in Vorde, Jylland (Denmark). Printed in Kristensen, *Danske sagn* 5 (1897), 405.

27. Ghosts

Whereas revenants are dead people returning to haunt the living for various reasons, ghosts usually appear as impersonal spooks. Most often they appear at night, making their presence known by shouting or wailing, seizing hold of people, stopping horses on the road, or by other undefined movements and actions. The encounter with ghosts often causes sickness and, at times, even death.

27.1 Fooling Around

Around Gåladal there were supposed to be ghosts. People could hear them fooling around.

"Have you heard about the man from Gudbrandsdalen who made love to a girl on a breadboard?"

And they laughed when they shouted that nonsense.

> This is the most characteristic manifestation of ghosts. Their presence is indicated only by voices.
>
> Told by Liv Bratterud, Bøherad, Telemark (Norway). Printed in Moltke Moe, *Folkeminne frå Bøherad* (1925), 70.

27.2 The Ghost without a Head

There were ghosts in Finsta'vøllen in Svarthølte. A girl who was staying at the summer dairy saw a man without a head by the well one evening when she was going to get water. She took the herding boy back with her, but he saw nothing. That summer dairy is no longer in use.

> During the summer the cattle were driven to grazing grounds in the mountains. Usually the dairymaid and the herding boy would stay at the summer dairy throughout the entire season.
>
> Collected by Lars M. Fjellstad in Elverum, Hedmark (Norway) between 1920 and 1927. Printed in Fjellstad, *Gammalt frå Elvrum* (1945), 67.

27.3 "Is My Eye Red?"

Once, it happened that both the tailor and the shoemaker went to the Kanta farm in Veddige at the same time. You can imagine there was a lot of talking in the evening. It was in autumn when the nights were dark.

One evening they talked about ghosts and about people who were afraid of the dark. There was a servant girl who insisted that she had never been afraid of the dark in her life. The workmen did not believe her, but she stood her ground. They made a bet that she would not dare go to the cemetery by herself. The servant girl said that she would. And so they agreed that she was to bring one of the knobs from the fence around a grave. In the olden days in Veddige, they used to put low wooden fences around the graves, and there were turned knobs on top of the fence posts. The knobs were loose, so it was easy to take one of them off.

The servant girl went right away. She had no trouble getting into the cemetery and taking a knob. But when she had gotten out on the road again, she heard someone calling after her.

"Is my eye red?" the person asked.

"Is my ass black?" the girl answered and walked on without turning around. But it came closer, whatever it was that was after her, and then she began to run. When she got back to the house at the Kanta farm, she threw the grave knob on the shoemaker's table and said:

"Well, you see, I am not afraid of the dark!"

Later there was a terrible uproar outside. Something banged the walls and crashed around the lumber stored on the farm, and there were screams.

The servant girl became sick and lay in bed for three days.

> In the old days, craftsmen would work their way from farm to farm. They were often good storytellers as well as bearers of current news. The challenge to fetch something from the cemetery is a frequent motif in folk traditions. The text is an example of the belief that evil powers could be warded off by some obscene gesture or expression. There is also the folk tradition that the revenant would gain power over anyone turning around and looking at it.
>
> Collected in 1927 by Johan Kalén from Johan Andersson, Veddige (Sweden) (born 1852). Ms. in IFGH (870), 26–27. Printed in Bengt af Klintberg, *Svenska folksägner* (1972), 176.

27.4 The Spook in the Grain House

At Nabb on Skaldö, there was a spook in the building they used for drying their grain. People thought it was a child crying. Some girl had probably killed her child there.

One evening I walked by there with another boy. We heard the crying, too.

To get rid of the spook, they burned down the grain house and built a new one. But there is a spook in the new building, too.

Collected by V. E. V. Wessman in 1918 in Ekenäs (Finland). Printed in Wessman, *Sägner* 3.2 (1931), 36.

27.5 Keeping Company with a Ghost

Jens Krog had lived in Tistrup, but he sold his farm there and moved to Simested. One afternoon he went to his old farm to visit the folks who had bought it from him. It got late and he did not head home before nightfall. He had to pass right by Tistrup cemetery, and by the time he got there, it was around midnight.

Suddenly a woman crossed the cemetery wall, and Jens got very frightened. He kept to the right side of the road, while she walked on the left, and they continued this way all the way to town. There was a path off the road, and she took that and entered a farm. That is how they parted company, but he knew that he had shared the road with a woman who used to live there but had died quite a while ago.

All the way from the cemetery, he walked in a cold sweat and did not dare to look anywhere but straight ahead because he knew that his companion was not the most pleasant sight. When he finally got home to his wife, sweat was dripping off him. He became quite sick and threw up when he saw the lights of his own house.

Collected by E. T. Kristensen in Jylland (Denmark). Printed in Kristensen, *Jyske folkeminder* 8 (1886), 216–17.

27.6 Ghosts Dancing

Quite a while ago, there was a man by the name of Ole Bakken who lived all alone in a hut. One day he left for work, but when he came back in the evening, he heard loud noises coming from the hut. There was music and such trampling and bustling that Olav stood there wondering what was going on. He had locked the door in the morning, and never before had anyone entered the hut without asking him first. All the same, he had to find out what was going on. He screwed up his courage and peeked in through the window. The hut was filled with people he knew, but they had all died years before. They were dancing in there. All of a sudden, it fell quiet and they all disappeared. When he entered the hut, everything was just the way he had left it.

Collected by Edvard Grimstad in Lom, Gudbrandsdalen (Norway). Printed in Grimstad, *Etter gamalt. Folkeminne frå Gudbrandsdalen* (1953), 44–45.

27.7 The Farmhand Who Danced with the Ghost at Kittebuske

On the north side of the tavern called Snurran, there stood a bush people referred to as Kittebuske. One evening some men were sitting there, drinking. One of them was a fellow who was something of a joker. They were talking about that bush.

Eventually they were done with their drinking and all went home. But when that fellow walked by Kittebuske, he said:

"Come on, Kersten, let's dance!"

Then a woman came up to him, and she put her arms around him and danced with him. He could not see how late it was, but they danced for a long time.

He was wearing beautiful new boots, so he was well equipped. And he thought it was fun to dance. He sang and carried on. But after a while, he got tired and wanted to quit.

Yet they danced until the cocks started crowing. He did not hear anything, but she said:

"Now crows the white cock, but we don't give a damn!"

He was really tired now, and his clothes were dripping with sweat. But when the cock crowed the second time, she said:

"Now crows the black cock; I am still dancing with you, Morten!"

And when the cock crowed for the third time, she said:

"Now crows the red cock; now the dead return into the earth!"

Suddenly the woman disappeared, and he was all alone. But when he looked around, he had no soles left on his boots or on his socks, and he had nearly danced the skin off his feet.

This man's name was Morten Jakobsson. His grandson Jakob Tuason told us this story when we were children. He said that it had happened to his grandfather. He lived in Svenstorp.

It was generally believed that ghosts were afraid of the cock's crow. By daybreak the dead had to be back in their graves. The legend is common in Denmark and in Skåne (Sweden).

Collected by B. A. Vifot in 1929 from Kersti Thor. Ms. in LUF 2566, 9–10. Printed in Bengt af Klintberg, *Svenska folksägner* (1972), 183.

PART III
Healers and Wise Folk

Part III illustration: "Often Finns provide merchants with wind . . . by selling them three magic knots." Olaus Magnus, *Historia de Gentibus Septentrionalibus* (History of the Northern People, 1555), book 3, chapter 16.

he healer and the so-called wise folk generally speaking occupied an ambiguous position in rural society. On the one hand, they had a useful and even necessary role to play in a prescientific context. They applied their magical skills to a variety of tasks, from healing humans and animals to ridding the house of mice and other pests, quenching fire, opening locks, tracking down thieves, creating wind for sailing, and so on. On the other hand, the special powers of the wise folk made them potentially dangerous in the eyes of the community, and at times they were suspected of being in league with the devil. Therefore the traditions of the healer and the wise folk often blend into those of the witch and the sorcerer.

Even today folk healers continue to play an important role in folk belief and in ethnomedicine.

See Carl-Herman Tillhagen, *Folklig läkekonst* (1958); Bente G. Alver et al., *Botare* (1980).

28. Healing Humans

The various activities of the healer were based on the conception that sickness is of supranormal origin, caused either by a preternatural being or by a person having special powers. A basic condition of healing was to discover the supranormal origin of sickness. The healing process involved the use of both magic formulas and rituals.

> See I. Reichborn-Kjennerud, *Vår gamle trolldomsmedisin* (1928–47); Carl-Herman Tillhagen, *Folklig läkekonst* (1958).

28.1 Kari Vrisdaughter

On Seland in Konsmo there lived a woman by the name of Kari Vrisdaughter. She had a neighbor named Berte Oddsdaughter. Berte was suffering from severe back pain, and she went to Kari to seek advice. Kari thought that she could drive the evil from Berte's back, but first all the others in the room had to leave. Everybody except for one boy went outside. He managed to hide in a corner where no one could see him.

When the others were gone, Kari took some rags and covered the windows so that no one could look in. Then she told Berte to take off her clothes and uncover her back. That done, Kari positioned herself behind Berte, and said:

Berte Oddsdaughter,
stand fast.
Ho he nid,

ho he did.
Out of the bone,
into the stone,
never come back.

Then she spat three times on Berte's back.

> The back pain afflicting Berte is of demonic origin. Therefore the procedure used in healing her consists of conjuring the offending power "out of the bone, into the stone." The efficacy of the ritual is dependent upon its being secret.
>
> "Ho he nid" literally means "She has a sting" (cf. Old Norse *hníta* = to sting), which is combined with a nonsense rhyme designed to reinforce the magic power of the words. To spit three times is a common procedure in all protective magic.
>
> See I. Reichborn-Kjennerud, *Vår gamle trolldomsmedisin* 4 (1944), 113–30, for "nid"; for "spittle," see Reichborn-Kjennerud, 5 (1947), index.
>
> Collected by Tore Bergstøl in Vest-Agder (Norway). Printed in Bergstøl, *Atterljom. Folkeminne fraa smaadalene kring Lindesnes* 2 (1930), 12.

28.2 Jens Kusk

Old Peder Kristensen in Bindeballe had a servant girl who drove the manure cart. One day the horses shied, and she broke her leg. In those days there were only village healers, and she had to go to one of them to have her leg fixed up.

Kristensen took the girl to Jens Kusk in Smidstrup. When they got just west of Smidstrup, he said:

"Now if we can only find that lazy fellow at home."

But when they got to the house, they found Kusk there, and he said to them:

"Well, it's a good thing you found this lazy fellow at home."

Kristensen and the servant girl did not like the sound of that, for now they understood that he was a little too clever for them.

To take care of the girl, Kusk put a salve on her leg and tied it up as best he could. Then he prepared a stick, put salve on it, tied it up, and put it away in the loft.

"Well, now you can go home," he said. "You don't need to come back because I can see from here whether your leg is getting better or not. I can take care of it from here."

The derogatory reference to Kusk reflects the ambivalent attitude of the community toward the healer, and Kusk's ability to over-hear people at a great distance demonstrates the healer's special powers. Jens Kusk, who lived between 1789 and 1846, was a well-known healer in eastern Jylland. He was regarded as a dangerous man to make fun of.

Kusk's method of treating the girl's leg constitutes a form of sympathetic magic. The stick represents the broken leg.

See Birgitte Rørbye *Kloge folk og skidtfolk* (1976), 127–29.

Collected by E. T. Kristensen in Gadbjærg parish, Jylland (Denmark) from Niels Zakariassen, Bindeballe Mark. Printed in Kristensen, *Danske sagn* 6, N.R. (1936), 107.

28.3 The Child Who Would Not Utter a Sound

I had a little brother who was seven months old, but as yet no one had ever heard a sound come from his mouth. People thought my mother might have come too close to the elder tree in the garden or dug in the ground near it when she was pregnant. Sometimes my mother saw a little woman walk past the window, but she would vanish near the door. Whenever that happened, the child would get cramps.

My family looked around for a wise woman and finally got hold of someone from Vendel. The woman's name was Edel. She lived in Ajbøl, which is part of Vestervig parish. When she visited us, she took a spoon and struck it three times on the table in front of the boy. Then she said:

"There is only one thing we can do." She turned to my father. "Dig a hole in the northwest corner of the dike at Kalgu, just big enough for the child to pass through. Then take the child's shirt and go to the church between midnight and two o'clock. Pass the shirt three times through the door handle of the church. When you get home, make a wooden cross. Then put the shirt on the child, and having done that, pull the child through the hole three times. But the last time your wife pushes the child through, she must throw the cross after the child, and leave it in the hole."

This was done. When the child passed through the hole the third time, it made a sound. But it was both the first and the last sound it ever made in its lifetime. My brother died three weeks later.

The boy's disability is identified with the preternatural beings living by the elder tree (*hylde* folk). The mother has broken an implied taboo against disturbing the ground around the tree.

The method of healing the child by pulling it through an opening in the ground or below a piece of turf has been interpreted in various ways. It may be a device to pacify the spirits of the earth or the dead. It has also been regarded as a form of rebirth.

The use of the shirt pulled through the door handle at the church applies the same model to mobilize the powers of the sacred.

See V. J. Brøndegaard, *Folk og flora* 4 (1980), 184–87; Bengt Holbek and Iørn Piø, *Fabeldyr og sagnfolk* (1967), 136; Carl-Herman Tillhagen, *Folklig läkekonst* (1958), 292–97; Nils Lid, "Jordsmøygjing," *Norsk aarbok* (1922), 81–88; I. Reichborn-Kjennerud, *Vår gamle trolldomsmedisin* 2 (1933), 103–4.

Collected by E. T. Kristensen from Mads Kristensen Grøntoft, Bedsted, Jylland (Denmark). Printed in Kristensen, *Danske sagn* 6, N.R., 273.

28.4 Olav Huse

Olav Huse was the name of a man who lived somewhere on the shore of Nordsjaa. He was a bloodstopper.

A girl in Porsgrunn, the daughter of a rich merchant, had cut herself in the thigh with a meat knife and was bleeding to death. Her family sent for the doctor, but he could not help her. Finally, after three physicians had been consulted and were unable to do anything for her, the merchant sent for Olav Huse. The messenger rode so hard that he almost ruined the horse. But even so, by the time he returned with Olav, the girl was nearly dead.

"I really have no business being here since you already have three doctors," said Olav when he came in through the door.

"If you can help her, just hurry up and do it," said the physicians. "We can't help her," they said.

Olav rushed to the girl and pinched the wound together. The bleeding stopped immediately and the girl recovered.

Olav demanded five dollars in payment, but the merchant gave him three hundred dollars because he had saved his daughter's life.

> The story is focused on the implicit faith in the ability of the healer, which at times was thought to exceed even that of the learned physician.

See, for a general description of the traditions and techniques
of stopping bleeding, I. Reichborn-Kjennerud, *Vår gamle trolldomsmedisin* 1–2 (1925–33); Carl-Herman Tillhagen, *Folklig läkekonst*
(1958), 268–74; Richard M. Dorson, *Bloodstoppers and Bearwalkers*
(1952).

Collected by Kjetil A. Flatin in Seljord (Norway). Printed in
Flatin, *Tussar og trolldom* (1930), 100.

28.5 To Stop Bleeding

Stay blood, stop blood
as the water stayed in Jordan's flood.
In three holy names: God, Father and God, Son
and God, the Holy Ghost.

Just as, according to apocryphal tradition, the water stopped
flowing when Jesus was baptized in the Jordan river by Saint
John, the bleeding is made to stop by the words of the healer.
This formula represents the conjuring type. The oldest known
version is in Latin and recorded in a Vatican manuscript dating
back to the ninth and tenth centuries.

See F. Ohrt, *Die ältesten Segen ueber Christi Taufe und Christi Tod
in religionsgeschichtlichem Lichte* (1938); Carl-Martin Edsman, "Folklig sed med rot i heden tid," *Arv* (1946), 145–76; Bengt af Klintberg, *Svenska trollformler* (1965), 103–5.

Collected by Moltke Moe in Bøherad, Telemark (Norway).
Printed in Moe, *Folkeminne frå Bøherad* (1925), 128.

28.6 May Bleeding Be Stanched

May bleeding be stanched for those who bleed;
blood flowed down from God's cross.
The Almighty endures fear,
from wounds tried sorely.
Stand in glory, even as in gore,
that the Son of God may hear of it.
The spirit and bleeding veins—
he (she) finds bliss who is released from this.
May bleeding be stanched—bleed neither without nor within.

With these words Saint John the Apostle stanched the blood on the lips of our Lord. . . . A stone called Surtur stands in the temple. There lie nine vipers. They shall neither wake nor sleep before this blood is stanched. Let this blood be stanched in the name of the Father and the Son and the Holy Ghost. *Filium spiritum domino pater.*

> Saint John was the last disciple to keep watch by the cross when Christ was crucified, but there is no biblical description of John stanching Christ's blood. This conjuring type formula is based on sympathetic magic. It is as impossible for the bleeding to continue as for a viper to wake and sleep simultaneously.
> Collected by Jón Borgfirðing, Reykjavik (Iceland). Printed in Jón Árnason, *Íslenzkar þjóðsögur og œfintýri* 3 (1958), 470.

28.7 Against Fever

Nine brothers were they,
Over land rode they;
They all met on a mill dam;
They met no other man
Than good Saint John.
Saint John the willow wound,
He all nine bound.

They promised God and Saint John,
They would not ride neither woman nor man,
Nor this man.

> The cause of the fever is personified by the nine demonic brothers exorcised by Saint John. The formula, which represents the epic type, derives from a fifteenth-century manuscript. It is well known in later Danish tradition.
> See F. Ohrt, *Da signed Krist-* (1927), 38–47.
> Printed in Ohrt, *Danmarks trylleformler* (1917), 196–97.

28.8 Against Snakebite

When someone had been bitten by a snake, good advice was dear. But it helped to spit in your hand, smear the saliva on the bite, and then squeeze out the wound. The best thing for snakebite, however, is to wash it out with urine and recite the following spell:

The snake wound itself around the birch root.
It bit our Lord Jesus in the foot.
"Why did you bite me?" asked Jesus.
"I did not know you were there," replied the snake.
Hurt and burn yourself, you who bit me,
and not I who was bitten!
In the name of God, the Father
God, the Son and God, the Holy Ghost!

One should say this three times while blowing on the urine. Then one should wash the wound three times. After doing so, one would be healed — usually, that is.

> Human breath, blood, saliva, urine, and other bodily secretions were thought to possess healing power. The power is further enhanced by this spell which describes Christ cursing the snake. The formula corresponds to the epic type.
>
> See I. Reichborn-Kjennerud, *Vår gamle trolldomsmedisin* 2 (1933), 134–39.
>
> Collected by Knut Hermundstad from Ingebjørg Torgesdatter Bakke in Vestre Slidre, Valdres, Buskerud (Norway). Printed in Hermundstad, *I kveldseta. Gamal Valdres-kultur* 6 (1955), 144–45.

28.9 Against Rickets

The mother makes a fire in the oven and, standing naked with her child in her arms, says three times:
"Here I stand with my child before the fire, to heal whore rickets, mother rickets, ladder rickets, and all kinds of rickets."

> Rachitis, which is known by various names in folk tradition, refers to bone deformities caused by nutritional deficiencies. In popular belief, however, moral causes or demonic influences are usually held responsible. The present formula is of the ritual type. It involves symbolic cleansing by fire and the spoken word.
>
> See I. Reichborn-Kjennerud, *Vår gamle trolldomsmedisin* 2 (1933), 100–107; Jonas Frykman, *Horan i bondesamhället* (1977), 25–54.
>
> Collected by J. M. Thiele (Denmark). Printed in Thiele, *Danmarks folkesagn* 3 (1860), 113. Reprinted in F. Ohrt, *Danmarks trylleformler* (1917), 183.

28.10 Healing a Sprain

As a child I once twisted my knee. At home in Ullann, there was a man named Truls Sønstebø who came from Sigdal. When he heard about my injury, he took two juniper branches and placed them crosswise over my knee. Then he told my father to ask him what he was doing.

I strike the sprain
from Sjur Ullann's knee,
out of the limb,
into the wood,

he said, and struck the branches with the knife. He did this three times. My father repeated the question, and he answered. I remember that it was very solemn and serious.

> The type of formula applied here was used for a wide range of afflictions from peritendinitis to sprains. The ritual of question and answer identifies the demonic cause of the problem and transfers it from the limb to some inanimate object.
>
> See I. Reichborn-Kjennerud, *Vår gamle trolldomsmedisin* 2 (1933), 150–56; Carl-Herman Tillhagen, *Folklig läkekonst* (1958), 228–32; John Granlund, "Curing *Knarren* (Peritendinitis or Tendovaginitis)," *Arv* 18–19 (1962–63), 187–225.
>
> Collected by Tov Flatin from Sjur Olsen Ullann in Sveene, Numedal (Norway). Printed in Flatin, *Gamalt frå Numedal* 5 (1923), 14.

28.11 Against Frostbite

K u l u m a r i s
K u l u m a r i
K u l u m a r
K u l u m a
K u l u m
K u l u
K u l
K u
K

> This formula conjures the frostbite referred to by the term Kulumaris. Klintberg suggests that the term derives from the Lat-

in *Calmaris*, meaning "Be still." In the ritual accompanying the spell, the formula was written line by line on strips of paper, which were fed to the patient, one each day. The frostbite diminished as the formula was consumed word by word and letter by letter.

See Sven B. Ek, *Tre svartkonstböcker* (1964), 16–20, 35; Bengt af Klintberg, *Svenska trollformler* (1965), 114–15.

Collected in Västmanland (Sweden) in 1926. Manuscript in Hammarstedtska arkivet, Nordiska Museet. Printed in af Klintberg, *Svenska trollformler* (1965), 76.

28.12 Against Inflammation

Noss and Toss were walking on the road
when they met Jesus himself.
"Where are you going?"
asked Jesus.
And they said:
"I am going to XYZ;
I shall tear his flesh,
and suck his blood,
and break his bone!"
"No," answered Jesus;
"I forbid you.
You shall not tear his flesh,
and suck his blood,
and break his bone.
You shall not do him any more harm
than a mouse does to a stone!"

In three holy names.
✝✝✝   Amen.

Noss and Toss are personifications of the demon causing the inflammation in the fingertips. The counterspell takes the form of a meeting between Christ and the demons.

See Carl-Herman Tillhagen, *Folklig läkekonst* (1958), 277–79.

Recorded in 1722 in Ale township, in the protocol of the trial against Bärta Andersdotter, Svångebo, Tunge, Västergötland (Sweden). Printed in Emanuel Linderholm, *Signelser ock besvärjelser från medeltid ock nytid* (1917–40), 863. Reprinted in Bengt af Klint-berg, *Svenska trollformler* (1965), 68.

29. Healing Animals

The procedures for healing animals are based on the same princi-ples as those used for healing humans. The specialist used formulas, rituals, and a variety of medicines to diagnose and treat disorders as-sumed to have been caused by supranormal influences of different origin.

See Paul Heurgren, *Husdjuren i nordisk folktro*, 1925.

29.1 Against Loss of Spirit in Animals

Jesus was walking along the road,
when he saw a cow by a fence, crying.
"What are you crying about?"
"They've taken my power and my spirit,
my flesh and my blood."
"You shall get back your power and your spirit,
your flesh and your blood.
Your power shall be a bear's power,
your spirit shall be a lion's spirit.
Your skin shall become as smooth as ice,
and your milk shall become like honey cake."

If a cow got sick, lost weight, or stopped giving milk, people be-lieved that some envious person or power had stolen the animal's "spirit." As af Klintberg points out, this formula demonstrates a common principle—namely, that the person or animal to be healed speaks for itself. This text represents the epic type of mag-ic formula.

See Bengt af Klintberg, *Svenska trollformler* (1965), 120–21; Paul Heurgren, *Husdjuren i nordisk folktro* (1925), 300–302; Per-Uno Ågren, "Maktstulen häst og modstulen ko," *Västerbotten* (1964), 33–68.

Collected in 1919 by Jon Johansen from P. Höglund, Holm parish, Medelpad (Sweden). Manuscript in Nordiska Museet, no. 4, 696. Printed in af Klintberg, *Svenska trollformler* (1965), 83.

29.2 Healing a Dried Up Cow

Niels Andersen in Kollemorten had a cow that would not get up or give any milk. He sent for Jens Kusk from Smidtstrup. But when Jens came, he straddled the oven and pissed right into the fire. Well, Niels's wife got mad and scolded him.

"What a fine pig you've brought into the house," she said to her husband. "I wish we were rid of him again."

"Go out and milk the cow," said Jens Kusk.

"Yes, that would be something," said the woman. "She hasn't given milk in two weeks."

"Do as I tell you. Go out and milk her."

The woman had to go. And there stood the cow straddling a huge udder, and she milked two full buckets. Everything was fine then, and the woman did not scold Jens anymore for having pissed into the fire. But it seems to me, the strange thing is that he never even touched the cow!

> (Cf. no. 28.2; it too deals with Jens Kusk.)
>
> Collected by E. T. Kristensen from Jørgen Madsen, Grejs, Nørvang, Jylland (Denmark). Printed in Kristensen, *Danske sagn* 6, N.R. (1936), 118–19.

29.3 To Heal a Bone Fracture

Recite the following spell:

Saint Olav rode in
green wood;
broke his little
horse's foot.
Bone to bone,
flesh to flesh,
skin to skin.
In the name of God,
amen.

> This formula corresponds to the so-called Second *Merseburger-spruch*, which is one of the few pre-Christian magic formulas that have survived. Saint Olav replaces the god Othin.
>
> See F. Ohrt, *De danske besværgelser mod vrid og blod* (Copenhagen, 1922); Reidar Th. Christiansen, *Die finnischen und nordischen Varianten des zweiten Merseburgerspruches* (FFC 18), 1914; F. Genz-

mer, "Da signed Krist—thû biguol'en Wuodan," *Arv* 5 (1949), 37–68; I. Hampp, *Beschwörung, Segen, Gebet* (1961), 110–14, 247–65.

Collected by Martin Bjørndal in Møre (Norway). Printed in Bjørndal, *Segn og tru. Folkeminne frå Møre* (1949), 98–99.

29.4 Against Finn Shot

If you shoot one, I shoot two,
if you shoot two, I shoot three,
if you shoot three, I shoot four,
if you shoot four, I shoot five,
if you shoot five, I shoot six,
if you shoot six, I shoot seven,
if you shoot seven, I shoot eight,
if you shoot eight, I shoot nine,
if you shoot nine, I shoot ten,
if you shoot ten, I shoot eleven,
and you none.

> Finn shot (also called magic shot) is a projectile sent by a preternatural being or sorcerer, which causes sickness. The shot can be returned to its origin either verbally or by firing a gun over the back of the animal.
>
> Foreign bodies found under the skin or in the stomach of an animal (agrophilae) were often diagnosed as Finn shot.
>
> Counting, as a magical device, usually regressed from the greater to the lesser number. In this formula, by contrast, the healer proceeds in the opposite manner. In form the spell represents the conjuring type.
>
> See Paul Heurgren, *Husdjuren i nordisk folktro* (1925), 326–34; Nils Lid, *Trolldom* (Oslo, 1950), 1–36; Bengt af Klintberg, *Svenska trollformler* (1965), 118–19; Lauri Honko, *Krankheitsprojektile*, (1959).
>
> Collected in 1927 by John Granlund from Anders Bjurström, Sävsnäs parish, Dalarna (Sweden). Ms. in IFGH (983), 26. Printed in af Klintberg, *Svenska trollformler* (1965), 82.

29.5 Turid Klomset

The mother of Johan Klumset's wife, Turid was her name, lived in the 1800's. She knew how to heal horses that had *riske* and other diseases. Nobody was allowed to listen or watch her when she worked. But one time somebody wanted to see what she was going to do, so he hid himself and watched.

Turid led the horse up the barn bridge, stroked it along and across its back, and said this spell:

Little wife, short wife,
lies under the barn bridge,
pinches the wood in the (harness).
Now she shall die!

When Turid had handled the horse this way for a little while, it was as if the sickness had been stroked right out of it.

> The Norwegian term *vendeskjei* (harness) is problematical. It may refer either to a wooden part of the gear or to the horse's back.
>
> *Riske* is a veterinary term for a disease causing the horse to roll over and scratch its back.
>
> By exorcising the "little wife," the healer eliminates the preternatural cause of the sickness.
>
> Collected by Kjetil A. Flatin in Seljord, Telemark (Norway). Printed in Flatin, *Tussar og trolldom* (1930), 103.

29.6 The Quack

A stranger passing through a farm was going to cure a cow of Finn shot. He got some cream porridge to give to the cow and went to the barn. Some people followed him secretly, wanting to see what he was going to do. He sat down on a milking stool on the barn floor and ate the cream porridge himself! And they heard him saying:

By the cow I sit,
eating delicious grits.
If the cow won't live by water and hay,
then let her die.

Well, they got mad and chased him out.

> This story parodies the traditional healing procedure of feeding cream porridge to the sick animal while reciting a spell against the Finn shot.
>
> See Svale Solheim, *Norsk sætertradisjon* (1952), 228.
>
> Collected by Ola Sandnes from his mother in Indre Sunnfjord (Norway). Printed in Solheim, *Norsk sætertradisjon*, 228.

29.7 Against Homesickness in Animals

The village has burned,
the farmer's been strung up,
the old woman, in a frenzy,
flies about in the woods.
And you are here.

> A newly acquired animal was protected against homesickness by
> whispering into its ear about how badly things were going at its
> previous home.
> See Paul Heurgren, *Husdjuren i nordisk folktro* (1925), 344–56.
> Collected in 1860 by Gustaf Ericsson in Åker and Öster-
> rekarne, Södermanland (Sweden). Printed in H. Aminson, "Om
> ladugård, stall, kreaturens sjukdomar och deras botemedel," *Bidrag
> till Södermanlands äldre kulturhistoria* 2.5, edited by H. Aminson and
> Joh. Wahlfisk (1884), 86. Reprinted in Bengt af Klintberg, *Svenska
> trollformler* (1965), 85.

30. Protecting House and Home

Many formulas and rituals deal with various needs arising in the
daily life and work on the farm. The control of fire, insects, rats, and
other pests, the opening of rusty locks, and many other activities,
from churning butter to bearing children, involve influences that can
be enhanced and manipulated through the use of magic. Some of the
magical practices called for the special knowledge and expertise of the
wise folk. But others were commonly known and applied by the
nonspecialist in meeting the challenges of everyday life.

30.1 Locking Doors

Come Christ, come to these doors.
Bless the bolts
of this house and the doors.
Lord God Himself!
Out evil spirits!
Come in God's angels!
All bolts are locked.

This prayer takes the form of a conjuring type formula. Collected by Stefán þorvaldsson, minister at Hítnarnes, from Svein þórðarsson, Laxárholt (Iceland). Printed in Jón Árnason, *Íslenzkar þjóðsögur og æfintýri* 3 (1958), 470.

30.2 Opening Locks

About four years ago they could not get the church door open. Nobody knew what was wrong with it. So they sent for Mads Grøntoft. He came and made some gestures. Then he struck the door three times and it opened immediately. This is really true. That is how Mads became famous.

> The dexterity required to open a lock was often ascribed to magic. In other texts, the wise folk open it by blowing into the lock.
> Collected by E. T. Kristensen from Otto Kristian Agisen, in Bedsted, Hassing, Jylland (Denmark). Printed in Kristensen, *Danske sagn* N.R. 6. (1936), 196.

30.3 Quenching Fire

The husband of Konge-Stina burned a field one day to get it ready for seeding rye. But the fire got out of hand. He began carrying furniture and other things from their cottage because he was sure that it would catch fire. But Stina became angry and said:

"Put that down, you! You've no reason to do that."

She then took a rope and tied a horseshoe to it. She told her husband to walk in front of her with the rope while she followed behind. And the strange thing is that the fire did not advance into the areas where the woman walked.

If you found a horseshoe on a road, and it had all six nails in place, you could put out forest fires by carrying it under your clothes against your bare chest.

> Because of the scarcity of manure, it was customary to prepare a field by burning it and then to drop the seed directly into the ashes.
> In popular tradition we encounter persons capable of quenching or limiting the spreading fire by walking around it. Either they were born with special powers or they used magic rituals and devices.
> See Nils-Arvid Bringéus, *Brännodling* (1963), 99–117, 157–58.

Collected by Arvid Ernvik in 1946 from E. S. Karlanda, Glaskogen, Värmland (Sweden). Printed in Ernvik, *Folkminnen från Glaskogen* 1 (1966), 115–16.

30.4 Wasp Spell

Brown man!
Brown man!
Brown man in the bush!
Sting stick and stone
but not Christian man's
flesh and bone!

In three names:
Father, Son, and Holy Ghost.

Say the Lord's Prayer.

Then spit three times in the direction of the wasp.

> The wasp spell belongs to the many formulas commonly used by ordinary people rather than by specialists only. In form it represents the conjuring type.
>   The term brown man is a noa-name used to avoid attracting the wasp by employing its proper name.
>   Collected by Magne Aurom from Edvard Torsud in Sør-Odal, Hedmark (Norway). Printed in Aurom, *Liv og lagnad. Folkeminne frå Sør-Odal* (1942), 52–53.

30.5 The Finn Who Exorcised the Rats

There was a place where there were many rats. Then a Finn came along. The folk asked him whether he could get rid of the rats for them. Sure, he could do that. He sat down by the shore and started muttering something. After a while a lot of rats came and plunged right into the water.

But to put the Finn to the test, they hid one of the rats. They kept it under a stone kettle. Then they went down to the shore and asked him:

"Are all the rats gone now?"

"No," he said.

At that moment they heard a loud bang. The stone kettle broke into pieces, and the rat ran past them and plunged into the water.

Finns were generally considered to have expertise in magic. Parallel legends tell about Finns ridding the community of snakes by conjuring them into the fire. The motif of the rat catcher is the same as the one in the well-known legend of the Pied Piper of Hamelin.

See Carl-Herman Tillhagen, "Finnen und Lappen als Zauberkundige in der skandinavischen Volksüberlieferung," *Kontakte und Grenzen* (1969), 129–43.

Collected in 1926 by Hulda Hammarbäck from Anna Karlsson, Västerlanda, Bohuslän (Sweden). Ms. in IFGH (VFF 1362), 60. Printed in Bengt af Klintberg, *Svenska folksägner* (1972), 218–19.

30.6 To Keep the Fire Burning

Ashes ball bag
Pussy ball mouse,
Never shall fire
Go out in my house.

> This formula was recited in the evening while stoking the fire. The sexual imagery suggests a kind of magic by association (sexuality = fire). Klintberg, however, has argued that the obscene references are intended to drive off demonic powers that might extinguish the fire.
>
> See Bengt af Klintberg, "Magisk diktteknik," *Ta'3* (1967), 20–27. Reprinted in af Klintberg, *Harens klagan* (1978), 7–21.
>
> Collected in 1930 by Gunnar Jonsson from Ad. Palmquist, Helge, Stenkyrka parish, Gotland (Sweden). Ms. in NM (EU 3255). Printed in af Klintberg, *Svenska trollformler* (1965), 96.

30.7 To Aid in Childbirth

Virgin Mary, gentle mother,
loan your keys to me;
to open my limbs
and my members.
†††

> This magic spell takes the form of a prayer. The background of the appeal to the Virgin is that Mary supposedly gave birth without pain. Keys made from silver were at times used as amulets to

aid in the birth process, and the flower called Maria's Keys (orchis maculata) was placed in the pregnant woman's bed. There is
evidence that after the Reformation use of the formula was forbidden in some areas of Scandinavia. This text was recorded in a
trial transcript from 1722 in Ale township, Västergötland
(Sweden), as reported by seventy-seven-year old Bärta Andersdotter, who claimed to have learned it from a chaplain.

See J. S. Møller, *Moder og barn* (1939–40), 131–33; Bengt Holbek, "Maria i folketraditionen," *KLNM* 11 (1966), column
367–68; Bengt af Klintberg, *Svenska trollformler* (1965), 130.

Printed in Emanuel Linderholm, *Signelser ock besvärjelser från
medeltid ock nytid* (1917–40), 209. Reprinted in af Klintberg, *Svenska trollformler*, 95.

31. Binding the Thief

Thievery has always been a problem in society. In folk tradition as
well as in learned tradition dating back to ancient Egypt, pictorial
magic and exorcisms were used to force a thief to return stolen goods
or to punish him or her, usually by striking out his or her eye. The
early Scandinavian formulas are mostly derived from printed German
Black Books.

See Adolf Spamer, *Romanusbüchlein* (1958), 223–76; F. Ohrt,
Trylleord. Fremmede og danske (1922), 22–27.

31.1 To Strike Out a Thief's Eye

I conjure and urge you, Devil and Beelzebub,
to strike out the eye of the thief who stole x from y.
Now strike the nail the first time.

I conjure and urge you, Beelzebub,
by all the devils that are in Hell and roam the world,
to strike out the eye of the thief who stole x from y.
Now strike the nail the second time.

Now I conjure you and urge you, Beelzebub,
to finally strike out the eye of the thief who stole x from y.

Now strike the nail all the way in,
in the name of the Devil, Beelzebub.

> The text describes a ritual based on sympathetic magic. The power of the devil is invoked while driving a nail into an image of the thief's eye.
>
> Derived from the so-called Hagholm manuscript, ca. 1800, Jylland (Denmark). Printed in F. Ohrt, *Danske trylleformler* (1917), 432.

31.2 The Cat Did It!

Once, my uncle, bookbinder Wiwel from Frederiksborg, was talking to the owner of an inn in town. They were saying how odd it was that the fish they had planned to eat for dinner had disappeared from the kitchen. Somebody must have stolen it because they had seen it a little earlier.

An old beggar happened to be at the inn, sitting by himself. People said that he could strike out a thief's eye. When they asked him, he did not deny it and promised to strike out the eye of whoever had stolen the fish.

With a piece of chalk, he drew a circle on the table and surrounded it with some scrawls. Then he took a hammer and nail and muttered something while he fixed the nail at the center of the circle.

"Now it is done," he said.

They sat and waited. Suddenly the black family cat came running. One of her eyes was all bloody and torn. There had not been anything wrong with the cat before, so they knew that the cat had been the thief.

> Collected by E. T. Kristensen from Niels Wiwel in Hellerup, Sjælland (Denmark). Printed in Kristensen, *Danske sagn*, N.R. 6 (1936), 182.

31.3 Caught in the Act

Jan Øye was on his way to town with a load of butter and cheese.

One evening he put his load down at a place called Spirille and walked up to a farm to spend the night there. The woman at the farm said:

"There are many thieves around here. You'd better not leave your load sitting there by itself."

Jan answered, "Let it sit where it sits. Anyone stealing from me isn't going to steal a second time."

When the woman got up the next morning, she saw a man standing by the load, balancing something on his back.

"Get up!" she shouted to Jan. "There is a man standing by your load, and he's got something big on his back."

"Oh, that's no problem. He'll stand there until I come," said Jan.

And the thief just stood there!

When Jan finished eating breakfast, he went down to the place where he had left his load. After hitching up the horse, he said to the thief, who by now was all blue and stiff from the cold:

"You can put that load down now! You've held it long enough. But remember not to steal from Jan Øye again."

He did not care to punish him any more.

> This legend, which is common throughout Scandinavia, focuses on the ability of the wise man to bind the thief in the very act of stealing. One purpose of telling the story may well be to scare off potential thieves.
>
> Collected by Knut Hermundstad from Jørgen Knutson Hermundstad, Valdres, Buskerud (Norway). Printed in Hermundstad, *Ættarminne. Gamal Valdres-kultur* 5 (1952), 117–18.

32. Wind and Weather

Given the changeable and often difficult climate in northern Scandinavia, it is not surprising that control of wind and weather would be a major concern of the practitioners of magic. Fishermen and sailors employed the services of wise folk to make favorable sailing wind. But beyond that, people quite commonly made use of spells and rituals to influence the weather.

32.1 Three Knots in a Handkerchief

A crew once sailed to Sweden with the very same ship that is lying in Tränjonkärr right now. The skipper wanted to sail back, but they got head wind. A fellow came along, however, who had a handkerchief which he had tied into three knots. He told them to untie the first and the second knots but wait to untie the third one until they could see the shore at home.

They did what he told them and got favorable sailing wind. But when the skipper saw that they were only a quarter of a mile from home, he thought they were safe. He opened the third knot, and the ship ran aground at Sandejde.

This happened a few hundred years ago.

> The legend about making sailing wind by tying three knots in a handkerchief or a rope is widespread in Europe. Its oldest printed variant, dating back to 1491, is found in Bartholomeus Anglicus's *De proprietatibus rerum* (15. 172), where it is identified with Finland or Finnmark.
>
> See John Granlund, "Vindmagi," KLMN 20 (1976), columns 98–100; W. Gaerte, "Wetterzauber im späten Mittelalter," *Rheinisches Jahrbuch für Volkskunde* 3 (1952), 226–73; Gunnar Norlén, "*Blås Kajsa*. Kring en svensk sjömanstradition," *Svenska landsmål* (1972), 61–83.
>
> Collected in 1915 by V. E. V. Wessman from Ulrik Thomasson in Pargas (Finland). Printed in Wessman, *Sägner* 3.2 (1931), 491.

32.2 If You Rule Today, I Rule Tomorrow

Often we would have stormy weather when old Jokum visited here, and it would be difficult for him to get back home.

One day he wanted to go home. So he walked down to the beach, took three stones, and threw one of them into the water, saying:

"If you rule today, I rule tomorrow."

He repeated this with the second and the third stone, and the next day the weather was calm.

> Collected by E. T. Kristensen from Maren Kristensen, Helnæs, Jylland (Denmark). Printed in Kristensen, *Danske sagn*, N.R. 6 (1936), 188.

32.3 The Finn Boy

When the rivers were flooding in springtime, Ola would float timbers. But the timbers lying in Elis river would not move unless there was a good northerly wind. The river was so calm that the current was barely visible. When there was no wind, the timbers would just lie still in the water.

Ola was hanging around with his lumberjacks and could not do anything except wait for a northerly wind.

"You really want wind from the north?" asked the Finn boy. He thought it was crazy to wish for cold weather. So Ola explained it to him.

Early the next morning, the Finn boy went out and crouched down on the north side of a spruce tree. Then he blew and hissed and mumbled something the others could not understand. But even before he got back up on his feet, there came such a wind from the north that it lifted the timbers up on the water.

People said that the Finn boy also knew how to protect the hay from rain. He held his sheath knife into the rain and split it. Not a drop fell on the hay spread out to dry, although the rain was pouring down all around.

> To provide the desired wind, the Finn boy applies a form of sympathetic magic (blowing = wind), combined with an unspecified spell.
>
> Collected by Sigurd Nergaard in Elverum, Hedmark (Norway). Printed in Nergaard, *Hulder og trollskap. Folkeminne fraa Østerdalen* 4 (1925), 56.

32.4 To Make the Rain Stop

Mary, Mary —
she sat
on the stair,
and prayed to Our Lord
to make the rain stop;
over peaks,
over trees,
over all God's angels.

> This spell represents the epic type in form.
>
> Collected in 1886 by Dr. Fritzner, the church dean in Lister, Vest-Agder (Norway). Printed in A. Chr. Bang, *Norske hexeformularer og magiske opskrifter* (1901–2), 618.

32.5 Rain from a Clear Sky

At Vanse there lived a church dean whose wife was a witch. They had a daughter, and the wife taught her witchcraft. The chaplain at Vanse got engaged to the daughter.

One evening the young folks went for a walk. The moon was shining brightly and the skies were clear. Then the daughter said to the chaplain:

"Would you believe that I can make it rain, even though the sky is clear?"

No, the chaplain could not believe that. But she crouched down and pulled her skirts over her head, and all at once it began to rain. They both got soaked.

> The story is a variant of the legend "The Daughter of the Witch." (Cf. no. 42.1.)
>
> Collected by Tore Bergstøl in Vest-Agder (Norway). Printed in Bergstøl, *Atterljom. Folkeminne fraa smaadalane kring Lindesnes* 2 (1930), 17–18.

33. The Trickster

Besides healers and other wise folk, we encounter in oral tradition individuals who possess the ability to hypnotize others. In most instances, these tricksters used their skills for entertainment wherever people gathered.

33.1 Maliser-Knut

There was a man named Maliser-Knut who understood the art of hypnosis. Once he was at a farm where a lot of people had gathered. They challenged Maliser-Knut to crawl inside a log that was lying in the yard. If he could do it, he would get a reward. But if he failed, he would get a beating from all the people who were watching.

Everybody gathered around, full of curiosity. They really thought they saw Maliser-Knut disappear into the log. It was slow going at first. He drilled for a long time before he got his head inside the log. But once his head disappeared, the rest of his body slipped in quickly. It was actually nothing but an optical illusion; in reality he was crawling along the outside of the log.

But now it happened that a woman came to the farm, leading a cow. She did not see Maliser-Knut until she was standing next to the others, so he did not have time to hypnotize her. The woman started to laugh.

"What are you standing here gaping at?" she asked. "What is so interesting about a man crawling back and forth on a log?"

When the others heard that, they got angry, and of course they struck Maliser-Knut. But he took revenge on the woman. He hypnotized her so that she believed she had come to a river, and the farther she went, the higher she thought the water was rising. The woman did not want to get wet, so she lifted up her skirt. The higher she thought the water rose, the higher she lifted, until finally she was walking with her skirt all the way up under her arms. You can imagine how people were grinning because the woman was really walking on dry ground!

Maliser-Knut was a man that no iron would hold. He was put in prison several times, but he got out every time. They eventually caught him and put him in a prison tower and erected a spiked fence around it. Knut managed to slip out of the irons that time, too. He tore his clothes into strips, tied them to a rope, and lowered himself down from the tower. But the rope was a little too short, so he had to jump. He had the bad luck to get hung up on one of the spikes. The guard found him there in the morning. The people wanted to take him down, but he asked to be allowed to hang there in peace until he died, and they let him. That is how Maliser-Knut ended his life. He is supposed to have lived in southern Norway, and what has been told here is only a small part of the stories about him.

> People obviously enjoyed being entertained but resented it when they were made the butt of the entertainer's tricks. The story demonstrates the exposed position of the outsider in traditional society.
>
> Collected in 1924–25 by Knut Strompdal from Eliseus Lomsdal, Velfjord, Nordland (Norway). Printed in Strompdal, *Gamalt frå Helgeland* 3 (1939), 60–62.

33.2 The Smith Who Hypnotized People

Some people can do all kinds of tricks. There was a smith who could take off his head and put it on the table to shave it.

It happened in Åkersberg. We were sitting in the bunkhouse— some of the drivers and a few others—when the smith came in.

"One has to make oneself pretty for the weekend," he said.

So he took off his head and put it on the table. We all saw it. It was the most awful thing any of us had ever seen.

The smith had a son. I asked him whether he could do any of the tricks his father did.

"Oh, yes," he said, "I've taught myself, but I don't want to have anything to do with it."

He drank a lot, that smith. One day he was drunk and the master struck him in the face. His head tumbled off his shoulders and rolled under the sofa. The master got scared and ran away. No wonder! Later on the smith didn't greet the master the way he was supposed to, and the master admonished him to do it properly. Then the smith took off his head and put it under his arm. From then on, he did this whenever he met the master.

I suppose he hypnotized people. If I had not seen it myself, I would never have believed it. Let me see, it all happened between 1869 and 1870, during the Franco-Prussian War.

> A smith was often thought to possess magic powers. Also, his skills as a craftsman made him indispensable. The interest of this legend rests not only on the skill of the trickster to entertain his audience but on his ability to make a fool of his superiors with impunity. Thus the narrative functions as a kind of protest against social privilege.
>
> See Carl-Herman Tillhagen, *Järnet och människorna* (1981), 195–220.
>
> Collected in 1926 by Margit Sjöberg from Valfrid Wijk, Beateberg parish, Västergötland (Sweden). Ms. in IFGH (737), 35–36. Printed in Bengt af Klintberg, *Svenska folksägner* (1965), 221–22.

PART IV
Witchcraft

Part IV illustration: "Witches have
the power to darken the light of
the moon, call up storms, uproot trees
and plants and weaken cattle and beasts
of burden." Olaus Magnus, *Historia de
Gentibus Septentrionalibus* (History of
the Northern People, 1555),
book 3, chapter 15.

he medieval literature of Scandinavia suggests that prior to Christianization the existence of individuals specializing in the use of supranormal powers was a generally accepted fact. In *Elder Edda* and in Snorri's *Saga of the Ynglings*, skills attributed to the god Othin are essentially the same as those identified in later tradition with the practitioners of magic, notably shape changing, magic flight, and the use of spells to control the elements and conjure the dead. A specially potent and malevolent form of magic was referred to as *seiðr*. It was used to rob its victims of their sanity, their health, even their life, and generally to cause misfortune.

The church rejected the notion of supranormal powers as illusory and passed numerous laws forbidding belief in witchcraft. Eventually the popular view regarding the witch was incorporated into official theology, however. Thus, according to the preamble to *Malleus Maleficarum* (The Witches' Hammer, 1486), the greatest heresy is *not* to believe in the power of the witch. *Malleus Maleficarum* was devised to identify witches and bring them to trial by a court of inquisition. In it numerous legends from recent folk tradition are cited as evidence concerning, for example, the witches' sabbath, the use of a familiar to steal milk, the passing of magic skills from mother to daughter, et cetera. The notorious witch trials in Europe, from the fifteenth to the seventeenth centuries, and in Scandinavia, from the end of the Reformation to the early eighteenth century, reinforced folk belief in the witch and her powers.

See Bente G. Alver, *Heksetro og trolddom* (1971); Norman Cohn, *Europe's Inner Demons: An Enquiry Inspired by the Great Witch Hunt* (1976); Heinrich Krämer and Jakob Sprenger, *Malleus Maleficarum* (1486).

34. Revenge and Envy

One of the stronger driving forces behind magic is the desire to bend others to one's will. Characteristically, harmful magic has its origin in feelings of envy and anger. Often individuals occupying low positions in society, the poor in general but also itinerant beggars and strangers—for instance, Lapps, Finns, and gypsies—used magic to force others to share with them certain necessities like food and lodging. People were afraid the gypsies would take revenge if they were denied. This mechanism was generally employed to explain sickness, accidents, and other misfortunes befalling the settled community.

> See Bente G. Alver, *Heksetro og trolddom* (1971), 160–71; Svale Solheim, *Norsk sætertradisjon* (1952), 288–339.

34.1 Sticking Pins into a Girl

In the parish of Tårs there was an old woman. People suspected that she was a witch. She became angry at her servant girl, and the girl got sick and had to take to bed. She felt as if someone was sticking pins into her, first on one side and then on the other. She became very ill.

One Sunday the old woman went to church to take communion. She forgot to lock her closet. Her husband opened it and looked inside. In it was a doll that was covered with pins all the way down to its thigh on one side. He pulled the pins out and went to ask the girl how she was feeling. She was fine! There was no longer anything wrong with her. Then he stuck the pins into the other side of the doll

161

and came back to ask how she was. She felt poorly once more, but this time the pain was on her other side.

The man freed the girl from her pain until the woman was expected to return from church. Then he went back and stuck the pins into the doll the way they had been before. He did not dare say anything to his wife. The old woman left the pins in place until she thought the girl had been sufficiently punished. When she took the pins out, the girl was free.

> According to folk belief it is possible to do harm to a person by inflicting injury on an image of that person. This form of sympathetic magic has well-known parallels in the African practice of voodoo.
>
> See Nils Lid and Matti Kuusi, "Biletmagi," *KLNM* 1 (1956), columns 540–42; Nils Lid, *Trolldom* (1950), 127–59; A. Hämäläinen, "Beiträge zur Bildmagie," *Mitteilung des Vereins für finnische Volkskunde* (1945), 15–27; Elizabeth Brandon, "Folk Medicine in French Louisiana," *American Folk Medicine* (1976), 215–34.
>
> Collected by E. T. Kristensen from Karen Marie Thomasdatter, Hallund Nymark, Vendsyssel, Jylland (Denmark). Printed in Kristensen, *Danske sagn*, N.R. 6 (1936), 264.

34.2 Øli Skogen

One day Øli came to Jamgrave and asked for a pail of milk. They refused to give it to her, and she went away angry.

A cow and her calf were grazing in the pen. Øli walked over and petted the calf's back. Then the calf grew wild. It bellowed and jumped and crashed into things. The farmer on Jamgrave, who had been watching, followed Øli to Skogen. He demanded that she remove the spell she had cast on the calf. If she did not, he would turn the law on her.

Øli stubbornly denied that she had done anything wrong. But right after the man left, she went and petted the calf's back once more. And immediately the animal was normal again.

> (Cf. no. 3.4; it discusses the power of the "evil hand.")
> Collected by Kjetil A. Flatin in Seljord, Telemark (Norway). Printed in Flatin, *Tussar og trolldom* (1930), 107.

34.3 Inger Petterst

Yes, that Inger Petterst was a nasty woman in more ways than one. She would go begging, and only the best was good enough for her. And woe if she did not get what she wanted. One could always expect one thing or another from her.

One time she visited my mother and asked for some clabbered milk. But it happened that the milk we had was a bit sour. My mother said as much:

"The milk I have is a little old, Inger. You'll have to settle for what I can offer."

And my mother put a wooden bowl and some flatbread on the table. But that was not good enough for Inger. She would not even sit down. She just muttered something below her breath, and out the door she went.

But she fixed things for us! The very same day we lost a goat. It fell over in the field and was dead instantly.

> The story gives credence to the widespread belief in the power of witches and their ability to take revenge if crossed. The willingness of people to give aid and comfort to itinerant beggars was often motivated by this fear.
>
> See Bengt af Klintberg, *Svenska folksägner* (1972), 36–37; Svale Solheim, *Norsk sætertradisjon* (1952), 288–98.
>
> Collected by Ragnvald Mo in Salten, Nordland (Norway). Printed in Mo, *Soge og segn. Folkeminne frå Salten* 3 (1952), 106.

34.4 The Lapp Woman

There was a Lapp woman who often came around here. I do not remember her name. It was in the days when old Jæger had his store on Mo. One Saturday night this woman came to sit with Jæger. She brought Jakob Jansa from Øvrenes with her. Jakob was something like a manager at the minister's place.

They had strong drinks. The woman was wild when she drank brandy and soon she was drunk. They came to exchange harsh words, and in the end, Jakob threw the woman out. She shrieked something foul. And the last time they saw her, she was crawling into a hay barn.

This occurred on Saturday night, as I said before. But Sunday morning, just when the folks at the minister's place were about to go to church, a strange thing happened. The cows keeled over! Now

Jakob understood what a mistake he had made. He found the woman
and asked her what to do about the cows. He got down on his knees
and begged her. Yes, that is how I heard the story. The woman was
amenable; she let herself be persuaded.

"If I have cast a spell on them, I can undo it, too," she said. And
she had the power to make everything all right again.

> The Lapps represented a different culture, and as strangers they
> were both ascribed special powers and regarded with implicit
> distrust.
>
> See Svale Solheim, *Norsk sætertradisjon* (1952), 290; Carl-
> Herman Tillhagen, "Finnen und Lappen als Zauberkundige in der
> skandinavischen Volksüberlieferung," *Kontakte und Grenzen*
> (1969), 129–43.
>
> Collected by Ragnvald Mo in Salten, Nordland (Norway).
> Printed in Mo, *Soge og segn. Folkeminne frå Salten* 3 (1952),
> 109–10.

35. Magic Shot

Magic shot, often called Finn shot, was the name given to projectiles supposedly causing sickness or sudden death. They were imagined to be sent in the form of bullets, insects, clouds or vapor, and
so on. Many legends are concerned with the means by which one
could protect oneself against this type of magic.

> (Cf. no. 29.4; it provides a formula by which to heal an animal
> suffering from the effect of magic shot.
>
> See Lauri Honko, *Krankheitsprojektile* (1959); Nils Lid, *Trolldom*
> (1950), 1–36.

35.1 Shooting the Trollman

A sailor from Lovisa was once staying in a town in Österbotten
while planks were being loaded on his ship. He got involved with a
girl. But when the ship got ready to sail, the girl's father, who was a
trollman, said that if the sailor did not return to marry the girl, he
would shoot him, no matter where he was. And this would happen
precisely one year later—to the day.

When a year had passed, the sailor was back in Lovisa and had no
mind to be married in Österbotten. But when the day drew closer, he
got nervous and went to a man named Holmström for help. Holm-

ström took the matter upon himself. He found an empty barrel in the
yard, turned it upside down, and told the sailor to sit quietly under
the barrel until it was over. Then he poured a few ladles of water
over the bottom of the barrel so that it formed a sort of mirror. He
fetched an old rifle from the house and positioned himself by the mirror. That way he was able to see the man in Österbotten getting
ready to shoot the sailor.

"Can you see him?" asked the sailor in the barrel. He was getting
nervous about how it would all end.

"Yes, now I can see him," answered Holmström. "He's just coming
out on the stairs with a gun in his hand. But I'm going to be the one
to shoot first."

And then he fired into the air.

"Did you hit him?"

"Yes. Now you can crawl out from under the barrel. He dropped
dead on the stairs," said Holmström.

> Conjuring up the image of an adversary in a mirror or on a sur-
> face of water was a common device in magical practice. By
> shooting or stabbing the image, the magician could harm or even
> kill. The present narrative deviates from this common pattern in-
> asmuch as Holmström sends a magic shot by firing into the air
> rather than into the mirror image.
>
> See Carl-Herman Tillhagen, "Finnen und Lappen als Zauber-
> kundige in der skandinavischen Volksüberlieferung," *Kontakte und
> Grenzen* (1969), 135–36; Nils Lid, *Trolldom* (1950), 149.
>
> Collected in Pärnå, Nyland (Finland). Printed in Josefina
> Bengts, *Från vargtider och vallpojksår* (1915), 103. Reprinted in V.
> E. V. Wessman, *Sägner* 3.2 (1931), 514–15.

35.2 *The Wizards of Vestmannaeyja*

When the Black Plague raged through Iceland, eighteen wizards
put their heads together and joined forces. They went out to Vestmannaeyja with the intention of protecting themselves from death as
long as possible. As soon as they could see that the plague had run
itself out on the mainland, they wanted to find out whether there
was anyone left alive. They agreed to send one of their group over,
and the wizard they chose for this was neither the most nor the
least skilled of them. They took him over to the mainland and said
that if he did not return by Christmas, they would send a Finn shot
to him that would kill him. This took place early in Advent. The

man set off, walked for a long time, and covered a lot of ground. But he did not see a single living soul. Farmhouses stood open with dead bodies lying about everywhere within them. He eventually came to a farm that was closed. He wondered about this and hoped that he might find someone. He knocked on the door, and a pretty young girl came out. He greeted her, and she threw her arms around him and wept for the joy of seeing someone—she said that she had thought she was the only one left alive. She asked him to stay with her, and he said he would. They went inside then and talked at length together. She asked where he had come from and where he had been headed. He told him about everything and about the fact that he had to be back before Christmas. She asked him to stay with her as long as possible. He felt so sorry for her that he promised to do so. She told him that in those parts no one was left alive—she had traveled from her home for a week in every direction and had found no one.

When it was getting close to Christmas, the man from Vestmannaeyja wanted to leave. The girl begged him to stay and said that his companions could not be mean enough to make him suffer for keeping her company, all alone as she was. He let himself be talked into staying, and soon it was the day before Christmas. Now he meant to go—no matter what she might say. She saw right away that her pleas would not be of any more use and said, "Do you really think you can get out to Vestmannaeyja tonight? Wouldn't it be just as good to die here with me rather than somewhere along the road back?" He could see that time had run out on him, so he decided to stay there to await his death.

The night passed and he was woebegone, but the girl was in a very good mood and asked whether he could see how the Vestmanna dwellers were getting on. He said that they were now ready to send the Finn shot across to the mainland and that it would arrive the next day. The girl sat down next to him on her bed, and he lay down next to the wall. He said that he was growing very drowsy and that that signaled the approach of the Finn shot. Then he fell asleep. The girl sat on the edge of the bed and kept trying to prod him awake so that he could tell her where the Finn shot was. But the closer it came, the more deeply he slept, and at last, when he said that the Finn shot had crossed the boundaries of the farm, he fell so deeply asleep that she could no longer wake him. It was not long before she saw a reddish brown cloud of vapor enter the farm.

This vapor drifted toward her bit by bit and took the shape of a human. She asked where it intended to go. The Finn shot told her what it had to do and asked her to get off the bed, "because you're in my way," it said. The girl then said that it would have to do something for her first. The Finn shot asked what that might be. The girl said that she wanted to see how big it could grow. The Finn shot went along with that and grew so big that it filled the entire house. Then the girl said, "Now I want to see how little you can be." The Finn shot said it could turn itself into a fly and in a flash did just that. Then it tried to zip under the girl's arm and into the bed where the man was, but it landed on a leg of mutton that the girl was holding and burrowed its way into it. And then the girl stopped up the hole with a plug. Afterward she put the leg of mutton into her pocket and woke up the man. He was instantly awake and marveled at the fact that he was still alive. The girl asked him where the Finn shot was, and he said he did not know what had become of it. The girl then said that she had suspected for a long time that the wizards in Vestmannaeyja were not very great. The man was very happy, and they both celebrated the holy days with great pleasure.

But, when the New Year approached, the man became withdrawn. The girl asked what was troubling him. He said that the men in Vestmannaeyja were readying another Finn shot, "and they are using all their magic on this one. It should arrive here on New Year's Eve day, and it won't be easy to save me." The girl said that she for one was not going to worry about something that had not happened yet, "and don't you be afraid of those Finn shots from the Vestmanna wizards." She was as merry as she could be, and he thought it would be dishonorable if he did not bear up. On New Year's Eve day, he said that the Finn shot had reached land, "and it is traveling fast because it has been pumped full of magic power." The girl said he should go for a walk with her. He did so. They kept walking until they got to a thicket. There the girl stopped and pulled up some twigs. A flat rock appeared, and she lifted it up. Below it was an underground chamber.

They went down into the chamber; it was dark and terrifying. There was a glimmer of light from a wick floating in a skull containing human fat. There, lying on a pallet near the light was an old man, frightening to look at. His eyes were like blood, and he was on the whole so hideous that the man from Vestmannaeyja was taken aback. The old man said, "Something must have come up, since you are up and about, my dear foster child. It's been a long time since I last saw you. What can I do for you?" The girl told him all about her doings and about the man and the first of the Finn shots. The old man asked her if he could see the leg of mutton. She gave it to him, and a change came over him when he took it. He turned it around and around in every direction and felt it all over. Then the girl said, "Now help me quickly, foster Father, because the man is beginning to grow drowsy, and that is a sign that the Finn shot is about to come." The old man took the plug out of the leg, and the fly crawled out. The old man stroked and patted the fly. Then he said, "You go and welcome all the Finn shots from Vestmannaeyja, and swallow them up." There was a gigantic crash, and the fly flew outside and grew so huge that one jaw reached up to heaven and the other down to the ground. It then took care of all the Finn shots from Vestmannaeyja, and the man was saved.

The man and the girl left the underground chamber and went home and settled on the girl's farm. Later they got married and increased and multiplied and peopled the earth.

> (Cf. nos. 60.1–60.15; they concern the Black Plague.)
>
> The motif of a person becoming drowsy when he or she is about to be attacked is frequently found in Icelandic sagas. The sleepiness is due to the *hug* of an enemy affecting his intended victim. The motif of catching a demon or devil inside a nut, a bottle, or a bag made from a child's or a foal's caul, is found both in folktales and in legends. (Cf. no. 54.9.) A powerful magician, like the old man in this text, could redirect or return the Finn shot.
>
> Collected in 1845 in Iceland. Printed in Jón Árnason, *Íslenzkar þjóðsögur og ævintýri* 1 (1862), 321–23. Reprinted in 1954.

36. The Whirlwind

In general, people regarded the whirlwind as the manifestation of the witch's or trollman's power. It was believed that the witch traveled in the whirlwind to inflict harm on people and cattle or to steal hay.

36.1 The Witch in the Whirlwind

There was an old woman named Aunt Håka-Per. She was a witch. And there was an old woman who lived at our place. Her name was Aunt Kari. She had never been married, and she was old and shaky.

One day, when she and my father were out raking, a whirlwind sprang up.

"Throw yourself down, Aunt Kari," my father shouted, "otherwise the wind will take you."

Then he pulled out his knife, spat on it, and threw it into the storm. Suddenly the wind subsided and the hay fell back down, out of the air. But the knife was gone, and my father had to go to Böle to fetch the knife from Håka-Per's wife. It was stuck in her thigh. But she laughed and said:

"It didn't occur to me that you might use your knife, Pelle."

> One of the ways to protect oneself against the whirlwind was to spit into the wind three times or to throw a knife into it. Steel and spit were common remedies against the demonic. The knife became stuck in the witch's thigh because she had been physically present in the whirlwind.
>
> See Joh. Th. Storaker, *Elementerne i den norske folketro* (1924), 13–15; I. Reichborn-Kjennerud, *Vår gamle trolldomsmedisin* 1 (1928), 20, 88, 173.
>
> Collected by Imber Nordin-Grip in 1938 from Per Olov Engman, Skog Parish, Södermanland (Sweden). Ms. in ULMA 12721 (29), 33. Printed in Bengt af Klintberg, *Svenska folksägner* (1972), 224.

36.2 Haying with a Whirlwind

Tobacco-Husin was a cotter in South-Etnedal. He became a soldier during the last great war. He owned and used the Black Book, people said.

Tobacco-Husin went haying with a farmhand and a girl. But the three of them just lay around inside the hay barn most of the day. Tobacco-Husin merely walked a ring around the barn.

During the night a whirlwind developed outside the barn. Hay came flying from all directions. It blew around the barn and right into the door. The next morning all the hay had been brought in.

> This story belongs to the folk tradition of trollmen using their Black-Book powers to carry out practical tasks, in this case, to bring in the hay.
>
> Collected in Etnedal, Oppland (Norway). Printed in Johan Skrindsrud, *På heimleg grund* (1956), 57.

37. Food Magic

In Snorre Sturlusson's *Prose Edda*, the god Thor magically reconstitutes the flesh of the goats he has slaughtered for his evening meals. Therefore he forbids his retainers to break the bones of the animal that is eaten.

In later folk tradition, it is the witch who magically replenishes food—usually herring. But people feared they would become thinner and thinner if they were fed the same food over and over again. For this reason it was considered a good precaution to break the bone when eating herring.

> See Bente G. Alver, *Heksetro og trolddom* (1971), 181–82.

37.1 *Ragnhild Blikka*

Ragnhild lived on Blikka, a large and beautiful farm in a cleft high up in the mountains, quite a bit north of the other farms in Svartdal. Ragnhild was known for her wealth and for her witchcraft. Her husband was named Gisle. He could do witchcraft too, people said.

In springtime when people were spreading manure on the fields down in Flatdal, Ragnhild would stand in her yard at home and conjure every bit of their manure onto her own fields on Blikka. In the fall the fields on Blikka were so beautiful that no one had seen the likes of it. But the fields on Flatdal were thin and scrawny.

Once Ragnhild had a serving boy. She had always been stingy with food. Every day when the boy was sent out to tend the livestock, she gave him a herring wrapped in a slice of bread. She admonished the boy that he must never break the herring bone. The boy did as he was told, and every evening he came plodding home with the bone in his food bag. But finally he realized that it was the same herring he ate every day, which always seemed like new the next day. Finally he got tired of that fare, and one day he broke the bone.

And in the evening, he found that Ragnhild's back was broken, too.

> This follows the belief tradition that the material projections of the witch's power are identified with her person; breaking the herring bone is tantamount to injuring the witch.
>
> Collected by Kjetil A. Flatin. Printed in Flatin, *Tussar og trolldom* (1930), 83–84.

37.2 Lisbet Nypan

When Lisbet Nypan's workmen ate salt herring, she ordered them to break the bone in the herring. If any of them cut the bone with a knife, she got very angry.

She had a trapdoor on the floor of her kitchen and below that door was an opening, a little room. She put the bones of the herring into that room, and the next day fat and shiny flesh had grown back onto the same herring bone from which they had eaten the day before. This way Lisbet Nypan got fresh herring every day.

> In this story, tradition has been modified so that the interdiction is against cutting the herring bone with a knife rather than against breaking it.
>
> Lisbet Nypan was burned as a witch in Norway in 1670. Legends about her are also well known in Sweden.
>
> See Bente G. Alver, *Heksetro og trolddom* (1971), 211. Bengt af Klintberg, *Svenska folksägner* (1972), 233, 339.
>
> Collected by Edvard Kruken in South-Trøndelag (Norway). Ms. In NFS Kruken (5), 33. Printed in Alver, *Heksetro og trolddom* (1971), 182.

38. Stealing Milk

People believed that if their cows gave little or no milk, or if they had poor success in churning, it was because envious neighbors used witchcraft to steal from them. By the same token, if someone produced more milk or butter than the average, it was usually explained to be the result of magic rather than superior animal husbandry.

> See Bente G. Alver, *Heksetro og trolddom* (1971), 184–95; Svale Solheim, *Norsk sætertradisjon* (1952), 311–13; *Atlas över svensk folkkultur II. Sägen, tro och högtidssed 2*, edited by Åke Campbell and Åsa Nyman (1976), 80–93.

38.1 Milking with a Knife

When our house burned down, we stayed with a woman in northern Ølgod. She told us about another woman in her neighborhood who could milk other people's cows with a knife. She did not live far from Skjærbæk mill in Ølgod, and at times she took so much milk that some of the cows at the mill would not give any milk at all.

The same woman had a little girl. When she went to school, she took some bread and cheese with her. But the cheese was always made from fresh milk. The other children said to her:

"How do you get cheese like that at your house? You don't have any milk to make the cheese!"

"Oh, yes, we do," said the girl. "My great-grandmother sticks a knife into a beam and puts a pot underneath and milks into it. That's what we use to make the cheese."

> The methods of troll milking from a pin or knife stuck in a wall or from a garter are the ones most frequently mentioned in folk tradition. Milking from a knife is referred to in *Malleus Maleficarum* (The Witches' Hammer).
>
> See Bente G. Alver, *Heksetro og trolddom* (1971), 24–33, 192–95; Svale Solheim, *Norsk sætertradisjon* (1952), 311–12.
>
> Collected by E. T. Kristensen from Niels Peter Rasmussen, Øse, Skads parish, Jylland (Denmark). Printed in Kristensen, *Danske sagn*, N.R. 6 (1936), 235.

38.2 Brandy from a Knife Handle

A Lapp woman came to a farm and asked for lodging, and she was permitted to stay. After a while she took out a sheath knife, stuck it into the wall, and put a bottle underneath it. Soon brandy began dripping from the shaft of the knife, as it does when you drill a hole into a tree and the sap comes trickling out. They went inside the house, but a little later the woman said to one of the boys:

"Go out and see whether it's still running."

He came back and said:

"Now it's half full."

"Well, let it run," said the Lapp woman. "That farmer's got plenty of brandy."

She was taking the brandy from another farm!

> This tale about stealing brandy by magic is parallel to the one about milking by witchcraft.
>
> Collected by Folke Hedblom in 1932 from a cotter known only as Virén, in Kjessmansbo, Valbo parish, Gästrikland (Sweden). Ms. in ULMA 10057, 8. Printed in Bengt af Klintberg, *Svenska folksägner* (1972), 221.

38.3 Witch Butter

There was a witch in Netland at the time when the minister Søren Schive was floating logs there. He said to his lumberjacks:

"Don't you buy any butter from her. She is a witch."

But there were some who did not listen to the minister. They bought butter from her anyway.

One day, when they sat eating by the river, the minister walked up to one of them.

"Did you buy butter from the witch after all?" he asked.

Then he plunged his knife into the butter. When he pulled it out, there was blood dripping from the blade.

> A method of testing whether butter had been churned magically was to cut it with a knife, preferably one with which a murder had been committed. The underlying assumption was that it would be dangerous to consume the butter because the power of the witch was identified with it.
>
> See Bente G. Alver, *Heksetro og trolddom* (1971), 189–90.
> Collected by Peter Lunde in Fjotland, Vest Agder (Norway).
> Printed in Lunde, *Kynnehuset. Vestegdske folkeminne* (1924), 156.

38.4 Churning

Once a woman from Brenneli attended a wedding. But they did not have enough butter at the reception. The woman sent a message home to the serving girl to churn some butter and bring it to her. But the woman warned her not to put more than one ladle of cream into the churn. Well, the girl thought that was too little, so she added another two ladles. And then she set to churning. But the cream began to overflow onto the floor, and the girl was almost beside herself.

The Finn woman sensed that something was wrong at home. She hurried back, but when she came in through the door, the cream stood higher than her shoes. And she became angrier than angry.

"Now what have you done?" she said to the girl.

"I thought that one ladle of cream wasn't enough, so I added another two."

Then the Finn woman whacked the girl on the ear.

"You should have done what I told you. Now you have taken all the cream from three parishes instead of just one."

> The story is based on pars-pro-toto magic. Each ladle represents the cream available in one of three parishes. The narrative also

shows the consequences people imagined to arise when someone incompetent in witchcraft used magic.

See Bente G. Alver, *Heksetro og trolddom* (1971), 184–92.

Legend type: ML 3040.

Collected by Lars M. Fjellstad in Eidskog, Hedmark (Norway). Printed in Fjellstad, *Haugfolk og trollskap* (1954), 43.

38.5 Hallvor Drengmann's Son

Hallvor Drengmann's son, named after his father, was a peddler who made his rounds in Telemark. A woman in Kvitseid owed him money for some goods.

One evening he thought he would go to her and collect. When he came to a river, which ran a little way from her house, he saw the woman sitting below a waterfall in the river. She was churning so that the cream spouted high in the air. Hallvor pretended not to notice anything but went straight to her farm and waited there.

After a while the woman arrived, carrying a big and beautiful piece of butter under her apron.

Hallvor stated his purpose, but the woman told him that she did not have any money and asked whether she could pay with some butter. Sure, he was satisfied with that and took the piece of butter the woman had brought from the waterfall.

But Hallvor of course suspected that there might be some witchcraft involved. To find out whether butter was made by a witch, one had to cut into it with a knife that had been used to kill a person. If it was witch butter, blood would run from the blade. There was a knife like that at Laupedalen in Brunkeberg. Hallvor borrowed it and tested the butter.

When he cut the butter with the knife, he clearly saw that blood ran from the edge. So there was no doubt about what kind of butter he had gotten.

Nevertheless, Hallvor took the butter to town and sold it there. And he never heard any complaints about it.

> In this instance churning by magic is made particularly dramatic by having it take place in a waterfall. But the story can be viewed as an example of decaying tradition. Even though the peddler knows full well that the butter was churned by witchcraft, he accepts it in payment and sells it at the market in town. His greed outweighs his fear.
>
> See Bente G. Alver, *Heksetro og trolddom* (1971), 189–90.

Collected by Kjetil A. Flatin in Seljord, Telemark (Norway).
Printed in Flatin, *Tussar og trolldom* (1930), 125–26.

38.6 The Neighbor Who Stole the Milk

Once Øli went to Aslaug's farm in Garvik to get some milk.
Aslaug said:

"You know, I don't understand what's the matter with my cows.
They're grazing in a field that hasn't been cut, and yet there's hardly
any milk in them. I get mostly blood all the time."

"Give me a couple drinks, and I'll show you who's been making
trouble for your cows. It's the evil eye of one of your neighbors that
does it."

"Oh, far from it. I just don't believe in that sort of thing," said
Aslaug.

Nevertheless, she gave Øli a couple drinks. The first one Øli drank
right away, the second she just sipped. Then she shook the glass for
some time while saying the names of all the people in the neighborhood. Finally she held up the glass in front of Aslaug.

"There she is!" said Øli, and Aslaug clearly saw one of her neighbors, standing on her head in the glass.

"May God have mercy on me!" said Aslaug. She could hardly believe her eyes.

> Whereas the farmer's wife is looking for a rational explanation for
> the fact that her cows are not producing much milk, Øli proceeds
> on the assumption that the milk has been stolen by magic. She
> makes use of a common method of revealing a thief by conjuring
> up his or her image in glass or a bucket of water.
>
> Brandy was the preferred liquid used both for magic rituals of
> this type and for payment of the specialist.
>
> Collected by Kjetil A. Flatin in Seljord, Telemark (Norway).
> Printed in Flatin, *Tussar og trolldom* (1936), 106.

39. Troll Cat

When stealing milk from her neighbors, the witch supposedly had
help from a familiar, variously referred to as a troll cat, milk rabbit,
troll ball, puck, et cetera.

> See Bente G. Alver, *Heksetro og trolddom* (1971), 195–209; Svale
> Solheim, *Norsk sætertradisjon*, 320–39; Jan Wall, *Tjuvmjölkande väsen*

2 vols. (1977–78); *Atlas över svensk folkkultur II. Sägen, tro och högtidssed 2*, edited by Åke Campbell and Åsa Nyman (1976), 80–93.

39.1 The Troll Cat

Every Thursday night Lispet Snipånn ordered her farmhand to cut brush for brooms. She was very anxious about the shavings from the brush he cut. She told him to pick up every bit and not to lose any of it. But after eating dinner on Thursday nights, Lispet would take the shavings away. The boy often wondered what she wanted with them.

So one evening he peeked in through the window. He wanted to see what she would do with the shavings. She rolled them into a ball, took a knife, cut her little finger, and let three drops of blood fall onto the shavings. Then she threw the ball across the floor and said:

"Now I have given you flesh and blood. May Old Nick give you power and life."

Then the ball of shavings became a troll cat, and it ran away.

> The folk believed that the witch created the troll cat from human hair, nails, wood shavings, and the like.
>
> Belief in the troll cat is connected with the observation of certain accumulations of matter, usually hair, passed from the stomachs of cattle (aegrophilae). Once this matter had dried on the ground, it was easily rolled across the yard or fields by the wind, giving the impression of a running animal.
>
> In this text Lisbet Nypan (cf. no 37.2) appears as Lisbet Snipånn.
>
> See Bente G. Alver, *Heksetro og trolddom* (1971), 196–99; Svale Solheim, *Norsk sætertradisjon* (1952), 321–25.
>
> Collected by Knut Strompdal in Frei, Nordland (Norway).
> Printed in Strompdal, *Gamalt frå Helgeland* 1 (1929), 159.

39.2 To Bring a Troll Cat to Life

Say the following spell while dripping your own blood on the troll cat:

I give you blood,
Satan gives you power.
You shall run for me on earth,
I shall burn for you in hell.

You shall travel through forests and fields,
gathering milk and cream.

> According to af Klintberg, the first four lines of the formula represent the normal type, whereas the last two lines are additions specific to this variant.
>
> This formula explicitly states that the power of the witch derives from a contract with the devil. He will serve her in this life, but the witch will go to hell after death.
>
> See Uno Harva, "Bjärans klotform," *Rig* 10 (1927), 161–72.
>
> Collected in 1908 by Levi Johansson from Margareta Svensson in Nybo, Haverö parish, Medelpad (Sweden). Ms. in NM, HA: Övernaturliga Väsen. Printed in Bengt af Klintberg, *Svenska trollformler* (1965), 87.

39.3 Marte Holon

Some 70 to 80 years ago there was a witch in Holon. Her name was Marte, and she was one of the most notorious witches in all of South Fron. She had the Black Book and a troll cat.

A troll cat is gray and round like a ball of wool, and it rolls along the ground. It sucks milk from the cows and sneaks into the houses to steal cream. When the troll cat sucks itself too full, it slobbers all over, and the spilled cream turns to gray paw butter, which people also call troll cat vomit and troll cat butter. One can see it on the ground in the morning after a foggy night; it covers planks and logs in the fields where the troll cat has run during the night.

You can force the owner of a troll cat to reveal herself if you know how! You take a little of the troll cat butter, put it down a gun barrel, and close it up well. Then you place the barrel into the fire until it starts glowing, and the owner of the troll cat comes rushing in and is terribly thirsty. Have something ready for her to drink, and while she is drinking, you must hit her with something sharp to make her bleed. If you do not manage to draw blood, she will take revenge.

One time things were going badly with the cows at Tofte. There was no milk, and the cows were restless at night. Folks found troll cat vomit outside the barn, so it was easy to see what was happening. Hans Tofte said he would take care of it; he would burn the vomit. He collected some and stuffed it into the barrel of a gun, closing it up tightly. He got a man to go with him to the smithy. It was four o'clock in the morning. They made a fire in the forge, put the gun barrel in it, and pulled the bellows to get a good draught going. Before long they could hear noises coming from the barrel, it banged and whimpered and whistled, and the men were quite frightened. All of a sudden Marte Holon came into the smithy, her shirt hanging halfway off her shoulder. I guess she did not have time to put it on all the way. Sweat was dripping off her, and she asked for something to drink. They had collected their own piss into a horn, and they offered this to her. Then Hans quickly took off his left shoe and hit her across the mouth so that two teeth fell out and blood flowed.

It is not easy to say whether it was Marte herself or her double. But when she left, she flew through the air over Tofte valley. She was riding on a broomstick, and there was a trail of sparks coming from the broom.

This must be the truth, too, because my grandmother once met Marte, and she saw that Marte was missing two of her front teeth.

> The gelatinous substance of certain fast-growing fungi (fuligo septica), as well as the white foam left by the spittle bug, were often associated with the droppings of the troll cat.
>
> Since the witch was identified with her troll cat, heating the "vomit" would make her thirsty and force her to appear. Drawing the witch's blood broke her power.
>
> It seems risky to offer one's urine to a witch. Tradition, however, is rarely self-consistent. Also, offering urine as a drink can be seen as an insult, and insults often play a role in countermagic.
>
> See Svale Solheim, *Norsk sætertradisjon* (1952), 315–16.
>
> Collected by Edvard Grimstad in Fron, Oppland (Norway). Printed in Grimstad, *Etter gamalt. Folkeminne frå Gudbrandsdalen* 3 (1953), 60–61.

39.4 Shot with a Silver Button

I do not remember exactly where this happened, but it was on some farm where the cows would not give any milk. Somebody else was milking their cows, and because the folk there had often seen a hare running across the yard, they thought right away that it was someone who had changed shape. They tried shooting the hare but could not hit it.

So one day they cut a silver button into small pieces and loaded the rifle with them. They shot the hare and hit it, too, but it ran off nonetheless, limping on one leg.

The next day there was an old woman in town who suddenly took to bed and could not get up anymore. They accused her, saying that she could do witchcraft and had been milking their cows. She stayed lame all her days.

> Besides making the familiar from inanimate materials, the witch herself could take an animal shape to steal milk. Traditions of the milk hare dominate in Denmark and southern Sweden; in Norway stories of the witch taking on the shape of a cat are more common.
>
> Silver was considered a particularly powerful means of dealing with the demonic.
>
> See Bente G. Alver, *Heksetro og trolddom* (1971), 207–9; Jan Wall, *Tjuvmjölkande väsen* 2 (1978), 64.
>
> Collected by E. T. Kristensen from Erik Eriksen, Borum, Jylland (Denmark). Printed in Kristensen, *Danske sagn*, N.R. 6 (1936), 215.

39.5 The Carrier

Once there was a farmer in the eastern part of the country who went on horseback one morning to fetch his cows; they had been left out in the open overnight. When he found them, he saw that a carrier, gray in color, was hanging at the udder of his best cow and was sucking her dry.

The carrier darted away at the farmer's approach, and he chased it on horseback. But it ran straight past some mounds and jumped over others, until it got home. There were some people out in the field, and the carrier dashed under the skirts of the farmer's wife. The man who was chasing the carrier jumped off his horse and tied up the woman's skirts to just below the place where the carrier was. Then the woman was burned.

> In Iceland the familiar is referred to as *tilbera* (carrier) or *snakkur* (spindle). The *snakkur* was made from a dead man's rib, stolen wool, and communion wine.
>
> See J. Simpson, *Icelandic Folktales and Legends* (1972), 170–74.
>
> Collected by Jón Árnason from Jón Bjarnason, Breiðuvík (Iceland). Printed in Árnason, *Íslenzkar þjóðsögur og æfintýri* 1 (1862), 433. Reprinted in 1954.

40. The Witches' Sabbath

According to folk tradition, witches met the devil on Blåkollen (Blue Mountain), in churches or in other places to celebrate the sabbath. This belief had its origin in the witch trials on the continent, where such events were considered to be factual. Bente Alver has pointed out that the legendary tradition of the witches' sabbath in Norway contains little of the sexual perversity we find in continental protocols. Nor are the activities of the witches actual parodies of the Christian mass. Throughout Scandinavia the motif that dominates legends about the sabbath is that witches write their names in the devil's book, share a festive meal with him, and dance on the altar and pews.

See Bente G. Alver, *Heksetro og trolddom* (1971), 209–19; Will-Erich Peuckert, "Der Blocksberg," *Verborgenes Niedersachsen* (1960), 103–10.

40.1 Steinar Aase

Steinar Aase, who lived in Brunkeberg around 1700, heard people say that every Easter night witches came to the church to scrape rust and copper off the church bell. One night before Easter, he hid himself in the church to find out whether this rumor about the witches was true. He had two pieces of sod, one to stand on and one to put on his head, so that the witches would not be able to see him.

Toward midnight three women came in, each riding on a broomstick. They clambered on the pews, from one pew to the next, all the way up to the altar. There the witches started to scrape the candlestick, and then they climbed the tower to get to the bell. It seemed to Steinar that he recognized them, and he was so eager to get a good look that he did not hold on to the sod on his head, and it fell on the floor. Now it was all over for Steinar. When the witches caught sight of him, they surrounded him and tore at him as if they were going to eat him alive. Now he could plainly see who the three women were. One was his own mother, another was the wife of the minister at Kvitseid, and the third was a rich and respectable woman from Morgedal. They hissed and shouted at Steinar, and it looked as if he was going to get his fill of their fun! None was worse than his own mother. She was quite ready to kill him. She put a finger into each of his nostrils and hung him out of a peephole in the church tower. Steinar begged for mercy and promised that he would never tell a living soul about what he had seen. So they let him go.

Easter morning Steinar was back at the church. When the service was over and the people came outside, Steinar walked over to an old gravestone, kicked it, and said:

"Something happened to me last night, which I have solemnly promised not to reveal to a living soul, and I will keep my promise. But I can safely tell it to you, because you're nothing but a stone and can keep quiet like a stone."

Then he recounted everything, from beginning to end, so that the minister and his wife and the whole parish heard it.

"I knew that I was born of sinful blood, but I didn't know that my mother was a witch," he finished.

> The preferred dates for the witches' sabbath were the night before Easter, Midsummer Night (Saint John's Eve), and Valborg's Eve. The witches were usually reported to ride to the sabbath on broomsticks, on animals, and even on human beings changed into animals.
>
> Steinar becomes invisible by placing pieces of sod on his head and under his feet. Symbolically, then, he is underground, that is, dead.
>
> The majority of individuals sentenced for witchcraft in Scandinavia belonged to the lower social classes. In legendary tradition the tendency is reversed; members of the immediate family and respected women in the community are often identified as witches. This may constitute a form of social protest, even revenge, by the lower classes.
>
> See Bente G. Alver, *Heksetro og trolddom* (1971), 210–13.
> Legend type: ML 3050
> Collected by Kjetil A. Flatin in Seljord, Telemark (Norway).
> Printed in Flatin, *Tussar og trolldom* (1930), 84–85.

40.2 The Burning Mill

There was a farmer who owned a small mill. But every Easter eve, the mill burned down and nobody knew why. Finally the farmer hired a young man to keep watch at the mill on the night before Easter.

In the evening he hid himself in the mill. Early that night the wind started howling, and he heard voices outside the mill. Then the door flew open, and a great many women came riding in on broomsticks. Four of them carried a young girl on a calfskin; she was going to be a witch too. Behind the girl another woman carried a table and a chair, and she put them in the middle of the floor. Then one of them said:

"The Master hasn't come yet."

And another one said:

"What is taking him so long?"

Some more time passed, but still the Master did not come. Then the women began to get angry because they had so much to do that night.

Finally the wind started howling again and a misshapen figure entered, carrying a book under his arm. It was the Master. The women upbraided him for being so late, but he excused himself, saying that he had been busy helping a girl kill her child. Then he put the book on the table, opened it, and sitting down, asked whether there were any newcomers to enroll.

"Yes, there is one," answered the women.

The boy who was hiding in the mill funnel thought they were talking about him, and he thought it would be wise to make a run for it. When he jumped up, both he and the funnel fell right on the Master's book and the women. Now they all got scared and took to their heels with frightful screams. But the young woman who had not learned witchcraft yet could not escape. The others were in such a hurry, they left behind not only the girl but also the table, the chair, the calfskin, and the Master's book.

Now the book, the table, and the chair began to burn. The boy collected his wits; he covered his hands with the calfskin and threw the burning things out, thus saving the mill. He took the young woman with him for questioning. She confessed that she had recently married and had wanted to learn witchcraft. Four of her neighbors had brought her to the mill to be instructed by the Master.

They were all discovered and punished for their witchcraft.

> The motif of the witches' sabbath in combination with the burning mill is common throughout Scandinavia. Parallel legends often substitute trolls or other supernormal beings for the witches.
> Collected in 1894 by I. A. Björkström in Sibbå, Nyland (Finland). Printed in V. E. V. Wessman, *Sägner* 3.2 (1931), 477–78.

41. Magic Flight

Whereas the Finn messenger achieves magic flight by sending his *hug* from his body while lying in a trance (cf. nos. 10.1–10.3), the witch typically uses her own body for flight, or she rides on a broomstick or some other inanimate object, or on an animal, which is often a human being whose shape she has changed.

Popular variants of stories about magic flight involve someone trying to imitate the witch's flight but using the wrong formula, often with dire consequences, or someone tricking the witch and riding upon her instead of the other way around.

The witch's power of flight is a function of her pact with the devil.

41.1 The Serving Boy

There was a wealthy farm in Sibäck. People said that the mistress of the house was a witch and flew to the sabbath on Easter. The servant boy heard about it, and one Easter night he stayed home to watch her.

Toward midnight he saw his mistress get up. She poured some salve from a horn and rubbed it on herself while she mumbled:

"Up and down, but run into nowhere."

Then she flew up through the chimney.

Now the serving boy wanted to try. He took the horn, rubbed himself with the salve, smeared a few drops on the fireplace, and said:

"Up and down, but run into everywhere."

Right away he flew out through the chimney. But he kept crashing into things until he finally came to a mill somewhere between Sibäck and Pörtom and flew inside. There sat his mistress at the end of a big table. At the center of the table sat a gentleman dressed in black, writing in a big book.

When the serving boy came in, his mistress asked him how he got there.

"Well, he said, "I rubbed some salve on myself just like you did and said 'Up and down, but run into everywhere,' but I have been crashing into all kinds of things and now I'm black and blue all over."

"You should have said 'Into nowhere,' then you wouldn't have bumped into anything at all and would have traveled smoothly."

Now the gentleman in black asked the woman to write her name in the book. When she had done so, he asked the serving boy to do the same. But he said no and wanted to go home.

"Oh, you'll get home all right," said the gentleman. "There is a black horse outside. Just sit on it, and it will take you home."

The serving boy did as he was told, and right away he took off over forests and fields. At home he put the horse into the stable, as the gentleman had instructed him to do, leaving the saddle blanket on the horse. The sun was just rising. He went inside and asked his master to come out and see what a big and fine horse he had gotten on Easter night. When they entered the stable, the master told the boy to take the blanket off so that he could really see the horse. But as soon as the serving boy did this, his mistress appeared in the stall where the horse had been.

"Well, well," said the farmer, "so it's you."

"Yes," she said, "I've been out on Easter night."

Well, there was nothing more to be said about it.

> In a number of legends, the witch rides the serving boy in animal shape to the sabbath, but the boy tricks her into trading places on the way home. In the present narrative, by contrast, it is the devil himself who imposes the horse shape on the witch.
> Legend type: ML 3045.
> Collected in Petalax, Österbotten (Finland). Printed in *Finska studentkårens album tillegnadt Elias Lönnrot* (Helsingfors) 1882, 151–52. Reprinted in V. E. V. Wessman, *Sägner* 3.2 (1931), 487–88.

41.2 Seeing Witches Fly

People said that witches rode to Troms Church on Valborg's Eve. If you wanted to see them, you had to go to a crossroads and sit beneath a harrow with a piece of turf on your head.

A man from Lund near Horsens wanted to try it, so he got himself situated. And sure enough, he saw the witches fly on rake handles! But he could not keep quiet.

"Now I've seen that witches can really fly!" he said. He should not have uttered a sound. The witches grabbed him and dragged him over hill and dale. He did not regain consciousness until he woke up the next morning, lying in his own bed.

Valborg's Eve is the night before May 1, the day on which the mass of Saint Walburga was celebrated. Bonfires were lit to protect the animals from witches and other demonic forces.

By placing a piece of turf on his head, the man made himself invisible. (Cf. the commentary to no. 40.1.)

See Julius Ejdestam, *Årseldarnas samband med boskapsskötsel och åkerbruk i Sverige* (Uppsala, 1944), 40–91; Nils-Arvid Bringéus, *Årets festseder* (Stockholm, 1976), 156–62.

Collected in 1911 by E. T. Kristensen from S. P. Petersen, Gjedsø, Jylland (Denmark). Printed in Kristensen, *Danske sagn*, N.R. 6 (1936), 220.

41.3 *Riding the Minister's Wife*

Once there was a minister, a handsome and well-to-do man. He was newly married, at the time of this story, and had a beautiful young wife of whom he was particularly fond. She was in every way the most exceptional woman thereabouts. There was, however, one problem in the marriage, which the minister did not regard as so very minor: she disappeared every Christmas Eve, and no one knew what became of her. The minister questioned her about this over and over again, but she told him that it was none of his business. This was the only thing they disagreed about.

A vagrant came along, and he got work in the minister's stable. He was not much, with regard to size and strength, but people reckoned he knew more about this and that than other ordinary folk. Time passed without anything of interest happening until it was almost Christmas. But on the day before Christmas, this fellow was out in the barn currying and tending the minister's stall-fed horses. Before he knew it, the minister's wife slipped in and started a conversation with him about various things. And when he least expected it, she pulled a bridle out from under her apron and put it on him. There was so much magic power in the bridle that the man was forced to let the minister's wife get on his back, and he took right off—just like a bird. He traveled over mountains and valleys, cliffs and moraines. It seemed to him that he was traveling through dense fog. Finally, they came to a little house. There she dismounted and tied him to a hitching post attached to the wall of the house. The minister's wife went to the door and knocked on it. A man came out and greeted her warmly. He took her into the house with him. When they were gone, the man loosened the reins from the post, managed to work himself out of the bridle, and stuffed it under his shirt. Then he sneaked up on top of the house and looked through a hole in the thatched roof. He saw twelve women sitting at a table, so, counting the man, there were thirteen people in all. He recognized his mistress among them. He saw that the women had a great deal of respect for the man and were in the midst of telling him various things about their tricks and cunning. Among other things, the minister's wife told them about how she had ridden a living man there, and the master of the house was very impressed because it takes the most powerful witchcraft to ride a living man. He said that she excelled at witchery, "because I didn't know anyone could do that but me." The other women were all over the master, begging him to teach them this trick. He placed onto the table a book which was gray in color and was written with fire or fiery-colored letters. There was no other light in the room but the glow that came from the letters. Then the master of the house began to teach the women from this book, explaining its contents to them—and the man on the roof learned everything the man uttered.

It was getting close to daybreak, and the women said it was time to go. The instruction ended then, and each woman took out a glass and gave it to the master of the house. The man could see that each glass contained something reddish, which the master sipped before handing back the glass. Then they bid him fond farewell and left the house. He saw then that each woman had her own bridle and mount. One had a horse's leg, another a jawbone, another a shoulder blade, and so on. Each one took her mount and rode off. But the minister's wife, it must be told, could not find her mount anywhere. She looked around the house in a rage, and when she least expected it, the man jumped down from the roof and slipped the bridle onto her. Then he got on her back and headed for home. He had learned enough during the night to be able to steer the minister's wife in the direction he wanted to go. We heard nothing about their journey until they returned to the very same stable they had departed from. There the boy dismounted and tethered the minister's wife in a stall. Then he went into the house and told the news about where he had been and where the minister's wife had ended up and how it had all come about. Everyone was shocked—not least of all the minister himself. Then the minister's wife was interrogated. She finally confessed that she and eleven other ministers' wives had for several years attended a school of black magic and were taught witchcraft by the devil himself, and they had only one year of instruction left. She said the devil had stipulated that they pay their tuition with menstrual blood—

which had been the reddish stuff that the boy had seen in the glass containers. The minister's wife was then suitably rewarded for her evil ways.

> The witch's name and her blood were the means by which she bound herself to the devil. Menstrual blood was considered unclean and therefore dangerous. Menstrual blood also played a certain role in healing.
>
> See I. Reichborn-Kjennerud, *Vår gamle trolldomsmedisin* 1 (1927), 265; 2 (1933), 78–80.
>
> Collected by Jón Sigurðarson, Gautlönd (Iceland). Printed in Jón Árnason, *Íslenzkar þjóðsögur og æfintýri* 1 (1862), 440–41. Reprinted in new edition 1 (1954), 427–28.

41.4 Fastri Hopen

A witch by the name of Fastri Hopen once sailed on a millstone across Saltfjord near Kolvereid. She stuck a broom handle through the hole in the millstone.

On her way she passed someone she knew and shouted to him not to call her by name. The man was stupid enough to do what she asked. If he had called her, she would have sunk.

> A witch was known to possess the ability to sail on a millstone.
>
> The magical identification of the name with the person is common in folk belief throughout the world.
>
> See Wolfgang Aly, "Name," *Handwörterbuch des deutschen Aberglaubens* 6 (1934–35), columns 950–61.
>
> Collected by Knut Strompdal in Helgeland (Norway). Printed in Strompdal, *Gamalt frå Helgeland* (1929), 160.

42. The Witch's Daughter

Folk tradition suggests that the magic abilities of the witch were imparted through initiation and instruction, but they could also be passed on genetically. The presumably innocent child of the witch typically inherited the powers of her mother and was held responsible for them.

42.1 The Little Girl Who was a Witch

Some gypsies arrived at a farm in Hedmark and asked for night lodging. The farmer did not want to have anything to do with them and told them to leave. But they made a circle around the houses and conjured up a great many snakes.

If they were permitted to stay there that night, they would drive the snakes away from the farm again.

Oh, yes, they could stay.

But the farmer thought it best to keep an eye on the gypsies. Around midnight one of the tramps got up and opened the door.

"Chee, chee, into the cellar!" he said, and a huge blackbird flew out the door. Then the tramp laid down again.

The next morning things were missing from the cellar, and the farmer sent for the sheriff. He arrested all the gypsies. Now, I suppose, they must have done a lot of evil because they were sentenced to be bled to death. But a little girl was left behind, and she was sent to the minister and stayed there.

One time she went with the minister to the fields where the farmhands were working. There were seven horses on the job.

"Would you believe that I can make the horses stand still so that nobody can get them moving again?" she asked the minister.

Well, he wanted to see that! She took some rowan twigs that were growing on a tree and stuck them into the harness pins. Nobody could budge the horses until the girl removed the twigs.

"Can you do other things, too?" the minister asked.

"I can milk the fence post, if I want to," said the girl.

"Well, do it then."

She ran to get a small pail and a bucket, drilled a hole into the post with her knife, and thrust a pin into the hole. She put the pail underneath it, and milked the pin until the pail was full. Then she emptied it into the bucket and milked some more. But suddenly she stopped.

"I'd better stop now," she said.

"Milk some more!" said the minister.

"The cow is going to milk blood."

"Let me see," said the minister.

And the girl milked again until nothing but blood came. Then she stopped.

"If I go on, the cow will collapse."

"Go on milking," said the minister.

She milked again, but nothing more came out.

"Now the cow is dead," the girl said.

And the same afternoon, they found one of the cotter's cows dead. He got another cow from the minister. But they took the girl and bled her to death, too.

> Gypsies, like other strangers, were ascribed the power of witchcraft. They were often thought to have the ability to conjure snakes.
>
> There is no evidence in any Scandinavian trial protocols indicating that convicted witches were ever bled to death. The motif appears in legends only.
>
> Both the motif of binding the horses by magic and that of milking from a fence post, are well known in legends about witches. (Cf. nos. 38.1–38.2.)
>
> The rowan was generally believed to possess both protective and harmful power, particularly when it took root on another tree (*flog-rogn*).
>
> See Bente G. Alver, *Heksetro og trolddom* (1971), 193–95; Ove Arbo Høeg, *Planter og tradisjon* (1974), 607.
>
> Legend type: ML 3035.
>
> Collected by Sigurd Nergaard in Østerdalen, Hedmark (Norway). Printed in Nergaard, *Hulder og trollskap. Folkeminne fraa Østerdalen* 4 (1925), 164–65.

42.2 The White Snake

At a cotter's place in Seljord a long time ago, there lived a woman who knew all kinds of witchcraft. She had able teachers. All the Finns who drifted into the village stopped by her place and stayed with her for weeks. She was not feeding them for nothing, that big shot!

Once she found a white snake. It was a rare stroke of good luck to find that kind of snake; it has the power to heal all manner of sickness. When you boil a white snake, three stars appear in the brine. The first makes you wise and the second gives you second sight, but the third makes you mad, and it spins around like a wheel.

The woman boiled the snake in the usual manner. Then she went out to the cow shed to take care of her animals. But her daughter Margit was alone in the house. She saw the pot sitting there, and being a child, she thought that it was broth. She took a piece of bread, dipped it into the pot, and got hold of the star that gives you second sight. When she had eaten the bread, she could see right through solid walls.

She ran down to her mother in the shed and shouted happily:

"Now I can see the color of the calf Golden Rose is going to have!"

"Oh, heaven help me, child, you haven't touched the pot?" cried the mother. She knew how much Margit would suffer if she had second sight.

And Margit did suffer. She saw all the evil that happened around her in the village. A man drowned at Svinesodden, and Margit saw it. She was almost beside herself with terror, screaming and moaning that someone should go and help the man.

She did not get any sleep night or day because of all the things she saw. In the end she nearly lost her mind. But luckily one of the Finns came to the farm. When she heard what was the matter with the girl, she took second sight from her and scattered it to the four winds.

> The white snake has been looked upon as a purely mythical motif but also as referring to a rare type of snake (coronella austriaca) found in southern Scandinavia. The motif has found literary application as far back as Eddic tradition, for example, in the story of Sigurd the dragon slayer, who gains the power to understand the speech of birds by drinking the blood of the snake. In folk tradition it is the broth that carries the magic power. The ability to see the unborn calf is the motif most frequently encountered.
>
> See I. Reichborn-Kjennerud, *Vår gamle trolldomsmedisin* 4 (1944), 177–79.
>
> Legend type: ML 3030.
>
> Collected in 1904 by D. Gadeholt from Anlaug Torsdatter Syftestad in Seljord, Telemark (Norway). Printed in Reidar Th. Christiansen, *Norske sagn* (1938), 66–67.

43. Social Sanction and Persecution

The most severe public reaction to the witch was to put her on trial for heresy and other violations of the law. In some instances this led to the witch's execution by burning at the stake. Nevertheless, relatively few individuals were ever burned in Scandinavia, in contrast to continental Europe where hundreds of thousands were executed. On the basis of the available legal documents, Bente G. Alver has determined that some 750 individuals, one-sixth of them men, were put on trial in Norway, and about one-fourth of this number were actually burned.

But short of legal persecution people tended to respond to the witch and her activities with a mixture of fear and loathing. She tended to become isolated and cut off from the community. The minister would deny her access to the holy rites of the church, or neighbors would vent their fear in physical abuse.

Even today stories circulate about individuals suspected of witchcraft. In recent tradition, however, the storytellers tend to question the evidence used to prove that someone is a witch.

See Bente G. Alver, *Heksetro og trolddom* (1971), 63–80.

43.1 The Trial of Quive Baardsen

On May 9, 1627, court was in session at Kassevog in the presence of bailiff Niels Knudsen and jury.

The bailiff called on a Finn by the name of Quive Baardsen and asked him what he did the time he made sailing wind for Niels Jonsen in Rognsund two years before. Then the latter answered and confessed that on the eighth day before All Saints Day, during the said year, the aforesaid Niels came to him in Rognsund and asked that he make sailing wind for him to get to Kassevog, saying that he would pay him when he came back.

He answered, yes, took off his right shoe, and washed his bare foot in the sea while the water was quiet and said:

"Wind to land! Wind to land!"

And then they got favorable sailing wind. And he asked them not to set too much sail before they passed Klubbenes; after that they could set as much sail as the boat would tolerate.

Soon thereafter, the Saturday before All Saints Day, Trine, the wife of Oluf Ørensen, came to him and asked him to make sailing wind so that her husband, who was with Niels Jonsen, could come home soon. And she promised to give him a jug of beer for his trouble.

He answered, yes, took a young pig, threw it into the sea, and said:

"Wind to sea! Wind to sea!"

But the pig squirmed too much in the sun, and the wind became too strong. Then he said to Trine:

"God have mercy on them! I am afraid that they have taken off too early and that the wind is too strong. If they took off at the beginning of the storm, may God have mercy, or they will not return."

The aforementioned Niels Jonsen, Oluf Ørensen, and three of Jensen's hired hands from Kasvog remained in that storm.

Then the bailiff asked if he had made sailing wind other times. He answered:

"Yes, I have often made wind for people, and a quarter of a year ago I made wind for a Hiemland ship lying before Kareken because they requested that I make wind for them. So I washed my foot, as I said before, and got a gentle southern wind."

Furthermore the bailiff asked whether he knew how to do sorcery. He answered that he had never taken anything for his runic spells. The bailiff asked him what the rune spells were.

"When one wants to cast rune spells, one takes a rune drum; it is made of pine root and covered with ox skin or buckskin. Then one uses a piece of wood as a handle under the drum, and hooves from every kind of animal in this country are hung around the drum. And nine lines are painted on the drum with alder bark, which is used to paint the seats of benches. The first line represents their god, the second the sun, and the third the moon, and then they mark all kinds of animals that can bring them luck or inflict harm on their enemies. And when two magicians want to test whose art is the strongest, they paint two ox reindeer on the drum, which butt each other with their horns. Whichever one turns out to be the strongest, his master is strongest and his art is best.

And when they want to ask their apostle something, they take some small pieces of copper and hang them on the wings of a copper bird, which they place on the drum. Then they beat it with a horn hammer lined with beaver skin. The bird hops around on the drum and finally stops on one of the lines. Then his master knows immediately what the answer is. And to protect the master or whoever else may be in the hut from accident, they beat the drum with the hammer. He whose bird falls from the drum will not live long.

Then he was asked how long ago he learned these things. He answered that when he was first introduced to such things he was only a little boy.

He was also asked how often he had been involved in beating such a drum. He answered that once many magicians came together to beat the drum to see whose art was strongest.

And he was also asked who taught him to make wind. He said:

"A Finn, now dead, by the name of Laurits Qoern, before the time of the war."

At the following court session he was condemned to death by fire and stake.

> The Lapp Quive Baardsen was clearly a specialist in making sail-
> ing wind by magic. His services were sought by the community.
> From the trial transcript, it appears that when his practice result-
> ed in the death of some of his clients, however, he was legally
> held responsible.
>
> Quive Baardsen describes how the Lapps used their rune
> drums to put themselves into trances in which to communicate
> with the spirit world. In the eyes of the court, these practices
> must have seemed heretical; they were reason enough to condemn
> the accused to death.
>
> See Bente G. Alver, *Heksetro og trolddom* (1971), 116–19.
>
> The original protocol of the trial of Quive Baardsen is found
> in manuscript form in the Statsarkiv, Trondheim (*Vardöhus Lens
> Justitsprotokol*). Printed in Hulda Rutberg, *Häxprocesser i norska Finn-
> marken* (1918), 25–27. Reprinted in Alver, *Heksetro og trolddom*
> (1971), 116–19.

43.2 Ingerid Erik's Daughter Kaaljørju

One evening Ingerid went to Per Finnøy and asked him for lodging, but Per refused. Just then Per's wife came out of the storehouse
with a cup of milk in her hand. Ingerid cast a spell, and Per's wife
jumped straight into the water and drowned before anyone could
stop her.

Per then sued Ingerid in court. He knew beforehand that there was
little hope of getting a judgment against this powerful woman. So he
went to her step-daughter and asked for advice.

On the day of the trial, when the matter was to be brought to
judgment, Per arrived early. He had drilled a hole through the
paneled ceiling over the door of the courtroom so that he could lie up
there unseen and look down at the people coming in. The step-
daughter, who was serving at the minister's, had told him that if he
managed to look at Ingerid first, when she entered the courtroom, he
would win the case. But if she saw him first, she would go free.

Per had not been lying up there above the ceiling for long, when
Ingerid entered, stylishly dressed. But at that very moment, she let
out an ugly scream and jumped. Per had seen her first. She had felt it
and knew well that there was no hope for her.

Per climbed down, and the court came to order. Ingerid was humble and begged for a settlement, but Per did not give in. Finally, she promised that if he let her go, she would bring Per's wife back, and he could keep her until he died himself.

"No," said Per, "I don't want my wife to suffer death twice, even if you have the power to do it. Anyway, you would probably give me the devil in the shape of my wife."

The trial ended with Ingerid being pronounced a witch and sentenced to burn at the stake. The judgment took place in Skien, and Ingerid sat in prison there until the sentence was executed. A stake was prepared near the monastery grounds, and along with the highest judges and jurors, a tremendous crowd gathered to watch. Ingerid was led out. She was blindfolded, and her hands and feet were bound, yet it was only with great difficulty that they got her up on the stake. But the fire would not touch her! It simply deflected to each side and did not come near her.

The judges did not know what to do. Three times they took her down from the stake and searched her, looking for some sorcery that might be protecting her against the fire.

Finally the judges asked Ingerid's step-daughter why she would not burn.

"She won't die by fire but she will by powder," said the girl.

At last, on the third day, they found a needle hidden in the thick flesh at the small of her back. As long as she had iron or steel on her, the fire would not touch her. They pulled the needle out, and then she asked that they remove the blindfold a little so that she might look toward the town. They were about to do it, but there were some who warned against it, so they did not dare. Then she asked to be allowed to look toward the woods and mountains beyond Porsgrunn River. The judges thought there could be no danger in that and pulled the blindfold aside a little bit on one eye. She had barely glanced over there, when a forest fire broke out. It crackled and burned in the tree tops as far as her eye could reach. They blindfolded her again and laid her on the stake, and the sentence was finally executed.

> Ingerid Eirik's Daughter Kaaljørju was burned as a witch at Klostergjorde, Skien, in 1661. According to this legend, she was brought to trial because she had caused the drowning of Per's wife.
>
> The narrative gives us two examples of the power of the eye to spellbind. Already in *Malleus Maleficarum*, the judges were ad-

vised to have the accused carried into the courtroom back first to neutralize her evil eye by looking at her first.

Iron protects against the power of the demonic. In this instance, however, the witch uses iron against fire.

See Bente G. Alver, *Heksetro og trolddom* (1971), 70.

Collected by Kjetil A. Flatin in Seljord, Telemark (Norway). Printed in Flatin, *Tussar og trolldom* (1930), 82–83.

43.3 Hilde Oluf's Daughter Blindheim

When I was a young boy my mother told me about an intelligent and energetic woman living at Blindheim in Vigra, who was almost burned as a witch. Later I dug through the trial transcripts from that period and found out the whole story.

The trial took place at Tennfjord in Vatne in 1667. Among the members of the jury were the following men from Vigra: Knut Rolnes, Oluf Rolnes, Jon Rørvik, Anders Rørvik, Eirik Synes, and Oluf Rørvik.

The accused was Hilde Oluf's Daughter Blindheim who had been reported by her neighbor Tore Oluf's Son Blindheim, for witchcraft.* The accusation consisted of the following:

1) Hilde had "bewitched" Tore's fishing gear so that he did not catch any fish.

2) She had conjured one of Tore's cows away from the herd so that the animal fell into a hole in a bog and drowned.

3) She had used witchcraft to heal a cow that had been near death on Rørvik.

Many witnesses were called. All of them were quite sure that Hilde served the Evil One and that Old Nick was helping her.

The only one who had some doubts was the judge. During the investigation it came out that the trouble started at a Christmas party. Both Hilde and Tore were there. They came to a heated exchange of words. Finally Hilde said that if she had her way, Tore would have little luck fishing the next spring. And it happened as Hilde had wished: Tore caught very few fish that season. The following spring, Tore lost a cow. The folks combed the area but could not find the cow. So they asked Hilde.

"Have you looked at Kolva?" she asked.

Kolva is a large bog on the other side of the mountain, near Rørvik. No, they had not done that.

"I wonder if the cow isn't there," she said.

They took off to look. Sure enough, there lay the cow in a hole in the bog.

The next year, during Lent, a man from Rørvik asked Hilde to take a look at a cow that recently had calved and now seemed critically ill. It was his best cow, too. Well, Hilde went with him. But when she got to Rørvik, there was a crowd of people gaping at the animal.

"She was lying there with outstretched neck and legs," said one of the witnesses.

"Yes, and her eyes were almost like those of a dead animal," said another.

Hilde chased the whole bunch out of the cow shed. She took the cow out of the yoke and moved her out onto the floor, which she covered with straw. Then she began to stretch and massage the udder and hind quarter of the cow, and she gave her something warm to drink. The cow responded immediately, and after a while, she got up and was led back into her stall.

One boy had the courage to climb up on the wall of the cow shed and peek in through a hole to see what Hilde was doing. He saw a black cat sitting on her shoulder while she was working with the animal. The cat was spitting now and then, and fire came from her mouth, said the boy.

This final testimony was the most serious for Hilde. Nevertheless, the judge — in "great doubt" — decided that she should be acquitted.

But most of the people then, and for a long time afterward, steadfastly believed that Hilde really was a witch.

> *People living on the same farm usually had the same surname. There is no indication that Tore Oluf's Son Blindheim was the brother of the accused.
>
> The text is not a legend but Martin Bjørndal's account of the trial of Hilde Oluf's Daughter Blindheim. The case provides an example of a person being subjected to persecution precisely because she is above average in intelligence and initiative.
>
> Printed in Martin Bjørndal, *Segn og tru. Folkeminne frå Møre* (1949), 22–24.

43.4 Two Witches

During my childhood there lived in Tise two very old women whom the minister and some other folks considered pious and God-fearing. But most of the villagers thought of them as nasty witches. They attended church regularly, but when they got too old to walk, the farmers had to take turns driving them. Most of the time, they were transported in a wheelbarrow or handcart, and some folks found them to be as light as feathers, while others found them to be as heavy as lead. People noticed that it was always their friends who thought of the two women as light. And, of course, that reinforced their belief that the women must be witches. But it was hard to find proof.

Finally they were brought to Junget Manor to be interrogated. But that did not lead to anything because the women denied that they knew the least bit about witchcraft. They were retained at the manor under strict supervision. A tutor came every day to read to them and instruct them in the true faith.

It happened that one day he got into an argument with one of them, and he kicked her in the face with his boot until the blood flowed. But the other woman said that he had better leave, or else it would go hard with him. This threat frightened the tutor and he ran up to his room, which was right above theirs. He had drilled a hole in the floor of his room so he could keep an eye on them without being noticed. He lay down there and looked.

After a while he saw a tiny gray man come in and busy himself with the women. The tutor knew right away that it was the devil himself, and now he no longer doubted that they were witches.

During the time the women sat captive at the manor, the owner became seriously ill several times. He sent a messenger for the minister, but by the time he reached the manor, the man was always well again. Then one day the nobleman became deathly ill. A wagon was sent for the minister, but that time too the sickness passed before the minister got to the manor. So they sent another messenger on horseback to tell him that he did not need to come because the man had gotten well again. When the minister got the message, he became rather impatient and exclaimed:

"To hell with it."

He turned around and drove home. But the nobleman died shortly thereafter, because when the minister had said those words, the witches had gained power over him and had used the opportunity to kill him.

Now the case against the witches was taken up in earnest, and even though the women refused to confess, they were sentenced to burn for their witchcraft. A stake was erected on Raven's Hill on Nørgård Field, and many people came to watch. The man who told me about it was ten or twelve at the time. He was there too.

They used good dry peat and firewood to make the pyre. But they could not get it to burn. So they sent for the minister, who told them that a little gray man sat between the two witches on the pyre. That was the reason why it would not burn, but he did not know how to chase him away. They were forced to take the witches down from the stake once more, and they brought them to a nearby farm for the night. But it did not go any better the next day. None of the ministers whom they asked for help could chase the little man away. Finally, on the third or fourth day, they got a minister who was so experienced in the black arts that he could drive the little man out. He was one of the few who had passed the entire course at the Black School. He had barely finished exorcising the little man when the pyre exploded into fire and the two witches were burned.

They were the last ones to be burned in that area. But still there were many around there who were reputed to be able to do witchcraft, and people were afraid of making them angry.

> The narrator of this story seems to sympathize with the two women. He suggests indirectly that the evidence against them is far from conclusive. Perhaps the story reflects the community's wish to be rid of two individuals who have become a burden.
>
> The reason that the tutor kicks one of the women in the face and draws blood may be related to the belief that making a witch bleed breaks her power. (Cf. no. 39.3.)
>
> The motif of the devil taking the shape of a little gray man is common in Danish tradition.
>
> Collected by J. P. Bønding from an unnamed 80-year-old man in Tise parish, Jylland (Denmark). Printed in E. T. Kristensen, *Danske sagn*, N.R. 6 (1936), 312–14.

43.5 The Witch Who Wanted to Take Holy Communion

Pastor Schytt retired from Fjotland parish in 1835. During the time he was minister there, a woman came from Veggjeland farm and wanted to take holy communion. But when the minister got near her with the chalice, he pushed her away, saying that she had no business being there.

Bernt Spillebrokk was deacon at the church. He asked what right the minister had to do this. The minister replied:

"Indeed I have the right because she is a witch."

Then Bernt asked what proof the minister had. He answered that when he came to the woman with the chalice, the wine rotated counterclockwise.

> Witches profaned the holy bread and wine and were therefore excluded from taking communion. The communal bread and wine were generally believed to possess magical power that could be used for various purposes, not only by witches. But the church considered any such use of the sacred elements to be a grave sin.
>
> See Oskar Rühle, "Abendmahl," *Handwörterbuch des deutschen Aberglaubens* 1 (1927), columns 42–55.
>
> Collected by Peter Lunde in Vest-Agder (Norway). Printed in Lunde, *Kynnehuset. Vestegdske folkeminne* (1924), 74.

43.6 Mette Bundet

On so-called Louse Hill, a little ways east of Dreslette Church, lies a house called Hill House. There, some two hundred years ago, lived a notorious witch by the name of Mette Bundet. She bore a grudge against a farmer whose name was Hans Pedersen and who was also a smith.

When Hans set about building a smithy on his farm, she said that he would not get much joy from it. But he built the smithy anyway. Shortly thereafter, he became seriously ill. He believed that Mette had caused this by casting a spell on him. He consulted a wise man who rid him of the sickness. But he gave Hans the advice that whenever he met the witch, he should greet her first. One morning they ran into each other, but she shouted from a long way off:

"Good morning, Hans."

Right away he got sick once more, and he neither got well nor ever worked in the smithy again.

One day a man walked down by Louse Hill and saw an egg rolling along the path. He hit it with his stick and tried stepping on it and finally squashed it to bits. This happened right outside Mette's house. She lay inside shouting and screaming in pain.

A farmer in the village by the name of Ole Hansen had much bad luck with his animals, and he believed that it was Mette's fault. One time when he met her on the road, he grabbed her and hit her until she bled from her nose and mouth.

> Here we encounter the underlying belief that the person speaking first has power over the other. (Cf. no. 43.2.)

The egg must be considered a demonic being identified with the witch herself. This is parallel to traditions about the witch taking the shape of the so-called troll cat or milk rabbit. (Cf. nos. 39.1–39.3.)

Collected by E. T. Kristensen from A. Jensen, Dreslette parish, Jylland (Denmark). Printed in Kristensen, *Danske sagn*, N.R. 6 (1936), 197.

PART V
The Invisible Folk

Part V illustration: "One day the king of Denmark and Sweden lost his way in the woods and came upon a hut belonging to the forest sprites." Olaus Magnus, *Historia de Gentibus Septentrionalibus* (History of the Northern People, 1555), book 3, chapter 10.

here are widespread traditions in Scandinavia about preternatural beings of various kinds. Although they are invisible, from time to time they appear to ordinary people, and when they do, they are in human shape. The "invisible folk" constitute quite heterogeneous groupings in the different geographical areas of Scandinavia and are called by a variety of names.

See Bengt Holbek and Iørn Piø, *Fabeldyr og sagnfolk* (1967); Bengt af Klintberg, *Svenska folksägner* (1972), 20–47; Åke Hultkrantz, ed., *The Supernatural Owners of Nature* (1961).

44. Origin and Hope for Salvation

Two questions raised in folk tradition concerning the invisible folk are how they were created and how they relate to the prospect of divine salvation.

See Katherine Briggs, *The Vanishing People* (1978), 27–38.

44.1 The Origin of the **Huldre** Folk

When Our Lord chased Adam and Eve from paradise, they did not have much cause for joy. And yet, they loved each other, got along well, and produced a lot of children.

One day Our Lord told Eve that He wanted to see her children. Eve thought it out of place to show all her children to Our Lord; she was ashamed that they had quite so many. So she hid half of them. The rest she showed to Our Lord when He arrived.

He looked at the children and praised them because they were beautiful, and He said as much to Eve.

"But tell me," He said, "are these all your children?"

"Yes, they are," said Eve.

"You don't have any others?"

"No, you see here all the children Adam and I have," she said.

She thought there were quite enough of them, she said.

"Well, yes," said Our Lord. "Let those who are hidden become *huldre*."

This legend explaining the origin of the *huldre* and similar beings is widespread in Europe. Another explanation found occasionally is that the *huldre* are descended from Adam's first wife, Lillith.

Because this narrative contains biblical motifs, it is at times classified as a religious folktale (AT 758) rather than as a legend.

See Katherine Briggs, *The Vanishing People* (1978), 30–31; Gunnar Granberg, *Skogsrået* (1935), 163–67.

Collected by Torkell Mauland from O. A. Lindal, Nærbø, Rogaland (Norway). Printed in Mauland, *Folkeminne fraa Rogaland* 1 (1928), 71.

44.2 The Origin of the Invisible Folk

When Our Lord expelled the fallen angels from heaven, they fell on the earth and became the troll folk we know. Some fell on the roof tops and became *nisse*; some fell in the water and became water sprites; some fell on the hills and became the hill folk; and some fell into the moors and became elves.

The belief that the various invisible folk are descendants of the fallen angels can be found not only in folk tradition but also in medieval theology. By finding a place for them within the framework of church-approved dogma, pre-Christian belief was assimilated into the biblical worldview.

See K. Beth, "Engel," *Handwörterbuch des deutschen Aberglaubens* 2 (1929–30), columns 826–36; Alfus Rosenberg, *Engel und Dämonen. Gestaltwandel eines Urbildes* (1967); Katherine Briggs, *The Vanishing People* (1978), 30–31.

Collected by E. T. Kristensen from M. Hansen, Hjallesø, Jylland (Denmark). Printed in Kristensen, *Danske sagn* 1 (1892), 3.

44.3 The Mound Folk Hope for Salvation

Jonskør is the name of the mountain pasture in Kasa and Strønd in Øye. Many people have seen and heard the mound folk there.

Once, a long, long time ago, a man from Kasa went to the mountains to look for his horses. He searched for a long time. Finally he came to a large rock. While he stood there, looking around for the animals, he clearly heard someone singing and praying inside the rock.

Now this man from Kasa was anything but godly. When he had been standing there listening for a while, he got mad and shouted:

"You're not going to find salvation no matter how much you sing and pray!"

With that he ran away from the church of the mound folk — that is what it was. But since that day, the man from Kasa got more trouble than he bargained for. Wherever he went, he thought that someone was following him, whimpering. He never had any peace.

One day the man went back to Jonskør to the same rock in which he had heard the praying and singing. Now he shouted at the rock:

"Yes, you'll find salvation if you sing and pray!"

After that day the man from Kasa was left in peace.

> The legend expresses the folk's widespread ambivalence concerning the *huldre*'s chances to find salvation. People were simply not sure whether the invisible folk were included in the divine plan for salvation. The usual pattern in this legend type is that the person first denies the possibility of the *huldre*'s salvation, but then feels sorry for them, is admonished by a minister, or witnesses a miracle which changes his or her mind.
>
> See R. T. Christiansen, "Gaelic and Norse Folklore," *Folk-Liv* (1938), 330–31.
>
> Legend type: ML 5050.
>
> Collected by Knut Hermundstad from Ingebjørg Larsdatter Øydgarden in Vang, Oppland (Norway). Printed in Hermundstad, *I kveldseta. Gamal Valdreskultur* 6 (1955), 138–39.

45. The Dangerous Encounter

The invisible folk were often considered demonic beings. Encountering them could be quite dangerous. If a child was retarded or sickly, for example, it was believed that the invisible folk had exchanged the healthy and normal human child for one of their own. Belief in the changeling is worldwide, and in Scandinavia it can be traced back to pre-Christian times.

It was also dangerous for adults to cross paths with the invisible folk. A person who disappeared or suddenly suffered from some mental disorder was often believed to have been "taken into the mountain" by a preternatural being.

> On the changeling, see Svale Solheim, "Byting," *KLMN* 2 (1957), columns 452–56; J. S. Møller, *Moder og barn* (1940), 233–78; Lily Weiser-Aall, *Svangerskap og fødsel* (1968), 13–14; Gisela Pi-aschewski, *Der Wechselbalg* (1935); Katherine Briggs, *The Vanishing*

People (1978), 93–103; Ilmar Arens and Bengt af Klintberg, "Bortbytingssägner i en gotländsk dombok från 1690," *Rig* (1979), 89–97.

On being "taken into the mountain," see Svale Solheim, *Norsk sætertradisjon* 340–46, 473–87; Katherine Briggs, *The Vanishing People* (1978), 104–17; Bengt Holbek and Iørn Piø, *Fabeldyr og sagnfolk* (1967), 111–20; H. F. Feilberg, *Bjærgtagen* (1910).

45.1 The Changeling

A woman was put into confinement. Then some troll folk came and exchanged her newborn child for one of theirs. When the woman woke up, she realized what had happened, and she told the serving girls to put the child out on the garbage heap.

Having done that her own child suddenly lay there, swaddled in the same way it had been in the cradle.

When it was born, she had made the sign of the cross on its forehead.

Collected by E. T. Kristensen from Ane Margarete Hansen, Havlund, Ølgod, Jylland (Denmark). Printed in Kristensen, *Danske sagn* 1 (1892), 297.

45.2 The Unbaptized Child

Once, in a house where a child had just been born, the midwife lay down on the bed with the mother, who held the child in her arms. The other women rested on a second bed. Everybody fell asleep immediately because they had been awake for a long time. But the mother, who probably was not sleeping as soundly as the rest of them, woke up feeling something move. To her horror she discovered that the child was gone. Looking around, she saw an elf woman sitting on the threshold, holding the child. She was trying to throw her leg over the threshold. You see, the elf woman was so short that this was the only way for her to get over it.

But the mother let out a loud scream and shouted:

"May Jesus forbid you!"

Then the elf woman let go of the child and disappeared. The mother jumped out of bed to retrieve her child, but the midwife and the other women got so scared they did not know what to do. The father did not hesitate for a moment. He fetched the minister, and the child was baptized right away.

As long as the child was not baptized, it was in danger of being abducted by the invisible folk. There are various explanations for why they wanted human children, for example, they wanted "fresh blood" or they considered human children more beautiful than their own. Placing steel, silver, or a hymnbook in the cradle would protect the child. It was believed that someone should always hold watch over the child, while burning a candle.

See J. S. Møller, *Moder og barn* (1940), 264–78.

Collected by E. T. Kristensen from Lars Dybdahl, Ty, Jylland (Denmark). Printed in Kristensen, *Danske sagn* 1 (1892), 294–95.

45.3 Burning the Changeling

In Skramgården, Fyn, there was a changeling who would not utter a word.

One morning the serving girl got up very early to do the milking, and she heard someone shout:

"Come Pinds! Come Pands!"

But when the girl came back to the house and told everybody what she had heard, the changeling suddenly exclaimed:

"That's my mother!"

The folks there were very surprised to hear it speak. But then the woman said:

"If she's your mother, you're going to burn!"

They fired up the oven and picked up the changeling, pretending they were going to throw it into the fire. Immediately its real mother appeared with the child she had stolen. Turning to the woman, she said:

"I have never treated your baby the way you treat mine!"

Then she took her own child and disappeared.

> If a child did not learn to talk, people concluded that it was a changeling refusing to speak because it did not want to be discovered. Threatening to burn the changeling would make the preternatural appear to reclaim it and to return the human child.
>
> Collected at Sødinge school, Ringe, Fyn (Denmark). Printed in E. T. Kristensen, *Danske sagn* 1 (1892), 307–8.

45.4 The Old Changeling

On a farm by the woods around Kvikne, there lived a man who was so old that no one in the village remembered him ever being any younger. The older villagers had heard from the old folks before them that nobody had ever seen him anywhere but in his armchair by the fire, nodding his head. They did not care much for the fellow, which was understandable because he was always cross and sulky, and it was not possible to get a proper answer from him. There had to be something strange about that old fellow because he never died.

So they went to see a wise man and asked for advice on how they might help this poor old body leave the world. The answer they received was that they should make him tell how old he was. Then he would die. Oh, yes, they tried. They asked the fellow in every possible way about his age. But he never gave them a straight answer, only whimpered and talked incoherently.

So they went back to the wise man and asked how they might get a real answer out of him. He said they had to try another tack. They should pretend that they were getting ready to brew. First they were to take a chicken egg and cut it in half. One half of the shell was to be used as a brewing vat, the other as a tub for the mash. Once they had done this, they were to wait and see what happened.

Well, they started their preparations as if they were getting ready for a great feast. They cut the eggshell to use the two halves for the brewing. Suddenly the old fellow by the fireplace woke up and burst into laughter:

"Now I've been around long enough to see Seven Miles Forest burn down and grow up again seven times, but never before have I seen beer brewed in an eggshell!"

Then a voice shouted through the wall:

"Are you through?"

"Yes," answered the old fellow.

And when they looked for him, he was gone. All that was left of him were some decayed bones lying in something like ashes in his chair.

An idea often found in legends about the changeling is that they are very old. One could get rid of them only by revealing their age, usually by tricking them into responding by confronting them with some unexpected situation. The motif of brewing in an eggshell is a favorite one in this connection.

See Ilmar Arens and Bengt af Klintberg, "Bortbytingssägner i en gotländsk dombok från 1690," *Rig* (1979), 93–95; Gisela Piaschewski, *Der Wechselbalg* (1935), 93; Robert Wildhaber, "Die Eierschalen in europäischem Glauben und Brauch," *Acta Ethnographica Academiae Scientiarum Hungaricae* 19 (1970), 435–57.

Legend type: ML 5085.

Collected by Sigurd Nergaard in Østerdalen, Hedmark (Norway). Printed in Nergaard, *Hulder og trollskap. Folkeminne fraa Østerdalen* 4 (1925), 227–28.

45.5 Where Are You Going, Killkrack?

Källmo is the name of a farm in the southern part of our parish. Once, a woman gave birth there. It was customary to place steel in the cradle of the newborn child, but this time they forgot.

Well, the mother was alone in her bed and the child in its cradle. All the others were gone. A beautiful woman appeared, and she took the child and put another in its place. It was a boy, big and coarse. They said it was a changeling because it never learned to talk.

A wise man advised them to take the changeling to the church and have the minister baptize it. On their way to the church, they crossed over Klippkrön, which is a nearby hill. Then they heard someone shouting from Kummel-Hill, a little ways off:

"Where are you going, Killkrack?"

"I'm going to church to become a better person," answered the changeling, who had never talked before.

Then they turned around, and they never did bring it to the church.

A Finn woman told them to put the changeling on the floor and sweep three Thursday nights in a row. The third Thursday they were to take the changeling and the sweepings and place them out on the garbage heap. They did this, and after a short while, the beautiful woman reappeared, holding their child. She put it in the cradle and took her own back.

"Here is your baby," she said, "I never treated it as badly as you've treated mine."

> This legend is found mostly in southern Sweden and Denmark. But it seems to have originated in Germany. The name Killkrack derives from the German word "Kielkropf," meaning cretin or deformed child.
>
> According to legendary tradition, baptizing the changeling or giving it holy communion would make it disappear. At other times it is implied that baptism would transform the changeling into a Christian so that it could be saved. However, something always interferes, and the baptism is never carried out.

See Bengt af Klintberg, *Svenska folksägner* (1972), 314; J. S. Møller, *Moder og barn* (1940), 258–60; Leander Petzoldt, *Deutsche Volkssagen* (1970), 247.

Collected by Maja Ericson in Lungesund, Värmland (Sweden). Printed in Carl-Martin Bergstrand, *Värmlands sägner* (1948), 81–82.

45.6 Taken into the Mountain

Once a herding girl disappeared in the summer pasture on Vetle Mountain in Dovre. She had been taken into the mountain.

They rang the church bells for her, and the girl returned. For a while she seemed rather strange, but gradually she recovered and became like other people once more.

> The expression "taken into the mountain" could refer to any sudden psychological change in a person. The change is usually associated with a traumatic experience such as getting lost on a mountain or in a forest. Ringing church bells was believed to force the invisible folk to release their captive.
>
> See Bengt Holbek and Iørn Piø, *Fabeldyr og sagnfolk* (1967), 111–20; Svale Solheim, *Norsk sætertradisjon* (1952), 473–87.
>
> Collected by Edvard Grimstad in Dovre, Oppland (Norway). Printed in Grimstad, *Etter gamalt. Folkeminne frå Gudbrandsdalen* 2 (1948), 82.

45.7 Dancing with the Elves

A boy named Jens Bovens was herding in the woods once, when he came to a place called the Dead Elves.

He did not return home with the cows by noontime. They went out looking for him, and when they found him, he was quite out of his mind. The elf folk had danced with him, and from that time, he grew no more. He never became any taller than a small boy.

> The invisible folk most frequently referred to in Danish tradition are the elves. They play a lesser role in other parts of Scandinavia. The elves were generally feared because they struck humans with sickness, as reflected in the term "elf shot" (Danish, *elveskud*, Norwegian, *alvskot*, Icelandic, *álfabruni*). The earliest known description of the elves dancing is found in Olaus Magnus's *History of the Nordic People* (1555). The dance of the elves is often imagined as a ring dance, based on the observation of certain fungi (marasmius

oreades) that typically grow in a circle. In English folk tradition, this is called a fairy ring.

See Bengt Holbek and Iørn Piø, *Fabeldyr og sagnfolk* (1967), 135–36; Nils Lid, *Trolldom* (1950), 1–36.

Collected by E. T. Kristensen from Jens Pedersen, Jævngyde, Jylland (Denmark). Printed in Kristensen, *Danske sagn* 2 (1893), 26.

45.8 The Boy Who Was Lured by the Elves

Once the folks from a nearby farm went to the moor to make hay. When evening came they were missing a half-grown boy named Niels. He was a little retarded. They thought that he must have gone home already, but when they did not find him there, they returned to the moor and looked and called for him. They heard a fine voice calling, now here, now there:

"Niels! Niels!"

And Niels, answering:

"Here I am!"

They followed the voice, but they could not find Niels. The same voice could be heard coming from different directions, so they nearly got lost themselves. At last they saw Niels running full-speed through the grass. He ran right past them without looking at them, and when they finally caught up with him, he was quite beside himself.

"Don't you hear how she's calling for me?" he shouted, trying to tear himself away.

He told them how a woman had called him from the moor, and how she had always run ahead of him while calling, enticing him deeper and deeper into the moor. People thought that she must have been an elf.

From that day on the boy seemed even crazier than before.

> The retarded boy insists that he has heard voices calling him. In the context of the narrative, it is important to note that the adults share his experience but without being enticed into the world of the elves, as the boy obviously is.
>
> See Bengt Holbek and Iørn Piø, *Fabeldyr og sagnfolk* (1967), 111–20.
>
> Collected by E. T. Kristensen from Anne Stolpe, Copenhagen (Denmark). Printed in Kristensen, *Danske sagn* 2 (1893), 20.

46. The Fairy Lover

Charcoal burners, lumberjacks, and half-grown boys and girls tending the cattle on the outlying summer farms often experienced the preternatural beings as erotically seductive. Legends reveal that people were simultaneously attracted and afraid of these beings. A young man might throw steel over the forest woman to bind her to himself, or he might use some protective magic to be rid of her. The marriage ceremony between a girl and a fairy lover might be interrupted at the last moment. There might be an actual liaison between a human and one of the invisible folk, resulting in the birth of a child, the disappearance of the person, or, inversely, the absorption of the supranormal being into human society. Sometimes, refusal of the erotic attentions of the fairy lover caused sickness, madness, even death. One of the important functions of legends about fairy lovers was to enforce certain rules of behavior on the men and women working in isolated areas.

> See Bengt Holbek and Iørn Piø, *Fabeldyr og sagnfolk* (1967), 111–20, 127–34; Svale Solheim, *Norsk sætertradisjon* (1952), 340–505; Gunnar Granberg, *Skogsrået* (1935).

46.1 The Hill Man

Ingebjørg Hovrudhaugen was often alone at the summer farm. She was a dairymaid on Breiset. One evening a hill man came to her after she had gone to bed. He wanted to get into bed with her. But she finally got rid of him. Before he left she said:

"There is an invisible bull who's after one of my cows. What can I do?"

He answered:

"Take woody nightshade and orchis and some tree sap and put it on her tail, then the invisible will leave her alone."

The next evening the hill man came back, but the girl had put the stuff on her own braids. And she had put a hymnbook under her pillow. The hill man would not even come close. He spat in the direction of the bed and said:

"Shame on you for doing that!"

Ever since then her health was bad. She got arthritis and suffered much.

Woody nightshade (solanum dulcamarae) and orchis (o. maculata), in combination with tree sap, was a commonly used remedy for protecting people and animals against the demonic. A fourth ingredient often mentioned is mezeron (daphne mezerum), which in Norwegian is called *tysbast* (Swedish, *tibast*). Hence this legend is often referred to as "*tysbast* legend."

See Svale Solheim, *Norsk sætertradisjon* (1952), 485–87; Gunnar Granberg, *Skogsrået* (1935), 183–202; Ove Arbo Høeg, *Planter og tradisjon* (1974), 307–13.

Legend type: ML 6000.

Collected by Knut Hermundstad in Valdres (Norway). Printed in Solheim, *Norsk sætertradisjon*, 486–87.

46.2 Courted by a **Hulder**

Once there was a man who was alone on a summer farm. One night he felt he had to go outside before he could go to bed. Suddenly a girl appeared, playing an instrument. The man had never heard anything so beautiful in all his life. He got scared and wanted to go inside, but the girl said:

"Wait a minute, let me talk to you for a little while."

They stood there talking, and in the end, the girl asked the man to marry her. But he soon understood what kind of woman she was, and he plainly said no, it could never be. She had to leave then.

Three nights in a row, she came back to tempt and court the man, but every time he said no, even though she was the most beautiful girl he had ever seen. He knew he had to send her away, and he finally got rid of her.

Collected by Olav Nordbø in Bø, Telemark (Norway). Printed in Nordbø, *Segner og sogur frå Bøherad* (1945), 48–49.

46.3 He Had to Go with the Forest Sprite

A forest sprite had gotten a man under her power. He went to the woods night after night. He looked tormented and gaunt. But then some other men got together and decided they would hold him back the next time. The forest sprite called, but he did not come. She came closer and closer, and he became quite wild, biting and foaming at the mouth.

Then one of the men went outside and took a shot at her. The other men did not dare shoot. Immediately other wood sprites appeared

and picked her up and carried her into the forest. But the man who
had shot her lost an eye. The eye he had aimed with simply disappeared. He was very old, though, and he said it did not matter to him
that he had lost an eye to save the man from the forest sprite.

> In Swedish folk tradition, the spirit of the forest (*skogsrå*) is most
> often described as a solitary woman who rules over the animals.
> When she encounters lumberjacks, charcoal burners, and hunters,
> she tries to seduce them, or she mocks them, causing them to lose
> their way. If they would not give in to her, she would take
> revenge.
>
> See Bengt Holbek and Iørn Piø, *Fabeldyr og sagnfolk* (1967),
> 129–31; Gunnar Granberg, *Skogsrået* (1935).
>
> Collected by Ragnar Nilsson in 1928 from Anders Petter
> Svensson in Eskilsäter, Värmland (Sweden). Ms. in IFGH (1220),
> 30. Printed in R. Nilsson and Carl-Martin Bergstrand, *Folktro och
> folksed på Värmlandsnäs* 3 (1962), 76–77. Reprinted in Bengt af
> Klintberg, *Svenska folksägner* (1972), 85.

46.4 The Girl and the Elf King

In the woods on Bogø, everybody's livestock grazed on the common. The dairymaids went together to milk the cows, and when they
were done, they always walked back together.

But one day when they were on their way home, they discovered
that one of the girls was missing. She did not answer, no matter how
much they called. They finally found her, sitting alone and bewil-
dered by Elves' Moor. They had barely gotten her home, when she
told them that she had met a handsome man. He had asked her to be
his sweetheart, and she had been charmed by him and could not get
away. He had told her not to answer when the other girls called.

After that she had to go to Elves' Moor every day. But someone
gave her the advice that when the elf king came, she should say three
times:

"Turn around so that I can see whether you are the same in back as
in front."

At their next meeting she did that, and then she saw that he was
hollow in the back, and shouted:

"No, for shame, you are hollow like a baking trough."

Then the elf king walked away and left her in peace.

> In folk tradition throughout Scandinavia, the invisible are thought
> to be beautiful in front but hollow or like a tree in back. Another

motif frequently found is that they have a cow's tail or some other animal trait.

See Bengt Holbek and Iørn Piø, *Fabeldyr og sagnfolk* (1967), 127–32.

Collected by E. T. Kristensen from a teacher named Hansen in Fårdrup, Jylland (Denmark). Printed in Kristensen, *Danske sagn* 2 (1893), 19.

46.5 Sleeping with a Forest Sprite

There was a farmer here in the village named Jan Nilsson. He and a serving girl went to Finröjningen to make hay. They both slept in the barn.

One night the girl saw a woman enter the barn and lie down beside the man. The stranger had beautiful eyes, but her back looked like the bark on a fir tree.

The next morning the girl asked the farmer who the woman was who had visited him during the night.

"Hush," he said, "today I'm going to get a great big buck."

After a while a huge bear came along and lay down on a rock just outside the barn. The man shot it without any trouble.

"There, you see? I've already been paid for sharing my bed with her," he said.

Of course it was a forest sprite he had slept with, the old folks said. No doubt this happened a long time ago.

> If well received, a wood sprite would reward a hunter with game.
>
> See Gunnar Granberg, *Skogsrået* (1935), 117–22, 142–54.
>
> Collected in 1912 by Levi Johansson from J. A. Nordin, Ortsjön, Njurunda parish, Medelpad (Sweden). Ms. in NM HA Övernaturliga väsen, 4. Printed in Bengt af Klintberg, *Svenska folksägner* (1972), 89.

46.6 The Interrupted Wedding with a Hill Man

My grandmother once told me that when she was growing up, the hill folk almost abducted a dairymaid. One day this woman was alone in the summer pasture, and they came and dressed her in bridal finery. But she managed to send the dog home. He ran to her brother's house and jumped up on the door. The brother knew, then, that something was wrong, and he took his horse and hurried to the mountain farm. When he came in through the gate, his horse started neighing, and the girl said:

"Thank God, I hear my brother's horse neighing!"

Quickly she made a cross with her arms over her chest and with her hands above her head. Then the hill folk disappeared, but they did not have time to take the bridal finery. When her brother entered the house, there she stood dressed as a bride.

> Probably the most common legend about life on the summer farms describes a girl being readied for a wedding with a fairy suitor. Usually her brother or fiancé intervenes at the last moment.
>
> One of the functions of telling this legend is to warn girls against staying on the mountain farm any longer than necessary.
>
> See Svale Solheim, *Norsk sætertradisjon* (1952), 491–96; C. W. von Sydow, "Trollbröllopet i säterstugan," *Fryksände förr och nu* 3 (1933), 99–103; Bengt Holbek and Iørn Piø, *Fabeldyr og sagnfolk* (1967), 113–16.
>
> Legend type: ML 6005.
>
> Collected in 1924 by Ella Ohlson from Göran Byman, Lillhallen, Berg parish, Jämtland (Sweden). Ms. in NM HA Övernaturliga väsen, 6. Printed in Bengt af Klintberg, *Svenska folksägner* (1972), 159–60.

46.7 Taken into the Hill

Kari was born on Svid near Kvistad in Hjørungafjord. She took service in Standal.

One day when she was out on the pasture tending the cattle, she was taken by the *huldre* folk into Midsæter Hill in Standal. There were three men in the hill — an old man and his two sons. The old man wanted Kari to marry the eldest son:

"We need fresh, new blood in our family" he said.

But Kari wanted to go home. She was already betrothed and she cried and begged them to let her go. Then the old man said:

"Well, you may go home, but if you stayed here, you would find happiness."

And suddenly she was at home again. Later, she married in Standal, but all her days, there was a sadness in her. Perhaps it would have been better for her to stay in the hill. She often sat there in the evening, dreaming.

It is unusual that a person considers from hindsight that it might have been better to stay in the world of the invisible.

See Svale Solheim, *Norsk sætertradisjon* (1952), 449–505.

Collected by Martin Bjørndal in Hjørungfjord, Møre (Norway). Printed in Bjørndal, *Segn og tru. Folkeminne frå Møre* (1949), 61.

46.8 Married to a Hulder

There was a boy who went haying on an outlying pasture. He slept in the barn there.

Late one night he was awakened by many people entering the barn. It was a wedding party. The bride was so beautiful that the boy could not take his eyes off her. So he threw his sheath knife over her. The others screamed and rushed out the door, and the boy was left alone with the bride. Then she became his.

He took her home, and they got married. She was an energetic and easygoing woman, and they got along well. But as time passed, he became stingy and complaining, and she was quite unhappy.

One day he was trying to shoe the horse. He was sulking because he could not fit it right. She asked what was the matter, and he answered that the shoe was too tight.

"Can't you widen it?" she asked.

No, he could not do that. There was nothing he could do but take the horse to the smith, he said.

"Let me have the horseshoe," she said.

He handed it to her, and she pulled it apart with her hands. When the man tried it on, the shoe was too wide.

"Can't you bend it back together?" she said.

She took the horseshoe once more and bent it together to make it fit just right. When she handed the horseshoe back to him, she said:

"If you are ever mean to me again, I'll do the same to you!"

After that they got along better.

> The legend about the fairy wife is widespread in Scandinavia. By virtue of the marriage ceremony, the preternatural being is assimilated into human society, but she retains her supranormal powers.
>
> See Hans-Egil Hauge, "Den sterke hustruen," *Arv* 2 (1946), 1–34; Svale Solheim, *Norsk sætertradisjon* (1952), 497–505.
>
> Legend type: ML5090.

Collected by Peter Lunde in Bjelland, Vest-Agder (Norway). Printed in Lunde, *Kynnehuset. Vestegdske folkeminne* (1924), 137.

46.9 The Abducted Bride

On Lower Lunde, a girl who was engaged to be married went outside one Christmas Eve. She was going to the storehouse to get some flatbread. She carried the big key to the storehouse in her hand. Nobody knows what happened, but the girl did not return. And they could not find her, no matter how much they searched for her.

On the next Christmas Eve, something happened that nobody had expected. The betrothed girl suddenly returned, with the key in her hand, and said:

"Don't think of me anymore, I am all right. I am living better than all of you."

After she had said that, she disappeared once more. They kept this key on Lunde for a long time, said Ola Lunde, the brother of my mother.

> The period just preceding marriage, as before any major life change, was considered a time of crisis when the betrothed individuals were especially endangered by preternatural powers.
>
> See Svale Solheim, *Norsk sætertradisjon* (1952), 490–93; Bengt Holbek and Iørn Piø, *Fabeldyr og sagnfolk* (1967), 114–16.
>
> Collected in 1928 by Knut Hermundstad from Elsa Lunde in Vang, Oppland (Norway). Printed in Hermundstad, *Gamle tidi talar. Gamal Valdreskultur* 1 (1936), 4.

46.10 The Boy Who Had a Child with a Tusse

There was a boy who was pursued by a *tusse* girl. One evening she appeared and wanted to sleep with him. He did not want to let her into his bed. But she would not give in; she absolutely wanted to sleep with him. There was no point trying to escape her, so the boy slept with the *tusse*. Sometime later the girl bore a child.

After she had given birth to this little one, she reappeared to the boy. She wanted him to come with her to the house where she lived. So he went along. He remarked how beautiful it was in her house. Then she said:

"Now I'll show you what a beautiful child I have."

The boy did not have much to say to that.

"I love this little child so much, I just wanted you to come and see it."

She did not want anything else from him. He was free to go. But she told him how to get out safely.

"As soon as you get through the door, you must jump to one side. There is a glowing iron in the fire. It will fly after you just when you leave."

He escaped unharmed. She did not want to hurt him.

> Legends about sexual intercourse with a fairy woman, resulting in the birth of a child, are not very common.
>
> The motif of the glowing iron thrown after the boy illustrates the fundamental ambivalence in the relationships between human beings and the preternatural powers.
>
> Collected by Andreas Mørch in Sigdal-Eggedal, Buskerud (Norway). Printed in Mørch, *Frå gamle dagar. Folkeminne frå Sigdal og Eggedal* (1932), 20–21.

46.11 Married to a Wood Sprite

A charcoal burner was out in the woods working his kilns. This was in Hartzberg Forest.

One evening a handsome woman appeared and talked to him. She said that she had just arrived in the area and wanted to go to Stripa but did not know the way. She was easygoing and nice. He thought that she could stay with him and help him with the kilns. So she stayed with him for three years, and they had three children. The youngest was a girl, and the woman named her Snorvipa.

But she made the charcoal burner promise that whenever he had been away someplace, he would first knock on a certain tree, which she pointed out to him, before coming home. He should knock three times.

One day, however, he forgot. When he got to the kilns, he saw her the way she really was. She stood there stoking the kiln with her nose and claws and damping the fire with her tail, which she dipped in a bucket of water.

He got very frightened because he now understood that he was living with a wood sprite. He did not say anything to her but turned around and went to an old Finn and asked him for advice. The Finn said:

"Take her and the children with you on a sleigh out on Lake Rasvaln. You must sit on the horse yourself, but put the harness pins in loosely so that you can kick them out with your heel. Don't tie any tight knots in the harness, everything must be loose. When you come to the middle of the lake, ride away from them and don't turn around until you get to the goldsmith's hut."

Now the charcoal burner went back and knocked on the tree as he usually did, and she was a handsome woman once more. He had brought the horse and sleigh. He said that they were going for a drive. He put her and the children in the sleigh, and he mounted the horse. When they got to the middle of the lake, seven white wolves appeared on the ice. When she saw them, and it dawned on her what he was going to do, she begged for mercy for herself and the children:

"If you don't have pity on me and the older two, at least have pity on little Snorvipa. If you are going to do what you are thinking of, I am going to call my brother in Hartzberg, my sister in Ringkälla, and my cousin in Stripa!"

But he rode away.

Then she called for help, and shots rained down from all three mountains and thundered like cannonballs, hitting the ice behind him. It was blue ice. But he rode away unscathed because he had tied all the knots loosely. The woman and her children, however, were devoured by the wolves.

> This legend is a folk tradition connected with the life of charcoal burners in Sweden. More generally it reflects the fear of involvement with preternatural beings. The brutality of the man's reaction shows that he considers the wood sprite a demonic being.
>
> See Gunnar Granberg, *Skogsrået* (1935), 174–78.
>
> Collected in 1932 by Ellen Lagergren from August Blomkvist, Angarne, Hed parish, Västmanland (Sweden). Ms. in ULMA (4008), 1–5. Printed in Bengt af Klintberg, *Svenska folksägner* (1972), 86–87.

47. Good Neighbors and Friends

Because the invisible folk were thought to live side by side with human beings, the work rhythms and daily needs of both groups overlapped in many ways. Thus, in many instances, legends tell us how the invisible folk help humans and vice-versa. People looked to preternatural beings for advice, special tools, and perhaps for help in emergency situations. The invisible folk requested aid from humans when, for example, a child was to be born.

It was important that contact between the worlds respected certain norms and limits. And in spite of generally good and neighborly relations, there remained an element of fear based on the realization that the invisible folk were more powerful than humans.

See Svale Solheim, *Norsk sætertradisjon* (1952), 340–505; Bengt Holbek and Iørn Piø, *Fabeldyr og sagnfolk* (1967), 107–38; Gunnar Granberg, *Skogsrået* (1935).

47.1 The Tusse Folk Help with the Harvest

It was sometime during the eighteenth century. One autumn Old Tore and Marte, who lived on Austaana in Kvitseid, had much trouble getting help to bring in the harvest. Their big, beautiful field was so ripe that the grain was dropping to the ground, and there was not a single person they could hire to do the mowing. They thought they might have to ask their neighbors for help, as they often did in those days whenever they were in a hurry with a job.

So Tore and Marte brewed and baked, as if they were preparing for a great feast. They brewed in the workhouse, and the evening before the neighbors were expected to come and help, the beer stood ready in a vat. But during the night, they heard the sound of cutting and tying in the field, and the sound of many feet shuffling and walking in the workhouse. And they heard voices mumbling and talking:

Everybody can mow,
but nobody can tie the cross.
We tie it straight,
and soon we can quit.

The next morning the folk on Austaana got a big surprise—the whole big field had been cut. But the sheaves had been tied in a way that no one in the village had seen before. Ever since that time, it has been called a "straight tie." The usual tie was in the shape of a cross, but the *tusse* could not tie that way.

When Tore and Marte went into the workhouse to fetch the beer, they found it was all gone except for a little bit of the dregs. The *tusse* had drunk the beer in payment for their labor. But when Marte flushed the dregs from the vat, she found three or four silver spoons on the bottom, which the *tusse* had left there. The spoons have been passed down on the farm from generation to generation, and they are engraved with Tore's name.

> One of the few fixed epic patterns in legends about the invisible aiding humans concerns the harvesting of the grain. The invisible cut the grain, but they cannot tie the sheaves in the shape of the cross because of the religious power associated with that shape. Traditionally sheaves were tied crosswise until the more efficient straight tie was introduced from Jylland, Denmark. In legendary tradition, this innovation is attributed to the *tusse*.
>
> For a general description of the grain harvest and customs, see Kristofer Visted and Hilmar Stigum, *Vår gamle bondekultur* 1 (1975), 227–46.
>
> Legend type: ML 6035.
>
> Collected by Kjetil A. Flatin in Seljord, Telemark (Norway). Printed in Flatin, *Tussar og trolldom* (1930), 41–42.

47.2 The Mound Folk Give Advice in Sewing

A herding girl once sat by a mound sewing a shift. When she got to the sleeves, she did not know how to sew them on so that they would turn right side out.

She was racking her brains to no avail, when suddenly she heard the women in the mound say:

Sleeves right side out
but the body left,
the sewing will be
skillful and deft.

Then the girl knew how to sew the sleeves onto the shift.

> Collected by E. T. Kristensen from K. M. Rasmussen, Linde, Jylland (Denmark). Printed in Kristensen, *Danske sagn* 1 (1892), 54.

47.3 The Huldre Folk Tell the Date

This happened during the time of the Black Death. Some folks who lived all alone were on their way to another village to find out what the date was. But along the road they suddenly heard the *huldre* say:

Dikka, dikka Tor,
bake bread for jul,

one night and
two days,
then it's jul!

When they heard that, they turned right around and hurried home
to get ready for jul.

> During the great epidemic called the Black Death (1349–50), half
> the population of Norway died, and in many areas people were
> left quite isolated. (Cf. nos. 60.10–60.15.)
>   Legend type: ML 6030.
>   Collected in 1889 by Moltke Moe from Åse Utbråtåen in Bø,
> Telemark (Norway). Printed in Moe, *Folkeminne fra Bøherad*
> (1925), 68.

47.4 *The Wood Sprite Woke Him Up in Time*

Some people say that a wood sprite is just like a *hulder*, except that
she lives by herself. Others believe that there is no difference between
them at all. They say that she calls people who have lost their way
and shows herself whenever someone needs help. They are quite sure
that she means well and would not harm anybody.

A man from Mo was looking for his horses one autumn day. He
had heard that they were somewhere around Wolf Bridge so he headed in that direction. He crossed over Gray Mountain and Snake Hill.
They had been there some eight days before and were running north.
He followed. He passed by Halvor's Mountain toward Grassland and
then north to Skyndal farm and Strømstad. By this time he had been
walking for several days and was exhausted. He lay down to rest by
the fireplace at Skyndal farm, intending to go on the next day. That
night a boy showed up who was heading toward Halvor's Mountain
to look for a mare of his own.

"If you wait a bit, I'll go along with you," the man said.

Yes, the boy would wait. But in the morning, when the herding
girl woke the man up, she said:

"Anders is already gone."

"What a troll that boy is. He's in such a hurry!" the man said. He
got some bread and set out after him.

When he came to Halvor's Mountain, the sun was so hot it made
him tired, and he wanted to take a rest. He sat with his back to a
spruce tree and put his stick into the ground in front of him so that
he would not lose his way. Then he fell asleep.

Suddenly he was awakened by a woman's voice resounding in the forest:

"You mustn't sit there any longer; your horses are passing on the other side of Halvor's Mountain!"

He jumped up, pulled up his stick, and took off. First he crossed a deep valley, then up one side of Halvor's Mountain and down the other. There were his horses, galloping by. If he had arrived just a moment earlier or later, he would have missed them. She knew exactly when to wake him up, she did.

> The figure of the wood sprite (*skogsrå*) in this story is borrowed from Sweden. The wood sprite is described as a solitary being. Her function in this particular legend corresponds to the Norwegian folk tradition about the *huldre* folk.
> See Gunnar Granberg, *Skogsrået* (1935), 61–66.
> Legend type: ML 6025.
> Collected by Sigurd Nergaard in Elverum, Østerdalen (Norway). Printed in Nergaard, *Hulder og trollskap. Folkeminne fraa Østerdalen* 4 (1925), 36–37.

47.5 Calling the Dairymaid

One night somebody called the dairymaid.

"Kari," the voice shouted outside, "you've got to get up now and go to the barn!"

But Kari did not want to get up. She just lay there quietly because the mound folk can get power over you if you answer them. After a while it shouted again:

"You've got to hurry to the barn before Kranselin strangles herself!"

Well, then she threw on a skirt and went to the barn. And it was high time she did! The cow had one foot stuck in her collar and was about to choke.

> Typically the invisible folk called the dairymaid if she had overslept or to warn her that there was something amiss with the cattle.
> See Svale Solheim, *Norsk sætertradisjon* (1952), 450–51.
> Legend type: ML 6025.
> Collected by Sigurd Nergaard in Aamot, Hedmark (Norway). Printed in Nergaard, *Hulder og trollskap. Folkeminne fraa Østerdalen* 4 (1925), 142.

47.6 Midwife to the Mound Folk

My wife's mother took service on Meløy for a few years. The folks she worked for owned a silver spoon, which the wife had received from the mound folk. She told my mother-in-law how that spoon came into their possession.

One evening the wife had gone to the storehouse. And just as she was about to return to the main house, a strange woman came up to her:

"I must ask you to come with me. My son's wife is having a baby," she said.

This happened so suddenly that the wife did not have time to ask any questions. She just thought of the woman who needed help and followed the other woman out of the storehouse. When they had gotten well beyond the stairs of the storehouse, the wife seemed to lose consciousness for a moment, and when she recovered, they were inside a house.

There were two people in there, an old man and a young woman lying in bed. The old man asked the wife for help.

The wife stayed there until the baby was born. But when she was ready to leave, the man said:

"When you get to your door at home, look on the ground. What you find lying there, you may have for coming here."

At the door the woman found the silver spoon I mentioned before.

> The legend about the wife who helps the invisible folk with childbirth is one of the most widespread in Scandinavia. As a reward she receives an item of value, usually made of silver.
>
> The woman in this legend acts from general neighborliness. Alternative reasons often found in this legend cycle are that the woman jokingly had promised her help to a toad or that the mother-to-be was her own daughter who had been "taken into the mountain."
>
> See H. F. Feilberg, "Alfekvinden i barnsnød," *Bjærgtagen* (1910), 69–84; Will-Erich Peuckert, *Sagen. Geburt und Antwort der mythischen Welt* (1965), 65–66, and *Deutscher Volksglauben des Spätmittelalters* (1942), 187–200; Reidar Th. Christiansen, "Midwife to the Hidden People," *Lochlann* 6 (1974), 104–17; *Atlas över svensk folkkultur II. Sägen, tro och högtidssed 2*, edited by Åke Campbell and Åsa Nyman (1976), 58–64.
>
> Legend type: ML 5070.

Collected by Ragnvald Mo in Salten, Nordland (Norway). Printed in Mo, *Eventyr og segner. Folkeminne frå Salten* 2 (1941), 129–30.

47.7 *She Threw Away the Shavings*

My foster mother told me another story about the mound folk.

One evening one of the mound folk pleaded with a woman to come and help his wife who was having a baby. The woman did, and when it was all over, the man in the mound said:

"Open your apron!"

He filled her apron with wood shavings, but she threw them away outside. The next morning one of the shavings was stuck to her apron, and it had turned to pure gold. Then she ran outside to look for the rest of the shavings, but they were gone.

> Often the midwife discards the gift she receives, believing it to have no value, only to discover too late that it was gold or silver. This is related to the belief that the world of preternatural beings is not what it appears.
>
> Legend type: ML 5070.
>
> Collected by E. T. Kristensen from N. J. Termansen, Holsted, Jylland (Denmark). Printed in Kristensen, *Danske sagn* 1 (1892), 348.

47.8 *The Grateful* Huldre *Mother*

One morning Mother Holla's servant girl went into the kitchen. There she saw a little mound woman swaddling her child. The maid came upon her so suddenly that she did not quite finish. The mound woman rushed out as soon as the girl came in, leaving a swaddling cloth behind.

The girl was smart enough not to touch the cloth. Instead she took a stick to move it aside, so it would not be in her way as she worked. After a while the girl had to go outside for a moment. When she came back, there was a silver spoon on the floor. It occurred to the girl that the spoon was for her because she had saved the swaddling cloth for the *hulder*. But she was not sure.

So she talked to Mother Holla about it. Mother Holla, however, said that the spoon was her own and took it away from the girl. But at that very moment, the girl heard someone say that the spoon was, indeed, intended for her. Mother Holla kept insisting that it was her own. But after that day, Mother Holla's fingers began to wither.

> According to folk tradition, if the girl had touched the cloth that was left behind, the *hulder* would not have been able to take it back.
>
> The description of the greedy mistress of the house and her punishment can be interpreted as a form of social comment.
>
> Legend type: ML 6020.
>
> Collected by Edvard Langset in 1919 from Frits Smith in Kristiansund, Nordmøre (Norway). Printed in Langset, *Segner-gåter-folketru frå Nordmør* (1948), 52–53.

47.9 Rynjus Is Dead

There was a dairymaid who kept shuttling back and forth between the village and the mountain farm all summer long. Once she had been back home and was on her way up the mountain, when something strange happened to her. While she was walking along and knitting, someone shouted to her:

"Tell them at the mountain farm that Rynjus is dead!"

When she got to the farm, she said to the empty air:

"I don't know whether to keep quiet or to speak, but someone shouted to me in Dale: tell them on the mountain farm that Rynjus is dead!"

As soon as she had said this, a woman appeared and said:

"Oh, no, is Rynjus dead?!"

"Yes, that's what they told me," answered the dairymaid.

"You wouldn't be so kind as to take care of things for me while I go to the funeral? My cattle are grazing among yours and my buckets stand among yours."

Then the mound woman—for that is what she was—was gone.

In the evening the cattle of the invisible came together with the dairymaid's cows, and she milked them and took care of them along with her own. After a few days, the mound woman returned, and her cattle disappeared. So she had taken over her own chores again. But the next evening a fine white goat wandered onto the farm. The dairymaid could not get rid of it. That was her pay for taking care of the cattle of the mound folk.

> Scholars have repeatedly suggested a historical connection between this narrative and the Legend of Pan's death according to Plutarch. I. Boberg, by contrast, has maintained that the motif of

a message about someone's death sent by the invisible folk is
Germanic rather than classical in origin.

See Inger M. Boberg, *Sagnet om den store Pans død* (1934);
Archer Taylor, "Northern Parallels to the Death of Pan," *Washington University Studies* 10, no. 1 (1922); Martti Haavio, "Der Tod
des grossen Pan," *Studia Fennica* 3 (1938), 113–36.

Legend type: ML 6070.

Collected by Knut Hermundstad from Synnøve Hermundstad
in Tangelo, Valdres (Norway). Printed in Hermundstad, *I kveldseta. Gamal Valdres-kultur* 6 (1955), 116–17.

47.10 The Mound Folk Gave Them Cake

The large hill called Lysbakken, in the parish of Tvilum, has been
under the plow for many years. The story goes that the first time it
was plowed, the farmhand and the servant boy found a fire rake and
a shovel, both of which were broken. They repaired them, and when
they came back the next day to finish the plowing, there were two
cakes lying on the ground.

The servant boy immediately ate one of them, but the farmhand
was afraid of the hill folk's cakes and would not touch them. The boy
was not harmed at all. On the contrary, he became so strong that
there was no one stronger for several miles around.

> The folk looked upon food and drink offered by preternatural beings with a certain ambivalence. They were afraid of being "taken
> into the mountain" (cf. nos. 45.6–45.8), but they were also hesitant about refusing a gift. In this instance, the boy benefits from
> accepting the food.
>
> See Svale Solheim, *Norsk sætertradisjon* (1952), 477; Bengt Holbek and Iørn Piø, *Fabeldyr og sagnfolk* (1967), 121–24; Inger M.
> Boberg, *Bjærgfolkenes bagning* (1938).
>
> Collected by E. T. Kristensen from Sven Peter Jensen, Vole,
> Jylland (Denmark). Printed in Kristensen, *Danske sagn* 1 (1892),
> 102.

47.11 Trading Fire and Tobacco with the Mound Folk

One holiday afternoon a farmer from Bjærgsted lit his pipe and
went out into the fields to look at the grain.

When he got to a mound by the field, a little man was sitting
there, filling his pipe.

"Can you give me fire?" the little man asked.

"Why, sure," the man answered and shook some coals into the other fellow's pipe.

"Now you can fill your pipe from my pouch," said the little man.

The farmer filled his pipe with tobacco from the little man's pouch and lit it. Then the little man disappeared.

The farmer insisted that he had never tasted better tobacco in all his life.

See Bengt Holbek and Iørn Piø, *Fabeldyr og sagnfolk* (1967), 121–24.

Collected by Anton Nielson in Munkebjærgby, Jylland (Denmark). Printed in Kristensen, *Danske sagn* 1 (1892), 96.

47.12 Moving the Stable

On Sylhus in Øvre, the farmer was forced to move his new cow shed.

He had torn the old one down and built a new shed on another site. But no matter how securely they tied up the cows in the new shed, two or three of them always tore themselves loose by the next morning. This went on the whole winter until spring came. Sometime before they were going to put the cows out to summer pasture, the farmer was standing outside one day, cutting wood, when a stranger came up to him.

"We are next-door neighbors, so to speak. Won't you come home with me and have a drink?"

Yes, the farmer went along with him. He understood full well what kind of man he was, but it did not look as if he intended any harm. Near the new cow shed, the stranger knocked on a steel pan the Sylhus man had never seen there before. Right away an opening in the ground appeared. They climbed down and emerged in a fine room. He was invited to the table, and it looked to him as if the table was made of silver. All kinds of food and drink were served. But just when they sat down, some dirty water ran down onto the table, and the man in the hill looked fiercely at the Sylhus farmer.

"Dear me, what's that?" the farmer asked.

"Oh, that's not difficult to understand. Your cow shed is right above us, you know."

"All right, I guess I put it in the wrong place; I understand that now," said the man from Sylhus. "I'll move it as soon as I put the cows out to summer pasture."

Well, they came to an understanding. In the summer the farmer got the cows out of the shed and went to work. And since then there were never any more problems with the cows.

> To ensure success in animal husbandry, it was considered neces-
> sary to be on good terms with the invisible folk. If a farmer
> abandoned a new cow shed or some other building, he was likely
> to explain that this was done out of consideration for his invisible
> neighbors.
> See Svale Solheim, *Norsk sætertradisjon* (1952), 366–69; Ella
> Ohlson, "Naturväsen i ångermanländsk folktro. En översikt,"
> *FmFt* 20 (1933), 87–88.
> Legend type: ML 5075.
> Collected by Sigurd Nergaard in Rendal, Hedmark (Norway).
> Printed in Nergaard, *Hulder og trollskap. Folkeminne fraa Østerdalen*
> (1925), 195–96.

47.13 Binding the Cattle of the Mound Folk

People were out in the woods someplace, bringing in hay. A woman came along, followed by a great number of fat cows.

"Get those iron hooks out of my way!" she said.

The woman meant that they should move their scythes out of the way. But one of the farmhands threw his scythe over one of the cows. He got to keep the cow because the woman was one of the mound folk.

Now the way it is with the cattle of the invisible, no matter how big a pail you have, you always milk it full. But you must never empty it and start milking again. These folks here remembered that, and all went well to begin with. But there came a time when they broke the rule, and the cow milked nothing but blood. They never got any more use out of her.

> Accounts of people seeing the cattle of the mound folk are com-
> monplace. Fairy cattle were considered superior to ordinary cat-
> tle. Solheim has suggested that stories about the cattle of the in-
> visible have their background in new breeds being introduced to
> a given area from the outside.
> See Svale Solheim, *Norsk sætertradisjon* (1952), 411; Ella Ohlson,
> "Naturväsen i ångermanländsk folktro," *FmFt* 20 (1933), 82.

Legend type: ML 6055.
Collected in 1912 by Levi Johansson from J. Bergström in Västanå, Njurunda parish, Medelpad (Sweden). Ms. in NM HA Övernaturliga väsen, 6. Printed in Bengt af Klintberg, *Svenska folksägner* (1972), 158.

47.14 Playing with the Children of the Mound Folk

To the south of Gudhjem lived a family who had a lot of children. The children played on the farm. Then there appeared a little girl nobody knew, and she played with them. When the mother gave her children some bread to eat in the afternoon, she also gave a little piece to the stranger. The little girl came every day, played with the children, and got a little something to eat.

But once the mother brought a big slice of bread and said:

"If you will tell me where you are from, I'll give you this piece of bread."

Suddenly a strange woman appeared, who angrily said to the housewife:

"If you want to give, then give, but don't ask questions of an innocent child."

Then she took the child by her arm and disappeared, and they never saw the child or her mother again.

But one day when the children were playing in the hills with children from the town, they heard a voice coming from a mound:

Pibel, put the pot on,
get the little chickies,
on the mound they run!

Then the children ran home and reported what had happened. And after that they never played near that mound again.

> The two encounters between the children, one within the limits of the village, the other out in nature, express the underlying ambivalence in the relations between humans and the invisible folk. The hill woman reacts against the conventional response of the mother, which emphasizes social rather than personal identity.
>
> Collected by E. T. Kristensen from G. Josefsen in Bornholm (Denmark). Printed in Kristensen, *Danske sagn* 1 (1892), 10.

47.15 The Boy Who Teased the Man in the Hill

My grandfather once told me how he had been playing with some boys near Toft Hill in Gadbjærg one afternoon. They were running around among the hills north of town. They got the idea to tease the man in the hill, so they shouted:

Nils with your nose,
Tulli with your toe —
Are you inside?
Out you go!

But then the hill opened, and many small people came running out. The boys headed back to town as fast as they could. The hill folk chased them until they came to the creek. When the boys crossed over the bridge, they heard splashing in the water, and then they did not see the hill folk anymore.

> The verse shouted by the children to tease the hill man is a traditional tongue twister. See Henning Frederik Feilberg, *Bidrag til en ordbog over jyske almuesmål* 2 (1894–1904), 687.
>
> Collected by E. T. Kristensen from a teacher named Nielsen in Tågelund, Jylland (Denmark). Printed in Kristensen, *Danske sagn* 1 (1892), 144.

47.16 The Cross Prevented Theft by the Mound Folk

In the old days, people used to make a cross in their grain after they were done threshing. That way the mound folk would not be able to steal any of it.

In Tjornede there was a farm where the mound folk would always go to borrow flour and oatmeal when they had used up all their own.

"You'll get it back when the folk at Bonnerup are done with their threshing," they always promised. "They don't make a cross in their seed.

And they kept their word.

> Making the sign of the cross was the most common protection against interference by the invisible folk, including theft.
>
> See Svale Solheim, *Norsk sætertradisjon* (1952), 34–35.
>
> Collected from Chr. Weiss, a teacher in Tingerup, Hvalsø, Sjælland (Denmark). Printed in E. T. Kristensen, *Danske sagn* 1 (1892), 121.

47.17 *The Hill Folk Borrowed Scissors and Knives.*

A man by the name of Steffen lived in a house west of Ry. He told me that he used to hear the door of his house open at night, and the next morning various items like scissors and knives were missing. He was certain that the hill folk had taken the things because they needed them to prepare their dead for burial, or something like that. A few nights later, the door would open again, and the things would all be returned.

These hill folk came from Skovsbjærg.

> An everyday occurrence such as losing or misplacing household items was commonly explained as "borrowing" by the invisible folk.
> Collected by E. T. Kristensen from Rasmus Mathisen, Ry, Jylland (Denmark). Printed in Kristensen, *Danske sagn* 1 (1892), 117.

47.18 *The Troll Hat*

A man called Hurdabaken had a troll hat. He dreamed that a *hulder* woman appeared to him. She put the hat on him, and it made him invisible.

"Don't show yourself to anyone when you're not wearing the hat," she said.

But that is exactly what he did. He showed himself at a dance in Vaset, and then it was all over for him. They ran him out and he slipped away into the hills.

For a long time they could not find him. But then they saw the tracks of his horse, so they followed him. Both horse and rider were invisible because he was wearing the hat.

Hurdabaken now rode full-speed through a river. They could see the water splashing around the legs of the horse, and they fired. The horse gave a jump so that Hurdabaken fell into the river, and the hat floated in the water. They captured him. Then they tied him between four wild horses and tore him apart. But before he died, he cursed everyone there. And the old folks were sure that there was a curse on the families of the men who took part in the killing.

They buried him on a small island by the river.

> Legends about a person getting a fairy hat that makes him or her invisible do not follow a distinct epic pattern.

The tradition about the man called Hurdabaken (or Hulabaken) is localized in Valdres and refers to a famous robber who was regarded by some as evil, by others as a kind of Robin Hood.

See Svale Solheim, "Segna om Hulabaken," *Tidsskrift for Valdres historielag* (1958), 67–75.

Legend type: ML 6050.

Collected by Johan Skrindsrud in Vestre Slidre, Valdres, Buskerud (Norway). Printed in Skrindsrud, *På heimleg grunn. Folkeminne frå Etnedal* (1956), 52.

47.19 The Drinking Horn

Halfway between the townships of Bø and Nes lies a hill called Vellar Hill. Some folks say that *draug* live in that hill. A man from Gjærnes, by the name of Gunnar, heard about it and wanted to put it to the test. One night he rode up to the hill and shouted:

Get up, *draug*,
in Vellar Hill,
give Gunnar Gjesmann something to drink!

"Sure, you'll get something!" came the answer from the hill.

Gunnar got scared and rode off as quickly as he could. But the *draug* chased him until they came to the river Greina. Then he threw the drinking horn after Gunnar so that it hit the back of his horse. Its contents spilled and burned both hair and hide off the horse.

Gunnar either turned around and grabbed the horn then, or he picked it up on the way home, I do not remember which. But he did get it and, as far as I know, the great horn can be found in Gjærnes to this very day.

> This legend is well known in Scandinavia, as well as in Germany and the British Isles. The earliest known variant was written down during the twelfth century by William of Newbury. In Denmark, Norway, and Sweden, it was first documented in the sixteenth century.
>
> In this particular text, the preternatural being in the hill is called a *draug* (revenant). More typically the hill dwellers are identified as trolls or simply as mound folk.
>
> See Rikard Berge, "Drikke joleskaal. Studie av ei norderlandsk villsegn," *Norsk folkekultur* 10 (1924), 1–53; Knut Liestøl, *Norsk folkediktning II. Segner* (1939), 206–7; Inger M. Boberg, "Des Knaben Wunderhorn—Oldenburgerhornet," *Festskrift til L. L. Hammerich* (1952), 53–61; Bengt Holbek and Iørn Piø, *Fabeldyr og*

sagnfolk (1967), 124–25; Bengt af Klintberg, *Svenska folksägner* (1972) 310–11; Inger Lövkrona, *Det bortrövade dryckeshornet* (1982). Legend type: ML 6045.
Collected by Moltke Moe from Halvor Skogen in the township of Bø, Telemark (Norway). Printed in Moe, *Folkeminne fra Bøherad* (1924), 63.

47.20 Hey, Look at the Pussycat!

Many trolls used to live in Brace Hill. The hill got its name because people put braces under the cliffs to keep them from toppling on people passing below. Once someone saw a long train of trolls marching out of the hill. When people were mowing the fields, the trolls showed up on the hill and did the same.

In earlier days the farms at Lycke lay nearer the trolls' abode, and the trolls came to Lycke more often to borrow one thing or another. But they always returned everything in good order. Christmas Eve the trolls would go to a farm and drive out the people sitting down for their meal. They would set the table with their own food and feast far into the night.

One Christmas Eve a man leading a show bear arrived. He asked for lodging. The folks answered that they did not get any rest on Christmas Eve themselves, and they told him the whole story. But the stranger said that he was not afraid of any trolls, and because he asked so intently, they let both him and his bear stay.

Everybody ate early that Christmas Eve and went to bed. The stranger lay down on top of the stove with the bear in front of him. After a short while, the door opened and a troll hag entered and looked around. A great number of other trolls followed her in. The hag set the table, and the trolls began their feast as usual. When they had finished eating and drinking, the hag who had come in first wandered around the room, until she discovered the bear on the stove.

"Hey, look at the pussycat!" shouted the hag. "The cat shall eat. We will give the pussy some food."

And she began feeding the bear. But the man lying in back of the bear nudged it from behind and thus provoked it. It charged after the trolls, who were fleeing in fright.

A year later, at Christmastime, the folks at the farm heard the troll hag at the window. She asked whether they still had that angry cat.

"We sure do," they answered, "and now she has seven kittens."

"Then we won't dare come to you again," shouted the troll, and she ran away.

> This legend is widely known in northern Europe. An early literary variant is found in a Middle High German poem. Scholars have variously identified trolls driving farm folk from their houses at Christmastime with nature spirits, the dead, or ancestor worship.
>
> See Reidar Th. Christiansen, *Kjætten paa Dovre* (1922), and *The Dead and the Living* (1946), 72–94; Lutz Röhrich, *Erzählungen des späten Mittelalters* 1 (1962), 11–26, 235–43.
>
> Legend type: ML 6015.
>
> Collected by K. O. Tellander in Hemsjö, Västergötland (Sweden). Printed in Tellander, *Allmogelif i Västergötland* (1891), 75–76.

48. The Spirit of the Farm

The protection and welfare of the farmhouse and its immediate surroundings found expression in traditions about a solitary being called by various names. The names *tomte* ("homestead man"), *gardvord* ("farm guardian"), and *tunkall* ("yard fellow") stress the identification of this being with the farmstead. Another common name is *nisse*, which is derived from the Scandinavian form of Nicholas. Its use in reference to the domestic spirit has been interpreted as a noa-name. The oldest literary reference to the farm sprite is found in the saga of Olaf Tryggvasson (twelfth century), in which he is called *ármaður* ("hearth man").

> See Bengt Holbek and Iørn Piø, *Fabeldyr og sagnfolk* (1967), 142–62; Henning Frederik Feilberg, *Nissens historie* (1919); Bengt af Klintberg, *Svenska folksägner* (1972), 24–25, 302; Lily Weiser-Aall, "Germanische Hausgeister und Kobolde," *Niederdeutsche Zeitschrift für Volkskunde* 4 (1926), 1–19; Andrejs Johansons, *Der Schirmherr des Hofes im Volksglauben der Letten* (1964); Martti Haavio, "Post equitem sedet atra cura," *Studia Fennica* 8 (1959), 11–22; Lauri Honko, *Geisterglaube in Ingermanland* 1 (1962), 161–251.

48.1 *The* Tusse *at Vreim*

Anund Smellupp was the name of a man from Bøherad. He tramped around in Telemark, fixing things and forging knife blades and hand drills. He was a master at sharpening blades. Anund was always talking about the *tusse* and knew many strange stories about them.

One autumn he was sleeping in a hayloft at Vreim in Bø. A *tusse* boy came in, gathered up an armful of hay, bundled it on his back, and left. But outside on the barn bridge, he met another *tusse* from the neighboring farm, carrying a load of hay to the barn at Vreim. Now a fight started, as you can well imagine. Both of them were mad as hell and tore into each other like two fighting cocks. Hay was flying about, thick as fog, on the barn bridge and in the yard. It did not take long before both loads of hay were spread to the wind. Then the two *tusse* disappeared in opposite directions.

"There'll be hay all over the yard tomorrow, I thought to myself," said Anund.

The next morning, however, you could not see a single straw of hay, either on the barn bridge or in the yard.

> According to legendary tradition, the domestic spirit (here called *tusse*, a general name for the invisible folk) at times steals from a neighbor to increase the prosperity of the farm on which he makes his home. This is often coupled with the motif of two farm sprites fighting each other.
> Legend type: ML 7000.
> See Henning Frederik Feilberg, *Nissens historie* (1919), 52–54.
> Collected by Kjetil A. Flatin in Seljord, Telemark (Norway).
> Printed in Flatin, *Tussar og trolldom* (1930), 35.

48.2 *The* Nisse *Who Stole Fodder*

On Hindø in Stadil, there lived a farmer who was quite well off, but one hard winter he ran out of fodder, and he grew worried.

One day he was sitting at the table, complaining about his trouble, when he heard a strange voice nearby:

"I am going to help you."

The farmer looked everywhere but could not find anyone. The man now waited for a few days. His cows seemed to be thriving even though he had no fodder for them! One day the farmer said:

"I'm going to take a chance and cross the ice to Stadil and buy some fodder there."

The farmer took off. When he had gotten to the middle of the ice, a strange little man appeared and asked:

"Where are you going, farmer?"

He said he was on his way to Stadil to buy some fodder.

"There is no need for that; I'm going to help you."

And with that he disappeared. The man wondered about this, but he turned around and went back home. Time passed, there was no hay, and yet the animals were doing fine. But eventually the man decided once more to go to Stadil.

But then light was shed on the matter. One late evening when the moon was out, he saw a little man pull the red cow out of the shed, cross the ice, and head for the other shore to a farmer in Sirsbæk. After a short while, the little man returned with the cow, and she was loaded down with fodder. Now the farmer understood that the little man was a *nisse*, and he had been fetching hay with the red cow.

After that the folks would amuse themselves by watching the *nisse*. One evening he returned from Sirsbæk with a big speckled cow. But a short piece from the shore, the cow slipped on the ice.

"If you can't walk here, you've got to go home again," said the *nisse*. He dragged the cow back and soon returned with the red cow. The *nisse* had wanted to give the big speckled cow to the farmer, but when she could not walk on the ice, nothing came of the trade.

See Henning Frederik Feilberg, *Nissens historie* (1919), 48.
Collected by E. T. Kristensen from Marie Sandal, Brande, Jylland (Denmark). Printed in Kristensen, *Danske sagn* 2 (1893), 50–51.

48.3 *The Heavy Burden*

One day Lavrans was down in Meås Valley, when he saw a *tusse* boy stumbling uphill to the barn with a single blade of grain on his back. He was groaning and panting, as if he was carrying a terribly heavy burden.

"What are you huffing and puffing about?" shouted Lavrans. "Your load isn't all that heavy!"

"If I'm going to carry as much *from* you as I have carried *to* you, you'll realize that the burden is heavy enough!" answered the *tusse*. And then he turned around and carried his load over to the neighboring farm, which was called Bakken. But when Lavrans looked at him from behind, he suddenly saw that the *tusse* was hauling a huge load of grain.

Before then the *tusse* had carried both hay and food stuffs from Bakken so that there was nothing but poverty and hardship there. But after he returned everything from Meås there was great wealth on Bakken. After that they had little luck on Meås. Lavrans died a violent death, and his family vanished.

> The success of human beings' relations to the farm sprite, as to any of the invisible folk, was based on respect and trust. Legends of this type describe how the farmer derides the activities of the spirit and thus loses his support.
>
> See Henning Frederik Feilberg, *Nissens historie* (1919), 50–52.
>
> Legend type: ML 7005.
>
> Collected by Kjetil A. Flatin in Seljord, Telemark (Norway).
> Printed in Flatin, *Tussar og trolldom* (1930), 43.

48.4 When the Nisse Got No Butter on His Christmas Porridge

One Christmas Eve many years ago, a servant girl wanted to tease the *nisse* by playing a trick on him. She hid the butter at the bottom of the bowl of porridge to be set out in the barn, knowing very well the *nisse* was greedy for the butter and would make a long face if he could not find it.

But when the *nisse* saw that there was no butter on the Christmas porridge, he became madder than the girl had imagined—he went straight to the cow shed and killed the best cow. That would show them how much he appreciated their begrudging him even a little bit of butter!

Then he went into the barn and ate the porridge anyway. And when the bowl was empty, he found the butter lying on the bottom. Now the *nisse* felt so bad about having killed the cow, he cried and carried on.

That same Christmas night, the *nisse* walked over to the neighboring farm, took the best cow he could find, led her back to Rød, and put her in the stall—the same stall where the other cow had been.

> A large cycle of legends describes how a mischievous person tampers with the porridge that the household spirit considers his or her due. Sometimes the spirit's revenge is comical, at other times quite serious. (Cf. nos. 48.5–48.6.)

See Henning Frederik Feilberg, *Nissens historie* (1919), 61–65.
Legend type: ML 7010
Collected by Erling Johansen in Østfold (Norway). Printed in
K. Weel Engebretsen and E. Johansen, *Sagn fra Østfold* (1947),
70–71.

48.5 Now Håkan Is Hot!

This happened at the ironworks in Ramnäs. The older smiths
talked about it when I was apprenticing there.

During the old days, when they used the German method in refin-
ing iron and got paid by the pound for it, the smiths got help from a
tomte. And he had to get his payment, too.

When Christmas Eve came, the master told one of the
journeymen—his name was Håkan—to carry a bowl of porridge
downstairs and put it on a tree stump for the *tomte*. But Håkan ate the
porridge himself, shit on the plate, and put it on the stump for the
tomte.

On the third day of Christmas, when the journeyman was firing
up the ovens, the *tomte* threw the journeyman into the furnace, pushing him in bit by bit, until only his wooden shoes were left outside.
Then he woke up the master and said:

"Up, master, up! Now Håkan is hot!"

> The so-called German method, a process of refining pig iron by
> smelting it with charcoal in a closed furnace, was introduced in
> Sweden during the 1600s and remained in use there for about
> 200 years.
>
> See Carl-Herman Tillhagen, *Järnet och människorna* (1980),
> 195–208.
>
> Legend type: ML 7010.
>
> Collected by Ellen Lagergren in 1933 from a smith named C.
> J. Blom, Färna Ironworks, Gunnilbo parish, Västmanland
> (Sweden). Ms. in ULMA (5957), 5. Printed in Bengt af Klintberg,
> *Svenska folksägner* (1972), 115.

48.6 The Farmhand Who Stole the Tomte's Porridge

On a farm someplace, they put out food for the *tomte* in the outer
room, and he came every night and ate it. But the farmhand slept in
that room, and when he saw all the good food they gave to the *tomte*,
he became jealous. He thought to himself:

"The food I get is not as good as what they give him."

And then he thought:

"This time I'm going to eat it before he gets it."

He never saw anyone, but the food was always eaten. So the farm-hand ate it himself. But then he saw the *tomte*, who had come for his food. When the *tomte* discovered that everything was gone, he heaved a great sigh, thinking that they had not given him anything. And then he thought:

"I have carried from seven miles far and seven miles wide, and much have I carried to this farm."

After that he did not come for several nights. The people thought this was too bad. They asked the farmhand whether the *tomte* had been there to eat, but he answered:

"I don't know."

But to himself he thought:

"I'm going to fix him."

The next night, when he was lying in the outer room again, he shit on the plate and put it on the table so the *tomte* would see it. Well, the *tomte* came and stood there with folded hands and heaved a sigh. Then he said:

"It's just as far coming as going. I have carried from seven miles far and seven miles wide, but now I'm going to take back as much as I have brought."

And since then there was no prosperity on the farm; they became poor in that house. But they chased the farmhand away because he had meddled with their *tomte*.

> (Cf. no. 48.4.)
> Legend type: ML 7010.
> Collected by M. Forss in 1897 in Petalax, Österbotten (Finland). Ms. in Svenska Litteratursällskapet i Finland (64). Printed in V. E. V. Wessman, *Sägner* 3.2 (1931), 265.

48.7 *The* Tomte *Who Baked Bread*

A servant girl was baking bread, and a *tomte* came to help her. She lay down on the kitchen bench and fell asleep and let the *tomte* do all the baking by himself. But he took all the dough and shoved it into the oven in one stroke, and then he called the girl:

"Up with you, girl. Now the whole mess is baked!"

When the servant girl saw what the *tomte* had done, she began to cry. Then the *tomte* felt remorse, and within two hours, he returned with a couple of baskets of fine, newly baked bread. He had taken it from someone else, of course.

> Here the domestic spirit teases the farm help rather than the other way around.
>
> Collected by P. Österlin in 1938 from Anna Fågelberg, Kristianopel parish, Blekinge (Sweden). Ms. in LUF (5903), 7. Printed in Bengt af Klintberg *Svenska folksägner* (1972), 113.

48.8 The Tomte Took Care of the Horse

When my father was young, he went into the stable one Monday morning to give some hay to the horse. He had been away, and it was already quite late in the day.

When he entered the stable, he petted the horse and saw that it did not have any hay. So he went up to the loft, but as he bent over the hay, someone grabbed him by the arms and carried him down the stairs so that his feet did not even touch the ground. He was set down in the middle of the stable floor. Now the horse was eating, even though he had not given it anything.

Every morning when they came into the stable, the horse was already cleaned and groomed, and they never needed to take care of it.

> This memorat exemplifies the tradition of the *tomte*, who not only takes care of the farm animals, especially the horses, but will not tolerate anyone else interfering with his work.
>
> See Henning Frederik Feilberg, *Nissens historie* (1919), 45–46.
>
> Collected in Korsholm, Österbotten (Finland). Printed in *Budkavlen* (1925), 83. Reprinted in V. E. V. Wessman, *Sägner* 3.2 (1931), 222.

48.9 How the Nisse Learned to Take a Rest

A man and his *nisse* once went out to steal some hay because the man had none left. They took it from someone who had plenty. When they had walked awhile, the man said:

"Shall we take a rest?"

"What's *that*?" asked the *nisse*.

"Well, that means you sit down, and after a while you get started again."

When they had rested awhile, the *nisse* said:

"If I had known that it felt so good to take a rest, I would have carried the whole barn on my back."

> This legend is popular throughout Scandinavia. The apparent stupidity of the *nisse* stands in comical contrast to his enormous capacity for work.
> See Henning Frederik Feilberg, *Nissens historie* (1919), 49–50.
> Collected by E. T. Kristensen in Hårup, Jylland (Denmark).
> Printed in Kristensen, *Danske sagn* 2 (1893), 53.

48.10 *The* Nisse's *New Clothes*

On Vaker they had a *nisse* who would go to the mill and grind all the grain for the farmer. The farmer did not have to do anything but load the wagon and hitch up the horses. The *nisse* drove to the mill and did the grinding himself.

When this had been going on for about a year, and they were getting another load ready for him, they decided to give the *nisse* something as a reward for being so helpful. So they sewed some new homespun clothes for him and put them on top of the load. When the *nisse* arrived to drive the wagon, he found the clothes. He was happy and put them on right away.

But seeing how fine he had become, he jumped down from the wagon and said:

"Now I am too elegant to do the grinding."

And since then the *nisse* did not grind the grain on Vaker anymore.

> This legend has been collected throughout western Europe. The background to the *nisse*'s decision to quit working may perhaps be found in folk traditions of paying off one's help at the end of a given period, usually at the end of the year. Often the payment was a new suit or a pair of shoes.
> Lutz Röhrich points out that in German folk tradition, a distinction is to be made between the domestic spirits, who defend their place in the household at all costs, and the dwarfs, who consider themselves laid off (*ausgelohnt*) when rewarded.
> See Röhrich, *Sage* (1966), 20–21.
> Legend type: ML 7015.
> Collected by Moltke Moe in Ringerike, Buskerud (Norway).
> Ms. in NFS Moltke Moe 20, 1.

48.11 The Troublesome **Haugbo**

At a certain farm, the *haugbo* was impossible to live with. The farmer decided to sell out and move to another place. Finally he had only some rubbish left at the old place, and he went back to fetch a load of it. Among other things there was a big tub. When the man got on the road with it, he discovered the tub was rather heavy. So he lifted up the lid to look inside. There sat the *haugbo* on his haunches.

"We're moving today, old man!" he chuckled.

> The term *haugbo* literally means "mound dweller." As the term is used here, it does not imply that the farm spirit lives subterraneously but that he is usually not visible.
>
> In legendary tradition it was considered impossible to force farm sprites to leave against their will. Klintberg argues that this notion derives from the ancient idea that humans cannot escape ill fate. In the expanded versions of the legend, however, the story ends differently: the farmer recognizes the domestic spirit as a bringer of luck and learns to live with him in harmony.
>
> See Henning Frederik Feilberg, *Nissens historie* (1919), 82–86; Bengt af Klintberg, *Svenska folksägner* (1972), 304; Archer Taylor, "The Pertinacious Cobold," *Journal of English and Germanic Philology* 31 (1932), 1–9.
>
> Legend type: ML 7020.
>
> Collected by Moltke Moe from Liv Bratterud in Bøherad, Telemark (Norway). Printed in Moe, *Folkeminne frå Bøherad* (1924), 62.

48.12 The **Tunkall** *at Tengesdal*

At Tengesdal in Hylsfjord there was a *tunkall* who lived in the bunkhouse. When strangers visited the farm, he would throw them on the floor as soon as they had crawled into bed.

The farmer at Tengesdal was named Njædl. He was an unusually strong fellow who wanted to be master in his own house. Once he decided to sleep in the bunkhouse himself. As soon as he lay down, the *tunkall* grabbed hold of him, trying to throw him out of bed. But Njædl put up a fight. He took his knife and cut and slashed and tore in all directions, hitting the walls and resisting with all his might. Then the *tunkall* got scared. He ran to the pigsty and hid himself. Njædl went after him; he did not want him there either. He did not give up until he had driven the *tunkall* from the farm.

When the *tunkall* had gotten a ways from the farm, he turned around and cried. The folks on the farm could hear him sobbing.

> Svale Solheim has documented this legend in western Norway, and Inger Boberg has pointed to parallels in Denmark. Solheim interprets the Norwegian materials as the remains of an ancient ancestral cult. According to Solheim, the *tunkall* represents the original owner of the farm and, thus, the sum of good luck and prosperity associated with the farm.
>
> Contrary to the foregoing legend, here the farmer actually drives the domestic spirit from the place. Solheim suggests that this results from a folk belief tradition dying out owing to changes in agricultural methods and house construction. When the outbuildings used as bunkhouses and for food storage disappeared from the typical farm, the *tunkall*, believed to have his bed there, was forced to leave, too.
>
> See Solheim, "Gardvoren og senga hans," *Maal og minne* (1951), 143–58. Reprinted in *Norveg* 16 (1973), 55–70; Inger M. Boberg, "Gardvordens seng i dansk tradition," *Maal og minne* (1956), 109–20.
>
> Collected by Torkell Mauland from Torjus Tengesdal, Ryfylke, Rogaland (Norway). Printed in Mauland, *Folkeminne fraa Rogaland* 1 (1925), 139.

48.13 The Nisse in the Church Tower

A *nisse* lives in Besser Church. He has his lair on a pile of rags, but on Sundays and other holy days he hides in a little mound nearby. He plays tricks on anyone who offends him.

One evening, when the sexton came to ring in vespers, the *nisse* had some fun with him. The sexton then discovered that a bundle of rags had been tied around the clapper of the bell. As he stood there wondering about this, he saw a little face with a red hat grinning at him from the top of the bell.

> In Denmark, Sweden, and Finland, a limited number of legends describe the guardian spirit of the church — the church *nisse* or *tomte*. This being is to be distinguished from the "church grim" — the revenant of an animal buried alive in the church's foundation. The "church grim" also has a protective function.
>
> See Bengt Holbek and Iørn Piø, *Fabeldyr og sagnfolk* (1967), 155, 222–24; John Pape, "Studier om kyrkogrimen," *Folkkultur* 6 (1946), 11–240.

Collected by E. T. Kristensen from Mikkel Sørensen, Samsø
(Denmark). Printed in Kristensen, *Danske sagn* 2 (1893), 43–44.

48.14 The **Nisse** *Woke Up the Ship's Mate*

A mate sailing on a big steamship once told a story about how
someone scratched him while he was sleeping. The big ship's lantern
had gone out, and another steamship would have smashed right into
them, if he had not been roused in time. It was a *nisse* who woke him
up.

> A variant of the domestic spirit who protects the farm is the spir-
> it who guards the ship. As long as the spirit is on board, the ship
> will not sink. Besides being called a ship's *tomte* or *nisse*, the spirit
> is often called *Klabautermann*.
>
> See Henning Frederik Feilberg, *Nissens historie* (1919), 101–4;
> Bengt Holbek and Iørn Piø, *Fabeldyr og sagnfolk* (1967), 160–62;
> Helge Gerndt, *Fliegender Holländer und Klabautermann* (1971); Rein-
> hard J. Buss, *The Klabautermann of the Northern Seas* (1973); J. Pau-
> li Joensen, " 'Lemperen' eller 'Manden ombord', " *Arv* 31 (1975),
> 74–108.
>
> Collected by Carl-Martin Bergstrand in Tjärnö, Bohuslän
> (Sweden). Printed in Bergstrand, *Bohusländska sägner* (1947), 81.

49. The Spirit of the Mill

In Norway, and in Sweden mostly along the Norwegian border,
folk traditions exist about *kvernknurren* (literally, "mill snarl," Swedish,
kvarngubben, "old man of the mill"). This preternatural being is known
to stop the mill if it is run at night or on a holy day. The implied
sanction against such inappropriate use of the mill is not unequivocal,
however, because the mill sprite is invariably pacified or driven away.

49.1 The Mill Troll

One winter night a farmer was grinding at the mill at Ner-Duåsen.
They used to have fire pits in the mills in the old days, where they
boiled pitch while watching the mill. That way they could both stay
warm and make good use of their time.

But while they were grinding, the mill suddenly stopped, and the
water started gushing up through the floorboards. The farmer took a

firebrand, and, shining the light down there, he saw a big old fellow holding on to the axle of the mill wheel. The farmer thrust the burning piece of wood into the fellow's beard, and it caught fire. Then the old fellow let go in a hurry and disappeared.

Not long afterward the farmer heard someone tramping outside the mill, and then the door tore open, and he saw a huge troll gaping in through the door. Its mouth was so big that the upper jaw touched the doorframe at the ceiling and the lower jaw touched the threshold.

"You've never seen such a big mouth before, have you?" shrieked the troll.

But the farmer grabbed the pot with boiling pitch and threw it into the troll's jaws.

"You've never tried such hot soup before, have you?" he shouted.

Now the troll disappeared, and it never tried to stop the mill at Ner-Duåsen again.

> This popular legend is told not only about trolls but also about mound folk, water sprites, farm spirits, and even mermaids.
>
> Collected in 1933 by Asbjørn Heggem from his father in Sørstranda, Romsdal (Norway). Printed in Olav Rekdal, *Eventyr og segner. Folkeminne frå Romsdal* (1933), 104.

49.2 A Little Man Held the Mill Wheel

Once they had a great deal of grinding to do at Bodanäs. They kept the mill going day and night, yet they could not get it all done.

One evening the mill stopped altogether, even though the water was running as usual. The miller checked in the wheel house, and there he saw a little old man holding the wheel. Then the miller understood what was the matter, and he threw a coin into the chute. After that the mill worked amazingly well, and the miller finished his grinding all at once.

> Collected by Maja Norlén in 1929 from A. W. Strandberg, Björkö parish, Småland (Sweden). Ms. in LUF (2857), 7. Printed in Bengt af Klintberg, *Svenska folksägner* (1972), 118.

50. The Spirit of the Mine

Mining legends constitute one of the largest categories in the folk tradition of continental Europe. They are not nearly as numerous in

Scandinavia because of the relative scarcity of mining activities there. In Norway and Sweden, the spirit of the mine appears most often as a solitary, female being. The *gruvrå* ("ruler of the mine"), *gruvfröken* ("lady of the mine"), or *sølvmora* ("silver mother") helps the miner find the ore and protects him while he is working in the shaft. But she is also believed to jealously guard the wealth hidden below ground, causing the loss of life and other disasters in the mine.

There are also folk traditions about the invisible folk exploiting the mines, a tradition which has its antecedents in mythological stories about dwarfs as miners and smiths.

> See Gerhard Heilfurth, *Bergbau und Bergmann in der deutschsprachi-gen Sagenüberlieferung Mitteleuropas* 1 (1967); Carl-Herman Tillha-gen, "Die Berggeistvorstellungen in Schweden," *The Supernatural Owners of Nature* (1961), 123–57, and "Gruvskrock," *Norveg* 12 (1965), 113–60.

50.1 The Silver Mother at Nasa

Nils Olson from northern Rana tells how his father once went over to look at the mines at Nasa. As it turned out, he stayed away for quite a long time, and when he finally returned, the people were just getting ready to come after him. They had feared that the silver mother in Nasa had taken him.

> The memorat is an example of folk traditions from the Norwegian-Swedish border about mining activities there. The Nasa mine is actually located on Swedish territory, but local folk tradition maintains that the Swedes acquired it by border manipu-lation.
>
> Collected by Knut Strompdal in southern Rana, Nordland (Norway). Printed in Strompdal, *Gamalt frå Helgeland* 3 (1939), 53.

50.2 Klett Mountain

There is silver to be found in Klett Mountain, but you have to know how to get to it.

Once some men walked to Nabset Sound. They called for the fer-ryman to take them across. He rowed them over in his boat. Each one of them was carrying a load of silver so big that the boat almost could not hold it.

"Where did you get all that silver?" asked the ferryman.

"We come from Klett Mountain," they answered.

"Is there silver in Klett Mountain?" he asked.

"Yes, there is a slope where you can find another seven loads of pure silver, if you dig down to the bottom," they answered.

They paid him when they got to shore but vanished as soon as they left the boat.

> This text exemplifies the preternatural beings themselves exploiting the mines.
>
> Collected by Sigurd Nergaard in Åmot, Østerdalen (Norway). Printed in Nergaard, *Gard og grend. Folkeminne fraa Østerdalen* 1 (1921), 110.

50.3 He Lost His Eyesight

According to legend the copper deposits at Ljusnarberg were discovered at the beginning of the seventeenth century by a man named Mårten Finne.

One day he went fishing and slept by his fire. He was awakened by the sound of hammering and pounding in the mountain. A rough voice shouted:

The first who our treasure espies,
will lose both eyes!

When he pushed aside the coals to quench the fire, the rock was laid bare, and there glistened the red ore. But as soon as the exploitation of the find began, Mårten Finne went blind.

> Here the invisible owners of the ore warn against its exploitation by humans.
>
> See Carl-Herman Tillhagen, "Gruvskrock," *Norveg* 12 (1965), 113–60.
>
> Collected in 1902 in Storå, Lindes parish, Västmanland (Sweden). Ms. in Västsvenska folkminnesarkivet, Göteborg (no. 201). Reprinted in Tillhagen, "Gruvskrock," 120.

50.4 They Got Help Finding the Ore

When they started working the silver mines in Hällefors Forest, the miners got help finding the ore. They were searching without finding anything, until one day they heard a clear voice in the mine:

"Keep to the left, otherwise you disturb the foot of my bed."
They did, and found the ore.

> In contrast to the foregoing text, here the lady of the mine actu-
> ally helps the miners locate the deposits.
> See Carl-Herman Tillhagen, "Gruvskrock," *Norveg* 12 (1965),
> 113–60.
> Collected in Hällefors, Västmanland (Sweden). Printed in
> *Bergslagsposten* (October 1939). Reprinted in Tillhagen, "Gruv-
> skrock," 136.

50.5 The Lady of the Mine Warned Them

In Klack Mountain there was a mining pit called Sunshine Mountain. My father heard from my grandfather, who worked there in his
time, that one day the miners had emerged from the mine and were
eating their noon meal in a shack. Suddenly a fine lady appeared and
said:
"Go down into the shaft, pick up your gear, and go home!"
The older men did as she told them, but the young fellows just
laughed and stayed. The mine collapsed and they were all buried under the rocks.
It was the lady of the mine who had warned them. Whenever she
showed herself, a miner would lose his life.

> In this instance the lady of the mine functions as the guardian of
> the mine workers.
> Collected in Norberg parish, Västmanland (Sweden). Ms. in
> ULMA, 8042. Printed in Carl-Herman Tillhagen, "Gruvskrock,"
> *Norveg* 12 (1965), 139.

51. The Water Sprite

The spirit of waterfalls, rivers, and lakes is most often called *nøkk*
(Swedish, *näck*; cf. English, "nix"). In Norway, the water sprite is also
referred to as *grim* (or *fossegrim*), a name that is applied to the guardian
spirit of the church and graveyard in Sweden and Denmark (cf. English, "church grim").
The water sprite appears variously in human or in horse shape. He
instructs fiddlers in their art but also threatens human life by drowning. The *nøkk* as often been looked upon as a demonic being and
therefore has absorbed certain traits identified with the devil. In the

English language, "nix" has become a noa-name for Satan (Old Nick). In older ballad tradition, the *nøkk* is usually depicted as a dangerous, erotic being.

See Tobias Norlind, *Studier i svensk folklore* (1911), 94–161; Lutz Röhrich, "Sagenballaden," *Handbuch des Volksliedes* 1 (1973), 101–56; Maja Bergstrand, "Näcken som musikaliskt väsen," *FmFt* 23 (1936), 14–31; Arne Bjørndal and Brynjulf Alver, *-og fela ho lét. Norsk spelemannstradisjon* (1966); *Atlas över svensk folkkultur II. Sägen, tro och högtidssed 2*, edited by Åke Campbell and Åsa Nyman (1976), 65–73; Jochum Stattin, *Näcken. Spelman eller gränsvakt?* (1984).

51.1 Learning to Play the Fiddle

Many years ago there lived a little boy by the name of Paul. He was working at the mountain farm here, herding cattle. The boy wanted very much to learn to play the fiddle; he walked around all day sawing on his little ragged instrument.

Then one evening he sat playing, close to where we are sitting now. Suddenly he heard beautiful sounds coming from that little waterfall over there. At first he was frightened, but then it sounded so very beautiful that he forgot his fear, took his little ragged fiddle, and began playing. It seemed that he had learned to play all at once; his fingers were more pliant and lighter, and the bow was dancing over the strings almost by itself.

When he had been sitting and playing for a while, a little old man appeared to him and said:

"If you will promise me one thing, Paul, I'll teach you to play so well that you will be the best fiddler in the whole village."

Paul asked him what that might be.

"Oh, nothing more," said the *grim*—for that is what he was—"than that you stop shouting and carrying on so in the meadows at night."

Well, Paul promised, and then he really learned to play.

See Tobias Norlind, *Studier i svensk folklore* (1911), 123–26; Bengt Holbek and Iørn Piø, *Fabeldyr og sagnfolk* (1967), 203; Arne Bjørndal and Brynjulf Alver, *-og fela ho lét. Norsk spelemannstradisjon* (1966), 132–45.

Legend type: ML 4090.

Collected by S. Sørensen in Flesberg, Buskerud (Norway). Ms. in NFS Sørensen (3), 11.

51.2 She Whistled the Tune

An old woman told me this story:
Once I was sitting by Women's Creek, tending cattle. I clearly
heard a *grim* playing a tune. As soon as he had finished, I ran home
and whistled the tune to my husband, who, at that time, was still a
bachelor and a fiddler.

> There are many fiddle tunes said to have preternatural origin.
> See Arne Bjørndal and Brynjulf Alver, *-og fela ho lét. Norsk
> spelemannstradisjon* (1966), 140–44.
> Collected by Olav Austad in Byggland, Setesdal, Aust-Agder
> (Norway). Ms. in NFS Questionnaire: Traditions about Preter-
> natural Beings (Austad).

51.3 He Gave a Gnawed Off Bone to the Water Sprite

Once there was a man who wanted to learn to play the fiddle from
a *näck*. One should always offer a water sprite something in return,
but the man just threw a bone into the river without anything on it.
Then the *näck* got angry and shouted:
"You'll learn to tune, but you'll never learn to play."

> This legend is widespread in western Sweden and Norway. The
> most common form of payment to the water sprite was a leg of
> mutton. In dealing with the water sprite, as with all preternatural
> beings, one must treat them with respect.
> See Jöran Sahlgren, "Strömkarlen spelar," *Namn och bygd* 23
> (1935), 42–55; Arne Bjørndal and Brynjulf Alver, *-og fela ho lét.
> Norsk spelemannstradisjon* (1966), 132–34.
> Legend type: ML 4090.
> Collected by Ingrid Settergren in Skredsvik, Bohuslän
> (Sweden). Printed in Carl-Martin Bergstrand, *Bohuslänska sägner*
> (1947), 18.

51.4 They Had to Keep Dancing

When I was young, I heard about a fiddler named Pelle who learned to play from a *näck*. Damn but it was easy for him!
Once he was playing at a dance on a farm. Later that night all the
folks became so crazy from his playing that each and every one of

them, young and old, had to get up and dance, whether they wanted to or not. And in the end, even the furniture in the house began dancing! That is what really happened! There was no end to the dancing, until they took Pelle's fiddle and cut the strings. If they had not done this, they would all have danced themselves to death.

> The musical impulse was often considered demonic and therefore dangerous. The fiddler had to play, and those who listened had to dance, whether they chose to or not. In many legends it is in fact not the water sprite but the devil who instructs the fiddler or plays himself. In some variants of the legend, the dancers dance themselves to death, leaving only their skulls behind.
>
> The compulsion to dance may be an elaboration of the dance epidemic first documented in Kölbigk, Germany, in the eleventh century. Legends and exempla describing this dance craze were widely distributed throughout medieval Europe. (Cf. nos. 54.13–54.14.)
>
> See Dag Strömbäck, "Den underbara årsdansen," *Arkiv för nordisk filologi* 59 (1944), 111–26. Reprinted in Strömbäck, *Folklore och filologi* (1970), 54–69, and "Kölbigk och Hårga," part 1: *Arv* 17 (1961), 1–48, and part 2: *Arv* 24 (1968), 91–132; A. Martin, "Geschichte der Tanzkrankheit in Deutschland," *Zeitschrift für Volkskunde* 24 (1914), 113–34, 225–39; see also Frederic C. Tubach, *Index Exemplorum*, no. 1419 (FFC 204).
>
> Collected by Sven Rothman in 1911 from a woman named Månsson in Västra, Harg parish, Östergötland (Sweden). Printed in Rothman, *Östgötska folkminnen* (1941), 95–96.

51.5 *The* Näck *Longed for Salvation*

There was a boy from Gylltorp who was walking home after a day's work at the manor. He came to the creek, and there he saw a *näck* sitting on a rock in the water. He was playing his fiddle and singing:

On Judgment Day, on Judgment Day,
I will receive God's mercy!
On Judgment Day, on Judgment Day,
I will receive God's mercy!

But the boy shouted:
"You will never receive God's mercy because you're much too foul!"

When the *näck* heard this he became very sad, and his crying could be heard a long way off. When the boy got home, his father was standing outside in the yard, and he asked about the noise down by the creek. The boy told him what it was all about, and the father said:

"Go back to the creek and tell the *näck*: my father is better read than I am, and he says that you will receive God's mercy."

Well, the boy did as he was told, and then the complaining stopped. Instead, the *näck* played beautifully on his fiddle and, finally, disappeared into the water.

> The oldest Scandinavian variant of this legend is found in a Danish book of devotions from 1509 by Gottfred of Ghemen. In a number of variants, the water sprite is identified with the fallen angels. (Cf. no. 44.2.)
>
> See Dag Strömbäck, "Näcken och förlossningen," *Varbergs museum årsbok* (1963), 77–85. Reprinted in Strömbäck, *Folklore och filologi* (1970), 115–22.

51.6 The Hour Has Come, but Not the Man!

Someplace in West Jylland, folks were cutting grass on a meadow by a river, when they heard a voice from the water:

"The hour has come, but not the man!"

Shortly after, a man came running as fast as he could and wanted to wade through the river. But they stopped him, saying that he must not cross the river; if he did, he would drown.

"Give me some water to drink, then," he said. "I'm so thirsty!"

They fetched some water for him, but as soon as he drank it, he collapsed and died.

> This legend combines two motifs, namely, that preternatural beings associated with the river demand sacrifice and that humans cannot escape their fate. The earliest known variant of this widely recorded legend is found in Gervasius of Tilbury's *Otia imperialia* (1214).
>
> See Robert Wildhaber, "Die Stunde ist da, aber der Mann nicht. Ein europäisches Sagenmotiv," *Rheinisches Jahrbuch für Volkskunde* 9 (1958), 65–88.
>
> Legend type: ML 4050.
>
> Collected by E. T. Kristensen in Rønslund, Vrads parish, Jylland (Denmark). Printed in Kristensen, *Danske sagn* 2 (1893), 159.

51.7 The Nøkk *in Horse Shape*

Once a shepherd girl was looking for some lost sheep. She had been walking for a long time and was exhausted. Then she caught sight of a gray horse, and, overjoyed, she fastened her garter onto it for reins, threw her apron over its back, and led it to a mound to climb on its back. But just as she mounted it, she said:

"I don't think I need to ride, after all."

Then the horse gave a start, jumped into a nearby lake, and disappeared. The girl now knew what kind of horse it had been—a *nøkk*—because *nøkks* can't stand to hear their own names and they will jump back into the lake if they do. You see, another name for the *nøkk* is "need," and the horse took off when the girl said "need."

> In legends throughout Scandinavia, the *nøkk* is described as taking the shape of a horse to lure people, especially children, into the water. Often the intended victims are saved by saying "*nøkk*," or something close to it.
>
> See Brita Egardt, "De svenska vattenhästsägnerna och deras ursprung," *Folkkultur* 4 (1944), 119–66.
>
> Collected by Magnús Grímsson, a minister in Mosfell, from Arnljótur Ólafsson, a minister in Bægisá (Iceland). Printed in Jón Árnason, *Íslenzkar þjóðsögur og æfintýri* 1 (1862), 137. Reprinted in new edition 1 (1954), 131.

51.8 *Riding the* Nøkk

One evening the children in Sørvágur had gone down to Leitisvatn to play. A *nøkk* appeared in the shape of a large horse, and they wanted to climb on its back. As soon as they got up, the horse carried them down to the water. The smallest boy, who had not been able to climb up on the horse, became frightened and called to his brother Niklas, who was sitting on the horse:

"Nika! Nika!"

The boy was so little that he still could not speak properly. But the *nøkk* thought its own name had been called and disappeared, so the children were saved.

It is said that when the *nøkk* hears its name, it loses all its power.

> (Cf. no. 51.7.)
>
> Collected by Jakob Jakobsen on the Faeroe Islands. Printed in Jakobsen, *Færøske folkesagn og æventyr* (1898–1901), 192.

51.9 Seven Women on a Horse

Once there were seven women on their way to visit a neighbor who had been brought to confinement. They came to a river and wondered how to get across, when suddenly they saw a horse. They decided to ride it across the river. They took off their garters and tied them together to make reins. But as soon as one or two of them had climbed on the horse, it grew so large that there was room for all seven women. They rode out into the river, but one of them said:

By Jesus' cross,
never have I seen so big a horse.

Then the horse vanished, and the women stood there in the river, holding on to their garters.

> (Cf. nos. 51.7–51.8.) In this instance it is the protective power of the holy name, rather than the name of the *nøkk*, that makes the water sprite disappear.
> The legend is known throughout Denmark and in Skåne (southern Sweden). The verse spoken by one of the women is traditional in this legend type.
> Collected by E. T. Kristensen from Kristen Ebbesen, Egtved, Jylland (Denmark). Printed in Kristensen, *Danske sagn* 2 (1893), 163.

51.10 The Näck as a Working Horse

Somewhere there was a farmer who did his spring plowing with the help of a *näck*. First he sent the servant girl to the field to get the horse. But she returned without it, saying that there were two horses on the pasture.

"Take the one that isn't ours," said the farmer.

She got the strange horse, and the farmer used it for all his spring work. But he never dared take the bit out of the horse's mouth. One time the servant girl was supposed to unharness the horse. She absent-mindedly took the bit out. As soon as the horse was rid of the bit, it ran right into the lake.

> One could bind the water sprite in horse shape by placing a bit on him, the same way a witch could be forced to stay in animal shape as long as the bit was on her. (Cf. no. 41.3.) The oldest

Scandinavian variant of this legend is found in *Landnámabók*, from
the twelfth century, which describes the settlement of Iceland.

See Dag Strömbäck, "Some Notes on the Nix in Older Nordic
Tradition," *Medieval Literature and Folklore Studies: Essays in Honor of
F. L. Utley* (1970), 245–56.

Collected by Elis Åström in 1941 in Kisa, Östergötland
(Sweden). Printed in Åström, *Folktro och folkliv i Östergötland*
(1962), 25–26.

51.11 Binding the Näck

Näck, näck, needle thief,
your father was a stable thief,
your mother was a whore,
did wicked things and more!
Näck, you are bound!

People protected themselves against a *näck* by binding him with
steel, throwing a stone in the water, and reciting a magic formula. This formula combines naming the preternatural being with
the magic effect of insult and accusation.

See K. Rob. V. Wikman, "Magiska bindebruk," *Hembygden*
(1912), 65–73, 116–17.

Collected by L. F. Rääf in 1801 from Samuel Ödmann,
Småland (Sweden). Printed in Rääf, *Svenska skrock och signerier*,
edited by Wikman (1957), no. 12b. Reprinted in Bengt af Klintberg, *Svenska trollformler* (1965), 98.

52. The Spirits of the Sea

The sea, like any other aspect of nature, was believed to be popu-
lated by various preternatural beings, both solitary and collective. As
a group they correspond in nature and function to the invisible folk
of forests, fields, rivers, and farmsteads, but they are modified to
reflect the environment of the sea. They include the *sjørå* ("sea ruler"),
mermaid and merman, *draug*, and other sea monsters, as well as the
inhabitants of fabulous islands.

See Bengt Holbek and Iørn Piø, *Fabeldyr og sagnfolk* (1967), 55–98;
Karl Rencke, "Havsfolket," *Bohuslänska folkminnen* (1922); Gwen

Benwell and Arthur Waugh, *Sea Enchantress. The Tale of the Mermaid and Her Kin* (1965).

52.1 The Cattle of the Mermaid

When I was a little girl, I had to go and watch the cattle. Every morning I herded the cows to a meadow called Salvig. One morning I saw the whole meadow filled with horses and cattle, but because it was so foggy, I could not quite see what they looked like. Then they all rushed into the water, and it made such a roaring sound that I was quite frightened. My cows followed behind, and one of them got all the way into the water.

Other people have seen these horses and cattle, too. My husband says this cannot be true, but it is.

> This memorat was collected by E. T. Kristensen from Kirsten Olesen, Ovrø, Horns parish, Jylland (Denmark). Printed in Kristensen, *Danske sagn*, N.R., 2 (1928), 105–6.

52.2 He Gave a New Mitten to the Merman

Once a skipper from Borre sailed by Sjøbjærg. There he found a large mitten. He took it home and knit a mitten to match it. Then he brought the pair of mittens back to Sjøbærg. Sometime later he was again sailing from Borre and passing by Sjøbjærg, when he heard a voice, shouting:

Listen, my mitten friend,
put your boat in at Borre,
'cause Tolk is spitting,
and the oaks in Norway groan.

The skipper turned around and sailed back to Borre, and there brewed a storm the likes of which nobody had ever seen. All the boats that were still out at sea were destroyed.

> Tolk is the name of a stretch of water off the shore of Denmark.
>   This legend is known in the coastal regions of all Scandinavia. It was first recorded in Olaus Magnus, *Historia de gentibus septentrionalibus* (1555), vol. 2, chap. 23.
>   See Bengt Holbek and Iørn Piø, *Fabeldyr og sagnfolk* (1967), 84–85.
>   Legend type: ML 4055.

Collected by Th. Jensen from Kirsten Andersdatter, Borre, (Denmark). Printed in E. T. Kristensen, *Danske sagn* 2 (1893), 144–45.

52.3 A Duel of Wits

A merman could take either human or fish shape, and sometimes it happened that fishermen would catch one. He might get trapped in the net or on a fish hook. He would be naked and cold and expected to be given clothes. Nobody could kill him; folks were to give him something to wear and throw him back into the sea. Otherwise he would take a terrible revenge.

The merman often came and talked to folks. If he got the last word in a duel of wits, he took them captive. Once a merman came across a farmer.

"Tonight two sons have been born to you," said the merman.

"That's good," the farmer said, "it makes the family grow."

"One of them died," the merman said.

"Then they won't fight over their inheritance," answered the farmer.

> In this description, the act of clothing the merman is motivated by fear rather than pity. Other legends indicate that catching a merman would bring luck in fishing.
>
> The idea that the preternatural being would gain power over his human opponent if he got the last word in a duel of wits is widely known from European legends, folktales, and myth.
>
> Collected by Johan Hveding in Hålogoland, Nordland (Norway). Printed in Hveding, *Folketru og folkeliv på Hålogoland* 2 (1944), 39.

52.4 The Mermaid and the Fisherman

Once a mermaid met a fisherman. She said he could put three questions to her. But the fisherman asked only some simple questions. Finally he asked about the strongest thing to use in making a flail.

"Calf hide, you crazy man," she said. "You should rather have asked what happens to your brewing water. The answer to that might have helped both you and your children."

The popularity of this legend seems to derive from the comical combination of trivial and enigmatic elements. Logically speaking, the question proposed by the mermaid is hardly more reasonable or important than the one actually asked by the fisherman.

A flail was a tool for threshing grain. It consisted of a wooden handle to which a shorter and stouter stick was tied to swing freely.

Legend type: ML 4060.

Collected by Olav Rekdal in 1923 from Guri Finnset in Eikisdalen, Romsdalen (Norway). Printed in Rekdal, *Eventyr og segner* (1933), 110.

52.5 The Mermaid at Stad

A man from Furestaven at Stad once came across a mermaid lying on the shore. He thought that she had been beached by the low tide.

She had scraped the area around herself free of seaweed and kelp, and had wrapped some seaweed around herself so that it looked like a belt.

The man stared at her for a long time. She smiled at him. Never in his life had he seen a woman with such beautiful eyes. She had long golden hair that reached down to her waist. He came closer. He was just about to place her on his lap, when he saw her fish tail. Below her waist she looked almost like a porpoise.

Eventually she rolled down to the edge of the water. Then she laughed aloud and disappeared into the waves.

> As in the case of an encounter between a man and a *hulder*, the response is ambivalent, blending erotic fascination with repulsion and fear of the mermaid's animal nature. (Cf. nos. 46.2–46.4, 46.11.)
>
> See Reidar Th. Christiansen, "Til de norske sjøvetters historie," *Maal og minne* (1935), 1–25.
>
> Collected by Kleofas G. Kvalsvik, Herøy, Møre (Norway). Printed in Martin Bjørndal, *Segn og tru. Folkeminne frå Møre* (1949), 83.

52.6 The Wind Knots

There was a skipper by the name of Rask. A beautiful woman came to him and asked him to load twenty-four bushels of rye for her and row them out to sea. When she instructed him that they were home, he was to unload the rye. The skipper should simply throw the sacks into the sea, she said. Then he should go with her and get his payment.

"Take my hand and jump," said the woman, and instantly they were in a big hall beneath the sea. There sat a blind old man.

"I smell the blood of a Christian," the old fellow said. "Come over here and let me finger wrestle with you."

The mermaid told the skipper that he should hand an anchor hook to the old fellow. This he did.

"Not bad, not bad at all," said the old man.

Then the skipper received a handkerchief in which three knots had been tied.

"When you get into a lull, you can open one knot. And if you want to go really fast, untie two knots, but never untie the third."

Once when the skipper had been to the city, he wanted to sail home, but the wind was still, the sails were slack, and his sloop was heavily laden. Rask was not quite sober. He untied the first knot and was determined to sail anyway. The sail filled with wind and everybody watched in amazement. Then Rask wanted to sail even faster, and he untied the second knot. The sloop went so fast, it made the water hiss. But he must have untied the third knot, too, because nobody ever saw him again.

> Many legends describe how humans supply grain or other goods to the hidden folk of the sea. Payment might take the form of some special power, the use of which, however, carried certain risks. The motif of the "wind knots" is best known from folk traditions about witches and other specialists in making sailing wind. (Cf. nos. 32.1–32.2, 43.1.)
>
> Collected by Carl-Martin Bergstrand from Helmer Olsson, Rolfstorp, Halland (Sweden). Printed in Bergstrand, *Hallands sägner* (1949), 35.

52.7 The Revenge of the Mermaid

The fact that mermaids are evil is shown by the following story:

People say that in the parish of Torp, toward the northern end of Hafsten, there once was a boy who got involved with a *sjørå*. Nobody knew about it except, of course, for the boy. But then he got engaged to a human girl. He and the girl were to go to Uddevalla to buy their rings. The *sjørå* told him that he could get everything that was customary to buy for one's betrothed except for one thing: he must not buy her the book. She meant the hymnal, which a groom always gave to his bride. The boy promised. But when they got to Uddevalla, the girl would not let him have any peace until he bought her the hymnal, too.

On their way home, the *sjørå* appeared to the boy, saying that he should not have bought it; he would see. And when the wedding took place, there was a big commotion and uproar at the farm, and then the bridegroom got sick and strange and never got well again.

> The legend ascribes demonic qualities to the mermaid. This is made explicit by the symbol of the hymnal representing both the conventional relationship of a groom to his bride and the sacred from which the preternatural being is excluded.
>
> Collected by Anton Abrahamsson (born 1845) in Torp, Orust, Bohuslän (Sweden).
>
> Printed in Carl-Martin Bergstrand, *Gammalt från Orust* (1962), 13–14.

52.8 The Seal Woman

Seals were actually people who of their own free will plunged themselves into the ocean and drowned. Once each year, on Twelfth Night, they get a chance to take off their sealskins, and then they look just like everyone else. They dance and play on the flat rocks by the shore and in the breeding caves near the beach, and they have a fine time. A legend tells how a boy from the southmost farm in Mikladalur heard people say that the seals got together on Twelfth Night in a cave on the breeding grounds not far from the village. So, in the evening, he went there to see if this was true. He hid behind a rock in front of the cave. After the sun went down, he saw seals swimming from all directions toward the spot where he was crouching. They took off their skins and put them on a flat rock on the beach. They did look just like ordinary people! The boy was fascinated with these creatures, but then he saw the most beautiful woman he had ever seen step out of a sealskin. He watched where she placed her skin, which was not far from where he was. The boy crept over and took it and returned to his hiding place. The seal folk danced all night long, but when it started to grow light, they returned to their skins. The beautiful seal woman could not find hers and wrung her hands and wailed because the sun was about to come up. But just before it did, she caught its scent near the hiding place of the boy from Mikladalur and pleaded with him to give it back to her. But he walked away from her, and she had to follow him to the farm. He took her as his wife, and they got on well together. But he always had to be careful not to let her get to her sealskin. He kept it in a locked chest and carried the key with him. One day he went fishing, and while he was sitting out at sea, pulling in fish, his hand happened to brush his belt where the key usually hung. He was dumbfounded when he realized that he must have forgotten the key at home. He cried out in his grief:

"This evening I'll be without a wife!"

The other fishermen pulled in their lines and rowed home as fast as they could. When the man from Mikladalur got to his house, his wife was gone. Only the children were there, sitting quietly. So that they would not hurt themselves while they were alone in the house, his wife had put out the fire and locked up all the knives and sharp objects. After that, she had run down to the beach, pulled on her sealskin, and plunged into the sea. She had indeed found the key and opened the chest, and when she saw the sealskin, she could not control herself and had to put it on. This is where the old saying comes from:

"He couldn't control himself any more than a seal that finds its skin."

When she leaped into the sea, her seal mate found her, and they swam away together. All these years he had been waiting for her to come back to him. When the children she had with the man from Mikladalur went down to the beach, a seal could be seen just off the shore watching them, and everyone thought that it was their mother.

Many years went by, and there is nothing to tell of the man on the farm and the children he and the seal woman had together. Then one day the villagers from Mikladalur went hunting for baby seals down in the breeding caves. The night before, the seal woman appeared to the farmer in a dream and said that if he went with the other villagers to hunt baby seals, he must make sure that they did not kill the male seal in front of the cave or the two seal pups that were lying at the very back of the cave. The male seal was her mate and the pups their sons, she said, and she told him how they were marked. But the farmer paid no heed to this dream. He went with the villagers to the cave, and they killed all the pups. As his share of the catch, the farmer got the entire male seal and the flippers of the pups, and for dinner they had boiled seal's head and flippers. Dinner was being served, when suddenly there came a loud noise and crashing, and the seal woman appeared in the kitchen in the shape of an ugly troll. She sniffed in the serving bowls and shouted in a rage:

"Here is the nose bone of the old man, and here, Hárekur's hands and Friðrikur's foot! Avenged it is and avenged it will be on the men of Mikladalur! Some will be lost at sea, and some will fall from mountain cliffs and ledges! And this will go on until so many have died that they can hold hands and reach all the way around Kalsoy!"

Then she disappeared with a great crashing sound and was never seen again. All too often men from Mikladalur perish at sea or fall from mountain cliffs, but it is said that there is still a foolish farmer on the southmost farm, and so it seems that the number of men that have perished is not yet enough to reach around the island.

> This legend has relatively limited distribution in Denmark, northern Norway, the Faeroe Islands, and Iceland. The motif of a woman in the shape of a seal, however, is known in much of northern Europe.
>
> Twelfth Night is the evening of January 6, the feast of Epiphany, or Twelfth Day, which is the concluding day of medieval Christmas.
>
> See Bengt Holbek and Iørn Piø, *Fabeldyr og sagnfolk* (1967), 64–65; G. Benwell and A. Waugh, *Sea Enchantress* (1965), 15–21.
>
> Legend type: ML 4080.
>
> Collected by V. U. Hammershaimb on the Faeroe Islands. Printed in Hammershaimb, "Færøiske folkesagn," *Antiquarisk tidsskrift, 1849–51* (1852), 190–93. Reprinted in Hammershaimb, *Savn* (1969), 134–37.

52.9 This One Suits Me, Said the Draug

A boat crew was on its way to Lofoten. They sailed into a storm and were forced to land on a small island, where they stayed for several days. They beached their boat in the usual way, but the oars were not left undisturbed. They were in order that night, but by the next morning, they had been moved. The leader of the crew hid himself to find out who might be messing with their boat. When it got to be night, a *draug* appeared, climbed into the boat, and started to poke around. He tried one rowing space after another, but he kept saying:

"Doesn't suit me."

Well, when he came to the head man's space, he said:

"This one suits me."

"Well, if it suits you, it suits me too," said the head man and drove a halibut spike right through the *draug*. The *draug* jumped into the sea so fast that phosphorescence shone around him. But that night the *draug* entered the shack where the crew was sleeping, and he dragged the head man out to sea.

> In Old Norse the term *draugr* primarily refers to a revenant. In recent Scandinavian folk tradition, various terms are used in reference to unidentified persons who have drowned at sea: in Danish, the common name is *strandvasker* ("beach washer"), in Swedish, *gast* ("ghost"). In Norwegian, the term *draug* refers to drowned persons as well as to malevolent preternatural beings of the sea.
>
> In this legend the *draug* both prophesies and becomes the material cause of the death of the fisherman.
>
> See Svale Solheim, "Den norske tradisjonen om draugen," *Norveg* 15 (1972), 43–57.
>
> Legend type: ML 4070.
>
> Collected by K. Strompdal from Halfrid Husje in Nesna, Nordland (Norway). Ms. in NFS Strompdal 11 (1935), 98.

52.10 The Kitchen Boy Beat His Mitten on the Draug

One day the kitchen boy from one of the shacks at Medfjord went down to the boat landing to beat his mittens. It was low tide and pitch black, too. He found a suitable rock covered with seaweed and began hitting the mittens against it. But to his horror, the rock was alive, and it jumped into the sea, spraying water behind it. The boy ran up to the shack and told them what had happened. Everybody realized that the boy had come across a *draug* and that the *draug* would be back to take revenge for the thrashing it had received. They agreed that right after supper they would all lie down with their feet toward the door and put the kitchen boy in between them.

At midnight the door flew open and a long arm with a hook reached in and took hold of the boy. But his comrades held on to him, and the *draug* let go. They never saw it again.

> The crew of fisherman described here are staying at one of the shacks set up for this purpose near the fishing grounds. It was customary to wash clothes by beating them with a stick or on a rock.

Collected by Arthur Brox from Kornelius Enoksen in Ytre Senja, Troms (Norway). Printed in Brox, *Folkeminne frå Ytre Senja* 1 (1970), 41.

52.11 The **Draug** *Shunned the Excrement*

Whenever people sailed anywhere, they had to take great care in tying up their boats because the *draug* would come and try to undo the knots. The only sure defense was to put human excrement on the rope with which they tied up their boats on shore.

Once some folks were on a trip and sought harbor somewhere. The skipper had seen a thing or two, so he knew about the *draug*. Therefore, when they had tied up on land, he shit on the rope. That night they heard a *draug* come out of the sea to undo the rope holding the boat. But that time it did not work.

"Damn, it's dirty!" they heard him say.

He had found the human excrement, and it had scared him off.

> The use of excrement and obscenity as a means of protection against preternatural beings and demonic powers is well documented in tradition.
>
> Collected by Knut Strompdal in Helgeland, Nordland (Norway). Printed in Strompdal, *Gamalt frå Helgeland* 1 (1929), 134–35.

52.12 The Dead Fight the **Draug**

A couple lived near the graveyard. One evening they were going to have herring for supper. The barrel with the herring stood just inside the door of the boathouse, but the woman did not dare go there. So the man grabbed a plate and went himself. He put his fist into the barrel and pulled out some herring. But suddenly he saw a creature with green eyes. The man got scared and hit it. There arose a terrible howl in the boathouse, and the man heard a flock of sea monsters come up on shore. The man threw away the plate of herring and ran through the field. When he got to the graveyard, he yelled:

"Up, all Christian folk, help me!"

Then he raced home and into the house. The next day he went to the graveyard to take a look. He found a big pile of seaweed and broken crosses from the graves.

In contrast to the foregoing text, it is the sacred that protects man against the malevolent *draug* in this legend. At times the *draug* are specifically identified with people who drowned at sea and, therefore, were not buried in sacred soil. There exists an implicit enmity between them and the dead who received Christian burial.

Reidar Th. Christiansen has pointed out parallels to this text in legends from France, Germany, and England, in which the dead rescue people from their living human pursuers.

See Christiansen, "Sjødraugene og landdraugene," *Jul i Salten* (1938), 15–17; Knut Liestøl, *Norsk folkedikting* 3 (1939), 199–200.

Legend type: ML 4065.

Collected by Arthur Brox from Kornelius Enoksen in Ytre Senja, Troms (Norway). Printed in Brox, *Folkeminne frå Ytre Senja* 1 (1970), 41.

52.13 The Sea Serpent

Once a sea serpent was lying across a fjord, thereby closing it to ships and boats, so that there was no way to get into town. They put sharp iron prongs on the bows of their ships and tried to kill or chase the sea serpent away. They managed to injure it, coloring the water blood red, but they could not get it out. Then they did not know what to do except hold a prayer meeting at church. From all the pulpits, prayers were said to free the town from this calamity.

Then a sea horse emerged from the ocean, and there was a fight to the death with the sea serpent. In the end the serpent let out a terrible howl and disappeared in the sea. The sea horse followed it, and since then, no one has seen either one of them.

> The belief in various kinds. of huge sea monsters is documented in legendary tradition, myth, and literature around the world. The sea horse was imagined to be a combination of horse and fish.
>
> See Bengt Holbek and Iørn Piø, *Fabeldyr og sagnfolk* (1967), 412–49; Elizabeth Skjelsvik, "Norwegian Lake and Sea Monsters," *Norveg* 7 (1960), 29–45.
>
> Legend type: ML 4085.
>
> Collected by Torkell Mauland in Rogaland (Norway). Printed in Mauland, *Folkeminne fraa Rogaland* 2 (1931), 7.

52.14 He Met the Sea Monster

People believed that there were monsters on the bottom of the ocean. They would surface, taking boats, people, and fish back into the depths with them. When they surfaced, they would first rise slowly, and then they would shoot up and collapse like a breaker.

Once a man was out in his boat, fishing with a handline. He paddled to a place where he knew there were a lot of fish. He hardly got bait on his hook before he caught one. But after sitting there for a while, he noticed that the water was becoming more and more shallow. He thought this was strange. He looked toward land to see whether he had drifted and lost his bearings. But, no, his position was exactly what it should be.

"It must be old Erik himself," he said.

And he hurriedly pulled up his line and rowed away as fast as he could. And it was high time, too. As soon as he got away, the waves crashed around him as if he had run into the worst breaker. He had encountered a sea monster. There are always a lot of fish just above it. But if a fisherman does not get away before the monster breaks through the surface of the water, he is doomed.

> See Bengt Holbek and Iørn Piø, *Fabeldyr og sagnfolk* (1967), 433–34.
> Collected by K. Strompdal in Helgeland, Nordland (Norway). Printed in Strompdal, *Gamalt frå Helgeland* 1 (1929), 132.

52.15 The Harbor on Utrøst

There was a sloop from Hålogaland that took off from Bergen rather late one year. It carried goods for the towns up north.

Time passed and it was already fall when the sloop entered the waters off Trondheim. It became critical then to make good use of the wind and to make the journey as short as possible. The skipper suggested they sail across the open sea from the Fro Islands to Lofoten. The others agreed and they steered the sloop out to sea.

On their way a terrible storm broke. They sailed and sailed and did not know where they were. They saw neither land nor shipping lanes, and everybody was sure they were going to shipwreck. All of a sudden, they saw land far ahead. They sailed closer but nobody recognized the land. It was low in contour and beautiful, and there were green meadows. They steered even closer and turned into a bay. It was still there, and the wind blew seaward. They stayed in the bay until the storm abated.

When they had raised anchor, the land disappeared. They were out on the lonely sea once more. So they sailed again for many days. Then they struck land at Lofoten Spit.

When the sloop returned, people talked much about that land. Nobody knew just where the sloop had been, but many surmised that they had sailed to Utrøst. Later the sloop was put up. Then it proved that people had been right. They found ears of barley around the steering lock. They had sailed over the grain fields on Utrøst.

> All over the world, folk traditions exist about hidden islands of bliss. In Western context the most famous is Atlantis, described by Plato in Timaios and Kritias (4th century B.C.) In Norway the best known is Utrøst, imagined to lie somewhere beyond the isle of Røst in northern Norway. Utrøst is populated by preternatural beings who live much like humans except that they are more prosperous and their environment is more beautiful and fruitful. Utrøst is visible to humans only in moments of mortal danger. Visitors are usually well received, and when they return home, good luck follows them.
>
> See Bengt Holbek and Iørn Piø, Fabeldyr og sagnfolk (1967), 229–54.
>
> Legend type: ML 4075.
>
> Collected by Johan Hveding from various sources in Tysfjord, Ofoten, and Lofoten, Nordland (Norway). Printed in Hveding, Folketru og folkeliv på Hålogaland (1935), 87.

52.16 Svínoy

There is a story about Svínoy that tells how it was originally a floating island, like some others in the Faeroes. It came from the north but was rarely seen because it brought foggy weather with it and was covered by mist. Now you shall hear how it happened that Svínoy came to lie still.

In the village of Viðareiði on Viðoy, the villagers had a sow but no boar, yet the sow had piglets every year. Everyone wondered about this and could not understand how it happened. People did say that she was not in the village sometimes, but she always came right back. One day she trotted off eastward through the village and over toward Eiðisvik. A woman managed to tie a bunch of keys to her tail. The sow jumped into the sea and swam away from shore. A little while after this, people on Viðareiði could see an island nearing them from south of the point. As quickly as they could, they manned a boat and rowed out to the island, and now they could see it and land on it. When the sow had carried iron onto that island, it had been fixed, and the fog had evaporated. And it has lain there ever since. People called it Svínoy because it was full of swine when they first went out to it and because a swine had fastened it to the ocean floor, so that it was not a floating island anymore. And it was out there that the sow from Viðareiði had found a mate.

> Both in Norway and on the Faeroe Islands, folk traditions exist about an invisible, floating island, which is found by an animal, usually a pig, carrying a metal object on its body. The metal disenchants the island.
>
> See Bengt Holbek and Iørn Piø, *Fabeldyr og sagnfolk* (1967), 246; Dag Strömbäck, "Att helga land," *Festskrift tillägnad Axel Hägerström* (1928), 198–220. Reprinted in Strömbäck, *Folklore och filologi* (1970), 135–65.

53. The Wild Hunt

In Scandinavian folk tradition, there are two chief types of night riders: the hunter and his dogs pursuing a woman, and the host flying through the air—especially at Christmastime. In Norway this host is usually called *oskorei* or *jolareidi* (Christmas riders).

> See Hilding Celander, "Oskoreien och besläktade föreställningar i äldre och nyare nordisk tradition," *Saga och sed* (1943), 71–175; Bengt Holbek and Iørn Piø, *Fabeldyr og sagnfolk* (1967), 99–106; L. Petzoldt, *Deutsche Volkssagen* (1970), 137–55, 393–401; Lutz Röhrich, "Die Frauenjagdsage," *IV. International Congress for Folk-Narrative Research in Athens* (1965), 408–23; *Atlas över svensk folkkultur II. Sägen, tro och högtidssed 2*, edited by Åke Campbell and Åsa Nyman (1976), 43–57.

53.1 *He Rode with the* Oskorei

Taddak Tveit once rode with the *oskorei* to Mykland. Taddak was an old man, and he had gone to bed. But before he knew it, he was on horseback in the middle of the host. They rode so hard that the sparks were flying. Nottov Haugann saw the light streaking across Grennes Hill. He counted thirty horses. At Lake Høvring the water was open. The horses went in up to their fetlocks. The *oskorei* stopped at Brenne and drank some Christmas beer. They did not dare tap from the barrel, so they thrust a knife into the wall and tapped from the shaft. Then the man on Brenna saw that Gyro had a tail.

"Pull in your tail, Gyro!" he shouted.

The host scattered and rode home. Taddak ran right into the corner of the storehouse so that the whole building was askew, and he knocked himself out. Suddenly he was in his bed once more, dripping with sweat. At the same moment, the host reached Mount Tveite. People heard it rattle when the *oskorei* rode into the mountain.

> This narrative is quite common. At times the host is led by Othin, the devil, or some other demonic being. Here the leader is Gyro (Gudrun), a preternatural being equipped with a tail like a *hulder*.
>
> Collected by Johannes Skar in Setesdal, Aust-Agder (Norway). Printed in Skar, *Gamalt or Sætesdal* 1 (1961), 414.

53.2 The Oskorei *Fetched the Dead Man*

On Aase in Flatdal, they were drinking and carousing one evening around Christmas time. Two men strapped themselves together with a belt and fought with knives. One of the men was stabbed and lay dead on the floor. Then the *oskorei* came riding in through the door, took the dead man with them, and threw a firebrand on the floor.

They left some reins behind on the attic floor. The reins have been kept at Aase ever since.

> In some areas of southern and western Norway, the *oskorei* are considered the host of the dead. They appear where a murder has been committed and take the dead body; sometimes they take the killer with them as well.
>
> See Hilding Celander, "Oskoreien och besläktade föreställningar," *Saga och sed* (1943), 78–81.
>
> Collected by Kjetil A. Flatin in Seljord, Telemark (Norway). Printed in Flatin, *Tussar og trolldom* (1930), 76.

53.3 Joen's Hunt

You can hear Joen's hunt in the air. It sounds like the baying of dogs. If someone whistled just when the hunt went by, it would land, and the dogs would bay.

When I was a child, we were always told not to whistle at night. "Otherwise Joen's hunt will come," my parents said.

In this text the aura of the demonic surrounding Joen's hunt is used to enforce the rule against whistling at night. The name Joen is derived from Odin (Othin).

See Hilding Celander, "Oskoreien och besläktade föreställningar," *Saga och sed* (1943), 139–51.

Collected by E. T. Kristensen from Jens Mark in Vokslev, Jylland (Denmark). Printed in Kristensen, *Danske sagn* 2 (1893), 105.

53.4 Horn's Hunter

As everybody knows, Horn's hunter was going to wipe out all the elf women.

At Lyngå a farmer had gone out early one morning to move his horses. When he was on his way home, he heard a terrifying roar in the air. It came closer and closer, and suddenly a man on horseback was standing before him. He shouted:

"Hold my dogs!"

The man obeyed. The hunter had three huge dogs tied with a silken thread. The farmer was looking at the thread when the hunter returned after a few moments. Over the back of his horse, he had slung two elf women who were tied together by their hair.

"Hand over my dogs and reach out your hand, and I'll give you a tip."

The farmer did, but the hunter thrust three fingertips into his hand, leaving three burn marks. Then he rode off with a roar, while the elf women howled and the dogs barked.

In a number of variants, a man is richly rewarded for helping the hunter. In this text, the burn marks on the man's hand underscore the demonic nature of the hunter.

Legend type: ML 5060.

Collected by E. T. Kristensen from R. H. Kruse, Fur, Jylland (Denmark). Printed in Kristensen, *Danske sagn* 2 (1893), 122.

53.5 The Chase of the Hind

I have an uncle who has seen the chase of the hind. He was a farmer and lived between Linköping and Mjölby. He was driving with a load of grain through the woods one day. Suddenly a woman ran past him. Her breasts were so long that she had to throw them over her shoulders, like this. A little later two dogs ran by and then two riders riding abreast. They asked him whether he had seen a hind. But he answered with a curse and said:

"I'm not going to tell you, no matter what I have seen."

Later he heard a shot, and then they came riding back. They had the woman hanging between them. One of the riders whispered into the farmer's ear:

"Kiss pussy! Kiss pussy!"

You see, the hunter said that because he had cursed at them.

> The folk tradition of the hunter pursuing a long-breasted woman is documented even in medieval texts. In later folk tradition, the hunters are variously identified with preternatural beings, Othin, or certain historical figures, such as, Diderik of Bern, King Arthur, and the Danish king Volmer.
>
> See Lutz Röhrich, *Erzählungen des späten Mittelalters* 2 (1967), 5–52, 393–407; Reidar Th. Christiansen, "Der wilde Jäger in Norwegen," *Zeitschrift für Volkskunde* (1938), 24–31; Bengt Holbek and Iørn Piø, *Fabeldyr og sagnfolk* (1967), 99–106; Helmer Olsson, "Odens jakt i Halland," *Vår bygd. Hallands hembygdsförbunds årsskrift* 25 (1940), 26–34.
>
> Legend type: ML 5060.
>
> Collected by Sven Rothman from juryman Öberg in Rommetorp, Hallestad, Östergötland (Sweden). Printed in Rothman, *Östgötska folkminnen* (1941), 72.

PART VI
The Devil

Part VI illustration: "A being more horrible to look at than anybody else . . . threw the poor woman on the horse and disappeared." Olaus Magnus, *Historia de Gentibus Septentrionalibus* (History of the Northern People, 1555), book 3, chapter 21.

he figure of the Devil, officially established in Christian dogma, was introduced to Scandinavian folk tradition through church iconography and exempla or sermon tales. During the sixteenth and seventeenth centuries the persecution of witches, whose powers presumably derived from Satan, further stimulated popular beliefs and traditions about the Devil. To some degree the role of the Devil became assimilated with that of preternatural beings, such as the troll, the *nøkk*, and the leader of the *oskorei*.

The legends express not only fear of the Devil but also a persistent fascination with the possibility of utilizing his power. A contract with the Evil One would bring material advantage in this life, but it would entail giving up one's soul and body in the next. A minister, by contrast, could make use of Satan's power with impunity. At the Black School at Wittenberg he acquired knowledge of the Black Book. In many jocular legends, the Devil appears as the fool duped by the minister. But there are also numerous legends about people other than the minister outwitting the Devil. A large cycle of legends is concerned with enforcing social sanctions, for instance, against fiddle playing, dancing, drinking, and card playing. This latter group of legends tends to emphasize the frightening and demonic aspects of the Evil One.

See Lutz Röhrich, "Teufelsmärchen und Teufelssagen," *Sagen und ihre Deutung* (1965), 28–58; Paul Danielsson, *Djävulsgestalten i Finlands svenska folktro* 1–2 (Bidrag till kännedom af Finlands natur och folk, vol. 83, 5 and vol. 84, 2) (1930–32); Barbara Allen Woods, *The Devil in Dog Form* (1959).

54.1 To Exorcise the Devil

Unclean spirit, you are commanded not by this sinful being but by the innocent Lamb and God's dear Son, Jesus Christ our Savior, who is Lord over all creatures and will be avenged on you and your kindred with fire!

Wicked Satan! By the Judge of Satan and all the dead and by the world's Creator! Yea, by Him who has power to cast you into hell's abyss, I command you to depart from this servant and creature of our Lord Jesus Christ. I command you not by my unworthy merit but by the power of the Holy Spirit to flee from this, his temple. Give way, foul and wicked Satan, seducer of deceit, and devilish fiend, give way to the Son of the highest God! The God of peace will soon place the Devil beneath our foot. To Him be honor now and in eternity. Amen.

Say this exorcism three times, recite the 29th psalm of David, as well as the Lord's Prayer, and a blessing.

> This formula, intended to drive out the Devil, answers closely to the concept of the Evil One as defined in church dogma.
>
> See Jacob Christian Jacobsen, *Djævlebesværgelse. Træk af Exorcismens Historie* (1972).
>
> The text was written down in Kvikne, Gudbrandsdal (Norway) in approximately 1860. Printed in A. Chr. Bang, *Norske hexeformularer og magiske opskrifter* (1901–2), 718–19.

54.2 Corporal Geremiæson's Contract with the Devil

I salute you, my Lord and God, Satan. I will be faithful to you and give you my body and soul if you will give me 300 dollars for the duration of 18 years. When the 18 years have passed, you may take me for as long as you wish. This is my desire, that you will write to me about my request tomorrow.

                                                    Johannes Geremiæson

> Similar contracts have been documented throughout Scandinavia. Written requests to the Devil were at times put in the keyhole of the church, which was considered to be the Devil's mailbox. If the sexton found it, however, it would end up in the hands of the authorities, and the offender would be held accountable. The above contract, penned by a soldier attached to a company in Voss (western Norway), was sent to Bishop Randulph by Christen Nilssøn Weinwich, the minister in Voss. It is not known what happened to the corporal after that. In a similar case reported from Sweden, a 15-year-old boy was initially sentenced to death, but his sentence was reduced to a short prison term on account of his young age. He grew up to become a professor of theology in Königsberg, Germany.
>
> See Bente G. Alver, *Heksetro og trolddom* (1971), 37–38; K. Rob. V. Wikman, "Förskrivning till djävulen," *Fataburen* (1960), 193–99; Paul Danielsson, *Djävulsgestalten i Finlands svenska folktro* 2 (1932), 48–92; Leopold Kretzenbacher, *Teufelsbündner und Faustgestalten im Abendlande* (1968).
>
> Printed in Amund Helland, *Topografisk-statistisk beskrivelse over søndre Bergenhus Amt* 1 (1921), 777–78. Reprinted in Alver, *Heksetro og trolddom,* (1971), 37.

54.3 Christen Pedersen's Contract with Satan

I give myself to Satan to be his own with body and soul. Just as Dr. Faustus became Satan's own, may I do the same. One thing shall Satan promise me, namely, that he will show himself to me whenever I desire and in whatever shape I wish. I promise, and in witness of my loyalty have signed with my blood, that I shall be his with body and soul in eternity. In return shall that spirit, the Devil, promise me money for my livelihood and whenever I have need for it, so that I may be rich all my life, and stop living in such

misery. If Satan will promise me this freely, I will freely pledge
never to forsake you, but be yours in eternity. This I Christen
Pedersen, promise as written. To confirm this contract, I have set it
down in blood. Christen Pedersen by his own hand. Written on
the second day of Saint Michael's Feast. Anno 1634.

> Dr. Johannes Faust (1480–1540), German magician and as-
> trologer, has in legendary tradition been credited with the author-
> ship of Black Books.
> See Gustav Henningsen, "Trolddom og hemmelige kunster,"
> *Dagligliv i Danmark i det syttende og attende århundrede* (1969),
> 191–92.
> This contract was written in Odense (Denmark), by a shoe-
> maker. Manuscript in the archives of the bishopry on Fyn,
> Odense. Printed in *Kirkehistoriske samlinger* (3d series), 4, 402.
> Reprinted in F. Ohrt, *Danmarks trylleformler* 1 (1917), 445.

54.4 You Can Take a Joke, Can't You?

Per Tværved needed some lumber for a carpentry job, and because
he did not care to buy it, he just went into Treschow's Woods to take
what he needed. It was winter and there was ice on Farris River, so
Per was able to walk across both ways. He took his time looking for
suitable lumber; he was not in any hurry, and besides, it was beautiful
in the woods.

But by the time he was done, dusk had already fallen, and when he
got on the ice with the lumber on his back, he got a little too close to
open water. Before Per knew it, he fell in, cursing and hollering,
while his lumber danced over the ice. No matter how much he struggled, Per could not get out because every time he tried taking hold of
the edge of the ice, it broke. There were no people around, so there
was little use in shouting for help. Finally Per thought he had better
call Our Lord, although he doubted that that would be of any use either, considering the nature of his errand. And whether it was on ac-
count of the lumber or something else Per had done, Our Lord did
not come, and Per remained there, flailing and struggling as before.

Then Per did not know what else to do but call on the Devil, and
to be on the safe side, he promised him his soul right away. And the
Devil did not wait to be asked twice. Hardly had Per spoken the
words before he felt someone grabbing him by the seat of his pants,
and then he danced across the ice, followed by his lumber. But when

Per had picked up all the pieces and tried sneaking away without so much as a thank you, Satan suddenly stood by his side and reminded him of his promise.

"You can take a joke, can't you?" asked Per.

Well, the Devil did not want to admit to anything less, and so he had to let Per go that time.

> This is a migratory legend, but here it is identified with a man who lived in the village of Farris in southern Norway and was well known for his practical jokes.
>
> Collected by Kristian Bugge from Hans Bredvej, a teacher at Larvik, Vestfold (Norway). Printed in Bugge, *Folkeminne-optegnelser* (1934), 56–57.

54.5 Making the Devil Carry Water in a Basket

Once a stranger approached a woman who was working in Priest Sæmundur's stable and offered to fetch water for her all winter, to muck out the stable, and all that sort of thing, if she would give him what she was carrying under her apron. The woman thought this was a fine bargain; she had nothing of value under her apron, and it did not occur to her that she might be pregnant.

But when the winter was nearly over, she realized her plight. She grew quiet and withdrawn, and Sæmundur asked her about the reason for her moodiness. In the beginning, she did not want to say anything, but finally she told him all about the bargain she had made with the stranger. Sæmundur let her know that her condition had been no secret to him, but he had done nothing about it before.

"Don't worry," said Sæmundur. "I'll show you how to break your bargain with the Devil. Tomorrow ask him to fetch water in the basket and walk past the gate to the cemetery, otherwise the bargain is off."

The woman did everything just as Sæmundur instructed her. The Devil took his basket and trudged off after water, but when he came to the churchyard, Sæmundur rang the bell, and all the water ran out. The Devil tried three times, but the same thing happened each time. Then he threw the basket away in a fit of rage and disappeared.

Later the woman gave birth to her child, and the Devil never bothered it. But he did think a lot about taking revenge on Sæmundur the priest because he had many things to pay him back for.

Sæmundur the Learned (1056–1133), Icelandic scholar and priest, was for a long time mistakenly regarded as the author of the *Poetic Edda*. He studied in France, and there are widespread folk traditions about him as an expert in black magic. (Cf. nos. 54.8 and 54.9.)

The motif of the child unwittingly offered in payment for the services rendered by the Devil or a troll is more common in folktales than in legends.

See B. S. Benedikz, "The Master Magician in Icelandic Folk Legend," *Durham University Journal* (1964), 22–34.

Collected by Magnús Grímsson, a minister in Mosfell (Iceland). Printed in Jón Árnason, *Íslenzkar þjóðsögur og æfintyri* 1 (1862), 498. Reprinted in new edition 1 (1954), 482.

54.6 Ignorant Use of the Black Book

Long ago there was a miller at Børrud Mill by the name of Linilla. People said that he had the Black Book, but he would never admit it, you know. He kept the book hidden at the mill.

One day a boy came to the mill to grind some barley. The miller went to check the mill race, while the boy stayed inside. There he found Linilla's book. He started reading and came across the formula for conjuring up the Devil. The Evil One appeared and asked the boy what he was supposed to do.

The miller heard the commotion the Devil was making at the mill and came running. He got there just in the nick of time; things would have gone awry for the boy. The miller asked the Devil to turn the waterfall around and make it flow upstream. That was a difficult job even for the Evil One. He stood there in the middle of the waterfall, flailing his long arms. What an uproar he made! You could hear it everywhere.

The miller took the book, and within a short time, the Devil was bound. The boy was more than happy. He escaped with only a scare that time.

> If one unwittingly conjured up the Devil, it was imperative to give him something to do. Otherwise he would have power over the person.
>
> See C.-M. Edsman, "Svartkonstböcker i sägen och historia," *Saga och sed* (1959), 160–68.
>
> Legend type: ML 3020.

Collected by Lars M. Fjellstad in Eidskog, Hedmark (Norway). Printed in Fjellstad, *Haugfolk og trollskap. Folkeminne frå Eidskog* 2 (1954), 21.

54.7 Burning the Black Book

Hans Kristian Munk, who used to be the bailiff at Bredballe, once found a Cyprianus among some old books at an auction. When he got home, his wife begged him to get rid of the book, but he said:

"I can't do it; even if I throw it into the fire, it will still be lying on the shelf."

One day, when the wife was baking bread, she threw the book into the oven, and it burned and did not reappear on the shelf. I suppose it was not a real Cyprianus, after all.

> The Black Book is often called a Cyprianus after the third-century African church father and martyr who claimed to be the author of the Black Book.
> Collected by E. T. Kristensen from Klavs Pedersen in Hornstrup parish, Jylland (Denmark). Printed in Kristensen, *Danske sagn*, N.R. 6 (1936), 34.

54.8 Last Man Out

In ancient times there was a school somewhere in the world called the Black School. There people learned witchcraft and various kinds of magic. The school had been set up in a building made of earth and stone. There were no windows, and it was always pitch black inside. There were no teachers, either, and the students learned from books written with fiery red letters that could be read in the dark. The students were not allowed to go outside or see daylight as long as they were there, and they had to stay from three to seven years to finish their studies. Each day a fur-covered gray hand reached through the wall and gave them their food. It was agreed that each year he who ran the school would receive the last graduate to leave the building. And because the students knew it was the Devil who ran the school, they all wanted to avoid being the last one to leave.

Once there were three Icelanders at the Black School, Sæmundur the Learned, Kálfur Árnason, and Hálfdan Eldjárnsson, who later became a minister in Fell in the district of Slettuhlíð. They were all to graduate at the same time, and Sæmundur volunteered to be the last one out of the building. The others were very pleased with this.

Sæmundur threw a long coat over his shoulders, leaving the sleeves dangling and the buttons unfastened. A ladder had been set up for the students to leave the school. When Sæmundur was climbing the ladder, the Devil grabbed his coat, and said:

"You're mine!"

But Sæmundur threw off the coat and scampered out. The Devil was left holding an empty coat. But just then the iron door slammed shut so close behind Sæmundur that his heel was injured. That is when he said:

"That door slammed hard on my heels!"

This has been used as a proverb ever since. And that is how Sæmundur the Learned escaped from the Black School with his friends.

Other people tell that when Sæmundur the Learned climbed the ladder and reached the doorway of the Black School, the sun cast his shadow against the wall. Just when the Devil was about to take him, Sæmundur said:

"But I'm not the last one out! Can't you see the guy behind me?"

The Devil grabbed the shadow, mistaking it for the real person, Sæmundur escaped, and the door slammed on his heels. And from that time on, Sæmundur went without his shadow because the Devil would never let him have it back.

> It was common that Scandinavian theologians-to-be studied in Germany. Often they were thought to acquire magical powers at the Black School supposedly located in Wittenberg. As the town where Martin Luther started the Reformation in 1521, it came to occupy a central position in popular tradition. Sæmundur the Learned in fact studied in France during the eleventh century, but in legends he is identified with post-Reformation Wittenberg.
>
> The motif of the lost shadow is widespread in legends as well as in folktales and in literature.
>
> See B. S. Benedikz, "The Master Magician in Icelandic Folk Legend," *Durham University Journal* (1964), 22–34; Bieler, "Schatten," *Handwörterbuch des deutschen Aberglaubens* 9 (1938–41), columns 126–42.
>
> Legend type: ML 3000.
>
> Collected by Magnús Grímsson, a minister in Mosfell (Iceland). Printed in Jón Árnason, *Íslenzkar þjóðsögur og æfintýri* 1 (1862), 490–91. Reprinted in new edition 1 (1954), 475–76.

54.9 *The Devil Took the Shape of a Fly*

Old Nick had it in for Sæmundur the Learned because it seemed that the minister always got the better of him. He tried every way he knew to avenge himself, but nothing worked. Once, he turned himself into a small fly and hid under the skin on the milk in a wooden tub of Sæmundur's, planning to sneak up on the minister and kill him. But when Sæmundur picked up the tub, he saw the fly, wrapped the skin of milk around it, packed everything into a caul, and put the whole bundle on the alter. There the fly had to cool his heels while Sæmundur recited the next scheduled office. When it was over, the minister opened the bundle and let Old Nick loose. People say Old Nick thought he had never gotten into a worse pinch than when he lay on the altar while Sæmundur held mass.

> The belief in the Devil's ability to change shape at will is well documented in European folk tradition.
> Collected by Magnús Grímsson, minister at Mosfell from Helgi Helgason, printer in Reykjavik (Iceland). Printed in Jón Árnason, *Íslenzkar þjóðsögur og æfintýri* 1 (1862), 495. Reprinted in new edition 1 (1954), 480–81.

54.10 *Petter Dass Traveled with Satan*

Have you heard what happened when Petter Dass traveled to Copenhagen? He was a merchant and a minister, you see. Once the king was in Bergen, and there he saw Petter Dass with his ship, selling fish. When the king heard that Petter was a minister, he wondered what kind of minister he could be. They said that Petter Dass was just as learned as any other minister, and then some, because he knew more than the others. So the king wrote a letter to Petter Dass, asking him to preach in the church at Copenhagen on Christmas Day. But he handed the letter to the bailiff with instructions to give it to the minister on Christmas Eve. He must not read it before then. Then he would see whether Petter Dass really knew more than other ministers.

So, early on Christmas morning, Petter Dass said to his wife:
"Today I'm going to preach for the king in Copenhagen."
"Why, sure," she said, "me too!"
She thought he was joking. But he told her to get his clothes ready, and she did, for she had seen enough to do what he said when

it became clear that he meant it. Then he sat down at a table and knocked three times, and someone came in.

"How fast can you carry me?" asked the minister.

"As fast as the bird flies."

"Not fast enough! Out again!"

He knocked again and someone else came in.

"How fast can you carry me?"

"As fast as wind and weather."

"Too slow! Out again!"

He rapped a third time, and there came yet someone else.

"How fast can you carry me?"

"As fast as human thought."

"Then carry me to Copenhagen right away."

"What payment will I get?"

"The souls of everyone sleeping in church today."

Then off they went through the air. But over the sea, the Evil One got tired and tried to trick Petter Dass into saying Jesus' name, because then he would have the power to throw him off.

"What does the baking woman say when she leaves the baking house at night?" he asked.

"Higher and faster! Straight to the gates of Copenhagen!" shouted the minister.

He arrived there in plenty of time, and the text was supposed to be lying on the pulpit. Petter Dass climbed into the pulpit, but there lay a white piece of paper that did not have a single letter on it.

"Here is nothing," he said and turned the paper over. "And there is nothing here, but out of nothing God created the world."

And then he preached a sermon the likes of which no one had ever heard before.

On the way home, his carrier was cross.

"Well, how many souls did you get today?" asked the minister.

"How could I get any souls, the way you were raving and carrying on?" snapped the Evil One.

> Petter Dass (1647–1707) was a minister, as well as the most popular Norwegian author of his time. In *Nordlands trompet* (The Trumpet of Nordland), he describes the land and people of his native region. But he was best known as the author of hymns based on holy scripture and the catechism. In legendary tradition, Petter Dass is characterized as the owner of the Black Book and a master magician.

This legend is widespread in Norway, but it is also known in Sweden and Denmark.

Legend type: ML 3025.

Collected by Sigurd Nergaard in Rendal, Hedmark (Norway). Printed in Nergaard, *Hulder og trollskap. Folkeminne fraa Østerdalen* 4 (1925), 202–4.

54.11 Traveling with the Evil One

Tore Rønningen from Gaustad once traveled with Satan.

How did it happen? Well, Tore had been in Christiania on an errand and was walking home. This was long before the railroad came, you know.

When Tore reached Grorud in the evening, someone drove by with a horse and sled. The stranger said "whoa" to his horse and stopped. It was too dark for Tore to see much of the man.

"Would you like a ride?"

"There is a good chance I would," answered Tore.

"How far are you going?" asked the man.

"I'm heading for Gaustad in Eidskog."

"I'm going to the same village. Stand on the back, but hold on tight: I drive fast."

Tore did as he was told, wondering what kind of fellow this could be. But he did not get much time to think about it because he got a ride like he had never had before.

They were traveling through the air as well as on the ground. Tore could barely hold on to the knobs of the sled. At one point one of the runners scraped on something.

"What was that?" Tore mustered his courage to ask.

"Oh, that was the steeple of Oppstad Church in Odalen," answered the man. On they went, faster and faster. After a while Tore asked:

"Where are you off to in such a hurry?"

"I'm going to your neighbor's house to hold the back of a girl giving birth to her child tonight."

Then the Devil laid the whip on his horse again. After a while he stopped.

"Now you are home, Tore."

Tore thanked him for the ride. He had had quite enough of it. He did not go home, however, but took a short cut to his neighbor's. He told them what the Devil was up to and advised them to keep an eye on the girl. And they did.

But when Tore got home, he met Satan at the gate. He was more than a little mad.

"Had I known you would trick me like that, I wouldn't have given you a ride."

Then Satan disappeared. But that night Tore could not get to sleep because the Devil was growling under the table in the shape of a dog. He showed himself for several nights, so Tore went to someone who knew more than others about such things. But that fellow could not get the Evil One out either. Satan was holding on to a post under the table.

"I'll find somebody who'll get you out," shouted Tore.

"That'll be Vingerstitten, for sure," answered the Evil One.

They sent for Vingerstitten, and he came right away. He was a man who knew more than just the Lord's Prayer.

"You've committed many sins," the Evil One said to the minister.

"It may be that I have sinned but not intentionally."

"You stole a hymnbook," said Satan.

"Only to bind you with it," said the minister.

"You also took a deck of cards."

"I use them the same way I use the hymnbook to bind you," answered Vingerstitten.

"And then you took a ball of yarn."

"That was to repair my pants when I was going to church in Matrand."

"And you put your socks on, left foot first."

"I can change that."

Well, then Satan understood that he could not get the better of Vingerstitten, and he begged for permission to exit by the door.

> If a girl gave birth to a child out of wedlock, it was believed that the Devil would come and be her midwife and try to entice her to kill the child.
>
> According to popular folk tradition, if a person dressed the left foot or arm first, he or she would have bad luck that day, or, worse, the Devil would gain power over him or her.
>
> See Barbara Allen Woods, *The Devil in Dog Form* (1959).
>
> Legend type: ML 3025, plus 3015. (Cf. also 5005.)
>
> Collected by Lars M. Fjellstad in Eidskog, Hedmark (Norway). Printed in Fjellstad, *Haugfolk og trollskap. Folkeminne frå Eidskog* 2 (1954), 56–57.

54.12 Driving on Three Wheels

A man, who in his younger days had been in the service of the minister at Gudbjærg, told my uncle this story:

I was his driver, and we took many trips together. Often it was not any farther than to the minister's house in Hesselager; they were good friends and had been through the Black School together. No matter how late it got, he never wanted to drive the upper road but always the shortcut over Sømaden and past Gorm Cliff, although that route was by far the worst.

Once we were taking the shortcut in the dead of night and with difficulty had made our way past that awful cliff, when the horses began panting and groaning as if the whole world was on top of the wagon.

"Whoa!" shouted the minister at once, and he jumped off the wagon, took the headgear off the horse on the left, looked through it while mumbling something I could not understand, and then put it back on the horse. After that he walked counterclockwise around the wagon, took off the right back wheel, and placed it in the wagon. Climbing back up, he said:

"You'll be the wheel now, until I release you."

We drove with three wheels to Gudbjærg, and the wagon rode like greased lightning. When the minister got off, he asked me to put the wagon in the watering hole by the gate out back. Hardly had I taken the gear off, when the minister shoved the wagon into the water. Then he laughed and said:

"Let him stay there tonight; it'll do him good. I expect he won't trouble us again very soon."

It was Old Nick who had been driving us, I could see that now. The next morning I got up late. The wheel was back on the wagon, but it was still standing out in the water.

> Removing the headgear from the horse and looking through it was a common way of discovering invisible beings, including the Devil.
>
> This legend is popular throughout Europe. An early use of the same motif occurs in Jacques de Vitry's collection of exempla from the thirteenth century, in which Saint Teobald makes the Devil carry the cart.
>
> Legend type: ML 3010.

Collected by E. T. Kristensen from Rasmus Haugen in Gudbjærg parish, Jylland (Denmark). Printed in Kristensen, *Danske sagn* N.R. 6 (1936), 44–45.

54.13 The Devil as a Dance Partner

Usually dancing is not a good thing. It happens that the Evil One shows up when it gets out of hand.

There was a girl by the name of Helge. She could never get her fill of dancing. No matter how far away the dances were, she ran to every one she heard about. But on one occasion a stranger asked her to dance. And then she got the dance of her life! He turned her so fast, they spun like a whirlwind, and she begged to be allowed to catch her breath. But he screamed so that it echoed in the house:

Hei, Helge, ho!
I shall turn you so!
You'll get your fill of dancing, ho!

And he danced more and more wildly. The fiddler got frightened and put down his instrument. But the fiddle played on by itself! The other dancers stood as if spellbound along the wall. The stranger continued until the girl hung limply in his arms, like a rag. They put the fiddle back on the wall, but it played on. The fiddler locked it in a cabinet, but the fiddle continued playing until the man stopped dancing and let go of the girl. But by that time, she was dead, and when they looked for the man, he was gone.

> This is obviously a didactic legend warning against excessive dancing. It shows Satan's punitive aspect. The compulsion to dance has also been associated with the water sprite and may have a historical background in a dance epidemic sweeping Europe in the early Middle Ages. (Cf. no. 54.14.)
>
> See Dag Strömbäck, "Kölbigh och Hårga II," *Arv* 24 (1968), 100; L. Kretzenbacher, "Freveltanz und Überzähliger," *Carinthia* 1 (1954), 843–66, and "Tanzverbot und Warnlegende," *Rheinisches Jahrbuch für Volkskunde* 12 (1961), 16–22.
>
> Legend type: ML 3070.
>
> Collected by Sigurd Nergaard in Elverum, Hedmark (Norway). Printed in Nergaard, *Hulder og trollskap. Folkeminne fraa Østerdalen* 4 (1925), 86.

54.14 They Danced to Their Death

In a village in Dalarna both the young and the old folk were always dancing on a mountain. Once when they were dancing, a stranger came with a fiddle under his arm and asked them whether he might play for them. He said that he was a good fiddler. The dancers happily invited him to play.

But when he played, they became as if possessed and started dancing wildly. They danced over sticks and stones and over holes in the ground at great speed, so that they soon got tired and wanted to rest. But it was impossible to stop. The fiddler played faster and faster, and before long, they had worn out their shoes and danced on their bare feet. They shouted to the fiddler to stop, but he pretended not to hear them and played even faster. Finally they had worn down their legs to their knees, but still they had to dance. They did not even get to stop when all that was left were their skulls jumping and dancing to the rhythm.

Finally a minister heard about the dancing on the mountain, and when he commanded the fiddler to stop, the man had to obey. But the folks who had followed the minister saw that it was Old Nick himself who sat there and played. He used his ass as a fiddle and worked it with the bow.

> The event described here is localized in Dalarna, but in fact the legend is derived from Norrland (northern Sweden) and has never been recorded in Dalarna.
> For commentary and bibliographical information, see foregoing text.
> Legend type: ML 3070.
> Collected by Olof Petter Pettersson in Vilhelmina, Lappland (Sweden). Printed in Pettersson, *Sagor från Åsele lappmark* (Svenska sagor och sägner 9 [1945]), 174–75. Reprinted in Bengt af Klintberg, *Svenska folksägner* (1972), 204.

54.15 The Devil as a Card Player

Where the road to Lake Hjulby splits off from the county road, there lies a gloomy-looking farm called Lindeborg. Once some men were playing cards and cursing terribly there. Later that night the door opened and an elegantly dressed gentleman came in and joined the game. After a while one of the men dropped a card to the floor and bent down to pick it up. To his horror he saw that the stranger had a cloven foot. Then they knew that he was the Devil, whom they had called so many times. They sent a messenger to the minister, who came right away. He drilled a hole through the window frame and forced the Devil to leave through it.

> The appearance of the Devil as an elegant gentleman with a cloven foot is a late development in Scandinavian folk tradition. In many variants to this legend, the devil sits under the table rather than participating in the game. He often takes the shape of a black dog. This legend purports to warn against activities, like dancing, which were considered sinful by many.
>
> See Martin Puhvel, "The Legend of the Devil-haunted Card Players in Northern Europe," *Folklore* 76 (1965), 33–38.
>
> Legend type: ML 3015.
>
> Collected by Valdemar Bennike in Hjulby parish, Vindinge, Fyn (Denmark). Printed in E. T. Kristensen, *Danske sagn*, N.R. 6 (1936), 61.

54.16 The Devil Took the Bride

Two young people on Fyn got engaged. The girl swore that if she deceived her betrothed, the Devil could have her on her wedding day. But she betrayed him anyway and got engaged to someone else. As so often happens, she did not think of her promise except at the moment she made it.

The time of her wedding arrived. All the guests sat down to eat. But there was a gentlemen no one knew, and he sat down at the table, too. The others did not pay much attention to him, although it seemed odd that he came uninvited, and there was something strange about him. Then one of the guests looked down and saw that he had a cloven foot. But when they got up from the meal, the stranger vanished with the bride, and everybody there was terrified.

> This legend reflects the traditional view that if a person breaks an oath, he or she is forefeited to the Devil.
>
> Collected by E. T. Kristensen from Nielsine Jakobsen, Kolding, Jylland (Denmark). Printed in Kristensen, *Danske sagn*, N.R. 6 (1936), 24–25.

54.17 The Devil Flayed the Dead

People were saying that an innkeeper at Hammenhög had sold himself to the Devil. Satan was to have his skin when he died. But when he died, the minister had his coffin brought into the church and placed by the altar railing. They hired a shoemaker to keep watch inside the railing. The minister said:

"Much will happen, but you will not be harmed."

The shoemaker lit a candle and waited. They came at midnight. There were many of them, and they took the lid off the coffin and set to work. He could see the knives moving. Then they hung the skin on the railing. But the shoemaker stuck an awl into the skin and pulled it toward himself. They tried to get the skin back. The Evil One even changed himself into the shape of the minister, but it did not work.

The man I was working for at Eastern Herrestad told me that the skin is hanging in the museum at Lund, with the fingernails still in place.

> The macabre motif of the devil flaying the dead is more typically found in folktales than in folk belief and legends. Cp. AT 810, "The Snares of the Evil One."
>
> Collected in 1922 in Hagestad, Löderup parish, Skåne (Sweden). Ms. in LUF (455, 1), 186–87. Printed in Bengt af Klintberg, *Svenska folksägner* (1972), 207.

PART VII
Trolls and Giants

Part VII illustration: "There are people who believe that the stone markers along the road used to be giants." Olaus Magnus, *Historia de Gentibus Septentrionalibus* (History of the Northern People, 1555), book 2, chapter 15.

n the oldest literature of Scandinavia, we find primordial giants identified with the origin and creation of the world. They are usually cast in the role of enemies of the gods and the human community. With the introduction of Christianity, they became enemies of the church as well. In more recent folk tradition, the giants usually appear as imaginary figures rather than as preternatural beings people actually believed in. They play a major role in *fabulats* and etiological legends explaining the origin of natural phenomena such as huge rock formations, lakes, and the so-called *jættegryter* ("giant potholes"). These giant beings are called *jätte* in Swedish folk tradition, *troll* and *jotun* (or *jutul*) in Norwegian, *trold* and *jætte* in Danish.

See Elisabeth Hartmann, *Die Trollvorstellungen in den Sagen und Märchen der skandinavischen Völker* (1936); Carl Wilhelm von Sydow, "Jättarna i mytologi och folktro," *FmFt* 6 (1919), 135–42; Marlene Ciklamini, "Journeys to the Giant Kingdom," *Scandinavian Studies* 40 (1968), 95–110; Bengt Holbek and Iørn Piø, *Fabeldyr og sagnfolk* (1967), 312–24; John Broderius, *The Giant in Germanic Tradition* (1932).

55.1 The Giant's Toy

In the parish of Gammalkils lies a mountain called Borre's Mountain, after the giant Borre. He moved there with his wife because he wanted to find peace from the intruding dwarfs.

One day the giant wife went out and saw a dwarf plowing a field in Kvarnlyckan near Björkhult's estate. She put the little man, along with his horse and plow, into her apron, and carried them home to their cave.

"Look at the critter I found out there," she said to her giant husband.

"Just carry it back," the old man answered, "otherwise something bad will happen. These creatures are supposed to live here and cultivate the earth after us."

The legend seeks to "explain" the disappearance of the giants and their replacement by the invisible folk of more recent folk tradition.

V. Höttges has documented the legend in Russia, Rumania, Germany, Denmark, Sweden, and Finland. An early allusion to it occurs in Georg Rollenhagen's *Froschmeuseler. Der Frösch und Meuse wunderbare Hoffhaltung* (1595), 93.

See Valerie Höttges, *Die Sage vom Riesenspielzeug* (1931); Helmer Olsson, "Sägnen om jätteleksaken," *FmFt* 22 (1935), 35–41.

Legend type: ML 5015.

Printed in Anton Ridderstad, *Östergötland 3. Fornsägner och kulturbilder från Östergötland* (1920), 3.

55.2 The Visit to the Old Troll

Once some fishermen from Långelanda were fishing by Jädern's
Reef northeast of Skagen. A storm drove them to the coast of Norway. They saw a light in a mountain and headed toward it. When
they entered the mountain, they found a blind old man sitting by the
fire. He said that he could hear by their speech that they were from
his old home district. Then he said to the man standing next to him:

"Give me your hand, I'd like to see whether there still runs warm
blood in the folks back home."

But the man took the giant's fire poker and gave it to him, and he
squeezed it so hard that the red-hot iron trickled out between his
fingers. He said:

"Not bad, but not quite like in the old days."

> Two prominent characteristics of trolls and giants are their great
> age and enormous strength.
> Legend type: ML 5010.
> Collected by Carl-Martin Bergstrand in Orust, Bohuslän
> (Sweden). Printed in Bergstrand, *Gammalt från Orust* (1962), 39.

55.3 The Ogress's Hole on Sandoy

By a bluff west of the village of Sandur, there is a big hole called
Gívrinarhol, and in it lives a giant woman. People tell of a man from
Sandur who went down into the hole to have a look at her. There
she stood grinding gold in a mill, and a child was sitting nearby playing with a golden stick. The old woman was blind, so the man tip-
toed over to the mill and took some of the gold. She did not see or
hear him, and yet she said:

"There's a mouse or a thief prowling around here, or something is
wrong with my old mill."

The man went over to the child, took away its golden stick, and
slapped it on the head so that it began to cry. Now the ogress knew
that something was wrong, and leaping to her feet, she groped
through the cave, trying to find what it was, but the man had already
climbed out, mounted his horse, and galloped home with the gold.
The giant woman could not find him, and so she called for her neighbor and asked for help in catching the thief. Her neighbor strode over
the lake at once; to this day her footprints can be seen in the rocks on
both sides of it. The man stayed ahead of her until he came to Volis-
mýri. Then she got so close that she grabbed the tail of his horse and

would not let go. The man spurred his horse so hard it lost its tail because the ogress was pulling in the other direction. The man threw himself forward, and at that very instant, he caught sight of the church in Sandur. So the ogress lost her power to do him harm and had to turn around and go home.

By Gívrinarhol you can still hear the blind, old giant woman grinding gold deep down in her cave.

> The wealth of trolls and giants is described in many legends. The story of the man freely entering the underground abode of the giant to steal the gold and escape, however, is more typical of the narrative structure of the folktale. (Cf. no. 47.19.)
> Collected by V. U. Hammershaimb on the Faeroe Islands. Printed in Hammershaimb "Færøiske folkesagn," *Antiquarisk tidskrift 1849–51* (1852), 196–97. Reprinted in Hammershaimb, *Savn* (1969), 140–41.

55.4 Trolls Shouting

One day the *jøtul* on Kall-Hill at Listeid shouted:
"There's a cow bellowing!"
Seven years later the *jøtul* in Dubingen on Duvold answered:
"Couldn't it just as well be a bull as a cow?"
Another seven years passed before the *jøtul* in Solslotte screamed:
"If you don't keep quiet and stop this commotion, I'll have to move!"

> Trolls were imagined to be dim-witted and slow to react.
> Collected in 1934–35 by Olav H. Westhassel in Lista, Vest-Agder (Norway). Ms. in NFS O.H. Westhassel 7, 67.

55.5 Håstein Reef

Once a giant was going to carry a huge rock across the sea. He put a rope around the rock, made a sling, and carried it about a mile beyond Tungeneset. But then he got so tired that he fell to his knees and dropped the rock. It so happened that he had eaten nothing but soup and porridge for his noon meal that day, and that is not enough for a workingman. When he fell, he said:
"Soup and porridge can bring a man to his knees."

The rock remained on the spot where the giant fell. Now it is a well-known reef. People call it the Håstein. On its side you can still see the wooden eye with which the giant tied his rope.

> Explanations of the origin of rock formations are typically tied to legends about giants and trolls.
> Collected by Torkell Mauland in Rogaland (Norway). Printed in Mauland, *Folkeminne fraa Rogaland* 1 (1928), 61.

55.6 The Trolls Scared a Fisherman

There was a man by the name of Jon. He used to fish on a lake ev'ry autumn and spring. Once he heard shouting from the mountains nearby:

"May I borrow your big kettle?"

"What do you want with it?" came the answer from another side.

"I want to cook Jon Long-Bone, who fishes on the lake ev'ry autumn and spring."

"Well, can I have the grease floating on top?"

"Sure, you can have the grease and the crust on the bottom of the kettle, too."

Hearing that, Jon hurriedly took his leave and never went back.

> At times trolls were described as cannibals.
> Legend type: ML 5000.
> Collected by Sophus Bugge from Gunnhild Røbakk in Telemark (Norway). Ms. in NFS Bugge 3, 75.

55.7 How to Scare Off a Poacher

Between Seljord and Sandland, there is a fishing lake that belongs to the folks from Sandland. But a man from Seljord was constantly stealing their fish. Finally two men from Sandland decided to scare off the poacher. They agreed to position themselves on different peaks in the surrounding hills and shout to each other.

In the evening when the thief came, one of them shouted:

"Can I borrow your kettle?"

"What do you want with it?" the other answered.

"I'm going to cook Jon Long-Bone, who fishes here ev'ry autumn and spring."

"Can I have the grease?"

"No, because I'm going to fry him over the coals."
Well, the man did not dare fish on that lake again.

> Here the tradition about the man-eating trolls is effectively em-
> ployed to scare off a thief.
> Legend type: ML 5000.
> Collected by Sophus Bugge from Olav Grasberg in Telemark
> (Norway). Ms. in NFS Bugge 4, 53.

55.8 Married to a Jätte

I took service on Kroken when I was fourteen. There I heard them
tell many stories about Vrål in Hästeskede.

In the old days, people often slept in outbuildings. Once a girl was
sleeping in a barn. Every night a woman would walk outside the barn
and talk about her three sons, Vrål, Navare, and Borr; she wanted the
girl to marry one of them. Finally the girl got tired of it and said she
would take Vrål. Next morning a huge *jätte* was standing outside. It
was Vrål. The girl married him.

A crofter at Näsinge said that Vrål was as strong as twelve men.
He fetched iron shares for twelve wooden plows and carried them all
at one time. He met an old woman who said:

"Sit down and rest awhile, Vrål; you're carrying such a heavy
burden."

Vrål sat down because he was tired.

"If I had known that it felt so good to take a rest, I would have
rested before this."

But when he tried to pick up his load again, he could lift only half
as much.

Vrål ate an awful lot. Once he was sitting and eating a huge tub of
porridge, when a smith came by and stirred horseshoe nails into the
porridge. Then he asked Vrål how the porridge tasted. Vrål answered:

"The porridge is fine, but there's some rather big bran in it."

Vrål said that anyone on Hästeskede bearing the name Halvard or
Olov would never be poor. And that turned out to be true.

Vrål said that when he died, they should get him to his grave at
the churchyard before sunrise, otherwise they would not reach the
cemetery. As it turned out, they were a little late, and while they
were still on their way, the sun rose over the highest mountain peak.
The wagon stopped abruptly. They got more horses, but the wagon

stood as if it was rooted. They had to dig a grave right there. Later they piled a huge mound of soil over it. Vrål's Mound is there to this very day.

> The cycle of legends about the good-natured giant Vrål, who was famous for his strength and enormous appetite, is found mostly in Bohuslän and partly in Dalsland, Sweden.
> The motif of someone learning about the virtue of taking a rest is more typically identified with folk traditions about the farm sprite. (Cf. no. 48.9.)
> Collected by Britt Adenius in Näsinge, Bohuslän (Sweden). Printed in Carl-Martin Bergstrand, *Bohusländska sägner* (1947), 50–51.

55.9 The Mowing Competition with a Jutul

A *jutul* and a man once competed in mowing. The *jutul* was to mow first, and the man was to walk along behind him.

But the man got something from a troll woman, which he smeared on his scythe so that it would stay sharp.

Soon the man caught up with the *jutul*.

"Why don't you whet your scythe?" asked the *jutul*.

"Mow today, whet tomorrow," said the man.

And so he beat the *jutul*.

> In competitions with trolls, humans usually win because of their superior intelligence.
> Collected in 1920 by Edvard Langset from Ola O. Hola in Nesset, Nordmøre (Norway). Printed in Langset, *Segner-gåter-folketru frå Nordmør* (1948), 47–48.

55.10 The Jätte's Wife Borrowed the Butter Churn

In the old days in Lilleberg, right next to Skallerud, there lived a *jätte*. This *jätte* had a wife who used to go down to Skallerud Farm to borrow the butter churn. She would say:

Dear mother, neighbor mine,
Loan me your roll-a-duck,
Roll it away, roll it home,
My roll-a-duck has gone to pieces.

This legend has been collected mostly in Värmland and occasionally in neighboring areas in Sweden, as well as in Norway.

"Roll-a-duck" here refers to the butter churn. Klintberg has suggested that the verse the *jätte's* wife recites is a riddle. The giants supposedly spoke their own secret language.

See Bengt af Klintberg, *Svenska folksägner* (1972), 307–8.

Collected by Ragnar Nilsson in 1928 from Britta-Maja Jansson in Skallerud, Grum parish, Värmland (Sweden). Ms. in IFGH, 1479. Printed in af Klintberg, *Svenska folksägner* (1972), 126.

55.11 The Master Builder

A casket maker was contracted to build the church at Vrejlev. But whatever he built during the day fell down again during the night. He became annoyed and discouraged and did not know how to deal with the situation of having promised to put up the building but not being able to do it. One day he was complaining about not knowing what to do, when a little man appeared and said:

"I can build the church for you, but you must promise me one of three things."

Well, the casket maker asked what he wanted. He wanted the sun, the moon, or the casket maker's heart. So they made a contract. But when the building was almost finished, the casket maker got very upset because he understood that it would cost him his heart—he knew he could not get the sun or the moon.

Then the little man appeared to him one day and said:

"If you can guess my name, I'll let you go."

Well, he could not guess it, so he decided to escape. One day he took off, and he walked and walked. He had taken some provisions with him, and when he got tired, he sat down by a mound to eat. Then he heard some children jabbering in the mound and a woman who said:

"Hush, hush, my little children, tonight your father Find will come home, and he'll bring you the sun or the moon or, perhaps, the heart of the casket maker."

Well, he had heard enough and went back home. When he met the troll, he said:

"You wanted me to give you my heart—but what are you going to do with it?"

"You can still get out of it, if you guess my name."

This time he was allowed three guesses. Well, he said a couple of other names first, but finally he asked:

"Isn't your name Find?"

Then the troll got so mad he ran to the east side of the church and tore out a stone. People say that it has been replaced, but it never stays put. The troll wanted to tear down the church, of course, but he did not manage to do that.

> In Scandinavia the legend about the troll who built the church first developed during the Middle Ages. In Trondheim (Norway) the troll is hired by Saint Olav, in Lund (Sweden) by Saint Laurentius. In German folk tradition, it is usually the devil rather than a troll who functions as the master builder. It has been suggested that the legend has its background in the Eddic myth about the building of the wall around the gods' abode (Asgarth). Other possible sources are certain Irish folktales, as well as the European cycle of tales about Titteliture, Tom-Tit-Tot, or Rumpelstiltskin. (Cf. no. 59.5.)
>
> See Carl Wilhelm von Sydow, "Studier i Finnsägnen och besläktade byggmästarsägner," *Fataburen* (1907), 65–78, 119–218; (1908), 19–27; and "Iriskt inflytande på nordisk guda- och hjältesaga," *Vetenskaps-societeten i Lund. Årsbok* (1920), 26–61; Jöran Sahlgren, "Sägnerna om trollen Finn och Skalle och deras kyrkobyggande," *Saga och sed* (1940), 1–50; (1941), 115–54; Waldemar Liungman, "Finnsägenproblemet," *FmFt* 29 (1942), 86–113, 138–54; Maja Fossenius, "Sägnerna om trollen Finn och Skalle som byggmästare," *Folkkultur* 3 (1943), 5–144; Inger M. Boberg, *Baumeistersagen* (1955); Niels C. Lukman, "Finn og St. Laurentius i Lund og i Canterbury," *Arkiv för nordisk filologi* 75 (1960), 194–237; Olav Bø, *Heilag Olav i norsk folketradisjon* (1955), 35–42.
>
> Legend type: ML 7065.
>
> Collected by E. T. Kristensen from Johanne Marie Kristensdatter in Søheden, Vendsyssel, Jylland (Denmark). Printed in Kristensen, *Danske sagn* 3 (1895), 181–82.

55.12 Gyðja and the Trolls

It is said that trolls visit people's homes, especially when they are standing empty. To the north of Núgvunes in Borgardalur on the island of Mykines, there is a hut the shepherds used as shelter when they were training the sheep to stay in the snow shelters and digging them out when they were snowed under. This mountain pasture is the farthest one from the village, which itself lies on the westernmost part of the island. One night one of the shepherds walked east toward the pasture in Borgardalur, when a fierce squall struck. He decided to take shelter in the hut. But when he approached, he heard noises. Looking in through the window, he saw that the hut was full of trolls dancing and singing:

Trum, trum, tra la la la!
Even trolls think it's chilly where it's hilly!
Nice and warm on the farm down at Skálavöllur!
Trum, trum, tra la la la!
Dance round and round, by window, wall, and door!

There were even worse doings at Trøllanes, the northernmost village on Kalsoy. On Twelfth Night each year, so many trolls swarmed from every direction that the villagers fled their homes and stayed in Mikladalur as long as the trolls carried on. This is how the village came to be called Trøllanes.

Once it happened that a very old woman was not able to flee with the other villagers. She hid under a table in the kitchen, hoping the trolls would not see her. Later in the evening, she saw trolls flocking through the doors like sheep into a fold, so many of them that she could not count them all. They began to kick up their heels. But just when the party was at its peak, the old woman cried out from under the table:

"Jesus have mercy on me!"
When the trolls heard the hated name, they howled:
"Gyðja broke up the dance!"

With that they left the house and have not disturbed the village since. When people returned from Mikladalur after the holy day, they expected to find old Gyðja dead, but she was still alive and told them how things had gone with her and the trolls.

(Cf. no. 47.20.)
   Legend type: ML 6015.
   Collected by V. U. Hammershaimb on the Faeroe Islands.
Printed in Hammershaimb, "Færøiske folkesagn," *Antiquarisk tidskrift 1849–51* (1852), 337–39. Reprinted in Hammershaimb, *Savn* (1969), 219–21.

55.13 The Troll and the Church at Skrea

The old troll on Butter Mountain could not stand the "bell cow" in Skrea. He threw a rock at it but did not hit his target. Then he moved out to an island. When a sailor arrived on the island, the troll gave him a necklace for a girl in Skrea, a box to be placed on the altar in the church, and a chest with seed he wanted them to sow.

When the sailor got home, they tied the necklace around an oak tree, and it flew up into the air and disappeared. Then they thought something might be wrong with the box, too. They put it on top of a hill and it burst into flames. But they did sow the seed, and from it grew a whole lot of troll heads. So they commandeered all the people in the village, and they grabbed their scythes and cut them off.

Throughout Scandinavia legends depict the trolls' resistance to the building of churches. The explanation given most often is that the trolls hate the sound of the bells. The church and its bell is often referred to as "bell cow."

The revengeful gift sent by the troll is frequently tied not only to his anger toward the church but also to an unsuccessful courtship. The same motif can be found in a legend from the ninth century about Saint Nikolas.

See Johan Kalén, "Hämdegåvan: några ord om en sägentyp," *FmFt* 22 (1935), 107–20; Hilding Celander, "En Nikolaus-legend och dess samband med sägnerna om Jätten på ön och Hämndegåvan," *FmFt* 22 (1935), 165–80.

Collected by Helmer Olsson in Skrea, Halland (Sweden). Printed in Carl-Martin Bergstrand, *Hallands sägner* (1949), 49.

55.14 The Jätte Who Moved to Norway

When they built the church in Mo, the giant there could not stand the ringing of the bells. So he moved to Norway. A few years later, some people from Mo visited Norway, where they saw the old giant himself. When they asked him why he had moved away from them, he answered:

In Borgås Mountain it was good to dwell,
except for the cow with the great big bell.

Collected by Arnold Olsson in Skee, Bohuslän (Sweden). Printed in Carl-Martin Bergstrand, *Bohusländska sägner* (1947), 55.

55.15 The Church at Ketilvellir

Bishop Gissur, second bishop of Skálholt, built a church at Ketil-vellir in the district of Laugardalur, which is in Árnessýsla. There it stood for a long time. Traces of the churchyard can still be seen there today. Later the church was moved to Miðdalur, where it has been ever since. The people from Laugardalur tell this story:

To the east of Miðdalur lies a canyon with dark clefts reaching up into the mountainside. In a cave in one of the clefts, there lived an ogress who every Christmas carried off the best man in Laugardalur. The people of Laugardalur talked to the Bishop at Skálholt, who counseled them to move their church as close to the canyon as possible and to ring the church bells every Christmas. This was done and the ogress fled the canyon.

Some people say that the ogress moved north to a place called Klukkuskarð. Bells were brought into the ravine, and the ogress was also driven from there by the ringing. That is how the ravine got its name. It lies on the road running north from Laugardalur to Skjold-breiður.

(Cf. nos. 55.13 and 55.14).

The motif of annual human sacrifice to an ogre is well known both in classical literature and in folktale tradition. Cp. AT type 300.

See Stith Thompson, *The Folktale* (1946), 24–33.

Collected in 1847 by Magnús Grímsson, minister at Mosfell from schoolboys from Southern Iceland. Printed in Jón Árnason, *Íslenzkar þjóðsögur og œfintýri* 1 (1862), 151. Reprinted in new edition 1 (1954), 145.

55.16 The Cleft in Horje Mountain

About a mile and a half north of Stavanger lies Tau. Big folk—both kings and giants—are supposed to have lived there in the old days. When the cathedral at Stavanger was being built, the giant on Tau got angry and wanted to tear it down even before it got finished. He uprooted a huge piece of rock and threw it, hoping to flatten the church. But there is an island halfway between Tau and the town. It is called Horje and is covered with towering mountains. The giant had thrown a little low, and the rock fell down on Horje, cutting a cleft into one of the peaks. As a result the rock did not reach its goal, but the cleft can be seen in the crest of Horje to this very day.

Here the traditional hostility of the trolls and giants toward the church serves to explain the origin of a mountain cleft.

See *Atlas över svensk folkkultur II. Sägen, tro och högtidssed 2*, edited by Åke Campbell and Åsa Nyman (1976) 33–36.

Collected by Oluf Løwold in Ryfylke, Rogaland (Norway). Printed in Løwold, *Præstehistorier og sagn* (1891), 170. Reprinted in Torkell Mauland, *Folkeminne fraa Rogaland* 1 (1926), 69.

55.17 The Troll Who Was Turned to Stone

Two men were riding south over the Kerlingarskarð. One was named Ólafur, but nobody can remember the name of the other man. On the pass they met a troll woman who said:

Ólafur the Mouth,
are you heading south?
Things will work out well.
But I predict, poor crooked jaw,
you'll leave without a straw.

Then Ólafur answered:
"Look to the east, there's a man riding on a white horse!"
The troll woman looked, but just then, the first rays of dawn appeared, and she was turned to stone.

(Cf. no. 59.1.)

In Snorri's *Edda* (thirteenth century), the sun is described as a horse called *Skinfaxi* ("Shining Mane"), whose mane illuminates the universe.

Collected by Jón Norðmann from Barður in Fljótar (Iceland). Printed in Jón Árnason, *Íslenzkar þjóðsögur og ævintýri* 1 (1862), 159. Reprinted in new edition 1 (1954), 156.

55.18 The Trolls Could Not Move the Faeroe Islands

To the north of the village of Eiði, at the mouth of the channel between Eysturoy and Streymoy, there stand two immense rocks in the sea called "The Giant and the Old Woman." In calm weather it is possible to row between them. There is a legend that tells how Iceland wanted the Faeroes moved northward into its own waters, and it sent the giant and his wife to do the job. They approached the Faeroes at the point of land to the northwest called Eiðskollur. The giant stood out in the ocean, while the old woman climbed up on the head to fasten a rope to it, and then to tip it so that he could heave it up on his back. The first time she took hold, she tugged so hard that the outer head was split off. Then she tried to fasten the rope someplace else, but the islands were rooted too firmly and were not going to be easy to move. The old woman was still atop the head when it started to turn light. Giants fear the daylight, and she climbed down to the giant waiting in the sea as quickly as she could. But they had lingered too long. When they met below the head to wade back to Iceland, the sun rose out of the sea, and both the giant and the woman were turned to stone. There they are still standing today, looking toward Iceland but unable to move.

Other people say that the giants were sent to fetch grain from the Faeroes because there was a famine in Iceland—indeed, it looks as if the old woman has a bundle or a sack on her back.

> Collected by V. U. Hammershaimb on the Faeroe Islands. Printed in Hammershaimb, *Færøsk anthologi* 1 (1891), 344–45.

55.19 *The Ogress Drowned in the Ocean*

Once a troll woman decided to wade all the way from Norway to Iceland. She knew there were trenches on the ocean floor. She even said to another troll woman, a neighbor who tried to discourage her from going:

"Iceland's trenches may be deep, but it is possible to wade across them!"

But she also said that there was one narrow trench in the middle of the ocean, so deep that she might get the top of her head wet. Then she set off. When she got to that trench, she tried grabbing on to a ship that was sailing by, to steady herself, but she missed the ship, lost her footing, plunged into the trench, and drowned. Her body was washed ashore here at Rauðisandur a while back. Lying dead and stiff on the beach, she was so huge that a man on horseback could not reach up and touch the underside of her bent knees with his riding crop.

> Collected by Skúli Gíslason, minister at Breiðabólstaður (Iceland). Printed in Jón Árnason, *Íslenzkar þjóðsögur og æfintýri* 1 (1862), 217. Reprinted in new edition 1 (1954), 206.

PART VIII
Buried Treasure

Part VIII illustration: "Desiring to own the buried treasure he fell upon the serpent." Olaus Magnus, *Historia de Gentibus Septentrionalibus* (History of the Northern People, 1555), book 5, chapter 22.

here is a core of historical fact behind the many treasure legends in Scandinavian folk tradition. Prior to Christianization, hoards of gold, silver, coins and other valuables were buried in graves for use by the dead in the afterlife, and both then and much later, people hid money underground for safekeeping. Legends frequently describe abortive attempts to find the hidden wealth protected by preternatural beings, believed to be the ghost of the original owner or perhaps the revenant of an animal sacrificed at the time of burial. Often the treasure was bound by various spells. It could be raised only at propitious times and if stringent conditions were met. The treasure hunter must be properly prepared—for instance, by fasting—and he must observe the taboo against talking or laughing. Sometimes strange apparitions lure the treasure hunter into breaking the taboo. At other times, someone burying the treasure is observed by a concealed witness who then retrieves the hoard.

See Hirschberg, "Schatz," *Handwörterbuch des deutschen Aberglaubens* 7 (1935–36), columns 1002–15; Leander Petzoldt, *Deutsche Volkssagen* (1970), 466; Bengt Holbek and Iørn Piø, *Fabeldyr og sagnfolk* (1967), 359–411; Bengt af Klintberg, *Svenska folksägner* (1972), 44–45; Carl Wilhelm von Sydow, *Sigurds strid med Fåvne* (1918), 17–19; Tobias Norlind, *Skattsägner* (1918); Waldemar Liungman, *Sveriges sägner i ord och bild* 5 (1961), 299–363; John Lindow, "Swedish Legends of Buried Treasure," *Journal of American Folklore* 95 (1982), 257–79.

56.1 A Spell for Binding Treasure

In the name of Jesus! The goods that I bury here in secret, I bind and chain with three chains of God: the Father, the Son, and the Holy Spirit. I command and conjure you, princes of eight hells: Lucifer, Belzebub, Astarot, Satanos, Stubis, Deis, Janus, Dracus Belial, to depart with all your following, and leave these goods in the hands of man.

> I stamp with my foot,
> Son of Mary, give power,
> give steadfastness to me and my goods,
> to remain here in the holy and blessed name,
> until I alone raise it again!
> In the name of God the Father, Son, and Holy Spirit. Amen.

> This conjuring type formula accompanies the ritual of burying treasure.
>
> From a Black Book from Eiker, Akershus (Norway), dating from 1800–1850. Printed in A. Chr. Bang, *Norske hexeformularer og magiske opskrifter* (1901–2), 709.

56.2 To Find Buried Treasure

On the eve of Maundy Thursday at dusk or on a Sunday morning at dawn just before sunrise—the first being preferable—take a twig from a rowan, cut it without the use of iron, make sure that it does not fall to the ground, and leave the bark in place. Using a needle or awl that has pierced through a black toad and the blood of a white hen, inscribe the following signs on the twig:

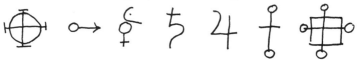

If carried over a place where a treasure is buried, the twig will reveal it by twisting in the hand of the bearer.

> This formula combines a magic ritual with the use of secret signs. Blood from a hen's comb was traditionally used as ink for these signs. The hen often appears as the guardian of treasures. The toad was generally considered an animal belonging to the Devil, and therefore dangerous, but it was also believed to possess magical powers. According to several variants in Rääf's collection, the nights of Easter week (Thursday through Sunday), as well as Midsummer Night, were the best times to find treasures. The divining rod employed in the ritual was preferably cut from the rowan because of the magical properties ascribed to that tree.
>
> See Hirschberg, "Schatz," *Handwörterbuch des deutschen Aberglaubens* 7 (1935–6), columns 1007–8; Tobias Norlind, *Skattsägner* (1918), 27–29.
>
> The text is derived from a manuscript from Småland (Sweden). Printed in Leonhard Fredrik Rääf, *Svenska skrock og signerier*, edited by K. Rob. V. Wikman (1957), 330.

56.3 The Fortress at Somnes

At Sømnes on Sørsømna, there is a place called Friborg Fortress. A lot of round stones can be found near it. According to legend, if a person dug down there, he or she would come to a big iron door underground, behind which lies a great treasure. On one side of the door is a dragon, on the other a lion. They have been put there to guard the treasure.

A woman known as the sybil has prophesied that the treasure is so great that it alone could feed all the people of Norway for thirty years.

> The dragon and lion as fabulous monsters guarding treasures date back to classical literature. The sybil also appears in ancient literature, but in European folk tradition, she is first documented during the Middle Ages. Sybils play an important role in Old Norse

literature, for instance, in the *Poetic Edda* and in a number of
Icelandic sagas.

See Will-Erich Peuckert, "Sibylle," *Handwörterbuch des deutschen
Aberglaubens* 7 (1935–36), columns 1655–59; Bengt Holbek and
Iørn Piø, *Fabeldyr og sagnfolk* (1967), 359–411; Carl-Martin Edsman, "Antik och modern Sibylla," *Vetenskapsamhällets i Uppsala
årsbok* (1971–72), 66–104.

Collected by Knut Strompdal in Sørsømna, Nordland (Norway). Printed in Strompdal, *Gamalt frå Helgeland* 3 (1939), 89.

56.4 I Will Catch Up with Him

Just beyond Øydnes Hill in Konsmo, by the old valley road, there
lies a big stone they call Rige Stone. There is supposed to be a kettle
of money buried under that stone.

Once some folks were out at Øydnes Hill, digging around the
stone to search for the kettle. When they had dug down so far that
they expected to hit the kettle at any moment, a man rode by on a
black horse. He was riding awfully fast. Right after him somebody
came along in a little boat, pushing himself forward on dry land with
a couple of sticks. But he went so slowly that he hardly moved at all.
He asked the people digging there whether they had seen a man on
horseback. Yes, he had gone past a little while ago.

"Oh, I see. Well, I guess I'll catch up with him," he said, as if talking to himself.

But one of the folks there cursed and said:

"That's what it looks like!"

All of a sudden the man in the boat grabbed the kettle with the
money and disappeared in the direction of Håbås Mountain.

This legend is an example of the preternatural guardian of a treasure creating a hallucination to fool the treasure hunter into breaking the taboo against talking.

See Tobias Norlind, *Skattsägner* (1918), 57–61.

Collected by Tore Bergstøl in Konsmo, Vest-Agder (Norway).
Printed in Bergstøl, *Atterljom. Folkeminne fraa smaadalane kring Lindesnes* 2 (1930), 53.

56.5 Seven Headless Roosters

The farmers at Kølby were digging for treasure on Visborg Hill.
But just when they got down far enough to reach the treasure, a car-

riage drawn by seven headless roosters drove by. One of the men said:

"That was a devil of a carriage that just drove by."

Then the treasure sank, and they never saw it again.

> Collected by E. T. Kristensen from Mette Printz in Nordby, Samso (Denmark). Printed in Kristensen, *Danske sagn* 3 (1895), 451.

56.6 The Treasure at Fagrihóll

Not very far from Stykkishólmur, there is a knoll called Fagrihóll. People say that inside it lies the buried treasure of the ancient monastery at Helgafell. Once an attempt was made to excavate the knoll. But when the diggers had gotten quite deep, they thought they saw the church at Helgafell in flames, and they rushed off to put out the fire. Later, there was another attempt to excavate the knoll, but this time the diggers saw an armed host arise from the ground and threaten them with death if they did not stop digging. After that no Icelander would excavate the knoll, so the diggers had to come from Denmark. The Danes' attempt was also a failure.

> Helgafell Monastery was sacked in the 1540s, when the Reformation was imposed on Iceland by the Danish king. In Icelandic legends, as in the saga, buried treasure is often guarded by the dead. In the saga, the treasure is usually raised by the hero, but in the Icelandic legends, it tends to elude the treasure seeker. Fagrihóll and the surrounding land was owned by a man named Egill Sveinbjarnason Egilsson, who related the above story to Konrad Maurer in 1858. The informant actually tried to raise the treasures of the ancient monastery but found nothing. Since no one from the local population was willing to work for him, he was forced to import Danish labor for the job.
>
> Collected by Konrad Maurer in Iceland. Printed in Maurer, *Isländische Volkssagen der Gegenwart* (1860), 72. Icelandic version printed in Jón Árnason, *Íslenzkar þjóðsögur og ævintýri* 1 (1862), 279. Reprinted in new edition 1 (1954), 268.

56.7 The Boy Who Raised the Treasure

In the old days, there was someone in Skrautvøl called the Ødde-Boy. One Midsummer Night he saw a gleaming light strike a mound. He dug up the mound the same night. They say he took his mother along on the dig. He had heard people tell that wherever a light like that struck, there was a treasure to be found.

He and his mother had been digging for a while, when suddenly an old crone drove by in a trough. She sat there, lurching forward now and then. That is how she moved. And all at once she said:

"I'll get there all right! I'll get there all right!"

I guess the old crone in the trough was trying to fool the boy into talking, because once he talked, there would be no use in digging any farther. But the Ødde-Boy held himself back, he did. And therefore he probably found the treasure. At least, it is certain that after that Midsummer Night he became a well-to-do man. Yes, that is what my father told me.

> Collected by Knut Hermundstad from Ragni Bjørnsdotter Rølloug in Nord-Aurdal, Valdres, Oppland (Norway). Printed in Hermundstad, *I kveldseta. Gamal Valdres-kultur* 6 (1955), 40.

56.8 *The Black Hen*

The farmer's wife at Vindbæk went to church at Elling one New Year's morning. I do not remember what year it was.

On her way to the church, she saw a black hen sitting on a copper kettle someplace near Remmen, close to where the mill is. The hen sat there brooding. The woman took her kerchief from around her neck and placed it next to the kettle. Then she put the hen on it. She took a few handfuls of silver coins from the kettle, wrapped them in her kerchief, and put the hen carefully back on the kettle. Then the hen said:

> If you hadn't picked me up so lightly
> and put me down so nicely,
> you wouldn't have received
> what you now may keep.

Since that day they have had nothing but prosperity at Vindbæk.

The old king's road used to run through Upper Remmen, east of where the Skagen road lies today. It was on this old road that the farmer's wife had been walking.

> In folk belief two explanations for the origin of the black hen are to be found; it represents either the dead owner of the treasure or the revenant of the animal sacrificed when the treasure was buried. In the legends, however, there is less concern with the ori-

gin of the hen than with the proper manner of treating it so that the treasure can be recovered.

See Bengt Holbek and Iørn Piø, *Fabeldyr og sagnfolk* (1967), 63; Tobias Norlind, *Skattsägner* (1918), 53–54, 73–74.

Collected by E. T. Kristensen from Niels Madsen in Bratten, Jylland (Denmark). Printed in Kristensen, *Danske sagn* 3 (1895), 455.

56.9 The Blood of Seven Brothers

Once a man buried a treasure near a mountain. But a child picking berries nearby watched him.

"Well, now," the man said when he had buried the treasure, "keep this safe for me until the blood of seven brothers has flown over it."

The child told his parents about what he had seen and heard. They took an ax and seven rooster chicks and went to the place. There they cut off their heads and let the blood flow over the spot. And then they were able to dig up the treasure.

My father's mother told me about it. She was born in Tving.

> The legend is known throughout Scandinavia. The number seven is considered magical.
>
> Collected by Sigfrid Svensson in 1924 from Ingrid Andersson in Tving parish, Blekinge (Sweden). Ms. in LUF (648), 30. Printed in Bengt af Klintberg, *Svenska folksägner* (1972), 264.

56.10 Plowing with a Hen and Harrowing with a Cat

My father told me about a farmer who once buried some money.

All the folks except the old farmer and a young herding boy were being tested on their knowledge of the catechism. The boy watched the old farmer, who crawled under the barn, dug a hole, and placed a small barrel filled with money in it. The he said:

No one may take this money up,
unless he plows with a hen
and harrows with a cat.

The boy pondered what he had seen. Eventually he left the farm, but after he was grown up, he returned and took service there. It was not difficult to make a little plow and a harrow and get a hen and a cat to pull them. He retrieved the money and kept as much as he wanted. He bought himself a farm and divided the rest of the money among the old farmer's relatives.

> Until a few generations ago, it was customary that once a year the local minister would make the rounds from farm to farm to question everybody about their faith and to test their knowledge of the church's teachings.
>
> Collected by Carl-Martin Bergstrand in 1954 from Emily Svensson in Forss parish, Bohuslän (Sweden). Ms. in IFGH (5849). Printed in Bengt af Klintberg, *Svenska folksägner* (1972), 264–65.

56.11 Buried Money

When people hid their money in the old days, they would secure it with a magic spell.

On a farm someplace, there was once a boy who watched the farmer bury some money. He hid it under the storehouse, saying that the money should lie there undisturbed until he retrieved it himself. But the farmer died not long after that. Then the boy carried the body to the storehouse, and, using the dead man's hand, he dug up the money. He kept it, of course.

> Collected by Knut Strompdal in Velfjord, Nordland (Norway). Printed in Strompdal, *Gamalt frå Helgeland* 3 (1939), 59.

PART IX
History as Seen from
the Village

Part IX illustration: "They saw the
trees in the forest . . . approach the
royal castle." Olaus Magnus, *Historia
de Gentibus Septentrionalibus* (History of the
Northern People, 1555),
book 7, chapter 20.

istorical legends comprise the largest single category in Scandinavian legend tradition. They are concerned with early settlements, local chieftains, kings, churches and ministers, epidemics, wars and soldiers, landowners, officials, thieves and strongmen, et cetera. The tradition tends to cluster around important events and individuals. For instance, Scandinavia experienced a number of destructive epidemics, but only the most catastrophic among them, the so-called Black Death (fourteenth century), is remembered in the legends. By and large, historical legends reflect the same worldview depicted in other legends, and they contain many supranormal elements. Thus the historicity of the so-called historical legends does not lie in the accuracy of factual data and information. Rather these legends depict the folk's interpretation of events, seen from a local perspective and filtered through traditional beliefs.

See Brynjulf Alver, "Historiske segner og historisk sanning," *Norveg* 9 (1962), 89–116; Vera K. Sokolova, "The Interaction of the Historical Legend with Other Folkloristic Genres," *Studia Fennica* 20 (1976), 58–66; Hildegunde Prütting, "Zur geschichtlichen Volkssage," *Bayerisches Jahrbuch für Volkskunde* (1953), 16–26.

57. Kings, Settlements, and Boundaries

Some of the early kings, thought of as national protectors, are depicted as almost mythical figures.

Legends telling about the first man to clear land and establish a farmstead are usually short and undeveloped. Often these pioneers are remembered as chieftains or kings, and the farm is named after them.

More developed narratives deal with border conflicts and changes in ownership of landholdings.

Jöran Sahlgren, "Ortsnamnssägner," *Saga och sed* (1945), 8–16.

57.1 Holger the Dane

Just south of Hjarne's Mound, in the parish of Tornby, there lies a huge flat rock in the middle of the field.

Once the owner of the field wanted to get rid of that rock because it was in his way. He sent four strong men armed with steel bars to move it. They finally managed to lift up one corner, when to their horror, they saw that it rested on four corner stones and covered a room made of stone. In it an old man with a white beard sat by a table. He had a big sword, and his beard reached all the way down to the table. He looked up and said:

"Is it time now? Give me your hand, my fellow countryman, so I can feel how strong you are."

One of the men handed him his steel bar, which the old man squeezed until it was flat. Then he said:

"There is still strength in the arms of the Danes, it isn't time yet. Greet my brothers and tell them that I am Holger the Dane. I will come and help Denmark in her hour of need."

Now they were able to let go of the rock. They ran home and told about what they had seen and heard. The rock lies there undisturbed to this very day.

> The folk tradition of the ancient king living in an underground or mountain abode is known in a number of European countries. In Germany, for instance, the reference is to Charlemagne, Frederik Barbarossa, and others, in England to King Arthur.
>
> See Donald Ward, "Berg," *Enzyklopädie des Märchens* 2 (1979), columns 138–46.
>
> Collected by E. T. Kristensen from Katrine Høeg-Højer in Hjørring, Jylland (Denmark). Printed in Kristensen, *Danske sagn 2* (1893), 333.

57.2 King Hjørd on Jørstad

In Jørstad on Umbo, one of the Sjødna Islands, there is supposed to have lived a king named Hjørd. This happened so long ago, an old man said, that it was at the same time Adam lived on Umbo and Eve walked around in wooden shoes. The farm is supposed to have taken its name from King Hjørd. There are many grave mounds on the farm, and in one of them, a lot of weapons and other ancient things were found.

> Collected by Torkell Mauland from Bjørn Eide in Rogaland (Norway). Printed in Mauland, *Folkeminne fraa Rogaland* 2 (1931), 27.

57.3 The King and the Crofter's Daughter

Once there were too many people in Sweden, and the king ordered some of them killed. But when the daughter of a crofter heard about this, she laughed at the king. He sent for her, commanding her to come neither during the waxing nor the waning moon, neither clothed nor unclothed, neither driving nor walking. So she dressed in a ragged fishnet and came during the moon's turning, with one foot on the back of a billy goat, the other on the ground.

The king asked her how she dared laugh at his command.

"His majesty has not given life and does not have the right to take life," she answered.

"What are we going to do with all the people, then?" asked the king.

"Give them a shovel and a bucket full of seed, and let them go to the place where there are no people," answered the girl.

The land where there were no people was Finland. This piece of advice pleased the king so much that he married the girl.

> Klintberg has suggested that this legend may have entered popular folk tradition through a school drama entitled *Disa*, written by Johannes Messenius, which was first performed in 1611. Parallels to the motif of solving overpopulation by mass killing date back to the Saga of Olaf Tryggvasson. The motif of the impossible task is more typically found in folktales (AT 875), but an early example exists in the saga of Ragnar Lodbrok.
>
> See Bengt af Klintberg, *Svenska folksägner* (1972), 346–47; L. Bygdén, "Några studier rörande Disasagan," *Samlaren* (1896), 21–74.
>
> Collected by J. E. Wefvar during the 1870s in Vörå, Österbotten (Finland). Printed in V. E. V. Wessman, *Sägner* 2.1 (1928), 2.

57.4 The Boundary Dispute

Once a boundary dispute arose between the people of Suntak and the folks at Valstad. A farmer at Valstad insisted that their parish extended all the way to Korsli. He was willing to take an oath at the place where he said the boundary was. He got some soil from the graveyard at Valstad and put it in his shoes. Then he swore that he was standing on the soil of his own parish. But when he swore, he sank into the ground. In the 1860s there was supposed to have been a stone marking the place where it happened.

> In other variants of this widespread legend, the punishment is not that the man sinks into the ground but that he must walk again after death. (Cf. nos. 26.1–26.7.)
>
> See Misch Orend, "Vom Schwur mit Erde in den Schuhen," *Deutsches Jahrbuch für Volkskunde* 4 (1958), 386–92.
>
> Collected by N. N. Sjöholm from Johan Möller in Korsberga parish, Kåkind, Västergötland (Sweden). Ms. in NM (EU 21806), 167.

57.5 The Boundaries of Klagstorp and Tåstorp

Near Skövde lie the two farms Klagstorp and Tåstorp. My mother's father comes from there, and he tells the following story.

At one time, when both places were to change hands, the new owners were to have as much land as they could traverse within a given time.

The man from Tåstorp walked reasonably fast and covered enough land to make a sizable manor; he returned within the set time limit, so he got the farm. Since then it has remained in his family's possession.

But the man who was to have Klagstorp was greedy. He wanted to have as much land as possible and ran around a huge piece of ground. He overexerted himself and fell down dead. That manor became bigger than Tåstorp, but it can never pass from father to son; it must forever pass into new hands.

> In the distant past, it was customary to ride, walk, or carry fire while encircling a piece of ground to be taken into possession. In this legend the ancient ritual functions to explain the relative size of the two farms, as well as the differences in owners.
>
> See Julius Eidestam, "Omfärd vid besittningstagande av jordegendom," *Svenska landsmål* 69 (1946), 86–114; Dag Strömbäck, "Att helga land. Studier i landnama och det äldsta rituella besittningstagandet," *Festskrift till Axel Hägerström* (1928), 198–220. Reprinted in Strömbäck, *Folklore och filologi* (1970), 135–65.
>
> Collected by N. Sjöholm from G. Andersson in Våmb parish, Håkind, Västergötland (Sweden). Ms. in NM (EU 17866).

57.6 The Borders of Sigdal, Krødsherad, and Snarum

When the boundaries between Sigdal, Krødsherad, and Snarum were to be marked, it happened in a special way.

There was never any peace between the villages because they could not settle on their borders. To end the conflict once and for all, they agreed that a man was to ride out from each village at dawn. The boundaries would be placed wherever the men met. So, off rode a man from Snarum, one from Krødsherad, and one from Sigdal. But the latter two took off too early, which is why the border came to be so far north and so close to Krødsherad. They met at Lake Håvardsrud in Finnerud's Wood.

Topographically unnatural boundaries were explained as resulting from deception in settling borders. In most variants of this migratory legend, someone circumvents the agreement by starting out too early. There are a number of parallels to this legend in classical literature.

See Lutz Röhrich, "Eine antike Grenzsage und ihre neuzeitlichen Parallelen," *Würzburger Jahrbücher für Altertumswissenschaft* 4 (1949–50), 339–69.

Collected by Andreas Mørch in Sigdal and Eggedal, Buskerud, (Norway). Printed in Mørch, *Frå gamle dagar. Folkeminne frå Sigdal og Eggedal* (1932), 78.

57.7 *The Boundaries of the Icelandic Bishoprics*

The bishops at Skálholt and Hólar could not reach an agreement about the boundaries of their sees, but they did set up a landmark between the counties of Þingeyjarsýsla and Norður-Múlasýsla to mark the northeastern border. Each of them was to start from the landmark and ride around the island, the Hólar bishop to the north and the Skálholt bishop to the south. The second marker was to be placed wherever they met. The bishop from Skálholt rode day and night as fast as his horses would go and arrived dead-tired at the place where the marker was eventually established. But the bishop from Hólar rode slowly and leisurely through the countryside and did not exert himself. He was bright-eyed and bushy-tailed when he met his colleague at the south end of Hrútafjöður. Ever since then the boundary between the two bishoprics has run through the middle of that fjord.

Iceland was divided into two bishoprics in 1106 A.D. The old bishopric of Skálholt retained three-fourths of the country, while the new bishopric of Hólar was assigned the remaining quarter.

Collected by Konrad Maurer from Runólfur Magnús Ólsen, Þingeyrar (Iceland). Printed in Maurer, *Isländische Volkssagen der Gegenwart* (1860), 213–14. Icelandic version in Jón Árnason, *Íslendzkar þjóðsögur og æfintýri* 2 (1864), 69–70. Reprinted in new edition 2 (1958), 74–75.

58. Churches

The numerous legends in this category indicate the central role of the church in traditional Scandinavian society. The most important and numerically speaking greatest subgroup concerns itself with the choice of building sites. The conflict between the church and supranormal beings is an important motif in this context. Other legends tell about the identification of the bells with a particular church. A further group describes the miraculous powers of holy images and how they came into the possession of a given parish.

> See Gunnar Smedberg, "Kyrksägnerna från Jämtland och Härjedalen," *Forum Theologicum* 17 (1960), 87–116.

58.1 Finding a Building Site for the New Church

When they were going to build the church in Vallerstad, they first intended to put it up on Lund's Hill. But that proved to be impossible. Whatever was erected during the day, was torn down again during the night by the troll. Finally the builders had to give up.

Because they did not want to pick another unsuitable building site, the folks in the parish agreed to leave it to Providence. They did what other people had tried before them: they loaded the foundation stone on a sled, harnessed a pair of wild oxen to it, and let them go wherever they wanted. The church was built where the oxen stopped.

> This legend is enormously popular throughout Scandinavia. Strömbäck has distinguished three subtypes, namely, that the church was built where floating timbers drifted ashore, where untamed oxen pulled the building materials, or where the invisible folk moved them at night. Parallels to this legend can also be found in early Scandinavian literature, for example, in the Icelandic *Book of Settlements* (twelfth century). A similar account in the Old Testament describes how the holy ark was returned to the Israelites (I. Samuel, chaps. 5–6).
>
> See Dag Strömbäck, "Den första kyrkplatsen i sägen och folklig tro," *Religion och bibel* 17 (1958), 3–13. Reprinted in Strömbäck, *Folklore och filologi* (1970), 123–34. *Atlas över svensk folkkultur II. Sägen, tro och högtidssed* 2, edited by Åke Campbell and Åsa Nyman (1976), 40–41.
>
> Legend type: ML 7060.
>
> Collected by Elis Åström in 1955 in Östergötland (Sweden). Printed in Åström, *Folktro och folkliv i Östergötland* (1962), 36.

58.2 Indulgences for Work on the Church

The church in Hälsinge was built during the Catholic period. Forgiveness of sins was granted to anyone who carried the larger stones to the wall.

> The dogma of indulgences was an important issue during the Reformation, which came to Scandinavia during the 1530s. It demonstrates the tenacity of folk tradition that a story based on that dogma survived for centuries after the practice of indulgences had been eliminated from the religious life of the population.
>
> See A. Chr. Bang, "Gjengangere fra hedenskabet og katolicismen blandt vort folk efter reformationen," *Theologisk tidsskrift* 10 (1885), 161–218.
>
> Collected by Filip Sundman in 1900 in Hälsinge, Nyland (Finland). Printed in V. E. V. Wessmann, *Sägner* 2.1 (1928), 266.

58.3 The Holy Image at Røldal Church

Once there was a blind fisherman. He was fishing on Cross Fjord, when he heard something in front of the boat. He crawled forward with the boat, feeling the water with his hand, and touched something that felt like a child's face. He tried to pull it into the boat but could not. He struggled until he was bathed in sweat. But he touched his face with the same hand that had touched the image, and suddenly he was able to see. He became so happy, he just had to get that image into the boat. He made a vow to give it to a certain church in Bergen, if he could only get it into the boat. That did not help either. He named all the churches he knew. But nothing helped until he named the church at Røldal. Then it almost seemed as if the image got into the boat by itself.

> Belief in the healing power of holy images was accepted dogma in Catholic belief. The migratory legend of the blind fisherman finding a crucifix floating in the sea is here adapted to explain how a particular image was brought to Røldal. The Røldal crucifix was famous throughout Norway. According to tradition, every Midsummer Night sweat dripped from the figure and was used to heal all kinds of ailments, including lameness and blindness. The last, unofficial Midsummer Night's mass was held at Røldal church during the nineteenth century.

See Kjell Bondevik, "Valfarting og lovnader," *Museet i Hauge-sund* (1925–35), 65–77.

Collected by Torkell Mauland from Hans and Inger Øverland in Suldal, Rogaland (Norway). Printed in Mauland, *Folkeminne fraa Rogaland* 2 (1931), 44.

58.4 They Could Not Move the Church Bells

Once they received a message that they were to move the church bells. I do not remember why. It was probably during the time the king owned the church. They pulled the bells down from the tower and loaded them on a sled, and a horse pulled them until they got to the road by the churchyard. But then the sled stood still and would not be moved at all. They harnessed two, then three, four, and final-ly, twelve horses in front of the sled. But it did not do any good. The sled remained immobilized. So they turned it around, and one horse easily pulled the bells back to the church.

> Attempts to move a bell that belonged to a given church usually proved futile. Either it became too heavy or fell into a river or lake while being transported.
>
> See Mats Åmark, *Kyrkklockor, klockare och klocksägner i Dalarne* (1928); Joh. Pesch, *Die Glocke in Geschichte, Sage, Volksglauben, Volksbrauch und Dichtung* (1918).
>
> Collected by J. I. Dalen in Vik, Sogn (Norway). Printed in Dalen, "Klokkorne i Hoprekstadkyrkja," *Tidsskrift utg. av Historie-laget for Sogn* 4 (1920), 54.

58.5 The Church Bell at Bergume

Three times the Danes used Bergume Church as a horse stable. Once they were going to transport the church bell over a bridge, but it fell into the creek. To this very day that place is known as the "bell hideout."

One time they were trying to raise the bell, but a hen came along, pulling a load of hay.

"I'm going to take this to town today," she said.

The men raising the bell thought this was so strange that they could not keep quiet any longer, so the bell sank once more.

You see talking is forbidden when trying to raise a treasure.

> (Cf. the section on treasure legends for commentary.)

Collected by Helmer Olsson in Vättle, Västergötland (Sweden).
Printed in Olsson, *Folkliv och folkdikt i Vättle härad under 1800–talet*
(1945), 190.

58.6 The Journeyman Who Cast the Bell

The great bell at Lerum was cast at Stora Härlanda. The master
had to take a trip to Alingsås, and so the journeyman finished casting
the bell on his own. Afterward he struck the bell to test its sound. He
saw three drops of blood appear on the bell. The sound of the bell
was so powerful that the master heard it on his way back home, and
he was still somewhere between Ingered and Tollered. When he got
home, the journeyman said:
"This bell will take three lives: mine and yours, and I don't know
whose will be the third."
But it was clear to the master that the journeyman had become an
even better craftsman than himself, and he said:
"You have taken my bread from me, I will take your life from
you."
And then he killed the journeyman. He was executed for what he
had done.
But sometime later the bell fell down and killed a man.

> This migratory legend is widespread in Europe. Bell casting
> demanded great skill and was a prestigious accomplishment for
> the craftsman. Bells were often considered sacred and endowed
> with prophetic powers.
> See N.-A. Bringéus, *Sägnen om Örkelljunga kyrkklocka* (1949).
> Collected by Helmer Olsson in Vättle, Östergötland (Sweden).
> Printed in Olsson, *Folkliv och folkdikt i Vättle härad under 1800–talet*
> (1945), 188–89.

59. Saint Olav

King Olav Haraldson, who ruled Norway from 1015 to 1030, is
largely responsible for the Christianization of that country. After his
untimely death at the Battle of Stiklestad, he was declared a saint and
rex perpetuus Norvegiae (perpetual king of Norway), a symbolic title
that emphasizes Olav's central position in the history of Norway.

In folk tradition, the figure of Olav has attracted various motifs from folk belief and legend, creating the image of a supranormal being rather than of a saint or king.

See Olav Bø, *Heilag-Olav i norsk folketradisjon* (1955).

59.1 Saint Olav's Spring at Torvastad

The parish of Torvastad is in the northern part of Karmøy. A valley runs from north to south through the parish. Today the valley bottom lies a few meters above sea level, but in the old days, the sea reached all the way in, so there was a sound separating eastern and western Torvastad.

Once Saint Olav sailed into the sound. When he had gotten about halfway in, he was told there was no water on board. Wearing his iron gloves, the king went ashore and thrust his hand right into the face of a rock. Immediately, clear, fresh water welled up and poured from the rock, and they all got to drink.

You can see the spring even today. It is called Olav's Spring, and it never runs dry. If you are sick, the water will heal you. And if you have warts, you need only go to Olav's Spring and dip your hands into the water a couple of times, and you will be rid of them. Yes, that is what the folks in Torvastad say.

> The veneration of sacred springs is widely known. After initial resistance, the church accepted the popular belief in the power of such springs and associated them with various saints.
>
> The most famous Olav's Spring is located in the cathedral of Trondheim in Saint Olav's burial chamber.
>
> The motif of the iron gloves is known from both myths and folktales. In other variants of this legend, Olav speaks to the mountain to make it bring forth water, or he strikes it with his staff, as Moses did according to biblical tradition.
>
> See Olav Bø, *Heilag-Olav i norsk folketradisjon* (1955), 111–44.
>
> Collected by Aamund Salvesou in Rogaland (Norway). Printed in Salveson, *Folkeminne* (1924), 49–50.

59.2 Saint Olav in Suldal

Once Saint Olav sailed his ship into Hylsfjord. Folks say that he was heading east to Setesdal to baptize the heathens there. When he got to the end of the fjord, he wanted to take a shortcut. Cleaving the mountain in two, he made the pass called Hyl's Pass today.

Saint Olav then sailed along the northern shore of Lake Suldal, until he was a little way beyond Lillehammer. You can still see a piece of his sail in a steep rock face there. He crossed over to the south side of the lake, climbed up Rolleivsdjuvet, and continued east to Setesdal. Folks who know the area well between Suldal and Setesdal have said that Saint Olav's ship is still in the mountains there.

> This etiological legend explains the origin of the mountain pass at Hyl. The motif of the ship that can travel through the air, on land, and over the sea is also known in myths and folktales. Legends about Saint Olav traveling in his magic ship were very popular.
>
> See Olav Bø, *Heilag-Olav i norsk folketradisjon* (1955), 60–95.
>
> Collected by Aamund Salveson in Rogaland (Norway). Printed in Salveson, *Folkeminne* (1924), 49.

59.3 The Troll Hag Spinning on Her Wheel

There is a valley in the outlying pastures belonging to Brommeland in Sand. It is called Gyvrodalen (Troll Hag Dale). There is a cleft in that valley, and on one side of its stands a huge rock that looks like a woman spinning on a wheel. People call the rock Gyvro (Troll Hag).

The legend tells that Saint Olav sailed right through the valley one day. The troll hag was sitting there spinning. She got angry at Olav and said:

"Why do you sail here and do me harm?"

To which Olav answered:

"Stay right there and turn to stone!"

And that is what happened. You can still see the troll sitting there to this very day.

> The ongoing confrontation with primordial trolls is a major theme in the legends about Saint Olav. Olav changes the ogress into a stone with the magic power of his word.
>
> The same story is also related in a folk ballad which, however, has been collected only in Denmark and Sweden (DgF 2, no. 50). Bø has suggested that the ballad is derived from an earlier variant of this legend.
>
> See Olav Bø, *Heilag-Olav i norsk folketradisjon* (1955), 50–59, 64–74.
>
> Collected by Aamund Salveson in Rogaland (Norway). Printed in Salveson, *Folkeminne* (1924), 50.

59.4 Saint Olav at Reinsfell

People say that once when Saint Olav had passed by the Seven Sisters, which is one of the few mountains that is usually visible, he got to Angersnes by Reinsfell. This was a real troll mountain because the notorious Reins troll lived there. He was so ill natured that he would suck up the southwesterly winds blowing north to Altensfjord and spit them out again, creating the storms that raged offshore at Ranafjord. It was tough for seagoing folk to sail their heavy square riggers past that troll. Many times they would see the *draug* grinning at them, leeward in his half-boat, and they would know what was in store for them.

But one evening near Midsummer's Night, Saint Olav landed his ship at Angersnes. One of his warriors went ashore and tied the ship's rope around a big rock on the beach; it was the same rock on which people made sacrifices to appease the Reins troll. Then the king went on land with his following, and there has never been a more beautiful sight. The village folk paid homage to the king, and he talked kindly to them. But when he heard about the evil troll, he gathered his men and led them off to the mountain. When they had gotten about halfway up, the king placed a silver arrow on his bow and shot into the mountain. At that very moment a huge rock slide fell with a great roar, and after the dust had settled, they saw an enormous black hole in the rock face. Everybody was sure the troll had met his death.

The great hole in the mountain is called Saint Olav's Shot to this very day, and you can still see the markings left by the ship's rope around the sacrificial rock. People call it Saint Olav's Rock.

> According to folk tradition in northern Norway, the *draug* sails in a half-boat. The *draug* is an omen of shipwreck and death.
> Collected by Hilmar Øren Båtstø, Holmvikja, Helgeland (Norway). Printed in Reidar Th. Christiansen, *Norske sagn* (1938), 34.

59.5 Saint Olav and the Master Builder

During the time Saint Olav was Christianizing Norway, he went to Karmøy to preach God's word. Before he left the island, he wanted to build a church at a place called Haldnes. It was to be a stone church with a tower. But the construction did not move as fast as the king had hoped. A troll who lived in a hill by Blood Field went to the king and offered to erect the church, tower and all, in a week's time. In payment he demanded the sun and the moon, or the king himself.

The king accepted the offer, thinking that no one could build that fast.

But it went up so quickly, no one could believe it. By Friday the work had progressed far enough that the church would be ready for Sunday services! There was no doubt about it. Saint Olav did not know what to do. He could not get the sun and the moon, and he surely did not want to sell himself to a troll. Olav did know that if he could find out the troll's name, he would be saved; if a troll hears its name from the lips of a Christian man, it bursts. But how could he find out the troll's name? He was in greater trouble than he had ever been before.

On Friday evening Saint Olav was walking along, brooding about this. He got to the hill by Blood Field. Tired and heavy of heart, he sat down on one of the mounds there. Then he heard something like a song. It was a troll woman rocking her child to sleep inside the mound. The king put his ear to the ground, and then he clearly heard these words:

Hush, my little chubby cheek,
Tomorrow comes your father, Sigg,
With the sun and the moon for my baby.

The king was very happy. He went home right away.

On Saturday the church was finished, tower and all. The *jutul* was just putting the last stone in place on the roof. The king stood there and watched, but all at once he shouted:

Watch out, Sigg, I say,
I hardly think that last stone will stay!

Instantly the troll fell down, hitting the ground so hard that his whole head sank into it. He turned to stone, and there by the wall of the church, he remains to this very day.

> As missionary king, Saint Olav no doubt had a good number of churches erected throughout Norway. But in folk tradition, many more churches are ascribed to him than he actually built.
> (Cf. no. 55.11, for commentary on the troll as master builder.)
> See Olav Bø, *Heilag-Olav i norsk folketradisjon* (1955), 30–59.
> Legend type: ML 7065.

Collected by Torkell Mauland on Karmøy, Rogaland (Norway). Printed in Mauland, *Folkeminne fraa Rogaland* 2 (1931), 39–40.

60. The Black Death

Black Death is the name the folk gave to the bubonic pestilence that ravaged Asia and Europe during the fourteenth century. The epidemic killed about one-third of the population in Sweden, two-thirds in Norway. Throughout the centuries other large-scale epidemics in Scandinavia have for the most part been assimilated into folk traditions about the Black Death.

The motifs most frequently found in legends about the pest are: omens; the spread of the disease through the arrival of a ship or through a personification of the plague in the shape of a woman, two children, or an animal; descriptions of the symptoms of the disease and of futile attempts to stop it; and folk traditions about survivors and the gradual repopulation of deserted areas.

See Carl-Herman Tillhagen, "Sägner och folktro kring pesten," *Fataburen* (1967), 215–30; Lauri Honko, *Krankheitsprojektile* (1959); I. Reichborn-Kjennerud, *Vår gamle trolldomsmedisin* 3 (1940), 74–131; Brynjulf Alver, "Historiske segner og historisk sanning," *Norveg* 9 (1962), 89–116.

60.1 The Pest Aboard a Ship

A ship beached at Vesterhavet. It had sailed in so quietly, people knew there was something amiss. Nevertheless the folks from Vesterhavet ran to plunder the ship. They found a great cargo, but all the people on board were dead. Everyone grabbed what they could, making off with all that wealth; they should have known something was wrong since the whole crew was dead. And indeed it did not take long before they all fell sick, and then the disease spread through the entire country.

You see, that is how the pest got here.

This legend reflects the most commonly held view of how the Black Death was brought to the shores of northern Europe.

Collected by E. T. Kristensen from Petrine Kristiansen in Møllerup, Jylland (Denmark). Printed in Kristensen, *Danske sagn* 4 (1896), 557.

60.2 The Pest and the Ferryman

The pest came to Fyr Lake by Svarteland and called for the ferryman. He came and took her across. She was wearing a red skirt.

The man asked for his life in exchange for ferrying her over.

"If you are not in my book, I'll let you go," she said.

She looked, but his name was there.

"No, I can't spare your life, but you shall have an easy death."

She pointed her staff at him, and he died on the spot. Then she made a clear sweep, and everybody there died.

> The Black Death was often personified as a woman carrying a broom and a rake. In places where she raked, only part of the population died, but where she swept, everyone fell victim to the disease.
>
> The legend exemplifies the belief that the pest could not traverse water without human aid.
>
> Legend type: ML 7085.
>
> Collected by Hans Ross in Fyresdal, Telemark (Norway). Ms. in NFS Ross 17, 105.

60.3 The King's Messenger Spread Cholera

A Swedish gentleman by the name of Viborg traveled around spreading cholera everywhere—in wells, and along the roads where people fared. You see, the Crown thought there were too many poor folk and sent out these messengers to kill them.

Viborg stayed at our house. We were terribly afraid of him, but he did not leave the cholera with us because we had given him lodging. He was in the service of the Crown.

> This chronicate is an example of more recent folk traditions about epidemics. (Cf. no 57.3, which exemplifies the notion that the king decreed death as a solution to overpopulation and poverty.)
>
> The motif that bearers of disease spare those who give them lodging is also prevalent in legends about the Black Death.
>
> Collected by V. E. V. Wessman in 1904–5 from Old Lundström in Pärnå, Nyland (Finland). Printed in Wessman, *Sägner* 2.2 (1924), 277.

60.4 Binding the Great Death

This happened in Värmland at the time when the Great Death was around. In the parish of Nyed there was a minister named Torellius. People said that he had dealings with the devil.

One day Torellius walked over Brattfors Moor, which lies between the parishes of Nyed and Brattfors. First he met a boy carrying a rake on his shoulder.

"Where are you going?" the minister asked.

"I'm on my way to Nyed to rake," the boy answered.

Then he met a girl carrying a broom.

"Where are you going?" the minister asked.

"To Nyed to sweep," she answered.

You see, it was the pest; it had been to Brattfors, and all the people there had died.

"You are going to stay right here on the moor and rake and sweep all you want," said Torelius, and he tied them both to a juniper bush. After that there was no more pest in the country.

Now I have seen a dry juniper bush out on the moor, but I did not think there was anything out of the ordinary about it. The old folks, however, believed that the pest was bound by that bush, and they said that no heather would grow near it. Yet it seemed to me that it grew about as well there as it did anyplace.

> It was believed that the pest could be bound by magic. The dialogue between the minister and the pest personified by the boy and the girl is patterned after formulas commonly used in healing. (Cf. no. 28.12; nos. 54.10, 54.12, and 54.14–54.15 further exemplify the magic skills often ascribed to ministers.)
>
> See John Lindow, "Personification and Narrative Structure in Scandinavian Plague Legends," *Arv* 29–30 (1973–74), 83–92.
>
> Legend type: ML 7080.
>
> Collected by Levi Johansson in 1908 from Johan Otterström in Borgsjö parish, Medelpad (Sweden). Ms. in NM HA, 1: *Sjukdomar V*.

60.5 Here You Shall Stand!

In the parishes around here, the folks died almost to a man. Then they got Old Copper Leg to bind the pest when it reached Iron Woods. The minister drove after the green man and the little old woman. When he caught up with them on Skönnerud Moor, he commanded them to stand still. He took out his Black Book and recited his spells until they submitted. Then he bound them to a big pine tree by the country road, saying:

Here you shall stand
for as many a year
as there are hairs
on the skin of this mare.

People say that a light shines every night from the trunk of that pine tree.

> Legend type: ML 7080.
> Collected in Järnskog parish, Värmland (Sweden). Printed in Edvard Olsson, *Värmländska folkminnen*. Edited by David Arill (1932), 127.

60.6 Sacrifice to Stop the Black Death

The legend says that the people in Ålsgjeld were spared the Black Death. But that is probably not true. Surely the epidemic raged there as much as it did in other places in Hallingdal.

When the terrible disease was laying the valley waste, the folks from Ålsgjeld got together, killed a blameless young man, and placed his body across the road by the boundary between Gol and Ål. They believed the pest could not cross over the dead body of this guiltless young man.

But his innocent blood was revenged. As a punishment, there have been many knifings and murders in Ålsgjeld every since.

Yes, that is how the legend goes further up in the valley.

> This legend is quite rare in Norway but widespread in southern Sweden and Denmark.
> Scholars have maintained that in extreme cases, individuals were actually buried alive to stop the plague. It appears that in earlier folk tradition, people believed the victim carried the pest demon in his body. Live burial, then, confined the pest in the grave. In the surviving variants of the legend, however, none of which are more than a century old, the victim is killed as a form of sacrifice.

See Hans-Egil Hauge, *Levande begravd eller bränd i nordisk folkemedisin* (1965), 223–25; Carl-Herman Tillhagen, "Sägner och folktro kring pesten," *Fataburen* (1967).

Collected in Hallingdal (Norway). Printed in A. Mehlum, *Hallingdal og hallingen* (1943), 20.

60.7 They Burned the Pest

There is a legend about an epidemic that devastated Helgeland during the early 1600s. But it did not reach Vefsn. This is why:

When the *Vefsn* was sailing home from Bergen, probably in 1618, people heard strange noises on board. They thought it came from the cargo hold.

One of the crew, a Finn, thought it might have something to do with the hemp they were carrying. He said he would take a look, but nothing was done until they sailed into outer Vefsn in South Fjord. Then such a racket came from the hold that everyone was terrified.

They decided to bring the hemp up on deck. The Finn pointed to a bundle and said that is where the evil sat. He said they should set fire to it and throw it into the sea. And that is what they did.

This happened just outside Korsnes. When the hemp caught on fire, the crew saw something that looked like two little boys jumping and kicking in the fire. They were screaming and making terrible noises.

It was the pest, which had taken human shape, but now it was being destroyed. That is why the pest did not get to Vefsn.

> The epidemic referred to here is said to have occurred some 300 years after the Black Death, but the description is the same. The legend combines the motifs of the pest arriving by ship and being personified by two children with the notion that it could be stopped by fire. Finns were traditionally looked upon as possessing magic skills.
>
> Collected by Reidar Svare in Vefsn, Nordland (Norway). Printed in R. Svare, *Far etter fedrane. Folkeminne innsamla i Vefsn* (1950), 67.

60.8 God Bless You!

In central Sjæland old folks say that when people fell victim to the Black Death, they would sneeze just before they died. As soon as the

afflicted began sneezing, their family and friends knew that the end
was near, and they would say:
"God bless you!"
Since then people have always said "God bless you!" whenever
someone sneezes.

> Sneezing has long been regarded as an omen of death. It became
> secondarily associated with the Black Death.
>
> See I. Reichborn-Kjennerud, *Vår gamle trolldomsmedisin* 3 (1940),
> 92; Carl Wilhelm von Sydow, "Prosit!—Gud hjälp! Några folkli-
> ga föreställningar om nysning," *Skånska folkminnen. Årsbok* (1929),
> 12–18.
>
> Collected by E. T. Kristensen from Henrik Pedersen, Maribo,
> Jylland (Denmark). Printed in Kristensen, *Danske sagn* 4 (1896),
> 558.

60.9 Førnes Brown

There is a dance tune called "Førnes Brown." It dates back to the
time of the Black Death.
At Møsstrånna there were so few people left, there was no one to
walk with the horse carrying the dead. One person stood by the
church—it was the Rauland Church—and dug graves all the time.
Another put the dead on the sled and tied snowshoes to the horse's
feet, and then it went off by itself. As soon as it returned to the
church, the horse was sent back to collect another body.
But one time one of the snowshoes came off, right on the mountain, and then things went badly for the horse. It limped on one leg.
You can clearly hear in the tune how it limps along.
Yes, "Førnes Brown" will never be forgotten.

> See Rikard Berge, "Førnesbrunen, segni og slaatten," *Norsk
> folkekultur* 21 (1935), 3–18.
>
> Collected by Moltke Moe from Liv Bratterud in Bøherad,
> Telemark (Norway). Printed in Moe, *Folkeminne frå Bøherad*
> (1924), 74.

60.10 Now It Will Be Fun to Live

People talk about the last man alive in Bø—how he looked at
everything the others had left behind.
"Now it will be fun to live in Bø," he said.
But at that very moment he fell down, dead.

Collected by K. Nauthella in Austevoll, Hordaland (Norway). Ms. in NFS Nauthella (1), 92.

60.11 The Black Death on Kirjala

At the time of the so-called Sudden Death, there was someone in my father's family who lived in Kårlax on the island of Kirjala. He was the smith there. Many people died, and he had to make the nails for all the coffins. Finally he got so worn out from working that he carried his anvil into the woods. He wanted to be left in peace. He did not want to make nails anymore.

In Skrobbå so few people were left that the whole place was deserted.

It happened that people collapsed on the road and died. A number of them are supposed to have died on the road outside Södergård.

> This text combines three dites depicting the epidemic on Kirjala Island.
>
> Collected by V. E. V. Wessman in 1915 from the director Frederiksson in Pargas, Åboland (Finland). Printed in Wessman, *Sägner* 2.2 (1924), 276.

60.12 Hukebu Haukeli

Hukebu Haukeli was the only person left alive in Haukeli after the Black Death. She needed 24 ells of homespun cloth to make her skirt. Her husband had used 12 ells to make his pants.

And it was Hukebu Haukeli,
She looked out over the fell,
It's sad to be alive in the world,
Gone is he I loved so well.

> The verse in this story takes the form of the *gammelstev* (old verse), a traditional form of folk verse containing four lines that rhyme XAYA.
>
> Collected by O. T. Vinje in Vinje, Telemark (Norway). Ms. in NFS Vinje (4), 84.

60.13 The Survivors

Nearly all the people died from the Great Death. There was a man from Ås who went to Padis — originally it was called Paradis — and found a woman there. They became man and wife.

Then there was a man from Mark — he could not find a living soul in all Frillesås. But when he got to Stocken, he saw the footprint of a human being, and he fell to the ground and kissed it.

> This legend is known throughout northern Europe.
> See Brynjulf Alver, "Historiske segner og historisk sanning," *Norveg* 9 (1962), 106–9.
> Legend type: ML 7090.
> Collected by Carl-Martin Bergstrand in Veddige, Halland (Sweden). Printed in Bergstrand, *Hallands sägner* (1949), 182.

60.14 She Rang the Church Bell

Somewhere in the area of Esbo, everybody died except a monk and the girl who kept house for him. When her parents had died, the monk had taken her in. But finally the monk died as well, so the girl climbed up in the church tower to ring the bell for the soul of the dead.

A boy heard the sound of the bell. He had thought he was the only one left alive. He found the girl, and they married without any church rites. The people of Esbo are their descendants.

> Legend type: ML 7090.
> Collected by V. E. V. Wessman in 1906 from a farmer named Weckström in Esbo, Nyland (Finland). Printed in Wessman, *Sägner* 2.2 (1924), 275.

60.15 The Deserted Church in Landet

There was a church in Landet, which nobody found until some three hundred years after the Black Death. Skeletons were lying about in the pews, and in front of them were hymnals, open to the song "In This Hour of Our Greatest Need." The doors were dangling from the hinges, and there was a bear slinking in and out of the church.

People said that an omen appeared then — it was an angel. They heard a voice saying that death such as that would happen again.

This legend is told about various churches throughout Norway. The hymn referred to in the text actually dates from the Reformation, that is, some two hundred years after the Black Death.
Legend type: ML 7095.
Collected by Olav Rekdal in Romsdal (Norway). Printed in Rekdal, *Eventyr og segner. Folkeminne frå Romsdal* (1933), 134.

61. War Times

The wars that have had the greatest impact on legend tradition in Scandinavia are the Seven Years' War (1563–70) and the Great Nordic War (1700–1721), both involving Denmark-Norway, and Sweden, the Napoleonic Wars (1807–14), and Finland's war with Russia (1808–9). Especially in the older folk tradition, the different wars tend to blend into one another. The legends are rarely concerned with the political implications of the various conflicts. Rather they focus on the impact of the war experience on individuals—both the soldiers and the civilian population. The story is almost always told from the perspective of one person and his or her local community. At the same time, many of the motifs found in these legends are actually migratory.

See Olav Bø, "Tradisjon om ufredstider," *Norveg* 5 (1955), 197–212.

61:1 The Comet

There's a kind of star called a shooting star. It never prophesies anything good. My mother saw a shooting star just before the war between Denmark and Germany in 1864. I was only a little child then, and she carried me outside so that I could see it.

Comets or shooting stars are traditionally interpreted as omens of war and disaster.
In 1864 Denmark lost Slesvig-Holstein to Prussia.
Collected by Halldor O. Opedal in Eidfjord, Hordaland (Norway). Printed in Opedal, *Makter og menneske. Folkeminne ifrå Hardanger* 2 (1934), 17.

61.2 *The Sound of Drums*

This happened in 1905. A man from Grov was staying overnight in a shack at Sletning, where he had been fishing. He had not yet heard that Norway had broken its ties with Sweden.

That night, while he was lying there in that little shack, he had dozed off a bit and suddenly he heard riders approaching—a whole army of them. He could even hear the sound of their drums. But the next day, when he returned to his village, people told him that the troops had been mobilized.

> According to folk tradition, preternatural beings at times aided people in armed conflicts with foreign enemies. Their drums (*dystetromma*) could be heard in the distance, presaging the coming war.
>
> Norway declared itself independent of Sweden in 1905. Both countries mobilized, but there were no armed hostilities.
>
> Collected by Knut Hermundstad from Ola Olsson Sveji in Vang, Valdres (Norway). Printed in Hermundstad, *Kvorvne tider. Gamal Valdreskultur* 7 (1961), 55.

61.3 *The Swedes in Mannfjord*

Once on the night before Christmas, a Swedish troop was going to plunder Tysfjord. In the mountains they met a Finn, who was hunting for some meat for Christmas dinner. They forced him to be their guide because they were not familiar enough with the terrain to find their way down to the village. They were all on skis. The Finn understood only too well what they were up to. He led the troop straight along a mountain ridge between Mannfjord and Grunnfjord. Furthest out on the promontory is a peak, which since then has been called Swedish Peak. The peak fronts on a steep precipice, several hundred meters high, that plunges straight down to rock-strewn slopes or into the sea.

It was dark that Christmas Eve when the Finn neared the edge of the mountain. He fired a torch and gathered the Swedes around:

"Just follow my torch," said the Finn. "The trail goes straight down to the valley. I'll ski ahead."

Then the Finn took off with the torch in his hand. All the Swedes followed. The Finn knew the area very well. Just when he reached the precipice, he tossed the torch ahead and then threw himself to the side with all his might. But the Swedes all continued forward, fell off he precipice, and were crushed.

The Finn took the trail back through the mountains and got to the base of Mannfjord on Christmas morning. The folks were sitting at their Christmas dinner, when the Finn came in and greeted them. He stood by the door.

"A blessed Christmas to you!" said the folks.

But the Finn raised his rifle and fired a shot over their heads. They jumped up.

"What's the matter?" they asked.

"Last night you were much closer to death than this," said the Finn.

Then he told them everything that had happened. Even today you can find bones below Swedish Peak.

> This migratory legend is told in Norway about conflicts with the Swedes, Russians, or Finns, and in Denmark about the wars with Sweden during the seventeenth century.
>
> See Svale Solheim, "Historical Legend—Historical Function," *Acta Ethnographica Academiae Scientiarum Hungaricae* 19 (1970), 341–46. (In Norwegian: "Historisk segn—historisk funksjon," *Norveg* 16 (1973), 141–47.)
>
> Legend type: ML 8000.
>
> Collected by Johan Hveding in Tysfjord, Nordland (Norway). Printed in Hveding, *Folketru og folkeliv på Hålogaland* (1935), 82–83.

61.4 The Guide Who Led the Enemy into Death

Once when there was war in this country, a troop of enemy cavalry came upon a man who was from Lemvig, and they forced him, with a sword held to his head, to show them the way to the town. He jumped on the back of a horse and rode ahead of them into the dark night. With flying speed, they followed him to a cliff and went right over the edge into the fjord. They all drowned, including the man. He had wanted to save his town.

> Legend type: ML 8000.
>
> Collected by E. T. Kristensen from Karen Marie Rasmussen in Linde, Nørhald, Jylland (Denmark). Printed in Kristensen, *Danske sagn*, N.R. 5 (1932), 55.

61.5 The Forest Moves

At Hälsingborg the Swedes took the Danes by surprise. They cut the tops of spruce and fir trees, and when night fell, they carried them in front of themselves so they looked like a forest.

"The forest is moving," said the Danes and thought it strange. But suddenly the Swedes were upon them, and the Danes had to flee in a hurry!

This was Magnus Stenbock's victory in 1710.

> This migratory legend is based on an ancient stratagem. Shakespeare used the motif in *Macbeth* Act V, scene 5.
>
> Magnus Stenbock's victory occurred during the Great Nordic War, when he foiled a Danish attempt to wrest Skåne from Sweden.
>
> Collected by Helmer Olsson in Vinberg, Halland (Sweden). Printed in Carl-Martin Bergstrand, *Hallands sägner* (1949), 185.

61.6 The Witch Who Blunted the Swedish Guns

In the war between the Swedes and the Finns, an old Finnish woman sat down between the two armies, rolling a ball of yarn. The bullets of the Finns found their mark, but the Swedish guns would not carry any farther than the place where the woman sat. Then a Swedish colonel walked up to her, circled her three times, and spat with each turn. The he ordered the Swedes to aim at the woman, and she was killed.

> Threefold circumambulation and spitting are traditional magical rites.
>
> Collected by Helmer Olsson in Vinberg, Halland (Sweden). Printed in Carl-Martin Bergstrand, *Hallandsägner* (1949), 186.

61.7 Feathers Turned into an Army

There was a man from the Lilja family. He knew more than other people about a lot of things. Once he was riding on Angere Hill, when he saw the Danes encamped below at Hisingen. He cut up a down comforter and shook it so that the feathers went flying, saying:

Horse and riders,
where before were feathers!

And the feathers turned into a great army, and when the Danes caught sight of it, they turned tail.

Once the Danes threatened Lerum. Then Ole from Alekärr shook out a down pillow and said:

Horse and riders,
where before were feathers!

And the Swedish cavalry suddenly got so big that the Danes were defeated.

> The ability to create hallucinations is well known in Scandinavian traditions about witchcraft.
> Collected by Helmer Olsson in Vättle, Västergötland (Sweden). Printed in Olsson, *Folkliv och folkdikt i Vättle härad under 1800–talet* (1945), 193.

61.8 Children Dressed Up as Sheep

Once the Danes were laying siege on Halmstad. They tried to drive the Swedes out by starving them. But the Swedes dressed some children in sheepskins and had them walk back and forth on the ramparts. Then the Danes decided there was no use in trying to starve out the town, since there were so many sheep there.

> This and similar ruses designed to fool the enemy into believing that a beleaguered city is stocked with food are well known in European legends and in classical literature.
> See Adolf Stender-Petersen, "Quamadmodum efficiatur, ut abundare uideantur, quae deerunt," *Festskrift til L. L. Hammerich* (1952), 230–41.
> Collected by Helmer Olsson in Vapnö, Halland (Sweden). Printed in Carl-Martin Bergstrand, *Hallands sägner* (1949), 183.

61.9 Charles XII, King of the Swedes

No bullet could hit Charles XII. He would free his soldiers for twenty-four hours at a time, and no bullet could hit them during that time period either.

In Idefjorden he would take his boots off whenever they were full of bullets, saying that it was hard to walk with all those "blueberries" in his boots.

He went to a ball in Halden. There he noticed that he had lost a button. He said to himself, then, that it would soon be over. And it was, too.

> Charles XII (1682–1718) was king of Sweden from 1697 until the end of his short life. Mostly because of his youth, Russia, Poland-Saxony, and Denmark in turn challenged Sweden's supremacy over the Baltic. In the Great Nordic War, Charles XII emerged victoriously time and again, but his eventual defeat at Poltava cost Sweden its rank as a great power. In popular folk tradition, the king is nevertheless remembered as a great hero. It was prophesied that he could be killed only by a bullet made from his own button.
>
> See Albert Sandklef et al., *Carl XII:s död* (1940), and, *Kulknappen och Carl XII:s död* (1941); Barbro Klein, "The Testimony of the Button," *Journal of the Folklore Institute* (1971), 127–46.
>
> Collected by Carl-Martin Bergstrand in Hogdal, Bohuslän (Sweden). Printed in Bergstrand, *Bohuslänska sägner* (1947), 176.

61.10 A Louse on a King

Once Charles XII stopped at a house and stayed overnight there. The next morning when he was about to leave, the woman in the house discovered some big lice on the king. But she did not want to talk about lice because she thought that it was a disgrace. So she said:
"I believe there is a flea on the king."
"What?" asked the king.
"I believe the king has got a flea," the old woman said again, and then the king understood what she meant. He became irritated and answered:
"No, dear mother. A flea on a dog but a louse on a king."
Ever since then this has been a proverb in our village.

> Collected by Sven Rystrand in 1944 from Georg Myström in Bro parish, Bohuslän (Sweden). Ms. in NM, EU 25732, Sägner om svenska kongar. Printed in Bengt af Klintberg, *Svenska folksägner* (1972), 272.

61.11 Charles XII and the Finnish Soldiers

During Charles XII's war with Poland, he once found himself alone with only ten Finnish soldiers facing one hundred Poles. The Finns defended themselves as best as they could. Among them was a huge fellow who was the drummer. The Finns killed all the Poles and sat down to take a rest by a small hill. Then a Jew came walking along and started to plunder the dead Poles, but the Finns saw him and went over to keep him from stealing. The Jew got scared and asked for mercy. They gave him reprieve but stuck him into the drum—he was very little.

But then twice as many Poles showed up. The drummer gave the Poles' heads one whack, and his drum another, but he hit so hard that the drum burst. Then the little Jew was freed. When the Poles saw him, they thought it was the Devil himself jumping out of the drum, and they ran. Thus the Finns carried the day.

> Charles XII fought a successful campaign in Poland in 1704. Soldiers from Finland were among his troops.
>
> The motif of the greedy Jew is a stereotype in European folk tradition.
>
> Collected by V. E. V. Wessman in 1905 from Mr. Sivander in Strömfors, Nyland (Finland). Printed in Wessman, Sägner 2.2 (1924), 11.

61.12 Tordenskjold

He was such a daredevil, that Tordenskjold. He cut right into the Swedish fleet and began firing. So the Swedes took him captive and brought him to the admiral's ship. Tordenskjold asked whether he might offer them a drink—he had used 24 barrels of malt to brew one barrel of beer. He got them so drunk, they all collapsed on the floor. Then he locked them up and took off with the entire fleet—he just shouted at the men on the other ships to follow his lead.

When the Swedes regained consciousness, they banged on the door and asked where they were.

"We are almost at Helsingør," answered Tordenskjold, but they were headed straight for Copenhagen.

He was such a big shot, the King himself had to lead him ashore .

> Baron Peder Wessel Tordenskjold (1691–1720) was a Norwegian naval hero. His most famous exploit was the capture of a superior Swedish naval force at Dynekilen (1716), described in legendary form here. Tordenskjold was eventually killed in a duel.
>
> Collected by Johannes Skar in Setesdal, Aust-Agder (Norway). Printed in Skar *Gamalt or Sætesdal* 1 (1961), 336.

61.13 The Women Who Carried Their Husbands out of Captivity

Most of the time, the farms in Ljørdal were vacant during the summer because the women were in the mountain pastures, and the men were hunting in the woods. They hid their silver in the river, while they were away.

But one summer day, when the men happened to be home, the Swedes invaded. The men put up such resistance that the Swedes got mad, took them prisoner, and carried them off, along with everything they could lay their hands on. The women found out what had happened and pursued them into Sweden, all the way to Kopparberg, people say. There they found the thieves and begged and begged them. The outcome was that, since they had come such a long way and gone through so much trouble, they were allowed to return to Ljørdal with as much as they could carry. Then each woman hoisted her husband onto her back and headed home.

> This migratory legend, also known as "The Women at Weinsberg," allegedly originated from the siege of a castle in Swabia, Germany, in 1140. In the most widespread version, the women negotiated the surrender of the castle on the condition that they were permitted to leave with their dearest possessions. To the surprise of the conquerors, they took their husbands, carrying them on their backs.
>
> The farms at Ljørdal were plundered by the Swedes during the so-called Gyldenløve Wars (1675–79) between Denmark-Norway and Sweden, and the Ljørdal farmers were brought to Sweden.
>
> See Leander Petzoldt, *Historische Sagen* 2 (1977), 323–24.
>
> Collected by Sigurd Nergaard. Printed in Nergaard, *Ufredstider*. *Folkeminne fraa Østerdalen* 2 (1922), 8.

61.14 They Killed the Child in the Cradle

Once when the Swedes were ravaging Fyn, they burst into a house. The woman fled, but she did not have a chance to grab her baby. It was lying there, smiling happily at the soldiers breaking in through the door. One of them got so mad that he rushed to the cradle and thrust his sword through the child.

> This is a rather common war legend told in various places.
>
> Collected by E. T. Kristensen from J. P. Olesen in Herrested, Fyn (Denmark). Printed in Kristensen, *Danske sagn*, N.R. 4 (1932), 37.

61.15 The Kalmycks

People say that during the Great War, the Russians counted some Kalmycks among their troops. It has been said that they cut women's breasts off and drank blood from them. They were also said to have a keen sense of smell, like dogs, and to make a strange whistling sound with their teeth. This sound was so terrible that for a long time afterward parents would not allow their children to whistle.

> The Kalmycks, originally a Mongol tribe, are described as demonic beings—half dog and half human, in European folk tradition. For example, Adam of Bremen wrote in 1075 in his *Gesta Hammaburgensis Ecclesiae Pontificum*: "There are places along the shore of the Baltic where children can be seen playing, the boys have the heads of dogs, but the girls are quite attractive creatures. One finds dog-headed people in Russia, too, and when they speak, they bark out their words."
>
> See Leopold Kretzenbacher, *Kynokephale Dämonen südosteuropäischer Volksdichtung* (1968); K. Völker, ed., *Von Werwölfen und anderen Tiermenschen* (1972); Gun Herranen, "Historical Legends Expressing Nationalism in a Minority Culture," *Folklore on Two Continents* (1980), 334–39.
>
> Collected by V. E. V. Wessman in 1917 from Samuel Öling in Maxmo, Österbotten (Finland). Printed in Wessman, *Sägner* 2.2 (1924), 9.

61.16 Fooling the Enemy

In 1807 when the English controlled the Little Belt, the people of Als feared that they might come ashore and start plundering. Then some of them used a ruse they remembered from previous wars. They tore up their bedding and let the feathers fly about. They believed that if the enemy came, they would think that the house had been ransacked already, and would pass by.

> In 1807 the English captured the entire Dano-Norwegian fleet in Copenhagen and put a blockade around Denmark and Norway. Little Belt is the strait between Fyn and Jylland.
>
> Collected in 1904 by Peter J. Petersen in Tandslet, Sønderborg, Jylland (Denmark). Printed in E. T. Kristensen, *Danske sagn*, N.R. 4 (1932), 35.

61.17 The Minister at Finnby Church

On the fields a battle took place between the Russians and the Swedes. That is why everything grows so well there to this very day.

The Russians wanted to set fire to the church, but they said they would wait until the minister had finished preaching. Hoping to save the church, the minister continued his sermon, while they sent a messenger to the Russian commander who was staying at Dalsbruk. And the messenger returned with the order to spare the church. But the minister is said to have lost his mind from preaching for so long.

> Collected by V. E. V. Wessman in 1915 from Johan Trygg, Kimito, Åboland (Finland). Printed in Wessman, *Sägner* 2.2 (1924), 21.

61.18 The Man Who Killed the Corporal

The man who owned this farm during the Swedish Wars was quite well-to-do, and the Swedes knew it. One day a Swedish corporal said to him:

"Where did you hide your money?"

They had already ransacked the house and come up empty.

"Out with it, or it will cost you your life!"

"All right," said the man, "I will tell you. I have a sheep cote down in the southern pasture. That's where I have buried my money and my silver too."

"Well, let's go out there."

There was a big plot of moorland south of the farm. That is where they went. When they got to the sheep cote, the door was low and small, and the Swede ordered the man to enter. But the man said:

"No, it's customary that the stranger enters first."

When the Swede bent down to go in, the man pulled out a big cudgel and hit him across the back of his neck so that he collapsed, and then the man finished him off and buried him right there. But the Swedes missed their countryman, of course, and one day a troop of soldiers came to the farm, took the man prisoner, and demanded to know what he had done with the corporal. They tied him up in the alley between the dikes east of here and tortured him terribly. Finally he died. The place is still called Death Alley. The dikes have been razed now, but the name has stuck.

Collected by E. T. Kristensen from Knud Martin Pedersen,
Randbøl parish, Tørrild, Jylland (Denmark). Printed in Kristensen,
Danske sagn, N.R. 4 (1932), 53.

61.19 They Took His Silverware

A woman who is more than eighty years old has said that as far as
anyone can remember, this farm has always been owned by the same
family. One of the former owners, who lived here during the Thirty
Years' War, fled to Haderslev to escape the fighting. He buried his
silver in the garden and put a servant girl in charge of the farm.

But the girl told the enemy where the silver was hidden, and when
the owner came back, he complained bitterly about it. He would have
preferred them to burn down the farm rather than steal his old silverware.

> The Thirty Years' War (1618–48) pitted the Protestant nations of
> northern Europe, including Sweden and Denmark-Norway,
> against the Catholic South.
>   Collected by E. T. Kristensen from Marie Skau, Sommersted
> parish, Haderslev Øster, Jylland (Denmark). Printed in Kristensen,
> *Danske sagn*, N.R. 4 (1932), 58.

61.20 The Swedes in Ure

When the Swedes invaded Ure, the people fled to Kjær Banks,
northwest of the town, and they took their silverware and other be-
longings with them. At night they slipped home to tend to their
farms.

But there was a girl who made friends with the Swedes. She stayed
in town and took care of everything that had been left behind. Well,
to make a long story short, she got to be on such good terms with
the Swedes, she ended up with a child. The Swedes began plowing
and making themselves at home. When they finally left, the Spanish
arrived, and they were much worse. They were crazy about eating
cats, and they ate almost all the cats in town.

> Collected by E. T. Kristensen from Erik Pedersen in Brande par-
> ish, Nørvang, Jylland (Denmark). Printed in Kristensen, *Danske
> sagn*, N.R. 4 (1932), 50.

61.21 He Did Not Stay the Night

After the battle of Poltava, the remainder of the Swedish army was carried off and put into captivity in Siberia. But many of them escaped, and after much suffering, they finally got home. No fewer than five soldiers from the parish of By were lucky enough to return. They were Drake and Clemetz from Fornby, one man from Dubben in Morshyttan, one from Trulsos in Västanhede, and one from Månsos in Västmossa. His wife had married again, after not hearing from her husband for many years.

When he returned late one evening, she did not recognize him. After looking around for a while in the house, he turned to a place by the door and said:

"There used to be a nail here that I hung my hat on."

Then the wife realized who he was. But when the man found out that his wife had remarried, he left. He did not even stay the night.

> Charles XII of Sweden suffered his first and decisive defeat at the hands of the Russians in 1709 at Poltava. Much of the army was taken prisoner.
>
> Collected by O. Östlund in 1932 from J. Joh. Johansson in By, Dalarna (Sweden). Printed in Östlund, *Från By Sockengille* 6 (1932), 18.

61.22 Home from the War

Kjetill Frøysnes was a soldier during the Eighteen Years' War. His son was no more than a small child when he left; when he finally came home, he was a grown man.

At Christmastime Kjetill returned. His wife was away, visiting at Nordgarden—she was originally from Nordgarden in Åraksbø. There was nobody home but a servant girl. She was scared because she thought he was a vagabond.

"Find me some food," he said angrily.

She set out some food.

"Tap some beer into a bowl," he said.

She tapped some beer.

"Is there a horse?" he asked.

Yes, there was a horse.

"Find me a bridle," he said.

And she found a bridle for him. Then he rode over to Nordgarden.

"Where are you from?" they asked.

"I'm from eastern Norway," said Kjetill, "I've been to the wars."

"Did you see Kjetill Frøysnes?" asked his wife.

"I've been with him the whole time," answered Kjetill.

When she heard this, she invited him to come home with her to Frøysnes. Well, there was a young man courting Kjetill's wife — everybody had been so sure her husband was dead, and he visited Frøysnes just then, too. When the beer went to his head, he sat in the high seat.

But Kjetill grabbed him by the seat of his pants and threw him across the floor.

"Kjetill Frøysnes will be master over the high seat himself," he said.

> The Eighteen Years' War mentioned here refers to the so-called Great Nordic War, which actually lasted from 1700–1721, but Norwegian soldiers were not involved in the early phase of the conflict.
>
> Legend type: ML 8005.
>
> Collected by Johannes Skar in Setesdal, Aust-Agder (Norway). Printed in Skar, *Gamalt or Sætesdal* 1 (1965), 337.

61.23 The Boy from Luoma

Once during the time of the Hussars, two boys were playing by the door outside a shed at the Luama homestead in the village of Storkyra Luakko. Suddenly the Russians were upon them. The older boy escaped, but they took the younger one with them — all the way to the river Don. There he became an errand boy and then went into the service of a general and cooked his meals. After some 13 years, he managed to escape and went home. At first his brother did not recognize him. But when he told him who he was, his brother arranged for a great feast to welcome him.

> The "time of the Hussars" refers to the Finno-Russian War (1808–9).
>
> Collected by J. E. Wefvar in the 1870s in Vörå, Österbotten (Sweden). Printed in Wessman, *Sägner* 2.2 (1924), 32.

61.24 The Soldier and the Jusska

Tollei Tolleison Heiæ from Fjotland went to war. Old Tollei followed his son to the Tollei Stone and stood there watching until he lost sight of him on the other side of the valley.

Tollei came home when the war was over. He had been betrothed to a *jusska* in Denmark, and she followed him to Norway. She was so refined that people just gaped at her in Øya. She was very unusual in the valley in those days.

Her name was Karen. She and Tollei got married. But she did not belong on a farm. She could not do anything. She could press roses into a handkerchief, but that was the *only* thing she could do.

When she was out of sorts, she wished only that she was back in Jylland.

The old folks were mean to Karen. Once when she was getting ready to make butter, they put animal droppings in the churn.

> A *jusska* (or *jysska*) was a girl from Jylland, hence, any Danish girl or woman.
>
> See Olav Bø, "Tradisjon om ufredstider," *Norveg* 5 (1955), 201.
>
> Collected by Peter Lunde in Vest-Agder (Norway). Printed in Lunde, *Kynnehuset. Vestegdske folkeminne* (1924), 174.

61.25 Darnel Soup

There was a time when there was so little food on Kråkerøy that people had to go to the woods and strip bark off the trees to mix it in their flour.

A woman at Trolldal was all out of food and did not know what to do. She had a big flock of children, and most of the day, they screamed and whimpered that they wanted something to eat. Many times she would put sand and water into a pot and stir it, while she sang:

Now you will soon get food,
Yes, now you will soon get food,
until they fell asleep.

Finally the woman found a solution, doing what many others had done before her. When the children could not sleep because their hunger was too great, she gave them darnel soup. It was made from a grass that grew wild in the fields. People also call it "dizzy weed." After tasting the soup, the children fell into a stupor and slept. That is probably how the weed got its name.

During the Napoleonic Wars, there were widespread famines in Norway, caused partly by the English blockade and partly by massive crop failures in 1807-8.

Darnel (*lolium temulentum*) is a poisonous grass. It is also called *svimling* ("dizzy weed").

See Ove Arbo Høeg, *Planter og tradisjon* (1970), 430.

Collected by Erling Johansen in Østfold (Norway). Printed in K. Weel Engebretsen and Johansen, *Sagn fra Østfold* (1947), 74.

61.26 The Hungry Soldiers

The Swedes were ravaging Norwegian villages, stealing and slaughtering cattle and carrying off the meat. They supplied themselves well, making off with many wagonloads of provisions. But this time we got it away from them and indulged ourselves; we had not tasted food for three days and were as hungry as wolves. It was almost impossible to get close enough to the food to get a bite. The soldiers teemed around the wagon like a swarm of mosquitoes, and they tore and ripped and pushed and jumped like wild animals. Finally I climbed up on somebody's shoulders and crawled forward from man to man, and they shoved and pushed me, until I landed on my back, right on top of the load. They took me and threw me off again, but I quickly grabbed a shoulder of meat. However, by the time I got out again, almost all the meat had been clawed off.

Not only the civilian population but also the soldiers were victimized by the lack of food. Statistics indicate that greater numbers of soldiers died of starvation than on the battlefield.

Collected by Kjetil A. Flatin in Seljord, Telemark (Norway). Printed in Flatin, *Gamle hermennar fraa Telemork* (1913), 74-75.

61.27 The Norwegian and the Swede

Once when the war had reached Kråkerøy, a Swede was lying behind a tree stump and a Norwegian behind a rock, shooting at each other. The Swede fired first, but he missed. Then the Norwegian shot, but he did not hit either. The Swede loaded again and fired another shot, but that did not hit either because the Norwegian got up from behind the rock and shouted to the Swede:

"Are you firing at me, you Swedish good-for-nothing?"

But the Swede stepped forward, bowed, and shouted back:

"Is it you, my good fellow? Could I buy some potatoes from you?"

Collected by Erling Johansen in Østfold (Norway). Printed in K. Weel Engebretsen and E. Johansen, *Sagn fra Østfold* (1947), 73–74.

62. Squires and Landowners

Legends about the rural aristocracy and landowners usually stress their harsh treatment of servants, tenants, and poor people in general. In the stories, a well-deserved punishment is meted out for arrogance, cruelty, and ungodliness. The legends thus function as a form of social protest and compensation.

62.1 The Rich Lady on Torget

On Torget in Helgeland, there lived a lady who was so rich that she had seven cargo ships, which sailed back and forth to Bergen. She had plenty of gold and silver in her house and was proud and haughty. Once she took a ring off her finger and threw it into the sea.

"It is just as impossible that I will ever find that ring again as it is that I will ever be poor," she said.

Shortly after that a fisherman came and sold the lady some fish for her dinner. When they cut one of the fish open, they found the ring the lady had thrown into the sea.

Many years passed. And the lady had bad luck. Every one of her seven cargo ships was shipwrecked. All her wealth vanished, and she spent her final years in great poverty.

> The earliest known variant of this widespread legend is found in Herodotus's story (fifth century B.C.) about Polykrates, king of Samos.
>
> See Johannes Künzig, "Der im Fischbauch wiedergefundene Ring in Sage, Legende, Märchen und Lied," *Volkskundliche Gaben: John Meier Festschrift* (1934), 85–103; Helge Søgaard, "Sagnet om den forsvundne og genfundne ring," *Sprog og kultur* 19 (1952), 69–79.
>
> Legend type: ML 7050.
>
> Collected by Johan Hveding from M. Salomonsen. Printed in Hveding, *Folketru og folkeliv på Hålogaland* (1935), 107.

62.2 Lady Anna of Pintorp

To punish a cotter, Lady Anna ordered him to fell the biggest oak in the woods. He went to the woods and sat down, listening. Then a little man came along and asked him why he was sitting there. He told him all about his trouble. But the little man said:

"The biggest oak is right here. Just strike three blows, and it will fall."

The cotter did as he was told. Then the little man said:

"Now sit on top of it. It will carry you home."

He sat on the oak, and it began to move. He did not see any horses, but he heard somebody driving and saying:

"Giddyap, Erik and Svante!"

Erik and Svante were Lady Anna's brothers. The tree kept moving, and when it got to the gate, it tore it right off the hinges. This frightened the Lady.

A little while later, a gentleman dressed in black came for her in a coach. Lady Anna knew who he was. She was getting ready and asked for a little extra time.

"No, right away. The horses are waiting."

Then she got dressed. The minister was to go, too.

"He's mine already," the gentleman said.

"Giddyap, Erik and Svante," said the man who was driving. The Lady shuddered. Erik and Svante had been evil men. When they reached their destination, the gentleman danced with her until she was quite hot. Then a trapdoor opened and down she went. The minister followed her.

But Lady Anna gave a ring to her chambermaid, whom she had brought along. When the maid put the ring on, her finger burned off. It took her three full years to walk all the way back to Ericsberg.

The folks there thought that someone in disguise had kidnapped the Lady and killed her. Since then the folk have been singing a ballad about her fate.

> A cycle of legends tells about the infamous owner of Pintorp Manor, Lady Anna Gyllenstierna, who died in 1552. The legends, later identified with Lady Beata Gyllenstierna (1618–67), became widely known through a broadside ballad printed in 1860 (ULMA 4863).
>
> See Imber Nordin-Grip, *Pintorpafrun* (1942) (Sörmländska handlingar 8).

Collected in 1932 in Bettna, Södermanland (Sweden). Printed in Nordin-Grip, *Pintorpafrun* (1942), 50.

62.3 The Sunken Manor

There is a bog by Lake Pade called Pade Hole. The water is quite deep there. Once the folk tied seven swaddling bands together, weighted it on one end, and sank it in the bog, but still they could not reach the bottom. And when they pulled the rope up, the weight had been replaced by a goat's horn.

People say that there used to be a manor where the bog is now, but it sank into the depths. They had sent a messenger to the minister asking him to come and prepare the Lady for death, but they put a sow into her bed, as a joke. The minister came and said the rite, but when he discovered what was going on, he left, and immediately the manor began to sink. Soon clear water covered everything. The minister managed to reach dry land. He said the manor would be damned forever because they had made fun of the sacrament. The chair on which he had placed his hymnal was sailing along with it, and when he removed the hymnal, the chair sank, too.

> This legend is particularly popular in Denmark, but it is also found in Germany along the shores of the Baltic Sea and the North Sea.
> See Warren R. Maurer, "German Sunken City Legends," *Fabula* 17 (1976), 189–214.
> Collected by E. T. Kristensen from Karl Kristiansen in Skovby, Fyn (Denmark). Printed in Kristensen, *Danske sagn*, N.R. 3 (1931), 163.

62.4 Sir Fleming on Svidja

Sir Fleming on Svidja was a very cruel man.

Once it happened that while they were brewing, the nursemaid entered the brewing house with the master's child on her arm.

"What punishment would I get if the child fell into the brewing vat?" the girl asked. And then the child fell in!

Sir Fleming had both the maid and her own child boiled to death in the same vat. The child was frightened and cried out that the water was too cold. But the maid said:

"Hush, hush, my little one. It will get warm in a little while."

People say that, to punish himself, Sir Fleming took his own life.

There is a whole cycle of legends about Sir Fleming on Svidja
and his inhumane treatment of people.

Collected by V. E. V. Wessman in 1906 from Amalie K. Fyrkvist
in Sjundeå, Nyland (Finland). Printed in Wessman, *Sägner* 2.2
(1924), 318.

62.5 Sir Fleming's Death

The cruel master on Svidja, who ordered his nursemaid and her
child boiled to death, had a brother in Sweden who was a duke.
When the duke heard what had happened, he summoned his brother
to answer for what he had done. But Sir Fleming did not go, so the
duke went to Finland instead.

Sir Fleming was standing in the doorway when the Duke arrived.
Pulling out a bottle, he drank from it, collapsed, and died. The duke
grabbed him by the beard and shook him:

"I don't know what punishment I would have given you if you
had lived."

Sir Fleming was buried in a silver casket and now rests below the
castle on Svidja.

Collected by V. E. V. Wessman in 1919 from Amalie K. Fyrkvist
in Enstad, Nyland (Finland). Printed in Wessman, *Sägner* 2.2
(1924), 319.

63. Thieves and Outlaws

Thieves and outlaws were a threat to the community, but at the
same time, in the popular imagination, they were surrounded with an
aura of fascination. At worst they were thought of as rapists and can-
nibals, at best as social heroes who stole from the rich and gave to the
poor. Most frequently the legends describe how the criminals are
caught and brought to justice.

See E. J. Hobsbawm, *Primitive Rebels* (1971).

63.1 Til, Til, Tove

In the really old days, there were some robbers or convicts who
had escaped from the authorities and were holing up on Dugurdsmål
Hill. Near the top of that hill was a cleft. That is where they were

hiding. They had even built a stone rampart in front. You can still see that rampart today.

There was a serving girl from Narum. She was taking care of the cattle on the summer pasture in the hills. One day when she was herding, she ran into these outlaws. They killed her cattle and the big oxen and hanged the watchdog, and they wanted to rape her. They dragged her to the cleft and would not let her go. But one day she climbed up on a ridge, played the lur and sang down to the village:

> Til, Til, Tove,
> twelve men in the woods,
> twelve men they are,
> twelve swords they bear,
> the big oxen they've stabbed,
> the bell cow they've tied,
> the dog they've hanged,
> the little child they've thrashed,
> and me they've raped.

"What are you singing?" the robbers asked. Then she began naming her cattle instead:

> Lillie and Blackie,
> Susie and Mary,
> bellow in the woods,
> and want to go home.

The folks in the village heard her and many men climbed the hill. When the robbers saw how many there were, one of them grabbed the girl by her apron and dragged her down to a small lake. He was going to drown her. But the apron string he was holding broke, and the girl got away. The men took all the robbers prisoner. Later the girl gave birth to a child.

> This is probably the most popular legend about robbers in Norway and Sweden. It is also widely known as a lullaby and a herding song, often played on the lur.
> Legend type: ML 8025.
> Collected in Sigdal-Eggedal, Buskerud (Norway). Printed in Andreas Mørch, *Frå gamle dagar. Folkeminne frå Sigdal og Eggedal* (1932), 68–69.

63.2 The Outlaws Who Kidnapped the Girl

A girl was kidnapped by some outlaws and taken to an island known as Robbers' Isle. She was there for seven years. During that time she was the mistress of all the robbers and every year gave birth to a child. The king of the robbers killed the children and ate their hearts.

But one Christmas Eve she went out to look for some Christmas straw. The outlaws were dead drunk and had forgotten all about her. She went home and told the folks what had happened. She had dropped pieces of straw along the way, so the villagers could retrace her steps and find the hideout. They surrounded the hideout and took the robbers prisoner. They were so drunk, they did not even put up any resistance. In prison the robbers' king admitted what he had done. As punishment he was walled in alive near the gate of Åbo castle. There are seven hearts cut in the wall where he is. If he had eaten the hearts of just two more children nobody would have been able to capture him.

> The so-called Christmas straw was traditionally spread on the floor, and the entire household would sleep there on Christmas Eve. The custom is pre-Christian in origin.
>
> Acquiring supranormal powers by eating human hearts is a motif also known from heroic legend and folktales.
>
> See Nils-Arvid Bringéus, *Årets festseder* (1976), 43–47; Lily Weiser-Aall, *Julehalmen i Norge* (1953).
>
> Collected by V. E. V. Wessman in 1915 from Wilhelmina Wikström in Finnby, Åboland (Finland). Printed in Wessman, *Sägner* 2.1 (1928), 244.

63.3 The Master Thief Who Did Both Good and Evil

Liven was a master thief who stole from the rich and gave to the poor. Once he met an old woman.

"Have you ever seen Liven?" he asked her.

"No, I haven't; he has done me neither good nor evil," answered the woman.

Then Liven shoved a pole through the sleeves of her jacket, and there she stood with her arms outstretched. Before he left he stuck a ten-crown note into her mouth and said:

"Now you can say that you have seen Liven, and he has done you both good and evil!"

Yes, there are many stories about that Liven fellow.

> This legend has been told about a number of different thieves.
> See Imber Nordin-Grip, *Mellösa i Sörmland. Folkminnen* (1964), 316–17.
>
> Collected by Carl Segerstahl in 1921 from Hanna i Bruket, Ydre härad, Östergötland (Sweden). Ms. in LUF (1950), 65.
> Printed in Bengt af Klintberg *Svenska folksägner* (1972), 280.

63.4 The Outlaw on Grasøya

Once an outlaw was living on Grasøya Island. His wife was staying with him. He often poached sheep in Fløstrand and took them over to the island. He had a big kettle in which he cooked the meat.

But then the folks at Fløstrand sent a message to Alexander, the gypsy sheriff in Borgund. They asked him to put an end to that thieving rabble on Grasøya.

So Alexander disguised himself as a fisherman and took a boat over to the island. He crept forward on the island until he was in firing range.

"I hear something clicking," said the outlaw's wife.

"Oh, it's just the fire crackling, Mother," said the outlaw.

"I smell a Christian," said the woman.

"That's the odor from the kettle," said the outlaw.

But just then a shot rang out, and the outlaw fell.

"I told you so, I told you so!" the woman shouted and threw herself headfirst into the sea.

> This outlaw legend is very common in Norway. The woman's ability to smell a Christian indicates that she is a witch. The gypsy sheriff had the task of keeping beggers and transients out of the district.
>
> Collected by Martin Bjørndal from Benjamin J. Runde in 1937 in Møre (Norway). Printed in Bjørndal, *Segn og tru. Folkeminne frå Møre* (1949), 30.

63.5 How to Catch a Thief

A pedlar met Jens Long-Knife in the woods, and he knew right away who he was.

"I might as well give you my wares," said the pedlar, and he undid his box and hung it over Jen's shoulder. Jens was only too willing to have it. But then the pedlar grabbed his stick and hit Jens across the legs so that he fell to the ground.

"Now I feel better," he said, "but how are things with you?"

Collected by E. T. Kristensen from Karen Marie Kristensdatter in Horns parish, Jylland (Denmark). Printed in Kristensen, *Danske sagn*, N.R. 4 (1932), 384.

63.6 Shoemaker Point

On Inner Amdal farm in Nedstrand, near the sea, there is a steep cliff topped by a sharp outcrop that people have named Shoemaker Point.

Once a shoemaker had been condemned to death for some crime. But he was told that if he could sit on top of that outcropping and make a pair of shoes, he could go free. The shoemaker crawled up onto the point, and it did not take him long to finish both shoes. But just when he was fixing the last nail in place, the hammer slipped out of his hand. He bent forward to grab it—and fell to his death.

Collected by Aamund Salveson in Ryfylke, Rogaland (Norway). Printed in Salveson, *Folkeminne* (1924), 52.

PART X
Urban Folklore Today

he industrialization of the Scandinavian countries, beginning in the nineteenth century and culminating after World War II, gradually transformed a basically rural society into an urban one. Traditional forms of folk belief and oral literature were at least in part replaced by new ones. But legends reflecting the worldview and concerns of contemporary society continue to flourish. One important trait of modern oral tradition is its decidedly international character and rapid dissemination through the mass media and tourism.

See Bengt af Klintberg, "Folksägner i dag," *Fataburen* (1976), 269–96; Jan Harold Brunvand, *The Vanishing Hitchhiker. American Urban Legends and Their Meanings* (1981).

64. Outsiders and Strangers

Outsiders and strangers have always been looked upon with suspicion, fear, and a certain fascination. In older folk tradition, transient beggars and Finns were often considered thieves, but at the same time, they were ascribed supernormal powers. More recent folk tradition focuses on the inability of migrants to adapt to a modern urban environment. Foreign cultures and subcultures in one's own country are seen not only as exotic but also as dangerous.

> See Magne Velure, "Rykten och vitsar om invandrargrupper," *Kulturell kommunikation* (1979), 144–50.

64.1 Potatoes in the Living Room

An immigrant family — grandmother and all — moved into an apartment house here in Eskiltuna. After some time the neighbors living downstairs noticed something suspicious. The ceiling was leaking and there were wet spots on the walls of their living room. They called the health department, and someone from there was sent out to check on the immigrant family. On the wood floor, which had been torn up in places, the foreigners were growing potatoes; they roasted their meat on a spit and cooked all their food there, too. It is incredible what some people will do.

> During the 1950s this and similar stories were told about Swedes moving into the city from the rural districts. Later the same story was told about various groups who immigrated to Sweden from southern Europe and Finland.

379

See Magne Velure, "Rykten och vitsar om invandrargrupper," *Kulturell kommunikation* (1979), 144–56; Bengt af Klintberg, "Folksägner idag," *Fataburen* (1976), 273.

From a questionnaire circulated by Bengt af Klintberg for Nordiska Museet, Stockholm (Sweden). Printed in Velure, "Rykten och vitsar," 147.

64.2 Rat Meat at the Restaurant

I was in Paris in the fall of 1971, when a French lady I knew told me this story about her sister-in-law.

The sister-in-law went out to eat at a Chinese restaurant and got something stuck in her teeth and could not get it out. She had to see a dentist, who managed to get it loose, and he found that it was a splinter from a rat's tooth. Later the police raided the restaurant, and there they discovered fifty rats in the deepfreeze.

After hearing this I would not eat at Chinese restaurants in Paris anymore. I was afraid those strips of meat in Chinese dishes might be rat meat.

> This migratory legend, frequently reported in the U.S. and in much of western Europe, reached Scandinavia in the 1970s. It is told about ethnic restaurants abroad as well as in Scandinavia.
>
> See Bengt af Klintberg, "Folksägner idag," *Fataburen* (1976), 273–76.
>
> Collected in Stockholm (Sweden). Printed in af Klintberg, "Folksägner idag," 275.

64.3 Spider

A lady from Bergen went on vacation somewhere in the South just before Christmas. But when she got home a few weeks later, she was in for a real shock.

A boil appeared on her right cheek. The physician did not think it was anything serious and prescribed an ointment, but it did not help at all. The boil on her cheek just kept getting bigger. Then one morning, when she was standing in front of the mirror trying to camouflage it with some powder, the boil burst open and out came—a big spider.

> Tourists in tropical countries are known to have experienced skin infestations from insects and larvae. More fantastic versions of

similar experiences have been circulated in oral tradition as well as in press reports.

See Bengt af Klintberg, "Folksägner idag," *Fataburen* (1976), 277–78.

Reported in the Norwegian daily *Bergens Arbeiderblad* (March 18, 1980) and picked up by the Norwegian News Agency (NTB) the same day.

64.4 *The Snake in the Banana*

My brother's wife told me this. It happened somewhere outside Borås.

A friend of hers had bought a bunch of bananas. She gave one to her little boy and said:

"Now you sit here and eat your banana!"

Then she went into the kitchen. Suddenly she heard him calling:

"Mama, the banana bit me!"

"Yes, sure," said the mother. She thought he was making it up. But when she went back into the room, the boy was lying there, dead. He had been bitten by a snake about 4 to 5 centimeters long — a miniature cobra.

Now I always check before I eat a banana to make sure there is not a snake in it.

> Rumors of bananas being infested with snakes caused the sale of the fruit to drop appreciably in both Sweden and Finland during the early 1970s.
>
> See Bengt af Klintberg, "Folksägner i dag," *Fataburen* (1976), 276–77.
>
> Collected by af Klintberg from a 16-year-old girl in Borås (Sweden). Printed in af Klintberg, "Mordet på balkongen och andra skrönor från storstadsdjungelen," *Vi* (1978), no. 50, 35.

64.5 *A Torn Off Finger*

I heard this story from the wife of a lawyer. She had heard the story from an acquaintance who worked at the police station in Hørsholm.

A woman was driving on Hørsholm Road (now Helsingør Road), on her way home from Copenhagen. When she got to an area where there are not many houses, a gang of motorcyclists drove up behind her. Her car was small and not very fast. The motorcyclists passed her and tried to push her to the side of the road. They were trying to get her to stop, and she knew they would probably rape her. Just to scare her, one of them drove right up to her slowing car and struck the windshield with a chain, knocking a hole in it. Of course she was terrified, but she pushed the gas pedal to the floor and drove away from the motorcyclists. To her surprise they did not follow her. She drove to the nearest police station to report what had happened. There she realized that the chain was tangled in the windshield, and two of the motorcyclist's fingers were stuck to one end of it.

> Versions of this story have been documented in North America and Europe. It was first reported in Scandinavia when "long-haired" (*raggar*) hitchhikers and motorcycle gangs appeared on the scene.
>
> See Bengt af Klintberg, "Folksägner i dag," *Fataburen* (1976), 278–80.
>
> Told on March 18, 1974 by Bengt Holbek, Danish folklorist. Ms. in Nordiska Museets Arkiv. Folkeminnesamlingen, Stockholm (Sweden).

65. The Supernatural

Despite the fact that people today attest to a rationalistic world-view, stories about ghosts, revenants, *hug*-messages, and the like are common in contemporary tradition. Other typical themes in current tradition deal with the appearance of Jesus, flying saucers, and visitors from outer space.

65.1 The Dead Woman

A man bought a cottage on a deserted island. One day he went out to see it. He was going to stay only for the day. That evening, just when he was getting ready to go home, he took a picture of the cottage. But when he had the picture developed, he discovered something strange. In front of the cottage stood a woman he had never seen before. He went to the police and showed them the picture. They told him that the woman had died a number of years before.

> In this story modern technology is employed to confirm the traditional belief in revenants.

Collected in 1969 by Magne Velure from Geir Olsen (10 years old) at Christi Krybbe School, Bergen (Norway). Ms. in EFI, Velure, 1969.

65.2 An Omen of Death

Two boys were on their way home from school. One of them was walking the other home. It was a dark evening. When they got to the cemetery, they saw a light, but there was nobody holding it. One boy asked the other what it could be. He answered that the light showed itself whenever someone was going to die. The light would wander along among the graves, and when it got to the church door, it would show the face of the one who was going to die. The other boy did not want to believe him, but he said he was going to see for himself. He stood near the church door and watched the light getting closer and closer, but nobody was holding it. When it got to the church door, he saw a face; it looked familiar, but he did not know who it was. He got scared and ran home. A week later he got sick and came down with pneumonia. He sent word to his friend that now he knew whose face he had seen. It had been his own.

> Seeing oneself is a traditional omen of death (Cf. nos. 9.5–9.6.). Today this story is reported among children, perhaps reflecting their concern about a subject that has become taboo in contemporary society.
>
> See Reimund Kvideland, "Historier om døden som del av barns kompensatoriske sosialisering," *Tidsskrift for samfunnsforskning* 20, (1979) 565–72; in English: "Stories about Death as Part of Children's Socialization," *Folklore on Two Continents*, edited by Nikolai Burlakoff et al. (1980), 59–64.
>
> Collected in 1969 by Magne M. Velure from Kjersti Sjøtun (13 years old) at Christi Krybbe School, Bergen (Norway). Printed in Kvideland, "Historier om døden," 568.

65.3 I Saw Jesus in Vadstena

When I was a child, I always went to church on Sundays. It was natural and fun for us kids to be with the grownups at all kinds of occasions: at mushroom outings, in the sauna, and at parties. I did not see the difference between adults and children, and there were never any problems.

I suppose I had seen a picture of Christ in a white gown some-where. One day, when I was six years old, my mother sent me to the grocery. I was jumping and skipping down the road, when suddenly I saw Jesus himself in the middle of the street. I stopped abruptly be-cause, you know, he was taller than any of the houses! I was not amazed, really, I just thought to myself:

"Well, well, today Jesus is coming to Vadstena to say hello!"

And I wanted to curtsy and greet him and tell him that I knew who he was. So I continued down the street by his side; I was on the sidewalk, and he walked in the middle of the street. When we had walked for a while like this, he sort of faded away, from his head on down, bit by bit, very slowly. Finally only his feet were showing, but I could see them, step by step. When the feet had vanished, I turned off at the corner where I was supposed to turn anyway. I did not think there was anything strange about it, I guess. I thought that gods could come and disappear like this because they were not hu-man, but I believed that they existed just as we do. I did not tell any-body at home about it because I thought that Jesus probably took a walk in Vadstena every so often.

> This memorat was told by a 65-year-old woman on a Swedish television program in 1972 about "inexplicable" experiences. The informant, a nurse by profession, did not consider herself a reli-gious person.
> See Bengt af Klintberg, "Jag såg Jesus i Vadstena. Berättelser om oförklarliga händelser," *Tradisjon* 3 (1973), 31–50.
> Printed in af Klintberg, "Jeg såg Jesus," 40.

65.4 Jesus' Second Coming

There were two women driving in a car. Along the road they saw a young woman, who was hitchhiking. Normally these women would not pick up hitchhikers, but this girl looked so sweet and friendly, they gave in to a sudden impulse and stopped to pick her up. She climbed into the back seat, and for some time, they drove in silence. Suddenly the girl leaned forward and said:

"Jesus is coming soon." But when the two women turned around, the back seat was empty.

This experience made a strong impression on both of them. I heard the story from my aunt, a teacher in her fifties, and she emphasized that the two women were quite religious. The story became very popular in Norway during the summer of 1973. In religous circles many people took it as a sign that the last hour was at hand. They believed it was a true story, a message from heaven.

> Stories about the Second Coming have been told ever since early Christianity. They tend to flourish during periods of social unrest and when there are threats of war, as well as at the end of the millennium.
>
> See Bengt af Klintberg, "Folksägner idag," *Fataburen* (1976), 290–91.
>
> Collected in 1975 by af Klintberg from Reimund Kvideland, Bergen (Norway). Printed in af Klintberg, "Folksägner idag," 290–91.

65.5 Jesus as Hitchhiker

A married couple was driving on a country road. They were going to a wedding. They saw a young man standing by the side of the road, hitchhiking. They stopped to pick him up. Their car was a two-door, and the woman was wearing a long dress—after all, they were going to a wedding—and so, she got out to let the young man climb into the back seat. When they took a good look at him, they were a bit surprised. He was barefoot and had long hair and a beard. Usually they would not pick up anyone who looked like that. But he had a nice face, so they gave him a lift.

They did not know what to say to him, because they were not used to giving rides to hippies. Then all of a sudden, after driving about ten to fifteen minutes, the young man said:

"Do you know Jesus?"

Well, the man and the woman, you know, were sort of conventional Christians. They got embarrassed by his question and did not know how to answer him. Finally the wife said:

"Yes, we do."

"Well, that's good," said the young man, "because, Jesus, that's me."

They shuddered and did not know what to say to that. Finally the wife turned around to look at the young man, but he was gone! They stopped the car and looked at each other in bewilderment. Then they got out and looked around. They were someplace on Western Jylland where the country is flat and empty on all sides. They got back into the car, feeling very ill at ease. Later when they stopped at a gas station to fill up, they told the attendant about their experience because they felt a need to talk about it. The man looked at them and said:

"Yes, you are the tenth family today who's told me about this."

See Bengt af Klintberg, "Folksägner idag," *Fataburen* (1976), 291. Collected in 1975 by af Klintberg from Inge Adriansen, Sønderborg, Jylland (Denmark). Ms. in Nordiska Museet, Stockholm (KU 6192, 103).

66. Horror Tales and Antitales

Horror tales as a genre flourish primarily among teenagers and students. They are told for entertainment and to generate a sense of fellowship. In the so-called antitales, the element of horror is given a surprising and often absurd turn.

66.1 The Murdered Boyfriend

I know a story about a boy and a girl; it is supposed to be true.

This happened in Germany. A boy and his girlfriend were out for a drive. In the middle of the woods, they ran out of gas, and he went to find a gas station. Before he left he told her not to open the car doors for anyone. While the girl sat waiting in the car, she heard a warning on the radio about an insane man. He had broken out of an asylum nearby. She sat there waiting for a long time. Suddenly she heard a scraping noise on the back of the car. It got quiet for a while, and then she heard a rhythmic thumping on the roof. Just then a police car drove up, and its sirens were on. The police officers got out of their car. They shouted to her through a megaphone to get out of the car and walk toward them. Under no circumstances should she turn around. She opened the car door and got out; she could still hear the thumping noise. But when she had walked some distance, she did what she was not supposed to do. She turned around, and she saw the insane man on top of the car. He held her boyfriend's head in his hands, and he was thumping the roof of the car with it.

I heard this story from a buddy the first time, but I have heard it many times since then. No matter who tells it, they always say that they are going to tell something ugly and then you get this story. I do not think the story is all that ugly anymore, but that is only because I have heard it so often. When I heard it the first time, I thought it was the worst thing I had ever heard, and everyone insists that it is true.

This story was first collected in the U.S. in 1964 and probably reached Scandinavia in the 1970s.

Collected from a schoolgirl in Borlänge (Sweden) in 1975. Printed in Bengt af Klintberg, "Folksägner idag," *Fataburen* (1976), 288.

66.2 The Trip to Mallorca

This is a story about a couple who was going to vacation on Mallorca. They had made arrangements with a babysitter. When she did not show up on time, they harnessed the child to its playpen and drove off because they had to catch their flight. When they got home two weeks later, they found the child choked to death in the playpen.

The babysitter had gotten into a car accident while en route to their house, and she was unconscious when the ambulance took her to the hospital. She still lay there unconscious when the couple returned home.

This story, which was first documented in Norway during the early 1970s, has been turned into a serial novel published in 1978 in the family weekly *Hjemmet* (The Home). In the novel, a dropout finds and takes care of the abandoned child, thus giving the story a socially desirable ending.

Collected in 1972 by Reimund Kvideland from Jon Foldøy in Bergen (Norway). Ms. in EFI, Modern Legends.

66.3 A Knife in the Heart

A little girl was celebrating her eighth birthday. Her mother asked her to fetch the cake from the basement. The girl went downstairs, but in the basement, there was a red hand, and it said:

"If you take the cake, I'll kill you."

The girl ran upstairs to her mother and told her what had happened. The mother did not want to listen to the girl, and she told her to go back downstairs. The same thing happened again, so then the mother had to go down into the basement. When she was about to take the cake, the red hand said:

"If you take the cake, I'll kill you."

"What nonsense," said the mother, and she brought the cake upstairs. That evening she said to the girl:

"You see, nothing happened with that red hand."

The girl went to bed reassured. But in the morning, when she was pulling her slippers out from under the bed, she found her mother there, a knife stuck in her heart.

> See Reimund Kvideland, "Stories about Death as Part of Children's Socialization," *Folklore on Two Continents* (1980), 59–64.
> Collected by Magne Velure in 1969 from Mona Bugge (13 years old) at Fridalen School, Bergen (Norway). Ms. in EFI, Velure, 1969.

66.4 *There Was Blood on the Stairs*

There was blood on the stairs, all the way up, there was blood on the stairs, all the way up, on all the stairs — and on the top of the stairs there lay *(with a high and happy voice)* — a blood orange.

> This antitale is a parody of a story describing how a child finds his father on top of the stairs with a knife stuck in his chest. Antitales frequently make use of formulaic repetition to generate suspense.
> Collected in Bergen (Norway). Printed in Reimund Kvideland, "Stories about Death as Part of Children's Socialization," *Folklore on Two Continents* (1980), 59–64.

66.5 *Blenda Washes Whiter*

Once there was a woman who was alone at home. Her husband had gone on vacation. One day she took a nap at noontime. When she woke up, she saw that the bed sheet was full of blood, and on it was written:
"Wash by twelve o'clock."
That evening the lady went to a party and did not get home until half-past ten. She came across the sheet again and took it down into the basement and scrubbed and scrubbed it. The sweat was pouring off her. The clock struck eleven, eleven-thirty, one minute to twelve, when suddenly she hear steps behind her, and a voice said:
"Blenda washes whiter."

> Blenda is the trade name of a well-known laundry soap in Norway.
> Collected by Magne Velure in 1969 from Ronny Hansen (11 years old) at Landås School, Bergen (Norway). Printed in Reimund Kvideland, "Stories about Death as Part of Children's Socialization," *Folklore on Two Continents* (1980), 59–64.

66.6 It Was a Dark, Dark Night

(*With a low, rough voice*):

It was a dark, dark night,
in a dark, dark wood,
there was a dark, dark house,
there was a dark, dark hallway,
there was a dark, dark stair,
there was a dark, dark door, which opened quietly,
and a voice said (*with a high voice*):
Mama, I've got to pee.

> This antitale is common among Scandinavian children, Ms. in
> EFI, barnetradisjon (Bergen, Norway).

67. Adulterers and Thieves

Contemporary legends about adultery and theft tend to emphasize
the comical aspects of a given situation. At the same time, they convey a sense of uneasiness about the disintegration of traditional norms
and values in modern society.

67.1 A Terrible Revenge

A man in Bergen, who sometimes after his regular job drives a
ready-mix cement truck, drove by his house the other day and saw
his friend's car parked outside. He stopped the truck and went inside
to say hello. Certain sounds from the bedroom made it clear that the
friend had stopped by not to visit him but his wife. Without the couple in the bedroom noticing, the man left the house and went to the
friend's car. He pushed back the sunroof and backed up his cement
truck. Then he opened the chute and filled the car with about two cu-
bic meters of ready-mix. When the lover was ready to leave, he could
not drive off because the cement had solidified.

Later that evening the car was towed away. The incident has not
been reported to the police.

> An older version of this legend was found in the U.S. in the
> 1920s. In 1960 the story was disseminated by the American news
> agency AP. In Scandinavia it is widely reported in oral tradition
> and has appeared as a news item from time to time. A few days

after the story was published in *Bergens Arbeiderblad* (Bergen Labor
News, March 6, 1973), a reader sent the following note to the
editor (March 15, 1973):

> Just what he deserved!
> Considering what is going on in many marriages these
> days, the story recently published in *Bergens Arbeiderblad* about
> the husband's revenge, is most appropriate. Nobody thinks
> about those who suffer in silence, end up in the psycho ward,
> start drinking, or take their own life. Isn't it high time that the
> husband gets a chance to strike back without threat of punish-
> ment? Then these unhealthy relations would seem less ap-
> pealing.
>
> Signed: Cuckold

But on March 14, 1973, *Bergens Arbeiderblad* reported that in
Kristiansand a sympathizer had started a collection to replace the
ruined vehicle.

See Reimund Kvideland, "Det stod i avisa! Når vandrehistorier
blir avismeldingar," *Tradisjon* 3 (1973), 1–12.

67.2 Grandmother Was Stolen

A few years ago, I am not sure when, I heard this story from one
of my sons:

A young couple from Holte was vacationing in Spain, and they
had taken the husband's mother along. During a car trip high up in
the Pyrennees, the mother-in-law got sick from the cold and the thin
air, and within a short time, she died. Because the temperature was so
low, the body became rigid rather quickly, and not being able to get
her back into the small car, they wrapped her in a tent they had
brought, and put her on top of the luggage rack.

They now drove as quickly as possible to the nearest town to report the death to the authorities and to take care of all the necessary
formalities.

Because of language difficulties, it took some time before they
managed to tell their story to the police. But the worst was yet to
come! When they went back outside, they found the car had been
stolen, and it has not been found yet!

Imagine the thief's fright when he found the dead mother-in-law
inside the tent. What did he do with the body?

The one who is the most interested in this question is, of course,
her son. He cannot prove to the Danish authorities that his mother is

dead, and, consequently, he cannot claim his inheritance, which supposedly amounts to around 300,000 Kroner.

Who can help this unhappy man?

> This story, which is widespread in the Western world, received its present form during or after World War II. Linda Dégh has suggested that the story has its background in folktales from the eighteenth and nineteenth centuries about the mistaken theft of a dead body.
>
> See Carsten Bregenhøj, "Svigermor i bagagerummet." *Folkeminder* 14–15 (1969–71), 9–14; Dégh, "The Runaway Grandmother," *Indiana Folklore* 1 (1968), 68–77; Alan Dundes, "The Psychology of Legend," *American Folk Legend. A Symposium* (1971), 33–36.
>
> Collected by Nikolai Andersen in 1966. Printed in Bregenhøj, "Svigermor i bagagerummet," 13–14.

67.3 A Turkey under Her Hat

One day a woman went to Åhlen's grocery store to shop. After walking around the store for a while, she stopped by one of the deep freezers and took out a frozen turkey and stuffed it in her hat without anyone noticing. It was a big broad-brimmed hat. Then she put it back on and continued to shop as if nothing had happened.

But there was a line for the cashier, and she had to wait. While she was standing there, she suddenly passed out. Her hat fell off, and the turkey rolled out onto the floor. The cold turkey had been too much for her, and therefore she had lost consciousness.

> This legend has been documented in Scandinavia and Germany.
>
> See Hans Ohlsson, "Kycklingen i hatten. En modern sägen och dess bakgrund," *Nord-Nytt* (1976), 51–70.
>
> Collected by Hans Ohlsson in Stockholm (Sweden). Printed in Hans Ohlsson, "Kycklingen i hatten," 60.

67.4 Free Tickets

A married couple was returning home from Spain or some other country in the South. I guess they had been away for quite a while.

They were glad to be back in Norway. They drove their heavily loaded car through Oslo to their villa, somewhere in Holmenkollen or in some other fashionable place a little way beyond the city.

They unloaded their bags and blankets and soon had taken possession of the old homestead once again. They tried the red wine they had smuggled across the border, and I imagine that the wife fried some eggs Norwegian-style and unwrapped the goat cheese she had bought on their way home. The husband happened to be looking out the window, when suddenly he gasped.

Their car was gone!

He rushed into the street and asked children and neighbors whether anybody had seen the thieves. No one could help him, and he raced back into the house, cursing this miserable country of thieves and crooks. He called the police, and they said they were sorry, very sorry. If they got the chance, they would happily arrest the crooks.

But the next morning, the man gasped once more. While he was sitting at the breakfast table, he looked out the window and saw that the car had been returned! The couple rushed outside and unlocked their beloved car. The thieves had left a note on the steering wheel. And there they read these lines:

"We are terribly sorry that we stole your car. Can you forgive us! We filled up the gas tank. And we enclose two tickets to the Chat Noir for tonight. Please use them! Then we'll know that you are not angry anymore."

The couple was very moved. There were still sweet and honest people in this country after all! And those theater tickets, what a great idea!

They decided to celebrate by dressing up in tux and evening dress. A half an hour before showtime, they drove off, and three hours later, they returned and found their house—stripped. Everything had been taken from the villa. The neighbors had seen the moving van to be sure, but they had assumed that the "foreigners" had decided to leave the place for good!

> The Chat Noir is a popular music hall and vaudeville theater in Oslo.
> Printed in *Farmand* 29 (1975), 19–20.

BIBLIOGRAPHY

Abbreviations

AT	Antti Aarne and Stith Thompson, The Types of the Folktale, 2d revised edition, FFC no. 184 (Helsinki, Suomalainen Tiedeakatemia, 1973).
Ballad type	Jonsson, Bengt R. et al. (ed.). The Types of the Scandinavian Medieval Ballad. A Descriptive Catalogue. (Skrifter utg. av Svenskt Visarkiv 5). Sth. and Oslo: Svenskt Visarkiv and Universitetsforlaget.
EFI	Etno-folkloristisk institutt (Department of Folklore), University of Bergen, Norway.
FFC	Folklore Fellows Communications (Helsinki, Suomalainen Tiedeakatemia).
FmFt	*Folkminnen och folktankar* (Lund, Göteborg, 1914–44), 1–31.
IFGH	Institutet för folkminnesforskning vid Göteborgs högskola (Folklore archive, Gothenburg, Sweden).
KLNM	Kulturhistorisk leksikon for nordisk middelalder (1956–78), 1–22.
LUF	Folklivsarkivet, Universitetet i Lund (Folklore archive, Lund, Sweden).
ML	Reidar Th. Christiansen, Migratory Legends, FFC no. 175 (Helsinki, Suomalainen Tiedeakatemia, 1958).
Ms	Manuscript.
NFS	Norsk folkeminnesamling, Institutt for folkeminnevitskap, Universitetet i Oslo (Folklore archive, Oslo, Norway).
NM	Nordiska Museet, Stockholm, Sweden.
NM EU	Nordiska Museet, Etnologiska undersökningen.
NM HA	Nordiska Museet, Hammarstedtska arkivet.
NM KU	Nordiska Museet Kulturhistoriska undersökningen.
N.R.	Ny Række (New Series).
ULMA	Dialekt- och folkminnesarkivet, Uppsala (Folklore archive, Uppsala, Sweden).
VFF	Västsvenska folkminnesföreningen (collections in Folklore archive, Gothenburg, Sweden).

Bibliography

Aakjær, Jeppe. *Jyske folkeminder.* Edited by Bengt Holbek (Danmarks folkeminder 76). Copenhagen: Munksgaard, 1966.

Aasen, Ivar. *Prøver af Landsmaalet i Norge.* Oslo: Feilberg og Landmark, 1852.

Abrahams, Roger D. "Genre Theory and Folkloristics." *Studia Fennica* 20 (1976), 13–19.

———. "The Complex Relations of Simple Forms." *Genre* 2 (1969), 104–28. Reprinted in *Folklore Genres.* Edited by Dan Ben-Amos, 193–214. Austin and London: University of Texas Press, 1976.

af Klintberg, Bengt. *See* Klintberg, Bengt af.

Ågren, Per-Uno. "Maktstulen häst och modstulen ko." *Västerbotten* (1964), 33–68.

Allardt, Anders. *Nyländska folkseder och bruk, vidskepelser m.m.* (Nyland. Samlingar utg. af Nyländska afdelningen 4). Helsingfors, 1889.

———, and Selim Perklén. *Nyländska folksagor och -sägner* (Nyland. Samlingar utg. af Nyländska afdelningen 6). Helsingfors. 1896.

Almqvist, Bo. "Niða[n]grisur. The Færoese Dead-Child Being." *Arv* 27 (1971), 97–120.

———. "Norska utburdsägner i västerled." *Norveg* 21 (1978), 109–19.

Alver, Bente Gullveig. "Conceptions of the Living Human Soul in the Norwegian Tradition." *Temenos* 7 (1971), 7–33.

———. " 'Du skal gå frisk herfra'. En etnomediciner og hans patientbehandling." *Tradisjon* 8 (1978), 27–36.

———. *Heksetro og trolddom. Et studie i norsk heksevæsen.* Oslo: Universitetsforlaget, 1971.

Alver, Brynjulf. "Category and Function." *Fabula* 9 (1967), 63–69.

———. "Dauinggudstenesta." *Arv* 6 (1950), 145–65.

———. "Historiske segner og historisk sanning." *Norveg* 9 (1962), 89–116.

———. "Tradisjon og minne." *Norges kulturhistorie* 4, 151–70. Oslo: Aschehoug, 1980.

Aly, Wolfgang. "Name." *Handwörterbuch des deutschen Aberglaubens* 6, columns 950–61. Berlin: de Gruyter, 1934–35.

Åmark, Mats. *Kyrkklockor, klockare och klocksägner i Dalarna*. En studie över *Dalarnes kyrkklockor i historien, kulten och folktron* (Dalarnes hembygds-förbunds skrifter 6). Strängnäs, 1928.

Aminson, H. "Om ladugård, stall, kreaturens sjukdommar och deras botemedel." *Bidrag till Södermanlands äldre kulturhistoria* 2.5 (1884), 84–109.

Andreassen, Eyðun. "Varsel om ulukker på sjøen på Færøyane." *Tradisjon* 7 (1977), 75–89.

Arbman, Ernst. "Shamanen, extatisk andebesvärjare och visjonär." *Primitiv religion och magi*. Edited by Å. Hultkrantz, 49–64. Stockholm: Bonnier, 1955.

Arens, Ilmar, and Bengt af Klintberg. "Bortbytingssägner i en gotländsk dombok från 1690." *Rig* 62 (1979), 89–97.

Árnason, Jón. *Íslenzkar þjóðsögur og æfintýri*. 2 vols. Leipzig: Hinrichs, 1862–64. New edition by Árni Böðvarsson and Bjarni Vilhjálmsson. 6 vols. Reykjavik: þjóðsaga, 1954–69.

———, and Magnús Grímsson. *Íslenzk æfintýri*. Reykjavik, 1852.

Asbjørnsen, P. Chr. *Norske Huldre-Eventyr og Folkesagn*. Oslo: Steensballe, 1870.

Åström, Elis. *Folktro och folkliv i Östergötland* (Acta Academiae Gustavi Adolphi 39). Uppsala, 1962.

Aurom, Magne. *Liv og lagnad. Folkeminne frå Sör-Odal* (Norsk folkeminnelags skrifter 48). Oslo, 1942.

Bang, A. Chr. "Gjengangere fra Hedenskabet og Katolicismen blandt vort Folk efter Reformationen." *Theologisk Tidsskrift* 10 (1885), 161–218.

———. *Norske Hexeformularer og Magiske Opskrifter* (Videnskabsselskabets skrifter. 2: Hist.-fil. klasse 1901, 1). Oslo, 1901–2.

Bascom, William. "Four Functions of Folklore." *Journal of American Folklore* 67 (1954), 333–49. Reprinted in *The Study of Folklore*. Edited by Alan Dundes, 279–98. Englewood Cliffs, N.J.: Prentice-Hall, 1965.

Ben-Amos, Dan. "Analytical Categories and Ethnic Genres." *Genre* 2 (1969), 275–301. Reprinted in *Folklore Genres*. Edited by Ben-Amos, 215–42. Austin and London: University of Texas Press, 1976.

———. "The Concept of Genre in Folklore." *Studia Fennica* 20 (1976), 30–43.

Benedikz, B. A. "The Master Magician in Icelandic Folk Legend." *Durham University Journal* (1964), 22–34.

Bengts, Josefina. *Från vargtider och vallpojksår*. Helsingfors: Söderström, 1915.

Benwell, Gwen, and Arthur Waugh. *Sea Enchantress. The Tale of the Mermaid and Her Kin*. New York: Hutchinson, 1965.

Berge, Rikard. "Drikke joleskaal. Studie av ei norderlandsk villsegn." *Norsk folkekultur* 10 (1924), 1–53.

———. "Folkesegni og den historiske kritiken." *Norsk folkekultur* 8 (1922), 21–32.

———. "Førnesbrunen, segni og slaatten." *Norsk folkekultur* 21 (1935), 3–18.
———. *Norsk sogukunst. Sogusegjarar og sogur.* Oslo: Aschehoug, 1924.
———. *Norske eventyr og sagn.* In collaboration with Sophus Bugge. 2 vols. Oslo and Copenhagen: Gyldendal, 1909–13.
Bergstøl, Tore. *Atterljom. Folkeminne fraa smaadalane kring Lindesnes* 2 (Norsk folkeminnelags skrifter 22). Oslo, 1930.
———. *Atterljom. Folkeminne frå smådalane kring Lindesnes* 3 (Norsk folkeminnelags skrifter 82). Oslo, 1959.
Bergstrand, Carl-Martin. *Bohuslänska sägner.* Göteborg: Gumperts, 1947.
———. *Gammalt från Orust. Folkminnen från Orust med närliggande öar.* Göteborg: Gumperts, 1962.
———. *Hallands sägner.* Göteborg: Gumperts, 1949.
———. *Värmlands sägner.* Göteborg: Gumperts, 1948.
Bergstrand, Maja. "Näcken som musikaliskt väsen." *FmFt* 23 (1936), 14–31.
Beth, K. "Engel." *Handwörterbuch des deutschen Aberglaubens* 2, columns 826–27. Berlin: de Gruyter, 1929–30.
Birkerod, Jacob. *Folketro og festskik, særlig fra Fyn (1734).* Edited by Inger M. Boberg (Danmarks folkeminder 43). Copenhagen: Det Schønbergske Forlag, 1936.
Bjersby, Ragnar. *Traditionsbärare på Gotland vid 1800-talets mitt. En undersökning rörande P. A. Säves sagesmän* (Skrifter utg. genom Landsmåls- och folkminnesarkivet i Uppsala. Serie B. 11). Uppsala, 1964.
Bjørkvik, Randi. "Gardfolk og plassfolk." *Norges kulturhistorie* 4, 41–68. Oslo: Aschehoug, 1980.
Bjørndal, Arne, and Brynjulf Alver. *-og fela ho lét. Norsk spelemannstradisjon.* Oslo: Universitetsforlaget, 1966. 2d revised edition, 1985.
Bjørndal, Martin. *Segn og tru. Folkeminne frå Møre.* (Norsk folkeminnelags skrifter 64). Oslo, 1949.
Bø, Olav. "Deildegasten." *Norveg* 5 (1955), 105–24.
———. *Heilag-Olav i norsk folketradisjon.* Oslo: Det norske samlaget, 1955.
———. "Tradisjon om ufredstider." *Norveg* 5 (1955), 197–212.
———. R. Grambo, Bjarne Hodne, and Ørnulf Hodne, eds. *Norske segner.* Oslo: Det norske samlaget, 1981.
Boberg, Inger M. *Baumeistersagen* (FFC 151). Helsinki, 1955.
———. *Bjærgfolkenes bagning. En sagnundersøgelse* (Danmarks folkeminder 45). Copenhagen: Det Schønbergske Forlag, 1938.
———. "Des Knaben Wunderhorn - Oldenburgerhornet." *Festskrift til L. L. Hammerich,* 53–61. Copenhagen: Gad, 1952.
———. *Folkemindeforskningens historie i Mellem- og Nordeuropa* (Danmarks folkeminder 60). Copenhagen: Munksgaard, 1953.
———. "Gardvordens seng i dansk tradition." *Maal og minne* (1956), 109–20.
———. *Sagnet om den store Pans død.* Copenhagen: Levin and Munksgaard, 1934.
Bondevik, Kjell. *Studiar i norsk segnhistorie.* Oslo: Aschehoug, 1948.

———. "Valfarting og lovnader." *Museet i Haugesund* (1925–35), 65–77.

Brandon, Elizabeth. "Folk Medicine in French Louisiana." *American Folk Medicine*. Edited by W. D. Hand, 215–34. Berkeley: University of California Press, 1976.

Bregenhøj, Carsten. "Svigermor i bagagerummet." *Folkeminder* 14/15 (1969/71), 9–14.

———. "Terrorisme, appelsiner og folkesagn." *Tradisjon* 8 (1978), 65–78.

Briggs, Katherine. *The Vanishing People*. London: Bratsford, 1978.

Bringéus, Nils-Arvid. *Årets fester*. Stockholm: LT's förlag, 1976.

———. *Brännodling. En historisk-etnologisk undersökning* (Skrifter från Folklivsarkivet i Lund 6). Lund: Gleerup, 1963.

———. *Sägnen om Örkelljunga kyrkklocka* (Skrifter utg. av Örkelljungabygdens hembygdsförening). Lund, 1949.

Broderius, John H. *The Giant in Germanic Tradition*. Chicago: The University of Chicago Libraries, 1932.

Brøndegaard, V. J. *Folk og flora. Dansk etnobotanik*. 4 vols. Copenhagen: Rosenkilde and Bagger, 1978–80.

Brox, Arthur. *Folkeminne frå Ytre Senja* 1 (Norsk folkeminnelags skrifter 105). Oslo, 1970.

Brunvand, Jan Harold. *The Vanishing Hitchhiker. American Urban Legends and Their Meanings*. New York: Norton, 1981.

Bugge, Kristian. *Folkeminne-optegnelser. Et Utvalg* (Norsk folkeminnelags skrifter 31). Oslo, 1934.

Burke, Peter. *Popular Culture in Early Modern Europe*. London: Maurice Temple Smith, 1978.

Buss, Reinhard J. *The Klabautermann of the Northern Seas. An Analysis of the Protective Spirit of Ships and Sailors in the Context of Popular Belief, Christian Legend, and Indo-European Mythology* (Folklore Studies 25). Berkeley, Los Angeles, London: University of California Press, 1973.

Bygdén, L. "Några studier rörande Disa-sagan." *Samlaren* 17 (1896), 21–74.

Campbell, Åke. "Det onda ögat och besläktade föreställningar i svensk folktradition." *FmFt* 20 (1933), 121–46.

———. "Halländsk bygdekultur." (Review) *FmFt* 12 (1925), 31–47.

———, and Åsa Nyman. *Atlas över svensk folkkultur II. Sägen, tro och högtidssed. 1 Kartor. 2 Kommentar*. Uppsala: Kungl. Gustav Adolfs Akademien, 1976.

Celander, Hilding. "En Nikolauslegend och dess samband med sägnerna om Jätten på ön och Hämndegåvan." *FmFt* 22 (1935), 165–80.

———. *Nordisk jul* 1. Stockholm: Hugo Gebers Förlag, 1928.

———. "Oskoreien och besläktade föreställningar i äldre och nyare nordisk tradition." *Saga och sed* (1943), 71–175.

Christiansen, Inger. "Likvakeskikken i Norge." *Norveg* 13 (1968), 32–72.

Christiansen, Reidar Th. "Der wilde Jäger in Norwegen." *Zeitschrift für Volkskunde* (1938), 24–31.

———. *The Dead and the Living*. (Studia Norvegica 2). Oslo, 1946.

———. *Die finnischen und nordischen Varianten des zweiten Merseburgerspruches* (FFC 18). Helsinki, 1914.

———. *Folktales of Norway.* Chicago: The University of Chicago Press, 1964.

———. "Gaelic and Norse Folklore." *Folk-Liv* 2 (1938), 321–35.

———. "Gårdvette og markavette." *Maal og minne* (1943), 137–60. Reprinted in *Eventyr og sagn*, 101–28. Oslo: Norli, 1946.

———. *Kjætten paa Dovre. Et bidrag til studiet av norske sagn* (Videnskapselskapets skrifter 2. Hist.-fil. klasse 1922, 6). Oslo, 1922.

———. "Midwife to the Hidden People. A Migratory Legend as Told from Ireland to Kurdistan." *Lochlann* 6 (1974), 104–17.

———. *The Migratory Legends. A Proposed List of Types with a Systematic Catalogue of the Norwegian Variants* (FFC 175). Helsinki, 1958.

———. *Norske sagn. Samlet ved Allers Familie-Journal.* Oslo: Aschehoug, 1938.

———. "Sjødraugene og land-draugene." *Jul i Salten* (1938), 15–17.

———. "Til de norske sjøvetters historie." *Maal og minne* (1935), 1–25. Reprinted in *Eventyr og sagn*, 129–60. Oslo: Norli, 1946.

Ciklamini, Marlene. "Journeys to the Giant Kingdom." *Scandinavian Studies* 40 (1968), 95–100.

Cohn, Norman. *Europe's Inner Demons: An Enquiry Inspired by the Great Witch Hunt.* New York: Heinemann, 1976.

Dahll, Vibeke. *Nordiske sagnregistre og sagnsystematik.* 2d edition (Nordic Institute of Folklore Publication 2). Turku, 1973.

Dalen, J. I. "Klokkorne i Hoprekstadkyrkja." *Tidsskrift utg. av Historielaget for Sogn* 4 (1920), 54.

Danielsson, Paul. *Djävulsgestalten i Finlands svenska folktro.* 2 vols. (Bidrag till kännedom af Finlands natur och folk 83, 5 and 84, 2). Helsingfors, 1930–32.

Dégh, Linda. "Folk Narrative." *Folklore and Folklife. An Introduction.* Edited by Richard M. Dorson, 53–83. Chicago and London: The University of Chicago Press, 1972.

———. "The Runaway Grandmother." *Indiana Folklore* 1 (1968), 68–77.

———. "UFO's and How Folklorists Should Look at Them." *Fabula* 18 (1977), 242–48.

———, and Andrew Vázsonyi. "Legends and Belief." *Genre* 4 (1971), 281–304. Reprinted in *Folklore Genres.* Edited by Dan Ben-Amos, 94–123. Austin and London: University of Texas Press, 1976.

Deneke, Bernward. *Legende und Volkssage. Untersuchungen zur Erzählung vom Geistergottesdienst.* Frankfurt am Main, 1958.

Dorson, Richard M. *Bloodstoppers and Bearwalkers.* Cambridge, Mass.: Harvard University Press, 1952.

Dundes, Alan. "On the Psychology of Legend." *American Folk Legend. A Symposium.* Edited by Wayland D. Hand, 21–36. Berkeley, Los Angeles, London: University of California Press, 1971.

Edsman, Carl-Martin. "Albert Eskeröd, Årets äring." (Review) *Rig* 32 (1949), 21–44.

———. "Antik och modern Sibylla." *Kungl. Vetenskapsamhällets i Uppsala årsbok* 15/16 (1971/72, issued 1973), 66–104.

———. "Folklig sed med rot i heden tid." *Arv* 2 (1946), 145–76.

———. "Svartkonstböcker i sägen och historia." *Saga och sed* (1959), 160–68.

Egardt, Brita. "De svenska vattenhästsägnerna och deras ursprung." *Folkkultur* 4 (1944), 119–66.

Ejdestam, Julius. *Årseldarnas samband med boskapsskötsel och åkerbruk i Sverige* (Skrifter utg. genom Landsmåls- och folkminnesarkivet i Uppsala. Serie B. 2). Uppsala, 1944.

———. "Omfärd vid besittningstagande av jordegendom." *Svenska landsmål* 69 (1946), 86–114.

Ek, Sven. *Tre svartkonstböcker* (Eslövs museums skriftserie 2). Eslöv, 1964.

Engebretsen, K. Weel, and Erling Johansen. *Sagn fra Østfold* (Norsk folkeminnelags skrifter 59). Oslo, 1947.

Ernvik, Arvid. *Folkminnen från Glaskogen. Sägen, tro och sed i västvärmländska skogsbygder* 1 (Skrifter utg. genom Landsmåls- och folkminnesarkivet i Uppsala. Serie B. 12:1). Uppsala, 1966.

Eskeröd, Albert. *Årets äring. Etnologiska studier i skördens och julens tro och sed* (Nordiska Museets handlingar 26). Stockholm, 1947.

Faye, Andreas. *Norske Sagn.* Arendal, 1833. 2d edition, *Norske Folke-Sagn.* Oslo: Guldberg and Dzwonkowskis Forlag, 1844. 3d edition (Norsk folkeminnelags skrifter 63). Oslo, 1948.

Feilberg, Henning Frederik. *Bidrag til en ordbog over jyske almuesmål.* 4 vols. Copenhagen, 1886–1914.

———. *Bjærgtagen. En studie over en gruppe træk fra nordisk alfetro* (Danmarks folkeminder 5). Copenhagen: Det Schønbergske Forlag, 1910.

———. *Jul.* 2 vols. Copenhagen, 1904. Reprinted Copenhagen: Rosenkilde and Bagger, 1962.

———. *Nissens historie.* (Danmarks folkeminder 18). Copenhagen: Det Schønbergske Forlag, 1919.

———. *Sjæletro* (Danmarks folkeminder 10). Copenhagen: Det Schønbergske Forlag, 1914.

Finska Studentkårens album tillegnadt Elias Lönnrot på åttionde årsdagen af hans födelse. Helsingfors, 1882.

Fjellstad, Lars M. *Gammalt frå Elvrom* (Norsk folkeminnelags skrifter 57). Oslo, 1945.

———. *Haugfolk og trollskap. Folkeminne frå Eidskog* 2 (Norsk folkeminnelags skrifter 74). Oslo, 1954.

Flatin, Kjetil A. *Gamle hermennar fraa Telemork.* Skien: Oluf Rasmussen, 1913.

———. *Tussar og trolldom.* Edited by Tov Flatin (Norsk folkeminnelags skrifter 21). Oslo, 1930.

Flatin, Tov. *Gamalt frå Numedal* 6 vols. Oslo, Risør: Nordli, Erik Gunleikson, 1913–28.

Forsslund, Karl-Erik. *Med Dalälven från källorna till havet. 1: Österdalälven. 8: Rättvik.* Stockholm: Åhlén and Åkerlund, 1922.

Fossenius, Maja. "Sägnerna om trollen Finn och Skalle som byggmästare." *Folkkultur* 3 (1943), 5–144.

Frazer, James. *The Golden Bough. A Study in Magic and Religion.* 12 vols. London: Macmillan, 1911–15.

Frykman, Jonas. *Horan i bondesamhället.* Lund: Liber, 1977.

Gaerte, W. "Wetterzauber im späten Mittelalter." *Rheinisches Jahrbuch für Volkskunde* 3 (1952), 226–73.

Geijer, Herman. "En gosses märkvärdiga upplevelser." *Svenska landsmål* (1913), 99–142.

Genzmer, Felix. "Da signed Krist- thû biguol' en Wuodan." *Arv* 5 (1949), 37–68.

Gerndt, Helge. *Fliegender Holländer und Klabautermann* (Schriften zur Niederdeutschen Volkskunde 4). Göttingen: Otto Schwartz, 1971.

Granberg, Gunnar. *Skogsrået i yngre nordisk folktradition.* (Skrifter utg. av Kungl. Gustav Adolfs akademien 3). Uppsala, 1935.

Granlund, John. "Curing *Knarren* (Peritendinitis or Tendovaginitis). A Popular Healing-Art." *Arv* 18/19 (1962/63), 187–225.

———. "Vindmagi." *KLNM* 20 (1976), columns 98–100.

Grimm, Jacob, and Wilhelm Grimm. *Deutsche Sagen.* 2 vols. Berlin: Nicolai, 1816–18.

Grimstad, Edvard. *Etter gamalt. Folkeminne fra Gudbrandsdalen* 2 (Norsk folkeminnelags skrifter 62). Oslo, 1948.

———. *Etter gamalt. Folkeminne fra Gudbrandsdalen* 3 (Norsk folkeminnelags skrifter 71). Oslo, 1953.

Grundtvig, Svend. *Gamle danske Minder.* 3 vols. Copenhagen: C. G. Iversen, 1854–61. Reprinted (Danmarks folkeminder 70). Copenhagen: Akademisk Forlag, 1970.

Haavio, Martti. "Der Tod des Grossen Pan. Mit Berücksichtigung neuen finnischen Materials." *Studia Fennica* 3 (1938), 113–36.

———. "Post equitem sedet atra cura." *Studia Fennica* 8 (1959), 11–22.

Hagberg, Louise. *När döden gästar. Svenska folkseder och svensk folktro i samband med död och begravning.* Stockholm: Wahlström and Widstrand, 1937.

Hämäläinen, Albert. "Beiträge zur Bildmagie." *Mitteilungen des Vereins für finnische Volkskunde* (1945), 15–27.

Hammarstedt, Nils Edvard. "Brödets helgd hos svenskarna, särskildt julbrödens, framställd i jämförande belysning." *Samfundet för Nordiska museets främjande. Meddelanden* (1893/94), 16–38.

———. "Kvarlevor af en Frösritual i en svensk bröllopslek." *Svenska landsmål* (1911), 489–517.

——. "Om smöjning och därmed befryndade bruk." *Samfundet för Nordiska museets främjande. Meddelanden* (1891/92), 34–45.

Hammershaimb, V. U. "Færøiske sagn." *Annaler for nordisk Oldkyndighed og Historie* (1846), 358–63. Reprinted in Hammershaimb. *Savn* (1969), 20–25.

——. Færøiske folkesagn." *Antiquarisk Tidsskrift* (1849/51), 170–208, 322–40. Reprinted in Hammershaimb. *Savn* (1969), 114–52, 204–22.

——. *Færøsk anthologi*. 2 vols. Copenhagen: Gyldendal, 1886–91. 3d edition. Tórshavn: Emil Thomsen, 1969.

——. *Savn úr Annaler for nordisk Oldkyndighed og Historie og Antiquarisk Tidsskrift*. Tórshavn: Emil Thomsen, 1969.

Hampp, Irmgard. *Beschwörung, Segen, Gebet. Untersuchungen zum Zauberspruch aus dem Bereich der Volksheilkunde*. Stuttgart: Silberburg Verlag Werner Jäckh, 1961.

Hartmann, Elisabeth. *Die Trollvorstellungen in den Sagen und Märchen der skandinavischen Völker*. Stuttgart und Berlin: Kohlhammer, 1936.

Harva, Uno. "Bjärans klotform. En komparativ studie." *Rig* 10 (1927), 161–72.

Hauge, Hans-Egil. "Den sterke hustruen." *Arv* 2 (1946), 1–34.

——. *Levande begravd eller bränd i nordisk folkmedicin. En studie i offer och magi* (Acta Universitatis Stockholmiensis. Stockholm Studies in Comparative Religion 6). Stockholm, 1965.

Hedberg, Gunnel. "Straffredskap." *KLNM* 17 (1972), columns 281–89.

Heilfurth, Gerhard, unter Mitarbeit von Ina-Maria Greverus. *Bergbau und Bergmann in der deutschsprachigen Sagenüberlieferung Mitteleuropas* 1. Marburg: Elvert, 1967.

Helland, Amund. *Topografisk-statistisk beskrivelse over Søndre Bergenhus Amt* 1 (Norges land og folk 12). Oslo, 1921.

Henningsen, Gustav. "Trolddom og hemmelige kunster." *Dagligliv i Danmark i det syttende og attende århundrede*. 161–96. Copenhagen: Nyt Nordisk Forlag Arnold Busck, 1969.

Hermundstad, Knut. *Gamletidi talar. Gamal Valdreskultur* 1 (Norsk folkeminnelags skrifter 36). Oslo 1936.

——. *Ættarminne. Gamal Valdreskultur* 5 (Norsk folkeminnelags skrifter 70). Oslo, 1952.

——. *I kvelseta. Gamal Valdreskultur* 6 (Norsk folkeminnelags skrifter 75). Oslo, 1955.

——. *Kvorvne tider. Gamal Valdreskultur* 7 (Norsk folkeminnelags skrifter 86). Oslo, 1961.

Herranen, Gun. "Historical Legends Expressing Nationalism in a Minority Culture." *Folklore on Two Continents. Essays in Honor of Linda Dégh*. Edited by N. Burlakoff and C. Lindahl, 334–39. Bloomington, Ind.: Trickster Press, 1980.

Heurgren, Paul. *Husdjuren i nordisk folktro*. Örebro, 1925.

Hirschberg. "Schatz." *Handwörterbuch des deutschen Aberglaubens* 7, columns 1002–15. Berlin: de Gruyter, 1935–36.

Hobsbawm, E. J. *Primitive Rebels: Studies in Archaic Forms of Social Movement in the 19th and 20th Centuries.* Manchester: Manchester University Press, 1959. 3d edition, 1971.

Hodne, Bjarne. *Å leve med døden. Folkelige forestillinger om døden og de døde.* Oslo: Aschehoug, 1980.

———. *Personalhistoriske sagn. En studie i kildeverdi.* Oslo: Universitetsforlaget, 1973.

Hodne, Ørnulf. "Trolldomssaken mot Spå-Eiliv. En undersøkelse av holdninger." *Norveg* 24 (1981), 7–40.

Høeg, Ove Arbo. *Planter og tradisjon.* Oslo: Universitetsforlaget, 1974.

Hofberg, Herman. *Svenska folksägner.* Stockholm: Fr. Skoglund, 1882.

Holbek, Bengt. "Maria i folketraditionen." *KLNM* 11 (1966), columns 367–73.

———. "Nordic Research in Popular Prose Narrative." (Commentaries by Satu Apo, Bjarne Hodne, and Jan-Öjvind Swahn.) (Trends in Nordic Tradition Research.) *Studia Fennica* 27 (1983), 145–76.

———, and Iørn Piø. *Fabeldyr og sagnfolk.* Copenhagen: Politikens Forlag, 1967.

Holmberg, Uno. See Harva, Uno.

Holmström, Helge. "Sägnerna om äktenskap med maran." *FmFt* 5 (1918), 135–45.

Honko, Lauri. "Folkmedicinen i utvecklings-perspektiv." *Tradisjon* 8 (1978), 1–26.

———. *Geisterglaube in Ingermanland* 1 (FFC 185). Helsinki, 1962.

———. "Genre Analysis in Folkloristics and Comparative Religion." *Temenos* 3 (1968), 48–66.

———. "Genre Theory Revisited." (Commentaries by Robert Austerlitz and R. Schenda.) *Studia Fennica* 20 (1976), 20–29.

———. *Krankheitsprojektile. Untersuchung über eine urtümliche Krankheitserklärung* (FFC 178). Helsinki, 1959.

———. "Memorates and the Study of Folk Beliefs." *Journal of the Folklore Institute* 1 (1965), 5–19.

———, and Orvar Löfgren, eds. *Tradition och miljö. Ett kultur-ekologiskt perspektiv* (Skrifter utg. av Etnologiska sällskapet i Lund 13 and Nordic Institute of Folklore Publications 11). Lund, 1981.

Höttges, Valerie. *Die Sage vom Riesenspielzeug.* Jena: Diederichs, 1931.

Hufford, David. "A New Approach to the Old Hag: The Nightmare Tradition Reexamined." *American Folk Medicine.* Edited by W. D. Hand, 73–85. Berkeley, Los Angeles, London: University of California Press, 1976.

Hultkrantz, Åke. "Miscellaneous Belief. Some Points of View Concerning the Informal Religious Sayings." *Temenos* 3 (1968), 67–82.

———, ed. *The Supernatural Owners of Nature. Nordic Symposium on the Religious*

Conceptions of Ruling Spirits (genii loci, genii speciei) and allied concepts (Acta Universitatis Stockholmiensis. Stockholm Studies in Comparative Religion 1). Stockholm, 1961.

Hveding, Johan. *Folketru og folkeliv på Hålogaland* 1–2 (Norsk folkeminnelags skrifter 33 and 53). Oslo, 1935–44.

Hyltén-Cavallius, G. O. *Wärend och wirdarna* 2 vols. Stockholm: Norstedt, 1863–68. 3d edition. Lund: Gleerup, 1972.

Jacobsen, Jørgen Carl. *Djævlebesværgelse. Træk af exorcismens historie.* Copenhagen: Gad, 1972.

Jakobsen, Jakob. *Færøske folkesagn og æventyr.* Copenhagen: Gyldendal, 1898–1901. New edition, Tórshavn: H. N. Jacobsens bókahandil, 1961–64.

Joensen, J. Pauli. " 'Lemperen' eller 'Manden ombord'." *Arv* 31 (1975), 74–108.

Johansons, Andrejs. *Der Schirmherr des Hofes im Volksglauben der Letten. Studien über Orts-, Hof- und Hausgeister* (Acta Universitatis Stockholmiensis. Stockholm Studies in Comparative Religion 5). Stockholm, 1964.

Johnsen, Birgit Hertzberg. "Her Ulve Mand har revet Aar Seksten Hundred Tolv. Tradisjon, miljø og verdirelatering — en sagn — studie." *Norveg* 23 (1980), 155–94.

Kalén, Johan. "Hämndegåvan: några ord om en sägentyp." *FmFt* 22 (1935), 107–20.

Kamp, Jens. *Dansk folketro.* Edited by Inger M. Boberg (Danmarks folkeminder 51). Copenhagen: Munksgaard, 1943.

———. *Danske folkeminder. Æventyr, folkesagn, gaader, rim og folketro.* Odense: R. Nielsens Forlag, 1877.

Klein, Barbro. "The Testimony of the Button." *Journal of the Folklore Institute* 8 (1971), 127–46.

Klintberg, Bengt af. "Folksägner i dag." *Fataburen* (1976), 269–96. Reprinted in af Klintberg. *Harens klagan*, 151–88. Stockholm: Pan/Norstedt, 1978.

———. " 'Gast' in Swedish Folk Tradition." *Temenos* 3 (1968), 83–109.

———. *Harens klagan och andra uppsatser om folklig diktning.* Stockholm: Pan/Norstedt, 1978. Enlarged edition, 1982.

———. " 'Jag såg Jesus i Vadstena'. Berättelser om oförklarliga händelser." *Tradisjon* 3 (1973), 31–50.

———. "Magisk diktteknik." *Ta* 3 (1967), 20–27. Reprinted in af Klintberg. *Harens klagan*, 7–21. Stockholm: Pan/Norstedt, 1978.

———. "Skall vi behålla våra genresystem?" *Folkloristikens aktuella paradigm.* Edited by Gun Herranen, 75–101. (Nordic Institute of Folklore Publications 10.) Turku, 1981.

———. *Svenska folksägner.* Stockholm: Pan/Norstedt, 1972.

———. *Svenska trollformler.* Stockholm: Wahlström and Widstrand, 1965. New edition. Stockholm: Tiden, 1980.

Kramer, Heinrich, and Jacob Sprenger. *Malleus Maleficarum.* (Speyer) 1485.

English translation (*The Witches' Hammer*) by M. Summers. London: John Rodker, 1928. Reprint. The Puskin Press, 1951.

Kretzenbacher, Leopold. "Freveltanz und Überzähliger." *Carinthia* 1 (1954), 843–66.

——. *Kynokephale Dämonen südosteuropäischer Volksdichtung.* Munich: Rudolf Trofenik, 1968.

——. "Tanzverbot und Warnlegende. Ein mittelalterliches Predigt-exempel in der steirischen Barockpassologie." *Rheinisches Jahrbuch für Volkskunde* 12 (1961), 16–22.

——. *Teufelsbündner und Faustgestalten im Abendlande* (Buchreihe des Landesmuseum für Kärnten 23). Klagenfurt, 1968.

Kriss, Marika. *Werewolves, Shapeshifters, and Skinwalkers.* Los Angeles: Sherbourne Press, 1972.

Kristensen, Evald Tang. *Danske sagn som de har lydt i folkemunde.* 7 vols. Århus, Silkeborg, 1892–1901. New series. 7 vols. Copenhagen: Nyt Nordisk Forlag Arnold Busck, 1928–39.

——. *Danske Skjæmtesagn.* Aarhus, 1900.

——. *Gamle Folks Fortællinger om det jyske Almueliv.* 12 vols. Kolding and Copenhagen: Gyldendal et al., 1891–1902.

——. *Gamle kildevæld.* Viborg: Bakkes Boghandel, 1927.

——. *Jyske folkeminder.* 13 vols. Copenhagen, Kolding, Århus: Gyldendal et al., 1871–97.

——, and Peter Olsen et al. *Gamle kildevæld. Portrætter af danske eventyrfortællere og visesangere fra århundredskiftet.* Copenhagen: Nyt Nordisk Forlag Arnold Busck, 1981.

Kulturhistorisk leksikon for nordisk middelalder. 22 vols. Oslo: Gyldendal, 1956–78.

Künzig, Johannes. "Der im Fischbauch wiedergefundene Ring in Sage, Legende, Märchen und Lied." *Volkskundliche Gaben John Meier dargebracht,* 85–103. Berlin: de Gruyter, 1934.

Kvideland, Reimund. "Det stod i avisa! Når vandrehistorier blir avismeldingar." *Tradisjon* 3 (1973), 1–12.

——. "Stories About Death as a Part of Children's Socialization." *Folklore on Two Continents. Essays in Honor of Linda Dégh.* Edited by N. Burlakoff and C. Lindahl, 59–64. Bloomington, Ind.: Trickster Press, 1980.

Landtmann, Gunnar. "Hustomtens förvantskap och härstamning." *Folkloristiska och etnografiska studier* 3 (1922), 1–48.

Langset, Edvard. *Segner, gåter, folketru frå Nordmør* (Norsk folkeminnelags skrifter 61). Oslo, 1948.

Lid, Nils *Joleband og vegetasjonsguddom* (Det Norske videnskaps-akademi i Oslo. Skrifter 2. Hist.-filos. klasse 1928, 4). Oslo, 1928.

——. *Jolesveinar og gröderikdomsgudar* (Det Norske videnskaps-akademi i Oslo. Skrifter 2. Hist.-filos. klasse 1932, 5). Oslo, 1933.

——. "Jordsmøygjing." *Norsk aarbok* (1922), 81–88.

——. "Magiske fyrestellingar og bruk." *Nordisk kultur 19. Folktru*, 3–76. Stockholm: Bonnier, 1935.
——. *Norske slakteskikkar* 1 (Det Norske videnskaps-akademi i Oslo. Skrifter 2. Hist.-filos. klasse 1923, 4). Oslo, 1924.
——. "Til varulvens historia." *Saga och sed* (1937), 3–25.
——. *Trolldom. Nordiske studiar*. Oslo: Cammermeyer, 1950.
——, and Matti Kuusi. "Biletmagi." *KLNM* 1 (1956), columns 540–42.
Lie, John, and Hallvor Lie. *Gaamaalt etti bestemor*. Edited by Rikard Berge (Norske folkeminnesamlarar 2, 5). Risør: Norsk folkekulturs forlag, 1925.
Liestøl, Knut. *Norsk folkedikting 3. Segner*. Oslo: Det norske samlaget, 1939.
——. *Norske ættesogor*. Oslo: Norli, 1922.
——. *The Origin of the Icelandic Family Sagas* (Instituttet for sammenlignende kulturforskning. Serie A. Forelesninger 10). Oslo, 1930.
——. *Upphavet til den islandske ættesaga* (Instituttet for sammenlignende kulturforskning. Serie A. Forelesninger 10a). Oslo, 1929.
Linderholm, Emanuel. *Signelser ock besvärjelser från medeltid ock nytid* (Svenska landsmål, B: vol. 41). Uppsala, 1917–40.
Lindow, John. "Personification and Narrative Structure in Scandinavian Plague Legends." *Arv* 29/30 (1973/74), 83–92.
——. *Swedish Legends and Folktales*. Berkeley, Los Angeles, and London: University of California Press, 1978.
——. "Swedish Legends of Buried Treasure." *Journal of American Folklore* 95 (1982), 157–79.
Lindqvist, Nat. *En isländsk svartkonstbok från 1500-talet*. Uppsala, 1921.
Liungman, Waldemar. "Finnsägenproblemet." *FmFt* 29 (1942), 86–113, 138–54.
——. *Sveriges sägner i ord och bild*. 7 vols. Stockholm and Djursholm: Vald litteratur, 1957–69.
Lixfeld, Hannjost. "Die Guntramsage (AT 1645A). Volkserzählungen vom Alter Ego in Tiergestalt und ihre schamanistische Herkunft." *Fabula* 13 (1972), 60–107.
Löfgren, Orvar. *Fångstmän i industrisamhället*. Lund: Liber, 1977.
——. "Fetströmming och lusmörtar. Folktro och kognitiva system i två kustbygder." *Sista lasset in. Studier tillägnade Albert Eskeröd*, 321–42. Stockholm: Nordiska museet, 1975.
Lövkrona, Inger. *Det bortrövade dryckeskärlet. En sägenstudie* (Skrifter från Folklivsarkivet i Lund 24). Lund, 1982.
Løwold, Oluf. *Præstehistorier og sagn*. Stavanger, 1891.
Ludvigsen, Peter. "Selvmord—sagn og virkelighed." *Tradisjon* 7 (1977), 91–102.
Lukman, Niels C. "Finn og St. Laurentius i Lund og i Cantebury." *Arkiv för nordisk filologi* 75 (1960), 194–237.
Lunde, Peter. *Folkeminne frå Søgne* (Norsk folkeminnelags skrifter 103). Oslo, 1969.

———. *Kynnehuset. Vestegdske folkeminne* (Norsk folkeminnelags skrifter 6). Oslo, 1924.

Lundell, J. A., M. Eriksson, and G. Hedström et al. *Sagor, sägner, legender, äventyr och skildringar av folkets levnadssätt på landsmål* (Svenska landsmål 3:3). Uppsala, 1881–1946.

Lüthi, Max. "Gehalt und Erzählweise der Volkssage." *Sagen und ihre Deutung*, 11–27. Göttingen: Vandenhoeck und Ruprecht, 1965.

———. *Volksmärchen und Volkssage: Zwei Grundformen erzählender Dichtung.* Bern and Munich: Francke, 1961.

Mannhardt, Wilhelm. *Wald- und Feldkulte.* 2 vols. Berlin: Bornträger, 1875–77.

Martin, A. "Geschichte der Tanzkrankheit in Deutschland." *Zeitschrift für Volkskunde* 24 (1914), 113–34, 225–39.

Mauland, Torkell. *Folkeminne fraa Rogaland* 1–2 (Norsk folkeminnelags skrifter 17 and 26). Oslo, 1928–31.

Maurer, Konrad. *Isländische Volkssagen der Gegenwart.* Leipzig: Hinrichs, 1860.

Maurer, Warren R. "German Sunken City Legends." *Fabula* 17 (1976), 189–214.

Mehlum, And. *Hallingdal og Hallingen.* Drammen, 1891–93. New edition. Røyse, 1943.

Mo, Ragnvald. *Eventyr og segner, barnerim, ordtak og gåter. Folkeminne frå Salten* 2 (Norsk folkeminnelags skrifter 54). Oslo, 1944.

———. *Soge og segn. Folkeminne frå Salten* 3 (Norsk folkeminnelags skrifter 69). Oslo, 1952.

Moe, Moltke. *Folkeminne frå Bøherad* (Norsk folkeminnelags skrifter 9). Oslo, 1925.

Møller, J. S. *Moder og barn i dansk folkeoverlevering* (Danmarks folkeminder 48). Copenhagen: Munksgaard, 1939–40.

Mørch, Andreas. *Frå gamle dagar. Folkeminne frå Sigdal og Eggedal* (Norsk folkeminnelags skrifter 27). Oslo, 1932.

Mundal, Else. *Fylgjemotiva i norrøn litteratur.* Oslo: Universitetsforlaget, 1974.

Nergaard, Sigurd. *Gard og grend. Folkeminne fraa Østerdalen* 1 (Norsk folkeminnelags skrifter 3). Oslo, 1921.

———. *Hulder og trollskap. Folkeminne fraa Østerdalen* 4 (Norsk folkeminnelags skrifter 11). Oslo, 1925.

Nielsen, J. E. *Søgnir fraa Hallingdal.* Oslo: Det norske samlaget, 1868. 3d edition by Reidar Djupedal. Oslo: Det norske samlaget, 1968.

Nikander, Gabriel. "Fruktbarhetsriter under årshögtiderna hos svenskarna i Finland." *Folkloristiska och etnografiska studier* 1 (1916), 195–315.

Nilsson, Martin P. "Julen." *Nordisk kultur* 22. *Årets högtider*, 14–63. Stockholm: Bonnier, 1938.

Nilsson, Ragnar, and Carl-Martin Bergstrand. *Folktro och folksed på Värmlandsnäs. Folkminnen från Näs härad* 3. *Sagor, sägner, visor och övrig folkdiktning.* Göteborg: Gumperts, 1962.

Nordbø, Halvor. *Ættesogor frå Telemark* (Det Norske videnskaps-akademi i Oslo. Skrifter 2. Hist.-filos. klasse 1928, 1). Oslo, 1928.

Nordbø, Olav. *Segner og sogur frå Bøherad* (Norsk folkeminnelags skrifter 56). Oslo, 1945.

Nordin-Grip, Imber. *Mellösa i Sörmland*. Mellösa: M. Eriksson, 1964.

——. *Pintorpafrun* (Sörmländska handlingar 8). Eskilstuna, 1942.

Nordland, Odd. "Mannbjørn." *By og bygd* 11 (1957), 133–56.

Norlén, Gunnar. " 'Blås Kajsa'. Kring en svensk sjömanstradition." *Svenska landsmål* (1972), 61–83.

Norlind, Tobias. *Skattsägner* (Lunds Universitets årsskrift. New series, part 1, vol. 14, no. 17). Lund, 1918.

——. *Studier i svensk folklore* (Lunds Universitets årsskrift. New series, part 1, vol. 7, no 5). Lund, 1911.

Odstedt, Ella. *Varulven i svensk folktradition* (Skrifter utg. genom Landsmåls- och folkminnesarkivet i Uppsala. Serie B. 1). Uppsala, 1943.

Ohlson (Odstedt), Ella. "Naturväsen i ångermanländsk folktro." *FmFt* 20 (1933), 70–112.

Ohlsson, Hans. "Kycklingen i hatten." *Nord-Nytt* (1976), 51–70.

Ohrt, Ferdinand. *Da signed Krist-. Tolkning af det religiöse indhold i Danmarks signelser og besværgelser*. Copenhagen: Gyldendal, 1927.

——. *Danmarks trylleformler*. 2 vols. Copenhagen and Oslo: Gyldendal, 1917–21.

——. *De danske besværgelser mod vrid og blod. Tolkning og forhistorie* (Det Kongelige Danske Videnskabernes Selskab. Historisk-filologiske Meddelelser 7, 3). Copenhagen, 1922.

——. *Die ältesten Segen über Christi Taufe und Christi Tod in religionsgeschichtlichem Lichte* (Det Kongelige Danske Videnskabernes Selskab. Historisk-filologiske Meddelelser 25, 1). Copenhagen, 1938.

——. *Trylleord. Fremmede og danske* (Danmarks folkeminder 25). Copenhagen: Det Schønbergske Forlag, 1922.

——. *Udvalgte Sønderjydske Folkesagn* (Danmarks folkeminder 21). Copenhagen: Det Schønbergske Forlag, 1919.

Olrik, Axel. *Nogle Grundsætninger for Sagnforskning*. Edited by Hans Ellekilde (Danmarks folkeminder 23). Copenhagen: Det Schønbergske Forlag, 1921.

——. *Nordens gudeverden*. 2 vols. Edited by Hans Ellekilde. Copenhagen: Gad, 1926–51.

Olrik, J. and H. Ræder, eds. *Saxonis Gesta Danorum*. 2 vols. Copenhagen, 1931–57.

Olsson, Edvard. *Värmländska folkminnen*. Edited by David Arill. Karlstad: Västsvenska folkminnesföreningen, 1932.

Olsson, Helmer. *Folkliv och folkdikt i Vättle härad under 1800-talet* (Acta Academiae Gustavi Adolphi 12). Uppsala, 1945.

——. "Odens jakt i Halland." *Vår bygd. Hallands hembygdsförbunds årsskrift* 25 (1940), 26–34.

———. "Sägnen om jätteleksaken." *FmFt* 22 (1935), 35–41.

Opedal, Halldor O. *Makter og menneske. Folkeminne ifrå Hardanger* 1–2 (Norsk folkeminnelags skrifter 23 and 32). Oslo, 1930–34.

Orend, Misch. "Vom Schwur mit Erde in den Schuhen. Die Entstehung einer Sage." *Deutsches Jahrbuch für Volkskunde* 4 (1958), 386–92.

Östlund, O. "Ur den gamla folktron." *Från By sockengille* 6 (1932), 17–19.

Pape, John. "Studier om kyrkogrimen." *Folkkultur* 6 (1946), 11–240.

Pentikäinen, Juha. "The Dead Without Status." *Temenos* 4 (1969), 92–102.

———. *The Nordic Dead-Child Tradition. Nordic Dead-Child Beings. A Study in Comparative Religion* (FFC 202). Helsinki, 1968.

Pesch, Joh. *Die Glocke in Geschichte, Sage, Volksglauben, Volksbrauch und Dichtung.* Dülmen: A. Laumann, 1918.

Petterson, Olof Petter. *Sagor från Åsele lappmark.* Edited by Herman Geijer et al. (Svenska sagor och sägner 9). Stockholm, 1945.

Petzoldt, Leander. *Deutsche Volkssagen.* Munich: Beck, 1970.

———. "AT 470: Friends in Life and Death. Zur Psychologie und Geschichte einer Wundererzählung." *Rheinisches Jahrbuch für Volkskunde* 19 (1968), 101–61.

———. *Historische Sagen. 1: Fahrten, Abenteuer und merkwürdige Begebenheiten, 2: Ritter, Räuber und geistliche Herren.* Munich: Beck, 1976–77.

Peuckert, Will-Erich. "Der Blocksberg." *Verborgenes Niedersachsen,* 103–10. Göttingen: Otto Schwartz, 1960.

———. *Deutscher Volksglauben des Spätmittelalters.* Stuttgart: Spemann, 1942.

———. *Lenore* (FFC 158). Helsinki, 1955.

———. *Sagen. Geburt und Antwort der mythischen Welt.* Berlin: Erich Schmidt, 1965.

———. "Sibylle." *Handwörterbuch des deutschen Aberglaubens* 7, columns 1655–59. Berlin: de Gruyter, 1935/36.

Piaschewski, Gisela. *Der Wechselbalg. Ein Beitrag zum Aberglauben der nordeuropäischen Völker* (Deutschkundliche Arbeiten. A. Allgemeine Reihe 5). Breslau, 1935.

Piø, Iørn. *Bank under bordet eller fem små kapitler af dagligdagens overtro.* Copenhagen: Foreningen Fremtiden, 1963.

Pontoppidan, Erik. *Fejekost til at udfeje den gamle Surdejg (1736).* Translated from Latin by J. Olrik (Danmarks folkeminder 27). Copenhagen: Det Schønbergske Forlag, 1923.

Prütting, Hildegunde. "Zur geschichtlichen Volkssage. Erscheinungsform und psychologische Struktur der volkstümlichen Geschichtsüberlieferung untersucht an den Sagen der Pfalz." *Bayerisches Jahrbuch für Volkskunde* (1953), 16–26.

Puhvel, Martin. "The Legend of the Devil-haunted Card Players in Northern Europe." *Folklore* 76 (1965), 33–38.

Rääf, Leonhard Fredrik. *Svenska skrock och signerier.* Edited by K. Rob. V.

Wikman (Kungl. Vitterhets historie och antikvitets akademiens handlingar. Filol.-filos. serien 4). Stockholm, 1957.

Reichborn-Kjennerud, Ingjald. *Vår gamle trolldomsmedisin*. 5 vols. (Det Norske videnskaps-akademi i Oslo. Skrifter 2. Hist.-filos. klasse 1927, 6; 1933, 2; 1940, 1; 1943, 2; 1947, 1.) Oslo, 1928–47.

Reinton, Lars. "Kildeverdien af historiske beretninger og andet traditionsstof fra eldre tider." *Fortid og nutid* 21 (1961), 185–97.

——. *Villandane. Ein etterrøknad i norsk ættesoge*. Oslo: Det Norske videnskaps-akademi i Oslo, 1939.

Rekdal, Olav. *Eventyr og segner. Folkeminne frå Romsdal* (Norsk folkeminnelags skrifter 30). Oslo, 1933.

Rencke, Karl. "Havsfolket." *Bohuslänska folkminnen*, Uddevalla, 1922.

Renvall, Lennart Torstensson. *Åländsk folktro, skrock och trolldom* (Svenska landsmål 7:9). Stockholm, 1890.

Ridderstad, Anton. *Östergötland 3. Fornsägner och kulturbilder från Östergötland*. Stockholm, 1920.

Röhrich, Lutz. "Die Frauenjagdsage (Motif E 501.5.1. Wild Hunters Pursue a Woman)," 408–23. (4th International Congress for Folk-Narrative Research in Athens.) Athens, 1965.

——. "Eine antike Grenzsage und ihre neuzeitliche Parallelen." *Würzburger Jahrbücher für Altertumswissenschaft* 4 (1949/59), 339–69.

——. *Erzählungen des späten Mittelalters und ihr Weiterleben in Literatur und Volksdichtung bis zur Gegenwart. Sagen, Märchen, Exempel und Schwänke*. 2 vols. Bern and Munich: Francke, 1962–67.

——. *Sage*. Stuttgart: Metzler, 1966.

——. "Sagenballade," *Handbuch des Volksliedes* 1, 101–56. Munich: Wilhelm Fink, 1973.

——. "Teufelsmärchen und Teufelssagen." *Sagen und ihre Deutung*. 28–58. Göttingen: Vandenhoeck and Ruprecht, 1965.

Rollenhagen, Georg. *Froschmeuseler. Der Frosch und Meuse wunderbare Hoffhaltung*. Magdeburg, 1595.

Rørbye, Birgitte. *Kloge folk og skidtfolk. Kvaksalveriets epoke i Danmark*. Copenhagen: Politikens Forlag, 1976.

——. "Nutidig folkemedicin." *Tradisjon* 8 (1978), 37–45. Also printed in *Unifol* (1977), 141–47.

Rosenberg, Alfus. *Engel und Dämon. Gestaltwandel eines Urbildes*. Munich: Prestel, 1967.

Rothman, Sven. *Östgötska folkminnen* (Skrifter utg. av Kungl. Gustav Adolfs Akademien 8). Uppsala, 1941.

Rühle, Oskar. "Abendmahl." *Handwörterbuch des deutschen Aberglaubens* 1, columns 42–55. Berlin: de Gruyter, 1927.

Russworm, Carl. *Eibofolke oder die Schweden an den Küsten Ehstlands und auf Runö*. Reval: Fleischer, 1855. Reprint, Hannover: Hirschheydt, 1969.

Rutberg, Hulda. *Häxprocesser i norska Finnmarken 1620–1692* (Svenska landsmål 16:4). Stockholm, 1918.

Sahlgren, Jöran. "Ortnamnssägner." *Saga och sed* (1945), 8–16.

——. "Sägnerna om trollen Finn och Skalle och deras kyrkobyggande." *Saga och sed* (1940), 1–50; (1941), 115–54.

Salveson, Aamund. *Folkeminne*. Stavanger, 1924.

Sandklef, Albert. *Kulknappen och Carl XII:s död*. Lund: Gleerup, 1941.

——, Carl-Fredrik Palmstierna, Nils Strömbom, and Samuel Clason. *Carl XII:s död*. Stockholm: Bonnier, 1940.

Schmidt, Leopold. *Die Volkserzählung. Märchen, Sage, Legende, Schwank*. Berlin: Erich Schmidt, 1963.

Schön, Ebbe. *Jan Fridegård. Proletärdiktaren och folkkulturen*. Stockholm: Wahlström and Widstrand, 1978.

Sigfússon, Sigfús. *Íslenzkar þjóðsögur og -sagnir*. 16 vols. Seyðfjöður and Reykjavik: Vikingsútgáfan, 1922–58.

Simpson, Jacqueline. *Icelandic Folktales and Legends*. Berkeley and Los Angeles: University of California Press, 1972.

——. *Legends of Icelandic Magicians*. Cambridge, Mass.: Brewer, 1975.

Skar, Johannes. *Gamalt or Sætesdal*. 8 vols. Oslo: Norli, 1903–16. New edition. 3 vols. Oslo: Det norske samlaget, 1961–63.

Skjelbred, Ann Helene. *Uren og hedning. Barselkvinnen i norsk folketradisjon*. Oslo: Universitetsforlaget, 1972.

Skjelsvik, Elizabeth. "Norwegian Lake and Sea Monsters." *Norveg* 7 (1960), 29–45.

Skrindsrud, Johan. *På heimleg grunn. Folkeminne frå Etnedal*. (Norsk folkeminnelags skrifter 77). Oslo, 1956.

Smedberg, Gunnar. "Kyrksägnerna från Jämtland och Härjedalen." *Forum Theologicum* 17 (1960), 87–116.

Søgaard, Helge. "Sagnet om den forsvundne og genfundne ring." *Sprog og kultur* 19 (1952), 69–79.

Sokolova, Vera K. "The Interaction of the Historical Legends with Other Folkloristic Genres." *Studia Fennica* 20 (1976), 58–66.

Solheim, Svale. "Byting." *KLNM* 2 (1957), columns 452–56.

——. "Tradisjonen om sjödraugen." *Norveg* 15 (1972), 43–57.

——. "Gardvoren og senga hans." *Maal og minne* (1951), 143–58. Reprinted in *Norveg* 16 (1973), 55–70.

——. "Historical Legend—Historical Function." *Acta Ethnographica Academiae Scientiarum Hungaricae* 19 (1970), 341–46. Norwegian edition: "Historisk segn—historisk funksjon." *Norveg* 16 (1973), 141–47.

——. *Norsk sætertradisjon* (Instituttet for sammenlignende kulturforskning. Serie B. Skrifter 47). Oslo, 1952.

——. "Segna om Hulabaken." *Tidsskrift for Valdres historielag* (1958), 67–75.

Spamer, Adolf. *Romanusbüchlein. Historisch-philologischer Kommentar zu einem deutschen Zauberbuch. Aus seinem Nachlass bearb. von Johanna Nickel*

(Veröffentlichungen des Instituts für deutsche Volkskunde 17). Berlin: Akademie-Verlag, 1958.

Stattin, Jochum. *Näcken. Spelman eller gränsvakt?* (Skrifter utg. av Etnologiska Sällskapet i Lund 14.) Lund: Liber, 1984.

Stender-Pettersen, Adolf. "Quemadmodum efficiatur, ut abundare uideantur, quae deerunt," *Festskrift til L. L. Hammerich*, 230–41. Copenhagen: Gad, 1952.

Storaker, Joh. Th. *Elementerne i den norske Folketro* (Norsk folkeminnelags skrifter 10). Oslo, 1924.

——. *Menneskelivet i den norske Folketro* (Norsk folkeminnelags skrifter 34). Oslo, 1935.

——. *Mennesket og Arbeidet i den norske Folketro* (Norsk folkeminnelags skrifter 41). Oslo, 1938.

——. *Naturrigerne i den norske Folketro* (Norsk folkeminnelags skrifter 18). Oslo, 1928.

——. *Rummet i den norske Folketro* (Norsk folkeminnelags skrifter 8). Oslo, 1932.

——. *Sygdom og Forgørelse i den norske Folketro* (Norsk folkeminnelags skrifter 28). Oslo, 1932.

——. *Tiden i den norske Folketro* (Norsk folkeminnelags skrifter 2). Oslo, 1921.

Strömbäck, Dag. "Att helga land. Studier i Landnáma och det äldsta rituella besittningstagandet." *Festskrift tillägnad Axel Hägerström*, 198–220. Stockholm: Almqvist and Wiksell, 1928. Reprinted in Strömbäck. *Folklore och filologi*, 135–65. Uppsala, 1970.

——. "Ein Beitrag zu den älteren Vorstellungen von der *mara*." *Arv* 32/33 (1976/77), 282–86.

——. The Concept of the Soul in Nordic Tradition." *Arv* 31 (1975), 5–22.

——. *Folklore och filologi* (Acta Academiae Gustavi Adolphi 48). Uppsala, 1970.

——. "Den första kyrkplatsen i sägen och folklig tro." *Religion och bibel* 17 (1958), 3–13. Reprinted in Strömbäck. *Folklore och filologi*, 123–134. Uppsala, 1970.

——. "Kölbigk och Hårga." *Arv* 17 (1961), 1–48; 24 (1968), 91–132.

——. "Näcken och förlossningen." *Varbergs Museum årsbok* (1963), 77–85. Reprinted in Strömbäck. *Folklore och filologi*, 115–22. Uppsala, 1970.

——. "Om varulven." *Svenska landsmål* (1943/44), 301–8.

——. *Sejd. Textstudier i nordisk religionshistoria* (Nordiska texter och undersökningar 5). Stockholm, 1935.

——. "Some Notes on the Nix in Older Nordic Tradition" *Medieval Literature and Folklore Studies: Essays in Honor of F. L. Utley*, 245–56. New Brunswick, N.J.: Rutgers University Press, 1970.

——. "Den underbara årsdansen." *Arkiv för nordisk filologi* 59 (1944), 111–26. Reprinted in Strömbäck. *Folklore och filologi*, 54–69. Uppsala 1970.

——, ed. *Leading Folklorists of the North. Biographical Studies.* Oslo: Universitetsforlaget, 1971. Also published in *Arv* 25–27 (1969–71).

Strompdal, Knut. *Gamalt frå Helgeland* 1–3 (Norsk folkeminnelags skrifter 19, 40, and 44). Oslo, 1929–39.

Summers, Montague. *The Werewolf.* 2d edition. New York: Bell Publishing Company, 1966.

Svare, Reidar. *Far etter fedrane. Folkeminne innsamla i Vefsn.* Mosjøen: Vefsn Historielag, 1950.

Sydow, Carl Wilhelm von. "Iriskt inflytande på nordisk guda- och hjältesaga." *Vetenskaps-societeten i Lund. Årsbok* (1920), 26–61.

——. "Jättarna i mytologi och folklore." *FmFt* 6 (1919), 135–42.

——. "Kategorien der Prosavolksdichtung." *Volkskundliche Gaben John Meier dargebracht*, 253–68. Berlin and Leipzig: de Gruyter, 1934. Also published in von Sydow. *Selected Papers*, 60–88. Copenhagen: Rosenkilde and Bagger, 1948. Swedish translation in A. B. Rooth. *Folkdikt och folktro*, 110–27. Lund: Gleerup, 1971.

——. "Prosit! —Gud Hjälp! Några folkliga föreställningar om nysning." *Skånska folkminnen. Årsbok* (1929), 12–18.

——. *Selected Papers on Folklore.* Copenhagen: Rosenkilde and Bagger, 1948.

——. *Sigurds strid med Fåvne* (Lunds Universitets årsskrift. New Series, part 1, vol. 14, no. 16). Lund, 1918.

——. Studier i Finnsägnen och besläktade byggmästarsägner." *Fataburen* (1907), 65–78, 199–218; (1908), 19–27.

——. "Trollbröllopet i säterstugan." *Fryksände förr och nu* 3 (1933), 99–103.

Taylor, Archer. "Northern Parallels to the Death of Pan." *Washington University Studies. Humanistic Series* 10 (1922), 3–102.

——. "The Pertinacious Cobold." *Journal of English and Germanic Philology* 31 (1932), 1–9.

Tellander, K. O. *Allmogelif i Vestergötland. Folklifsskildringar, sagor och sägner, visor, skrock och ordspråk.* Stockholm: Bonnier, 1891.

Thiele, Just M. *Danmarks Folkesagn.* 3 vols. Copenhagen: Reitzel, 1843–60.

Thompson, Stith. *The Folktale.* New York: Holt, Rinehart, and Winston, 1946. 3d edition. Berkeley: University of California Press, 1970.

Tillhagen, Carl-Herman. "Der internationale Sagenkatalog." (Tagung der International Society for Folk-Narrative Research, Antwerp, 6–8 September 1962. Berichte und Referate.) Edited by K. C. Peeters, 37–40. Antwerp, 1963.

——. "Die Berggeistvorstellungen in Schweden." *The Supernatural Owners of Nature.* Edited by Åke Hultkrantz, 123–57. Stockholm, 1961.

——. "The Concept of the Nightmare in Sweden." *Humaniora: Essays honoring Archer Taylor.* Edited by W. D. Hand and G. Holt, 317–29. Locust Valley, New York: J. J. Augustin, 1960.

——. *Fåglarne i folktron.* Stockholm: LTs förlag, 1978.

———. "Finnen und Lappen als Zauberkundige in der skandinavischen Volks-überlieferung." *Kontakte und Grenzen. Festschrift für G. Heilfurth*, 129–43. Göttingen: Otto Schwartz, 1969.

———. *Folklig läkekonst.* Stockholm: LTs förlag, 1958. 2d edition. 1962.

———. "Gruvskrock." *Norveg* 12 (1965), 113–60.

———. *Järnet och människorna. Verklighet och vidskepelse.* Stockholm: LTs förlag, 1981.

———. "Sägner och folktro kring pesten." *Fataburen* (1967), 215–30.

———. "Was ist eine Sage? Eine Definition und ein Vorschlag für ein europäisches Sagensystem." (Tagung der Sagenkommission der International Society for Folk-Narrative Research, Budapest, 14–16 Oktober, 1963.) Edited by G. Ortutay, 9–17. Budapest, 1964.

Tubach, Frederic C. *Index Exemplorum. A Handbook of Medieval Religious Tales* (FFC 204). Helsinki, 1961.

Tylor, Edward B. *Primitive Culture: Researches into the Development of Mythology, Philosophy, Religion, Art, and Custom.* 2 vols. London, 1871.

Uhrskov, Anders. *Sjællandske sagn.* Copenhagen: Gyldendal, 1932.

———. *Folkesagn.* Copenhagen: Aschehoug, 1922.

Vang, Andris Eivindson. *Gamla segner fraa Valdres.* Oslo: Abelsted, 1871.

———. *Gamla reglo aa rispo ifraa Valdres.* Oslo: Dybwad, 1850. New edition (Norsk folkeminnelags skrifter 111). Oslo: Universitetsforlaget, 1974.

Velure, Magne. "Hovuddrag i nordisk folketruforsking 1850–1975." *Fataburen* (1976), 21–48.

———. "Nordic Folk Belief Research: Schools and Approaches." (Commentaries by Ulf Drobin, Hallfreður Örn Eiríksson, and Anna-Leena Siikala.) (Trends in Nordic Tradition Research.) *Studia Fennica* 27 (1983), 111–44.

———. "Rykten och vitsar om invandrargrupper." *Kulturell kommunikation.* Edited by Nils-Arvid Bringéus and Göran Rosander, 144–56. Lund: Signum, 1979.

———. *Tradisjonen om fossegrimen og nøkken. Ein genreanalytisk studie.* Bergen: Etno-folkloristisk institutt, 1972.

Vinten, Elsebeth. *Islandske folkesagn og eventyr. Indsamling, tradition og traditionsmiljø* (Udgivelsesudvalgets samling af studenterafhandlinger 18). Odense, 1980.

Visted, Kristofer, and Hilmar Stigum. *Vår gamle bondekultur.* 3d edition. 2 vols. Oslo: Cappelen, 1971.

von Sydow, Carl Wilhelm. *See* Sydow, Carl Wilhelm von.

Vries, Jan de. *Altgermanische Religionsgeschichte.* 2 vols. Berlin: de Gruyter, 1970.

Wall, Jan. *Tjuvmjölkande väsen. 1. Äldre nordisk tradition. 2. Yngre nordisk tradition* (Studia ethnologica Upsaliensis 3 and 5). Uppsala, 1977–78.

Ward, Donald. "Berg." *Enzyklopädie des Märchens* 2, columns 138–46. Berlin: de Gruyter, 1979.

——. "The Little Man Who Wasn't There: On Encounters with the Supranormal." *Fabula* 18 (1977), 212–25.

Weiser-Aall, Lily. "Die Glückshaube in der norwegischen Überlieferung." *Saga och sed* (1960), 29–36.

——. "Germanische Hausgeister und Kobolde." *Niederdeutsche Zeitschrift für Volkskunde* 4 (1926), 7–19.

——. *Julehalmen i Norge* (Småskrifter fra Norsk etnologisk gransking 3). Oslo, 1953.

——. "En studie om vardøger." *Norveg* 12 (1965), 73–112.

——. *Svangerskap og fødsel i nyere norsk tradisjon* (Småskrifter fra Norsk etnologisk gransking 6/7). Oslo, 1968.

Wessman, V. E. V. *Sägner.* 3 vols. (Finlands svenska folkdiktning 2.) Helsingfors, 1924–31.

West, John F. *Faroese Folk-Tales and Legends.* Lerwick: Shetland Publishing Company, 1980.

Wigström, Eva. *Folkdiktning, samlad och upptecknad i Skåne.* Copenhagen: Karl Schønbergs boghandel, 1880.

——. *Folktro och sägner från skilda landskap* (Svenska landsmål 8:3). Stockholm, 1898–1914.

——. *Folktro och sägner från skilda landskap.* Edited by Aina Stenklo (Svenska sagor och sägner 11). Uppsala, 1952.

Wikman, K. Rob. V. "Förskrivning till djävulen." *Fataburen (1960),* 193–99.

——. "Magiska bindebruk." *Hembygden* (1912), 65–73, 116–17.

Wildhaber, Robert. "Die Eierschalen in europäischem Glauben und Brauch." *Acta Ethnographica Academiae Scientiarum Hungaricae* 19 (1970), 435–57.

——. "Die Stunde ist da, aber der Mann nicht. Ein europäisches Sagenmotiv." *Rheinisches Jahrbuch für Volkskunde* 9 (1958), 65–88.

Woods, Barbara Allen. *The Devil in Dog Form* (Folklore Studies 11). Berkeley, Los Angeles, London, 1959.

INDEX

Index

General Index

Adam of Bremen, 61.15n
Adultery, 67.1
Afterlife, 14.1–14.4, 15.1
Angel, 44.2, 60.15
Anti-legend, 66.4–66.6
"Armadr." *See* Supranormal beings, farm sprite
Arthur, king, 53.5n, 57.1n
AT 470, 89–90
AT 758 44.1
AT 875. *Cf.* 57.3
AT 1645A. *See* 11.1
Atlantis, 52.15n

Baptizing a murdered child, 25.1
Bartholomeus Anglicus, 32.1n
Beggar, 3.1
Berserk, 75
Binding the dead, 19.1–19.4
Black book, 54.3n, 54.6–54.7
Black Death: general description, 344, 35.2, 60.1–60.15
Black Plague. *See* Black Death
Black School, Wittenberg: general description, 279, 43.4, 54.8
Blasphemy, 62.3
Blessed island, 52.15
Blood stopping, 28.4–28.6
Boundary, 57.4–57.7
Boundary, ghost. *See* Revenant

Bürger, G. A., 91
Burial, dishonest, 112

Cap (shirt) of victory, 9.8–9.10
Changeling. *See* Supranormal beings
Charlemagne, 57.1n
Charles XII of Sweden, 61.9–61.11
Chinese restaurant, 64.2
Cholera, 60.3
Church bell, 58.4–58.6
Churches, 58.1–58.6
Chronicat: King's messenger spread cholera, 60.3
Comet, 61.1
Cyprianus. *See* Black book

Dance epidemic, 51.4n
Darnel soup, 61.25
Dass, Petter, 54.10
Dead, 85, 14.1–27.7: binding the dead 19.1–19.4; dead lover returns, 16.1; midnight mass of the dead, 93, 17.1–17.2; neglected provisions for burial, 21.1–21.3
Death, 13.1–13.3, 14.1–14.4
Denmark, Danes, 61.1, 61.5, 61.7–61.8
Devil: general description 279, 54.1–54.17; contract with the devil, 14.3, 54.2–54.3, 62.2; devil fetched the bride, 54.16; devil flayed the dead, 54.17
Diderik of Bern, 53.5n

419

Dog-headed people. *See* Kalmycks
"Draug." *See* Supranormal beings, revenant, sea sprite
Dream soul. *See* Soul
Drum of the fairies, 61.2

Edda, Elder or Poetic, 159, 56.3n
Edda, Snorri's or Prose, 159, 312
"Elsk." *See* Soul
English, war with, 61.16
English blockade, 61.25n
Envy. *See* Soul
Epidemic. *See also* Black Death, 60.3, 60.7
Evil eye, evil foot, evil hand, evil tongue. *See* Soul
Exorcism, 54.1

Fairy lover: general description, 214; 46.1–46.11
Fairy ring, 45.7n
Famine, 61.25
Faust, Johannes, 54.3n
Finland, 61.6, 61.17, 61.23
Finn, troll, 55.11
Finns, 10.1–10.3, 12.6–12.7, 12.9–12.10, 30.5, 34.4, 38.2, 43.1, 60.7, 61.3, 61.6
Finn-shot, 29.4, 29.6
Fire, quenching, 9.9, 9.10, 30.3
Fleming, Sir, 62.4–62.5
Food magic. *See* Witchcraft
Formula, magic, 4.2, 5.3, 18.2, 28.1, 28.5–29.1, 29.3–30.1, 30.4, 30.6–31.1, 32.4, 39.2, 51.11, 54.1, 56.1–56.2, 60.5
"Fossegrim." *See* Supranormal beings, water sprite
Frederik Barbarossa, 57.1n
Funeral singer, 18.7
"Fylgje." *See* Soul

"Gardvord." *See* Supranormal beings, farm sprite
"Gast." *See* Revenant
Giant. *See* Troll
Gottfred of Ghemen, 51.5n
Greed, 23.1–23.2, 57.5, 60.10
Grief, 6.3
"Grim." *See* Supranormal beings, water sprite

"Gruvfröken." *See* Supranormal beings, mine sprite
"Gruvrå." *See* Supranormal beings, mine sprite
Guntram, king of Burgundians, 73
Gyllenstierna, Anna, 62.2n
Gypsies, 3.1, 42.1, 63.4

Hallucination, 61.7
"Ham." *See* Soul
Handshake, the old troll's, 52.6, 55.2, 57.1
"Haugbo." *See* Supranormal beings, farm sprite
Healers, 28.1–29.7
Healing, 1.6–1.7, 3.1–3.3, 28.1–29.7, 58.3, 59.1
Healing power of the holy image, 58.3
Healing spring, 59.1
Hill folk. *See* Supranormal beings
Hill man. *See* Supranormal beings
Holger the Dane, 57.1
Holy image, 58.3
Homesickness, 29.7
"Hug." *See* Soul
Hypnosis, 33.1–33.2

Icelandic bishoprics, 57.7
Illness, 1.4, 1.6–1.7, 3.1–3.4, 9.4, 28.1–29.7
Immigrant, 64.1
Insanity, 9.4, 159
Invisible folk. *See* Supranormal beings
Iron work, 48.5

Jens Kusk, healer, 28.2, 29.2
Jesus, 65.3–65.5
Joen's hunt. *See* Oskorei
"Jolareidi." *See* Supranormal beings, oskorei

Kalmycks, 61.15
King, 57.1–57.3, 59.1–59.5, 61.9–61.11
Klabautermann. *See* Supranormal beings, sea sprite, 48.14n
"Kvarngubbe." *See* Supranormal beings, mill sprite
"Kvernknurr." *See* Supranormal beings, mill sprite

Last wish, 14.3
Lenore-motif, 91

Lilith, Adam's first wife, 44.1n
Lisbet Nypan, witch, 37.2, 39.1
Lock, closing, opening, 30.1–30.2
Longing. *See* Soul
Love magic, 2.1–2.5
Lullaby, 59.5
Lycanthropy, 75

Magic. *See* Binding the dead, Black book,
    Black School, Devil, Evil eye, Finns,
    Finn-shot, Fire, Formula, Healing, Ill-
    ness, Love, Magic flight, Magic shot,
    Magic sleep, Revenge, Rune drum, Self-
    transformation, Shamanism, Shapeshift-
    ing, Soul, Weather, Wind knots, Wise
    folk, Witch, Witchcraft
Magic flight. *See* Witch
Magic shot. *See* Witch
Malleus maleficarum, 159, 43.2n
Man-bear. *See* Soul
"Mare." *See* Nightmare, Soul
Mill sprite. *See* Supranormal beings
Mill troll. *See* Supranormal beings, mill
    sprite
Mine sprite. *See* Supranormal beings
Mongol, 61.15n
Mound folk. *See* Supranormal beings
Murder, 66.1, 66.3
Murdered child. *See* Revenant

"Näck." *See* Supranormal beings, water
    sprite
Nakedness, 12.1
Name, 12.3, 18.5
Nightmare. *See* Soul
"Nisse." *See* Supranormal beings, church
    sprite, farm sprite, ship sprite
"Nøkk." *See* Supranormal beings, water
    sprite

Obscenity, 27.3n
Olaus Magnus, 45.7n
Omen, 1.1–1.3, 1.5, 7.1–7.7, 9.5, 9.6,
    14.1–14.4, 20.4, 58.6, 60.8, 60.15,
    61.1–61.2, 65.2
"Oskorei," 53.1–53.3
Othin, Norse god, 159, 53.1n, 53.3n, 53.5n
Outlaw, 63.2–63.4
Outsiders, 64.1–64.5

Pan's death, 47.9n
Parody, 29.6n
Paulus Diaconus, 73
Pharaoh's dream, 15.1n
Pintorp, 62.2
Poland, 61.11
Poltava, 61.21
Polykrates' ring, 62.1n
Prayer. 5.1. *Cf.* Formula
Preternatural beings. *See* Supranormal
    beings

Revenant: binding revenant, 19.1; boundary
    ghost, 26.1–26.7; "draug," *see* Supranor-
    mal beings (47.19), (52.9–52.12);
    friendly revenant, 20.1–20.5; greedy
    person as revenant, 23.1–23.2; message
    of shipwreck, 20.4; messenger from
    heaven, 20.2; murdered child, 25.1–25.6,
    27.4; picture of revenant, 65.1; protec-
    tion against revenant, 18.1–18.9, 19.1,
    19.3; reconciliation of revenant,
    22.1–22.2; revenant forced to reveal his
    treasure, 23.2; revenant gives advice,
    20.3; revenant lover, 16.1; revenant
    nurses child, 20.5; revenant provided
    for, 21.1–21.3; revenant reveals crime,
    18.8; revenant wants child named after
    him, 18.5; revenging dead, 95,
    18.1–18.9; shooting the revenant, 19.3;
    suicide victim as revenant, 24.1–24.2
Revenge, 1.8, 2.5–2.7
Robbers, 47.18n, 63.1–63.2
Rune drum, 43.1
Russians, 61.15, 61.17, 61.23

Saemundur the Learned, 54.5, 54.8–54.9
Saxo Grammaticus, 19.1n
Sea horse. *See* Supranormal beings, sea
    sprite
Sea monster. *See* Supranormal beings, sea
    sprite
Sea serpent. *See* Supranormal beings, sea
    sprite
Sea sprite. *See* Supranormal beings
Seal woman. *See* Supranormal beings
Self-transformation, 12.6–12.7, 12.10
Settlements, 57.2–57.3
Shakespeare, W., 61.5n

Shamanism, 10.1–10.3
Shapeshifting, 74, 12.1–12.10
Ship sprite. *See* Supranormal beings
Sibyl, 56.3
Silver mother. *See* Supranormal beings, mine sprite
"Sjörå." *See* Supranormal beings, sea sprite
"Skogsrå." *See* Supranormal beings, forest sprite
Sleep, magic, 15.1
Sneezing, 60.8
Snorri Sturlason, 159
"Sølvmor." *See* Supranormal beings, mine sprite
Soul: general description, 41–42, 1.1–13.3; Christian soul, 13.1–13.3, 14.3; dream soul, 11.1; "elsk," 6.1–6.3; envy, 4.1–4.4; evil eye (evil foot, evil hand, evil tongue), 3.1–3.6, 34.2; "fylgje," *cf.* "vardøger," 9.1–9.10, 14.2n; "ham," "hugham," 5.1–5.5, 7.1–9.7, 12.1–13.3; "hug," 1.6–1.8, 2.1–2.7, 7.1–7.7, 10.1–10.3, *cf.* 1.1–13.3, 20.4, 35.2, 65.2; longing, 6.1–6.3; man-bear, 12.7–12.10; materialized, 13.1–13.3; nightmare ("mare"), 5.1–5.5, 12.1; "vardøger," *cf.* "fylgje," 8.1–8.3; thought, 1.1–1.8, 2.5–2.6; werewolf, 12.1–12.6
Spanish, 61.20
St. Laurentius, 55.11n
St. Olaf, general description, 339, 55.11n, 59.1–59.5
Stenbock, Magnus, 61.5
Strangers, 64.1–64.5
Stratagems, 61.5, 61.8
Suicide, 24.1–24.2
Supranatural. *See* Supernormal
Supernormal beings: "armadr," *see* farm sprite; changeling, 45.1–45.6; church grim, *see* church sprite; church sprite, 48.13; "draug," *see* sea sprite, revenant (47.19), 52.9–52.12, 59.4; elves, 45.7–45.8, 46.4; fairies, 44.1–44.3, 46.1–46.11, 47.1–47.20; fairy lover, 46.1–46.11; farm sprite, 48.1–48.12; forest sprite, 46.3, 46.5, 46.11, 47.4; "fossegrim," *see* water sprite; "gardvord," *see* farm sprite; "gast," *see* revenant; "grim," *see* water sprite; "gruvfröken," *see* mine

sprite; "gruvrå," *see* mine sprite; "haugbo," *see* farm sprite; hill man, 6.1, 46.6–46.7; "hulder," *see* fairies; "jolareidi," *see* "oskorei"; kalmyck, 61.15; "klabautermann," *see* ship sprite; "kvarngubbe," *see* mill sprite; "kvernknurr," *see* mill sprite; man-bear, *see* soul; "mare," *see* soul, nightmare; mermaid, 52.1, 52.4–52.7; merman, 52.2–52.3; mill sprite, 49.1–49.2; mine sprite, 50.1–50.5; "naekk," "nøkk," *see also* water sprite, 51.5–51.11; nightmare, *see* soul; "nisse," *see* church sprite, farm sprite, ship sprite; "oskoreia," 53.1–53.2; sea horse, 52.13; sea monster, 52.14; sea serpent, 52.13; sea sprite, 52.1–52.16; seal woman, 52.8; ship sprite, 48.14; silver mother, *see* spirit of the mine; "sjörå," *see* sea sprite; "skogsrå," *see* forest sprite; " sølvmor," *see* mine sprite; spirit of the church, *see* church sprite; spirit of the farm, *see* farm sprite; spirit of the mill, *see* mill sprite; spirit of the mine, *see* mine sprite; spirit of the sea, *see* sea sprite; spirit of the ship, *see* ship sprite; "strandvasker," *see* revenant; "tomte," *see* farm sprite; "troll," *see also* fairies; "tunkall," *see* farm sprite; "tusse," *see* fairies and spirit of the farm; "utburd," *see* revenant, murdered child; water sprite, 51.1–51.11; werewolf, *see* soul; wild hunt, 53.1–53.5; wood sprite, *see* forest sprite
Sweden, Swedes, 61.2–61.3, 61.5–61.14, 61.17–61.18, 61.20–61.21, 61.26–61.27

Theft, 67.2–67.4
Thief, 63.3, 63.5
Thief, binding, 31.1–31.3
Thor, Norse god, 170
Thought. *See* Soul
"Tomte." *See* Supernormal beings, farm sprite
Tongue twister, 47.15
Tordenskjold, P. W., 61.12
Tourism, 64.2–64.3
Trance, 10.1–10.3
Treasure, buried, general description, 317, 56.1–56.11
Trickster, 2.5, 33.1–33.2

Troll, general description, 299, 55.1–55.19, 59.3–59.5

Troll cat. *See* Witchcraft

Trolls as fairies. *See* Supernormal beings, fairies

"Tunkall." *See* Supernormal beings, farm sprite

"Tusse." *See* Supernormal beings, fairies, farm sprite

"Utburd." *See* Revenant, murdered child

"Utrøst," 52.15

"Vardøger." *See* Soul

Volmer, Danish king, 53.5n

Weinsberg, women at, 61.13

Werewolf. *See* Soul

Weather magic, 32.1–32.5

Wind-knots, 32.1, 52.6

Wise folk, 2.5–2.7, 3.1–3.2, 30.1–33.2

Witch, 34.1–43.6, 61.6

Witch trial, 43.1–43.3: Hilde Blindheim, 1667, 43.3; Ingerid Erik's Daughter Kaaljørju, 1661, 43.2; Quive Baardsen, 1627, 43.1

Witch's daughter, 32.5, 42.1–42.2

Witchcraft: general description, 159; envy, 34.2–34.4; food magic, 37.1–37.2; magic flight, 41.1–41.4; magic shot, 35.1–35.2; persecution, 190, 43.1–43.6; revenge, 34.1–34.4, 43.3, 43.6; rune drum, 43.1; troll cat, 39.1–39.5; whirlwind, 36.1–36.2; wind magic, 43.1; witch butter, 38.3

Witches' Sabbath, 40.1–40.2

Legend Types

(According to Reidar Th. Christiansen's The Migratory Legends)

ML 3000: Escape from the Black School, 54.8

ML 3010: Making the devil carry the cart, 54.12

ML 3015: The cardplayer and the devil, (54.11), 54.15

ML 3020: Inexperienced use of the Black Book, 54.6

ML 3025: Carried by the devil, 54.10–54.11

ML 3030: The white serpent, 42.2

ML 3035: The daughter of the witch, (32.5), 42.1

ML 3040: The witch making butter, 38.4

ML 3045: Following the witch, 41.1

ML (3050): At the witches' sabbath, 40.1–40.2, 41.2

ML 3060: Banning the snakes (rats), 30.5

ML 3070: The demon dancer, 54.13–54.14

ML 3080: The Finn messenger, 10.1–10.3

ML 4000: The Guntram legend, 11.1

ML 4005: The werewolf husband, 12.3, 12.5

ML 4010: Married to nightmare, 5.5

ML 4015: The midnight mass of the dead, 17.1–17.2

ML 4020: The unforgiven dead, 22.1

ML 4025: Infants killed before they were baptized, haunt mother, 25.1

ML 4050: River claiming its due, 51.6

ML 4055: Mysterious warning of approaching storm, 52.2

ML 4060: The mermaid's message, 52.4

ML 4065: The dead from the sea and those from the land, 52.12

ML 4070: Sea sprite trying out the seats of a boat, 52.9

ML 4075: Visit to the blessed island, 52.15

ML 4080: The seal woman, 52.8

ML 4085: The seahorse and the sea serpent, 52.13

ML 4090: Music taught by water sprite, 51.1, 51.3

ML 5000: Troll resents a disturbance, 55.6–55.7

ML 5010: The visit to the old troll, (52.6), 55.2, (57.1)

ML 5015: The plaything of the troll, 55.1

ML 5050: The fairies' prospect of salvation, 44.3, (51.5)

ML 5060: The fairy hunter, 53.4, (53.5)

ML 5070: Midwife to the fairies, 47.6–47.7

ML 5075: Removing buildings, 47.12

ML 5080: Food from the fairies, (47.10)

ML 5085: The changeling, 45.4

ML 5090: Married to a fairy woman, 46.8, (46.11)

ML 5095: Fairy woman pursues man, (46.2), (46.3), (46.5), (46.10)

ML 6000: Tricking the fairy suitor, 46.1

ML 6005: The interrupted fairy wedding, 46.6

ML 6015: The Christmas visitors, 47.20, (55.12)

ML 6020: The grateful fairy mother, 47.8

ML 6025: Calling the dairymaid, 47.4–47.5

ML 6030: Fairies give information as to the date, 47.3

ML 6035: Fairies assist a farmer in his work, 47.1

ML 6045: Drinking cup stolen from the fairies, 47.19

ML 6050: The fairy hat, 47.18

ML 6055: The fairy cows, 47.13

ML 6070: Fairies send a message, 47.9

ML 7000: Fighting nisse, 48.1

ML 7005: The heavy burden, 48.3

ML 7010: Revenge for being teased, 48.4–48.6

ML 7015: The new suit, 48.10

ML 7020: Vain attempt to escape from the nisse, 48.11

ML 7050: Ring thrown into the water, 62.1

ML 7060: The disputed site for a church, 58.1

ML 7065: The name of the masterbuilder, 55.11

ML (7070ff.): Church bells, 58.4–58.6

ML 7080: The plague with a rake and a broom, 60.4

ML 7085: The plague ferried across a river, 60.2

ML 7090: The survivors. A girl and a boy, 60.13–60.14

ML 7095: Rediscovery of a church, 60.15

ML 8000: Leading the enemies to their destruction, 61.3–61.4

ML 8005: Soldier returns in time to prevent his wife remarrying, 61.22

ML 8010ff: Hidden treasure, 56.4–56.11

ML 8025: The robbers and the captive girl, 63.1

Legend Types (Unnumbered)

binding the dead with needles in soles, 19.4

binding a thief, 31.3

Black Death, *cf.* legend type ML 7080–7095: binding the plague, 60.4–60.7; burning the plague, 60.7; "God bless you," 60.8; greedy person dies, 60.10; horse carries the dead, 60.9; the only person left, 60.12; the plague comes on a ship, 60.1; the plague ferried over a lake, 60.2; young man killed to stop the plague, 60.6

boundary dispute, 57.4, 57.6–57.7

boundary ghost, false witness, 26.3: ghost receives help in restoring boundary, 26.1–26.2, 26.5–26.6; ghost tries to remove boundary stone, 26.4

burial of an ungodly person, 14.3–14.4

burning troll cat butter, 39.3

burning mill, 40.2

changeling, *cf.* legend type ML 5085: pretending to baptize the changeling, 45.5; pretending to burn the changeling, 45.3; throwing changeling on the garbage heap, 45.1

child stolen by an elf, 45.2

church, *cf.* legend type ML 7060–7070: church bell took three lives, 58.6; church bells cannot be moved, 58.4; church bells cannot be raised, 58.5; holy image promised to church, 58.3; indulgence for work on a church, 58.2

church sprite ties rags around the clapper of the bell, 48.13

dead as messenger from heaven, 20.2

dead child complains of "elsk," 6.3

dead lover returns, 16.1

dead man's "fylgje" claims dead man's leg, 9.7

dead mother nurses child, 20.5

devil, *cf.* legend types ML 3000–3025, 3070–3075: devil fetched rich lady, 62.2; devil in shape of a fly, 54.9; devil must carry water in basket, 54.5; devil must take a joke, 54.4

draug, *cf.* legend types ML 4065–4070: boy hits mittens on draug, 52.10; draug shuns excrements, 52.11

duel of wits with merman, 52.3

elves dance with a boy, 45.7

elves lure a boy, 45.8

envy corrodes a stone, 4.4

evil hand harms a calf, 34.2

fairies, *cf.* legend types ML 5050–6070: fairies as silver miners, 50.2; fairies bake bread, 48.7; fairies offer food, 47.10; fairy lover, 46.2–46.11; origin of fairies, 44.2

426

farm spirit, *cf.* legend types ML 7000–7020: farm spirit driven from farm, 48.12; farm spirit learns to take a rest, 48.9; farm spirit steals fodder, 48.2
Finn exorcises rats, *cf.* legend type ML 3060, 30.5
Finn provides wind, 32.3
Finn transformed into a bear or wolf, 12.6–12.7, 12.9–12.10
friends in life and death, 15.1

ghosts: dancing ghosts, 27.6; is my eye red? 27.3; meeting a ghost causes sickness, 27.5
girl conjures her lover's "hug," 1.8
girl sees the "fylgjer" at a dance, 9.3

haying with the whirlwind, 36.2
healer overhears people at great distance, 28.2
"hug"-turning: boy throws away apple to avoid "hug"-turning, 2.4; he makes a girl undress, 2.5; they make a horse (pig) follow instead of person, 2.5–2.7; use of urine to turn girl's "hug," 2.3

island is disenchanted, 52.16

king: first king on Jørstad, 57.2; king and the crofter's daughter, *cf.* AT 875, 57.3; king sleeping in the mountain, 57.1

landowner: blasphemous landowner punished, 62.3; cruel landowner punished, 62.2; evil landowner, 62.2, 62.4–62.5

magical dance, 51.4
man bear raises child, 12.8
man understands howling of wolves, 12.4
master thief does both good and evil, 63.3
mermaid: lured man, 52.5; orders a load of grain, 52.6; takes revenge on unfaithful lover, 52.7; the wind knots, 52.6
message of death and advice, 7.5
message of shipwreck, 7.2
mill sprite disturbing miller, 49.1–49.2
mine sprite warns workers, 50.5
modern legends, 64.1–67.4

mound folk, *see also* fairies: mound folk borrow flour, 47.16; mound folk borrow scissors and knife, 47.17; mound woman gives advice in sewing, 47.2; playing with mound children, 47.14; trading fire and tobacco with mound man, 47.11
murdered child: kills calves, 25.3; reveals mother, 25.2, 25.4–25.6

nightmare, *cf.* legend type ML 4010: man frees girl from being a nightmare, 5.4

ore sprite: blinds first exploiter, 50.3; helps first exploiter, 50.4
"oskorei": fetched dead man, 53.2; riding with, 53.1
outlaws and thieves: greedy robber caught, 63.5; master thief did both good and evil, 63.3; outlaws killed by the sheriff, 63.4; robbers keep girl captive, *cf.* legend type ML 8025, 63.2; Shoemaker Piont, 63.6

Pied Piper of Hamelin, 30.5n

revenant: greedy person becomes revenant, 23.1; man marries dead girl, 18.4; protection against revenant, 18.1, 18.9, 19.1, 19.3; revenant forced to reveal treasure, 23.2; revenant provided for, 21.1, 21.3; revenant reveals crime, 18.8; revenging dead, 18.3–18.4; serving food to dead husband, 20.1

saved from finnshot, 35.1–35.2
sea monster, 52.14
shoemaker punished, 63.6
shooting troll cat, 39.4
shooting trollman, 35.1
St. Olaf: his ship, 59.2; his spring, 59.1; turned hag to stone, 59.3
sunken manor, 62.3
swearing with soil in his shoes, 57.4

"taken into mountain," 45.6, 46.7, 46.9
taking possession of land by riding around it, 57.5
three wind knots, 32.1

trickster: 'crawls through a log,' 33.1; makes a girl undress in front of people, 2.5; 'makes water rise,' 33.1; 'takes off his head,' 33.2

troll, *cf.* legend types ML 5000–5050: carries off a man every Christmas, 55.15; dialogue between, 55.4; drowns in Iceland's trenches, 55.19; the giant Vrål, 55.8; moves a rock, 55.5; moved because of the church bells, 55.13–55.15; mowing competition, 55.9; 'revengeful gift,' 55.13; stealing gold from, 55.3; throws rock against church, 55.16; tried to move the Faeroe Islands, 55.18; turned into stone, 55.17–55.18, 59.3; wife borrows churn, 55.10

urban legends, 64.1–67.4:
adultery: lover's car filled with ready-mix, 67.1
anti-legend: Blenda washes whiter, 66.5; blood on the stairs, 66.4; a dark, dark night, 66.6
horror and death: baby left behind, dies, 66.2; murdered boyfriend, 66.1; red hand in basement kills, 66.3; snake in banana, 66.4; torn off fingers, 64.5
strangers: potatoes in living room, 64.1; rat meat in Chinese food, 64.2
tourism: spider on cheek, 64.3
supernatural: dead woman in picture, 65.1; Jesus as hitchhiker, 65.5; Jesus' second coming, 65.4; seeing oneself, 65.2
theft: free tickets, 67.4; the stolen grandmother, 67.2; turkey under the hat, 67.3

war legends, *cf.* legend type ML 8000–8005:

boy returns from Russia, 61.23; Charles XII of Sweden invulnerable, 61.9; darnel soup, 61.25; dressed up as sheep, 61.8; farmer kills soldier, 61.18; feathers turned into an army, 61.7; fooling the enemy, 61.5, 61.7–61.8, 61.16; forest moves, 61.5; hungry soldiers, 61.26; Jew taken for devil, soldiers flee, 61.11; louse on a king, 61.10; minister preaches to save church, 61.17; soldier buys potatoes from enemy, 61.27; soldier kills child in the cradle, 61.14; soldier marries Danish girl, 61.24; soldier's wife had remarried, 61.2; soldiers steal silverware, 61.19; Tordenskjold captures the Swedish fleet, 61.12; witch blunts guns, 61.6; wives carry husbands out of captivity, 61.13

water sprite: riding on water sprite, 51.7–51.9; water sprite longs for salvation, *cf.* legend type ML 5050, 51.5; as workhorse, 51.10

white and black birds fight at death of dean, 14.2

witch, *cf.* legend types ML 3030–3065: blunting guns, 61.6; churning witch butter in river, 38.5; creating troll cat, 39.1; holy communion denied, 43.5; man rides minister's wife, 41.3; milking with a knife, 38.1; putting new flesh on fishbones, 37.1–37.2; sailing on a millstone, 41.4; stealing brandy with a knife, 38.2; sticking pins in a doll, 34.1; testing witch butter, 38.2, 38.5; troll cat reveals witch, 39.3–39.5, 43.6; witch revealed as milk thief, 38.6

witch's daughter makes it rain, 32.5

woman hears her husband's "vardøger," 8.1

Memorats

avoiding effects of envy, 1.4
cattle of the mermaid, 52.1
children teasing mound man, 47.15
dancing with ghost, 27.7
dead husband longs for namesake, 6.2
dead mother gives advice, 20.3
dead reconciled, 22.2
dead wants child named after him, 18.5
dead wants shroud for child, 21.2
dog thought to be boundary ghost, 26.7
farm spirit takes care of horse, 48.8
fiddle tune taught by water sprite, 51.2
healers, 28.1, 28.3–28.4, 28.10, 29.2, 29.5–29.6
healing English sickness, 3.1
illness caused by thought, 1.7
Jesus, vision of, 65.3
message of death, 7.1, 7.6

message of drowning, 7.3
message of escape from fire, 7.7
message of shipwreck, 7.4, 20.4
nightmare in shape of a cat, 5.2
nightmare was her husband, 5.1
quenching fire, 9.10, 30.3
revenge of beggar, 34.3
revenge of Lapp woman, 34.4
revenging dead, 18.6–18.7
seeing a person's "vardøger," 8.2, 8.3
shirt of victory stops fire, 9.10
silver mother, afraid of, 50.1
spirit of ship gives warning, 48.14
striking out a thief's eye, 31.2
suicide victim walks again, 24.1–24.2
unsuccessful healing of animal, 3.3
wild hunt, 53.5
wise-folk, 30.2

Reimund Kvideland

is a professor in the Department of Folklore and Ethnology at the University of Bergen, Norway. He has been editor of *Tradisjon* since 1975, and contributes to various other ethnology and folkloristic journals.

Henning K. Sehmsdorf

is professor of Scandinavian and comparative literature at the University of Washington. He is editor of *Northwest Folklore*, and has written numerous articles on folklore, mythology, and Scandinavian and comparative literature.